THE
LAST
CON

Center Point
Large Print

Also by Zachary Bartels and available from
Center Point Large Print:

Playing Saint

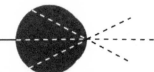

**This Large Print Book carries the
Seal of Approval of N.A.V.H.**

THE
LAST
CON

Zachary
Bartels

CENTER POINT LARGE PRINT
THORNDIKE, MAINE

This Center Point Large Print edition is published
in the year 2016 by arrangement with Thomas Nelson.

Scripture quotations are taken from the Holy Bible, New
International Version®, NIV®. Copyright © 1973, 1978,
1984, 2011 by Biblica, Inc.™ Used by permission of
Zondervan. All rights reserved worldwide.
www.zondervan.com. The "NIV" and "New International
Version" are trademarks registered in the United States
Patent and Trademark Office by Biblica, Inc.™

The text of this Large Print edition is unabridged.
In other aspects, this book may vary
from the original edition.
Printed in the United States of America
on permanent paper.
Set in 16-point Times New Roman type.

ISBN: 978-1-62899-832-0

Library of Congress Cataloging-in-Publication Data

Names: Bartels, Zachary.
Title: The last con / Zachary Bartels.
Description: Center Point Large Print edition. | Thorndike, Maine :
Center Point Large Print, 2016. | ©2015
Identifiers: LCCN 2015042179 | ISBN 9781628998320 (hardcover :
alk. paper)
Subjects: LCSH: Large type books. | GSAFD: Christian fiction.
Classification: LCC PS3602.A83855 L37 2016 | DDC 813/.6—dc23
LC record available at http://lccn.loc.gov/2015042179

For my wife Erin,
The most genuine person I know.

THE
LAST
CON

Prologue

Six years ago

Those last few hours of freedom are only precious in retrospect. Fletcher spent his at the Olympic Diner, shoveling down that barely edible breakfast food.

It was their ritual; they ordered "hippy hash" and black coffee and talked through the plan. Then they talked through it again, careful to touch on every contingency. There had been a time when Fletcher complained about the greasy food and dive setting. But Andrew had insisted they stick with the ritual, and before long the round corner booth became a source of comfort for Fletcher. If nothing else, the lard-encrusted eggs proved a convenient justification for the disquiet in his guts as the job drew near. After all, real grifters didn't get nervous—everyone knew that. There was no rule, however, against indigestion.

Andrew pushed his half-empty plate away firmly, as if to make sure the remaining food got the message. He patted a napkin against his mouth a few times and leaned back in the booth, the fabric of his fine Italian suit seeming to recoil from the cracking red vinyl of the seat.

"Let's go through it one more time," he said, running a hand delicately along his carefully quaffed hair, pushing a few errant strands back into place. Andrew had turned forty a month earlier, but Fletcher knew he could still pass for a college student if the job called for it as easily as he could embody a tenured professor.

"I think we've talked it to death," Fletcher said. "Simplest job of the year, man. Let's just go."

"Well, *I'd* like to talk about it some more," Happy said. He was sprawled in the booth, red hair disheveled, wearing cargo pants and an old flannel shirt, not caring what passersby might assume about two clean-cut men in suits keeping such unkempt and uncouth company. He leaned onto the table toward his two associates. "It's a church, you guys," he whispered. "This is the line we weren't going to cross, remember?"

"It's not a church," Andrew said.

"Right. Remind me what it's called again?"

Fletcher sighed. "It's called St. Bernadette's Church, but it was deconsecrated ten years ago. That means it's not really a church anymore. They rent the place out to groups like this Civic Pride thing tonight. That's it."

"Just seems messed up."

"You don't have to come," Fletcher said. "I already told you that."

"Whatever. I'm in." Happy slumped back in his seat. "So what am I doing?"

Fletcher shrugged. "Driving us there, waiting in the van, picking us up."

"Right, right. But what am I *doing?*"

"Nothing," Andrew answered. "It's the annual meeting of the Knights of Civic Pride. There's no retinal scan equipment, no motion sensors, and probably no spy satellites locked in on a gathering of the world's dullest crowd eating a rubber chicken dinner. If the word *church* is a deal breaker, head on home. Like Fletcher said, we don't need you tonight."

Happy grinned. "You said that last month in Royal Oak, and I seem to recall saving both of your butts."

Fletcher's phone rang in his pocket. He extracted himself from the booth and answered it. "Hello?"

"Am I interrupting something terribly exciting?"

Fletcher smiled involuntarily and walked out into the cool night, leaving Andrew to pick up the check.

"No, it's Yawnsville here," he said, looking back into the neon glow of the diner. "This anthropologist from Chicago is doing a slide-show. Like, with an actual slide projector—the kind with the carousel."

His wife laughed that cute little laugh. Inside, Andrew was paying the cashier and Happy was fiddling with his own phone.

"Yeah, and he's standing two feet away from the projector, but instead of just pushing the button, he keeps saying *sliiiide,* and Andrew was sitting behind the machine so he's been reduced to slide master."

"I bet he hates that," Meg said.

"Oh, it's a gong show. I was happy for the excuse to duck out. So what's up?"

Andrew and Happy came walking out of the diner. Fletcher pointed at his phone and mouthed *Meg*. They nodded, and the three quietly climbed into Happy's old van.

"I wanted to get your opinion on something," she said. "But first I have to tell you what Ivy said today."

"Hit me." Fletcher muted the phone while Happy turned the old van's ignition.

"Well, at school they're doing this project of free-associating in visual media."

"That sounds like a college class, not first grade." The van scraped the concrete below as they pulled out onto the street.

"It's just, like, making collages and drawings and things," Meg said. "Anyway, she was making a picture of her family, and she cut out a glossy of Charlize Theron on the red carpet for me and a picture of that old man from *Jurassic Park* for you."

"Old man? I'm thirty-two."

Meg laughed.

"Are they going to teach her to read at some point?" Fletcher asked. He'd been smarting at the hefty tuition payments being auto-drafted from his bank account while the children were allowed to do whatever they pleased most of the day.

"It's self-directed. When she's ready, she'll be reading. Anyway, I really called to ask what you'd think of putting a claw-foot tub where the vanity is now and then kind of switching the toilet to the opposite corner. It's just more balanced that way."

Meg had been knee-deep in bathroom renovation plans since finishing their kitchen overhaul a year earlier. The expenses were noisily tallying in Fletcher's mind, adding themselves to the tuition and the mortgage payments and drowning out any of his own reservations about robbing St. Bernadette's Deconsecrated Church.

"Hmmm. Let me mull that over. I better get back in there now. Andrew's going to wonder what's up."

"Tell him I said hi. I'll probably be asleep when you get home. I've got a callback in the morning."

"Okay. I love you."

"Love you more," Meg purred. "Night."

"Look at that stupid grin," Happy said from the driver's seat. "You been married for the better part of a decade. How are you still twitterpated?"

"I'm what?"

"Twitterpated. Like Thumper." He turned to Andrew. "Is she really that hot?"

Andrew gave a slight, knowing nod.

"Guys," Fletcher called. "I'm still here!"

Andrew laughed. "It's not just that she's beauti-

13

ful. She's smart, fun, the whole package. And that little girl is something else. Who knows what they're doing with a lousy grifter like Fletcher. Makes no sense."

The stupid grin evaporated. "If she knew what we really did, things would probably make a whole lot more sense, real quick."

The auditorium of the deconsecrated church had been cleared of pews and filled with standard-issue banquet hall chairs, save for the back of the hall, where a long table had been meticulously arranged with all manner of crackers, cheeses, and deli meats.

Andrew and Fletcher entered separately, a few minutes apart. Their target was locked up in what had been the sacristy, where the vessels and vestments of the church were kept. The two men mingled pleasantly, repeating the same contrived niceties as the rest of the crowd. Andrew made his way to the dais at the front of the hall, where he answered a phone call from no one and stepped into the north transept for some privacy. From there he slipped unseen into the sacristy.

Fletcher leaned against the wall and perused the program he'd been handed on the way in. If all was going according to plan, Andrew was even now cracking the safe—a cheap and outdated Gurnell Gun Safe that, according to tax records, had been donated to the church by a parishioner fifteen years earlier. It would take him all of three minutes to access what lay within.

Feeling that rumble in his stomach again, Fletcher refocused on the program. The Knights of Civic Pride would begin their meeting in approximately fifteen minutes, if they were on schedule. After some introductory comments from the chairman, the first order of business would be giving out the year's Civic Pride Award, which would be bestowed upon—

Suddenly stiffening, Fletcher let his eyes drift around the crowded room, searching for a tall black man in dress blues. Instead he saw Andrew, smiling and nodding, making his way through the crowd toward Fletcher. He held out a hand. "Cyrus Turk," he said. "And you are?"

Fletcher gave his hand a friendly pump. "I am . . . really looking forward to the award the *chief of police* will be receiving here in a few minutes." He held up the program with a panicked smile.

Andrew nodded again. "Well, so far everything is exactly as I expected here. They have my favorite cookies, and the package is open. In fact, there are four different kinds, and I can't make up my mind."

Fletcher bit his lip. "I can probably help you choose," he said, "but again, I'm thinking about the chief of police and his big award. Maybe we should get together for cookies another day?"

"No, tonight's good," Andrew said. His voice dropped to a near whisper as he leaned in and gave the kind of half hug one gives an acquaintance at a social function. "I propped the back door," he said. "Happy and I will bring the van around. You just slip in and get what we came for."

"All right." Breaking the embrace, Fletcher moved quickly and quietly out of the building, down the stone steps, and around to the back of the church. He entered through the propped door, which bore the stenciled words EMERGENCY EXIT ONLY.

Once inside, he clicked on a pen light and swept the room, quickly locating the open safe. As Andrew had indicated, there were four monstrances lined up inside—ornate gold vessels used to display the Host for adoration. Each was about eighteen inches tall, culminating with a round sunburst pattern with a circular void at its center where the consecrated bread of the Eucharist would be placed.

He felt a little tingle of excitement, which he assumed was not too different from the Presence of the Divine experienced by those who had worshiped an invisible God with the aid of these golden objects and a little wafer of bread. For Fletcher, it was about the history, the culture. He'd studied religion and philosophy as an outsider, motivated by his curiosity about what drove humans to be so . . . *human* . . . The same curiosity that now motivated him as a grifter.

Fletcher rubbed his whiskered cheeks and gazed into the safe. He had never heard of a church having more than one monstrance—let alone four—and to the untrained eye these were virtually identical. But that's why Andrew had brought him along.

He leaned in close and studied each of the gold stands in turn. The second one from the left. That was the Valletta Monstrance—the one they were after. Reaching up under his jacket, he pulled out a large, collapsible nylon bag and carefully slid the holy vessel in, hefting it onto his shoulder. It slipped off the first time, causing him to curse. He was feeling rushed, which he didn't like. Haste led to sloppiness, Andrew had emphasized again and again, and sloppiness gets you caught. That's why they weren't here in the dead of the night, breaking in as cat burglars. Instead, they were grifting, expertly working their marks, hiding in the midst of the crowd.

Before zipping the bag shut, Fletcher paused and shined the light around the inside of the large safe, illuminating a variety of smaller items. If there was anything else of value here, he might as well take it. No one would know, after all. And none of this stuff was doing anyone a bit of good locked away in the back of this no-longer-a-church.

That's when the door opened and the light came on overhead. Fletcher's eyes met the chief's, both men speechless and open-mouthed. The tall, muscular man wore a crisp dress uniform and held a small yellow notepad in his left hand, scribbled with notes for an acceptance speech. And then he had his sidearm in his right. Fletcher thought about grifting, talking, charming—but he could see in the chief's eyes that it would be pointless.

Thus ended his freedom for the better part of a decade. And, while he knew it made no sense, whenever Fletcher remembered that moment, he could see the vague flashing of police lights and hear the slamming of a cell door.

Chapter 1

Present day

Dante Watkins went to jail at least twice a week. It really didn't bother him.

Jail was familiar—the steps up to the brick-and-concrete edifice, the words COVNTY JAIL engraved over the entrance in block letters, the aging guard behind the desk—they were all commonplace and somehow neutral, like the newsstand outside his apartment or the train platform a block away.

And it was nothing like prison. Not to Dante.

Prisons were isolated compounds—little kingdoms unto themselves, wrapped in razor wire and surrounded by gun towers, where men were banished, often for life. The old county jail, on the other hand, was nestled in one of the nicer parts of downtown, between the new casino and the opera house. Driving by, a person could think it was an office building or high-rise apartment complex, so Dante could run in and out without so much as a blip in his mood.

But he had to be quick. Always. Because inside, the jail smelled like tenement and emergency room and disinfectant. And somehow, every surface was sticky. A bit of a germ freak, Dante kept his personal footprint as small as possible while inside, tight and professional, never sprawling in a chair or leaning on a table. In and out.

"Eighty degrees, and the preacher's in a three-piece suit!" The uniformed man at the desk stretched his mouth into a wide grin full of straight, off-white teeth. "Good to see you; we needed a little class in here today." He retrieved a clipboard from under the desk and slid it toward the thin man approaching him. "How are you this afternoon, Reverend?"

Dante mirrored the man's smile. "I'm blessed, James. But busy. Lots of folks need what I've got." He carefully set his bulky King James Bible on the desk and retrieved an ink pen from his jacket. He printed and signed his name on the log sheet before him. "I'm here to see a lost soul named Gregory Barnes," he said, copying the inmate number from an index card onto the form.

"If you're gonna save that soul, you better work fast. They're taking him to Jackson tomorrow." The guard punched a few buttons on an outdated computer and nodded his approval. "Looks like he's waiting for you in Consult 6. Go on through."

"Thanks." Dante tucked the worn Bible under his arm and stepped up to a reinforced door, where he paused. This was not the visitors' door with the walk-through metal detector. That wasn't for Dante. While security had been slowly tightening for a decade, attorneys and clergy were still subject to a mere visual search by the lobby officer. Any measures beyond that were at the officer's discretion. The wand might come out for a new lawyer or an out-of-towner with a smart mouth, but Dante and his Bible had been coming here for years and no one gave them a second thought. A grinding buzz sounded from the magnetic lock above, signaling the minister to pass through.

The light was greenish and low in the narrow hallway, occasionally flickering out, but Dante could have navigated the space blindfolded. Twenty-four steps, then through a door on his left and into a hub connecting eight small consultation rooms. An orange-clad inmate, lethargically mopping the floor, looked up at Dante with empty eyes before slowly dragging the mop and bucket out of his way. Each of the eight metal doors had been painted a sickly institutional green and bore a stenciled number beneath a small window. An armed guard at the far wall glanced up at the visitor with little interest and pointed to door number six.

Dante entered the bare room. A compact metal table filled the majority of the space, flanked by two cheap molded-plastic chairs. Gregory Barnes was wedged into one of them, tipping back, studying the ceiling. Dante lowered himself into the other and placed his Bible on the table between them.

"Are you a skinhead, Gregory?"

At six foot six, the inmate had to look down to meet Dante's gaze. "What?"

"You're going to a state penitentiary tomorrow. You look like a skinhead, you know? That's a statement you're making."

"No. I mean, I've been waxing my head, but—"

"Why?"

"Because it feels good. And it looks good."

"And you're going bald, right?" Dante said, pointing at the faint shadow of a receding hairline. "I can see it there."

"What is this?"

"This is your first stretch. You show up looking like a skinhead—that can set the trajectory for your entire stay. You got a skinhead-sounding nickname? What do people call you?"

"Gregory."

"Huh. That's like a four out of ten. You'll probably be okay." Dante unbuttoned his suit coat and adjusted his tie. "Anyway, enough with the pleasantries. I'm here for a spiritual visit, aren't I? Let's you and I pray together." He placed his hands out on the table, palms up. "Shall we?"

"Pray . . . *what?* They told me that you were the guy who—"

"This is how it's done, Greg. Be cool." He peered at Gregory for a moment over the top of his brow-line glasses, then felt the man's large, sweaty hands wrap around his own. The irony still amused Dante after all these years. Spouses, parents, children—they all had no-contact visitation with the inmates, through filthy, tiny windows lining a miserable corridor. They spoke on telephones from three feet away, pushed their hands up against the glass. But here in this room there were no barriers, no cameras, no one listening in. This was where confidential meetings—constitutionally protected meetings— took place, beyond the reach of prying eyes and listening ears. And yet it was clearly not human contact that Gregory Barnes was craving as he shifted uncomfortably in his seat.

"Big Guy in the Sky," Dante began, squeezing his eyes shut. "I pray for this skinhead-lookin' convict. May he land a plush cell at the state pen tomorrow, with a weak little roommate who likes him for who he is inside. You know, the *real* Greg. May the food not taste like gruel. May he keep his mouth shut, remembering the words of your Good Book, that *snitches get stitches.* And most importantly, may Gregory pay what he owes lest he reap what he sows." He paused. "I say again, *may he pay what he owes.*" Dante opened his eyes. "You're not praying, Gregory."

"I didn't come here to pray." He broke his hands free from Dante's grip. "You have something for me."

"I said be cool, Greg." Dante shook his head, annoyed. "They think we're praying in here, right? Otis didn't tell you how it's done? You slip it in my hand while we pray. You think I *want* to hang on to that big clammy mitt of yours? You pay what you owe or you reap what you sow. Now show me what you got."

Gregory sat back and surreptitiously pulled the zipper of his orange jumpsuit down to his chest and withdrew a small bundle, a few inches squared, wrapped in newspaper.

Dante bared his teeth and quietly chided, "Put it down low, next to the table, man. There may not be cameras, but there's a window, and the guard makes the rounds. What's the matter with you?"

"Fine," Gregory said. "I got it. See? Now give me the stuff."

"Open it up. Let me have a look."

Gregory snuffed and pulled open the bundle, fanning a stack of wrinkled tens and twenties.

Dante frowned. "Price is eight hundred fifty, Greg. Looks like you're trying to short me there."

The inmate closed his ample fist around the money. "It's four hundred bucks, but you're not getting it anyway. Deal's changed."

"Has it now?"

"New deal: you give me what I asked for and I won't tell the deputy warden about the game you're running in his jail. How about that?"

Dante smiled—not a malicious smile—and sat back in the chair. "You're going to turn me in? That's the plan?"

"Why not? I've been asking around about you, Preacher. And I think you're running a solo act. You come in here and jack up the price of everything while we're locked up and have no choice but to pay. But I won't be locked up forever."

"Seven years, from what I understand."

"Be out in three. Maybe I'll come visit you then. How about that? You think you can intimidate me? You come in here in your suit jacket and pants and those stupid glasses, looking like Malcolm X, talking about skinheads and how bad it's gonna be for me inside, and I'm supposed to forget what you really are?"

"What am I?"

"You're a weak little man with no pull. No connections. No muscle."

Dante's smile disappeared. "What do you think would happen if I called for the guard right now, Greg?" He opened the Bible, revealing a cutaway, and withdrew a small cardboard box. "What if I told him that you offered me this in exchange for a favor on the outside? Who do you think they'd believe?"

Gregory twisted his head to the side, cracking his neck and showcasing a network of steel cable muscles and tendons running under the skin. "There you go again with that intimidation," he said. "But it doesn't work on me. I'm not stupid like the rest of these dirtbags."

Controlled rage flickered behind Dante's eyes. "You're not like these dirtbags? Son, you're in an orange jumpsuit because you stole the Jaws of Life from a fire station and tried to crack open an ATM. You called 911 on *yourself.* How's the hand, by the way?"

Gregory rubbed his right hand, but said nothing.

"My services are a privilege, not a right. You've just lost that privilege." Dante rebuttoned his jacket, returned the little box to its place in the old Bible, and scooted his chair back.

"Nobody walks away from me," Gregory growled. "You don't want to give me what I got coming? What's to stop me from taking it from you right now?" He motioned at the Bible with his eyes. "Like you said, no cameras in here."

"So take it." Dante brought his hands up next to his face. "Go ahead."

The two men locked eyes for a moment.

"No?" Dante laughed. "You jumped right into that little speech you memorized, how you're not intimidated and all that. But you're a mess, Greg. I mean, it's not that hot in here, man; why's that bald head of yours raining like that? My guess: This isn't going the way you hoped when you rehearsed it in your cell. Now you're thinking about an exit strategy, some kind of back road out, but you didn't lay one." He scoffed. "Look at you—skin leakin' all over." He pulled his jacket up at the lapel and raised his arm over his head, his crisp shirt sliding against his skin. "Cool and dry over here, Greg."

With a sudden snatch, the inmate's massive right hand went for the Bible, connecting with the soft leather cover for just a moment before it was gripped hard over the pinky, turned backward, and pinned against his forearm. He resisted the hold for a second, then yelped and went limp.

"There you go," Dante said. "Just relax. Now, where were we? That's right. You were telling me how stupid you aren't. And I was about to tell you how everything you've done with your pathetic little life has been stupid. But this—this right here?—this is your stupidest move yet. You think I'd come in here week after week for almost twenty years unprotected? Unconnected?" He gave the big hand a little extra twist. "Answer me."

"You're not with"—Gregory gasped in pain—"any gang I heard of."

Dante leaned forward and looked the man in the eye. "You ever heard of La Bella Donna?" He pushed his glasses back up the bridge of his nose with his free hand. "I'm guessing by the panic in your eyes that you have. Do you have any idea what would happen to you if I told Bella Donna you tried to take her product without paying? You're locked in a cage, surrounded by her people, Greg . . . headed to a bigger, nastier cage also filled with her people."

Gregory's racing pulse was easily visible in his eighteen-inch neck.

"Did you even know *you* worked for Bella Donna? The only reason you even got through to me is because you run for Jay on Roosevelt. And Jay reports to D'Angelo, who answers to Big Mike, who answers to Marcus, who handles affairs for Bella Donna." He was suddenly aware that his voice had been rising steadily as he spoke. He breathed in slowly and let it out.

"I tell you what," he said. "I may be going soft, but I'm going to let you off the hook this time. I'm going to walk out of here with this"—he tapped his Bible—"and we'll just forget you tried something so stupid. Sound good?"

A frantic nod was Gregory's only response.

Dante released the man to resume rubbing his hand and stood, towering over the inmate, drawing his Bible up under his arm. "Aren't you forgetting something?" he asked.

"I'm sorry," Gregory mumbled, staring down at the table like a pouting child.

"I don't care if you're sorry." Dante reached his hand out. "Give it to me."

Gregory looked up, confused. "You said the deal was off."

"*New* new deal: I leave with the package *and* the money, and the boss never hears about this." Dante accepted the cash and slipped it into his pocket. "And don't ever call for me again."

His face resumed its kindly air as he passed through the door. He nodded at the guard with a smile and made for the exit.

Then stopped short.

To his left, in his peripheral vision, he could see a man standing there, staring at him. Dante had walked right past him, the oddness of the man's presence taking a moment to process. He studied the man's reflection in the wire mesh reinforced window before him. Small in stature—a good six inches shorter than Dante's five foot ten—but solid, the man was far from handsome. His head was balding and his face marked by a long nose and wide-set eyes. As if to compensate, his eyebrows reached inward so far as to just barely meet in the middle. But the oddest thing about him was his dress. Or rather, his robe. The man wore a long beige garment reaching to his ankles, with a darker tunic over that. In his hand he tightly gripped a dirty piece of cloth, hanging halfway to the ground.

Beyond the strange man Dante could see the reflection of the guard, sitting on his stool, paying no notice to anyone. Dante felt his heart kick up, although he was unsure why. There was something unnerving about this little man glaring at him, dressed like a monk or some kind of ancient philosopher, standing here where he shouldn't be. *When* he shouldn't be.

Dante forced himself to turn and face the man. He needed to know who he was. It made no sense, his being here, and Dante liked things to make sense.

The mopping inmate looked up from his bucket with the same vacant eyes as before, from precisely the place where the robed man had stood. Dante opened his mouth to speak, then closed it again. The guard perked up, put his hand on his sidearm.

"Everything okay?" he asked.

"Fine." Dante opened the door and stole another look back into the room. The sense of panic hadn't subsided, but he smiled all the same. "You gentlemen have a good day."

"You too, Reverend."

Chapter 2

April 1, 1765
Valletta, Malta

From without, the Cathédrale Saint-Jean-Baptiste de Lyon looked more like a fortress than a church —thoroughly monochromatic, starkly functional, and flanked by two unembellished towers. But inside, light gushed in through a series of strategically placed windows, bouncing off an arched ceiling and glistening against the gold that adorned almost every surface, accenting some of the most ornate carvings, paintings, and monuments in the Mediterranean world, if not all of Europe.

Count Cagliostro took it in with what he hoped was a sense of banality. As far as he knew, no one was watching, but that didn't matter. If he were to be accepted as a noble, an adventurer and mystic who had traveled the world, mastered forbidden arts, and learned manifold ancient secrets, he could not allow himself to feel even a private sense of awe.

To suppress it, he turned his attention to analyzing a particular panel beneath his feet— one of more than a hundred works of inlaid marble composing the chamber's floor. Each was large enough that he could have lain down on it with room to spare. He gazed down at the piece, admiring the craftsmanship despite himself. A skeleton holding a scythe and trumpet looked back up at him—oddly lifelike for a cold stone depiction of Death himself. Cagliostro's eyes drifted from panel to panel, finding most of them similarly decorated with skulls, crossbones, and skeletons.

"Welcome to the Island of Malta!" The greeting filled the perfect acoustics of the church. It was the voice of an old man, yet still full of life. He spoke Cagliostro's native Italian with an accent that did more to obscure his words than titivate them. Cagliostro looked up from the skeleton beneath him to see a man so old he seemed on the edge of meeting the Reaper firsthand. He walked with short, determined steps, causing his long black cloak to flap against his legs and the curls of his white wig to bounce against his high cheekbones.

Behind him, a burly man in a simpler black cloak belted the words, "His Most Eminent Highness, Grand Master Manuel Pinto da Fonseca, Prince of Malta."

There was an awkward moment while the Grand Master covered the remaining space between himself and his guest, clearly not wanting the young man to come to him. Cagliostro's eyes were drawn to the large white eight-pointed cross emblazoned on the man's breast—four arrowheads pointed inward. He felt his pulse quicken. This symbol represented everything that had drawn him here.

"I am delighted that you have come to our island," the Grand Master said. He held his hand out to Cagliostro, who stared at it for a moment, unsure of how to respond, before deciding to grasp it firmly—the sign of an equal.

"The pleasure belongs to me, Your Eminence," Cagliostro replied. He could sense in the old man's eyes that he had guessed correctly.

"Please," the old man replied, "my knights call me Grand Master Pinto. My subjects call me Your Eminent Highness. But my friends call me Fonseca, and I believe that you and I are to become friends." His smile widened. "Come, sit with me."

He grasped Cagliostro's stout arm as if to lead him to a seat, but it became quickly apparent that he needed the support of the younger man, who helped him over to a cushioned bench.

"I suppose," Fonseca said, his breath slightly labored, "I should have said, welcome *back* to Malta. I understand you have been here before."

"Indeed I have, although I do not remember it." Cagliostro leaned back and fixed his wide, round eyes on the Grand Master's. "You must understand that, while I am only twenty-two years of age, I have led an exceptional life.

"I was born of Christian nobles and abandoned

on the shores of this very island. At a young age I was brought to the holy city of Medina, where I was raised in the Muphti's palace and taught the mystical arts of necromancy, alchemy, and the kabala. Together with my servants and tutors I traveled to Mecca and then Egypt, where the temple priests took me into their confidence and entrusted to me many wonders, including the ancient rite of pure, untarnished Masonry." He paced himself, not wanting his words to betray themselves as memorized. "I have traveled widely throughout Africa and Asia and hold within myself many secrets—not the least of which is the Egyptian wine, which prolongs life." He smiled knowingly, his olive skin puckering. "I believe it is this secret that has earned me an audience with you."

Fonseca tipped his head toward his new friend and spoke quietly. "There is much we can do for each other, you and I. And much we can learn from each other. It is true that I am very old. Eighty-four years, and yet sound in mind and body." He looked down at his trembling right hand and quieted it with his left. "I would like to continue living, yes, but not just for the sake of living. I have been the Grand Master of the Knights of Malta for twenty-four years—far longer than anyone expected I should last. And yet . . ."

Cagliostro studied his face. "You fear you've been a disappointment to the order?"

"I should hope not," the Grand Master said, the words heavy. "When I was first elected to this office, I could sense that times were changing. We all could. And yet I ignored it, like the rest. I built cities in my name and pressed new coins for every occasion. But the truth is that all of this"— he gestured at the gilded hall around them—"is a veneer. Here we sit at the very crossroads of the world, where East meets West, with an army of the most powerful noble families in Europe—and yet our coffers are nearly empty.

"I have tried cultivating silk, expanding our cities, raising taxes. It's no good." He stared up into the murals above them. "For six hundred and sixty-six years we have survived and flourished as an order. I will not see that glory fade away, even as the life fades from this body." A fire seemed to rekindle in his eyes, and he turned again to face his companion.

"That is why you're here, Cagliostro. I have heard of your skills as an alchemist and a conjurer, that you can predict the future by way of dreams, and that you are very close to perfecting an Elixir of Life."

"This is true," Cagliostro said, as if it were nothing profound.

"Then you will have all of the remaining resources at my disposal." Fonseca straightened his spine and squeezed his bony knees through his cloak. "I have a group of nobles very much

34

interested in the occult, ready to aid you. And more importantly, I have this." He reached into his cloak and withdrew the sacred object. "Do you know what this is, my dear Cagliostro?"

The count was now on his feet, mouth agape, no longer able to hide his amazement. "Yes," he said, his voice barely a whisper. "Yes, I think I do."

Fonseca grinned. "The world may change," he said, "but we will cut it off at the pass."

Chapter 3

Present day

"You need to cook those first," Fletcher said. He was leaning on the counter in the cramped kitchen, less than a foot away from his wife, being helpful again.

"They're already cooked," Meg said.

"But not really. I mean, they're pink. Like raw-hamburger pink. When you cook them, they change color."

"What does this say? Right here?" She pointed at some smallish print on the label.

"No, but that's—"

"What does it say?"

" 'Classic wieners.' "

She laughed. "Down here. It says 'fully cooked.' "

"Who can read that? That's nothing."

She pulled a long knife from the block and gestured at him with her elbow. "You want to give me some space here?"

"They're cold, though. That's the thing."

She cut the package open and retrieved three hot dogs. "I leave it all on the stove so it warms up together. That's how she likes it." She sliced the hot dogs into half-inch segments and dumped them into a pot of macaroni and cheese bubbling on the stove. "You will eat it and you will like it."

"Can't wait. Third time this week." He didn't mention that he'd been keeping count since returning home three months earlier. Tonight would make thirty-two times that mac and cheese and hot dogs had graced the menu in the Doyle household, not counting leftovers for lunch.

Meg sighed. "It's cheap and it's one of about three things Ivy will eat, so yes, we have it a lot. We're used to it, Fletcher. And I would think you'd be used to a lot worse, so stop complaining."

"The food in the chow hall wasn't actually that bad." He scratched his head, further tousling his intentionally disheveled blond hair. "But the stuff people came up with on their own . . . This one guy, Little Domino, would make pizza—I mean, he called it pizza. The crust was crushed-up crackers and ramen noodles, and he'd put it in a trash bag and kind of knead it into shape."

"That's disgusting." She stirred the pot with a

wooden spoon, distributing the hot dogs. "What did he use as toppings?"

"Whatever he could get his hands on. Corn chips, salsa, ketchup, Slim Jims, sliced-up hot dogs. But even he had the sense to cook the things first."

"You think you're funny?" Her tone was sharp, but her smile gave her away.

"Maybe a little bit?"

Their eyes locked for a moment, and he considered moving even closer. She was wearing an old cotton T-shirt and no makeup, and her auburn hair was pulled back in a careless pony-tail. He wanted to put his arms around her and pull her in tight, like before. But he hesitated, and the moment passed.

Pathetic. Who ever heard of a confidence man who lacked the confidence to kiss his own wife?

They heard the front door swing open, and their daughter breezed in. She moved quickly past the kitchen, a rather full canvas bag in tow. To Fletcher, Ivy looked like a miniature version of his wife, his only obvious genetic contribution being her slightly cleft chin.

"Hello to you too!" he called out after her. Her footsteps stopped, then reversed, and she appeared in the doorway.

"Hello, Father. What's for dinner?"

"What do you think?"

She nodded her approval, a crooked smile on

her face, and Fletcher was suddenly fine with macaroni and cheese with hot dogs.

"What have you got there?" he asked.

"Just some stuff for my collection."

"More trash?"

Ivy rolled her eyes. "It's not trash, Father. It's from the recycle bin at the Dairy Mart."

"You really can call me Dad, you know."

"Got it." She looked down at the bag in her hands quietly for a moment.

"This is almost done, sweet pea," Meg said. "Why don't you go wash up?"

"Okay."

"And don't get sidetracked. We have to be at church in less than an hour."

Ivy twisted her face up. "Why are we having youth group tonight if we're spending a whole week with those people?"

"We just have to go over last-minute details," Meg said. "Besides, your dad is speaking tonight."

"You?" She looked at her father. "Really?"

"Yes, really," Meg said. "Now go wash up."

They had just dished out their meal and said grace when the doorbell rang. Fletcher sighed and dropped his fork back onto the table.

"It better not be him," he said.

"I'll answer it," Meg offered.

"No. I got it." He stood and repeated, "It better not be him."

It was him. "Him" being Brad Howard. Fletcher saw his smug face through the window from ten feet away, and by the time he opened the door he was already in a foul mood.

"We just sat down to eat, Brad," he said as curtly as he could. "What do you need?"

Brad smirked. "You know, on the outside we greet each other with words like 'Hello' and 'How are you?' "

Everything about Brad was loathsome to Fletcher, from his holier-than-thou attitude to his thinning, probably dyed ink-black hair, combed back in a bad attempt at a pompadour. Fletcher pegged him at somewhere between forty-five and sixty. It was hard to pin down precisely, as his skin was badly sun-damaged (from boating, no doubt), and he always seemed to be wearing the uniform of the ageless dork—pleated khakis, golf shirt, braided belt.

"Look, Brad, this thing at church was your idea, and we're a bit crunched for time. Do you need something?"

"It's about that. I wanted to make sure we're on the same page tonight. Can I assume you cleared this trip with your parole officer?" The way he drew out the words *parole officer* made Fletcher want to knock the smirk off the guy's face.

"Yes, Brad. Not that it's any of your concern, but yes."

"And your boss at the . . . Where is it you work again?"

"Labrenz Vending. Yes, I've taken the time off work."

Brad squeezed out a condescending little smile. "I think it's just terrific that you've been able to hold down a job for three months. I know it can be tough."

"I have a doctorate, Brad. I think I can probably handle refilling vending machines. Now, if you don't mind—"

"Just make sure you tell them you're sorry, okay? Tonight? Say those words. That's what we're going for."

"Tell who I'm sorry?"

"The parents and the youth group kids. That's why we're all getting together before the trip, Fletcher—a lot of the parents have come to me to voice their concern that there's a convicted felon accompanying their kids on a week-long trip. This is an opportunity to clear the air."

"Who voiced concerns?"

"A lot of people."

"Name one. Pastor Dave told me that everyone was fine with me and Meg going. So tell me the name of just one of these mystery people." Fletcher caught his anger rising and intentionally slowed his breathing. Very few people had successfully gotten under his skin in the past ten years, six of which had been spent in prison. And yet Brad managed to do it every time they spoke.

"Look," Brad said, "I don't want to make a big thing of it. It was a pretty big group, and I assured them that I would be going along as well to keep an eye on everything, and that you weren't that kind of criminal—you know, a sex pervert or something."

"Appreciate it, Brad."

"But if there's still significant concern after tonight, we may have to ask you to stay behind."

Fletcher gathered his anger in his chest, an old trick his mentor had taught him, and forced it all up into a smile. "Whether you like it or not, I'm going. I'm looking forward to spending time with Meg and Ivy, meeting new people, helping out, and I think it would be best if you and I just steered clear of each other."

"You don't think Ivy is too young for this trip, do you?"

"Three other twelve-year-olds are going. So, no."

"And what about you?" His face read overstated concern. "Is this too soon? Are you worried about going back into the city? Your old territory?"

"Nope."

"That's good. We wouldn't want you falling back in with the wrong element. Your old cronies or homies or whatever."

"I haven't seen any of those people in almost seven years. My PO is fine with this and I'm fine with it and Pastor Dave is fine with it. And you don't get a vote."

"Fair enough." Brad looked past Fletcher, into the house. "Well, I guess you should get some dinner in you. How's the range working, by the way? I know while you were locked up it would sometimes go on the fritz. I had to come by many a night and help make the macaroni and hot dogs a reality." He smirked again. Or was that just how Brad smiled?

"It's fine," Fletcher said, slowly closing the door.

"Okay. Just trying to do my part. See you at church, Fletcher."

Fletcher said nothing.

Chapter 4

Dante unlocked the metal accordion gate blocking off Broadmoor Outreach Tabernacle and slid it back just far enough to unlock the door. The storefront church was situated in a less-than-desirable neighborhood, and Dante kept his guard up while coming and going. The unwritten rule was that ministers were off-limits when it came to the local criminal element, but he took no chances. He locked the door behind him and deactivated the burglar alarm.

The day had been a waste. Dante had spent four hours at Mercy Hospital, waiting for some street-level punk to get out of surgery so he could waltz past the police into the recovery room, Bible in hand, and find out who had shot him. And, of course, deliver a firm reminder of just what would await the kid should he get chatty with the cops.

But the boy hadn't made it through surgery, and now Dante's back was killing him. What kind of sadist would fill a hospital waiting room with such criminally uncomfortable furniture? He stretched and groaned, feeling far older than his thirty-eight years.

"Welcome to Broadmoor Whatever Church. Please be seated."

A shot of alarm crackled up Dante's spine, and his mind went to the Glock in his desk drawer in the study. Then he saw the man standing behind the pulpit, partially obscured by shadows, but unmistakably Marcus Brinkman. The fear left Dante, leaving a low-grade dread behind.

"Have a seat, Trick," the man said. "We need to talk."

The last few rays of sun were spilling in on Dante through the window and seemed to lock him in place, holding him back from the darkness and the man on the platform.

"You know I don't like to repeat myself, Trick," Marcus said.

Dante suppressed his instincts and slowly approached the man.

Bella Donna's primary enforcer had to be at

least seventy years old, but Dante felt no shame in being terrified of Marcus Brinkman. The man looked like a cautionary tale, with the eyes of a corpse on a good day and a swollen head, shaved completely bald and covered in liver spots that reminded Dante of kill tallies on the side of a World War II fighter plane. His bulbous nose looked like it had been broken a dozen times.

Dante took a seat near the front of the make-shift sanctuary. Marcus dragged a chair around and sat facing him. He said nothing for several seconds, just sat there sucking his teeth.

"How are things, Marcus?" Dante asked. He'd been chewed out by this man before, and it was anything but pleasant. He wanted to move things along, get it over with.

"How are things?" the older man repeated. "I've got problems. Like anyone, I suppose. My doctor tells me I've got high cholesterol. Wants me to stop eating red meat like some kind of you-know-what."

"Vegetarian?"

"Sure. I tell him it's the twenty-first century and he can just give me some medicine to fix the problem. And he says they don't make medicine to lower this kind of cholesterol. I guess there's more than one kind of cholesterol now. So he's got me taking fish oil capsules, three every morning. And then all day long, I'm burping. I'm tasting fish all day."

"That's . . . I'm sorry to hear that, Marcus."

"So now I'm sitting in this phony little church of yours for two hours waiting for you to show, burping up fish. That's how things are over here. How you been, Trick?"

"I'm—"

"Not good, that's how. When I show up at your door, means the boss isn't happy."

"Okay?" Dante crossed and recrossed his legs.

"You've been taking liberties, Trick." He raised his eyebrows and waited a moment. Dante said nothing. "I hear you collected four hundred dollars from that Barnes kid yesterday. Funny thing is, it wasn't in the ledger."

Sweat began to crowd Dante's eyes. He blinked it away. "He didn't take the product, Marcus. I can't really put it in the ledger if he doesn't take the product."

"But you took his money."

"The guy had to learn—"

"What? What did he have to learn? The exact chain of command from his insignificant little carcass on the street all the way up to Bella Donna? Did he have to learn that? Because he's been bragging about that over at his new home in Jackson. Yappin' about it to anyone who'll listen. And that information could come in handy if, say, he wants to work out a deal for himself."

Dante opened his mouth, but decided that silence was his best tactic at the moment.

"You been around awhile," Marcus continued. "You've figured out how things work, and you think that makes you bulletproof. But it doesn't."

"I . . . I have the money here. And the product. You can have it."

Marcus frowned and shook his head slowly. "Nah, you keep it. We're not worried about one little transgression. What does concern us is what I like to call a pattern of sloppiness and over-stepping. And this time you've taken one step too far. Doesn't surprise me; I've been warning Bella Donna for years that you were eventually going to land in it, and now you have. You know how?"

Dante shook his head.

"Everyone says you can talk, Trick. Apparently you can't shut up. Last week you were dealing with another guy who needed to 'learn.' Only you decided that this guy ought to learn about a quarter-million dollar deal coming up through the tunnel. Then he started flapping his jaw to his fellow lowlifes, and before long word was everywhere and the deal fell through. Bella Donna lost two hundred twenty-five large in one day. Because of you."

Dante shifted. He felt like his head was full of helium and his feet full of bricks.

"But that's not all," Marcus said. "Cleaning up the mess and restoring good faith with the seller, that took another hundred grand and, as you well know, the boss is inclined to round up in such cases. Let's call this a half-million dollar problem."

With startling speed, the old man lurched forward and drove his fist into Dante's solar plexus, sending him to the ground gasping for breath. Marcus rose to his feet and reached up under his suit coat, pulling a handgun from the small of his back.

"I can make it up to her," Dante wheezed. Then he felt the muzzle of the gun pushing against his temple.

"Mm-hmm. Normally your brains would be abstract carpet art from here to the wall," Marcus said, "but you've been such a useful little cog in the machine that the boss wants to give you a chance to redeem yourself. You've got one week. Bring her the half million and turn from your wicked, wicked ways, and all will be forgiven."

"A week?" Dante was a master negotiator, but he knew better than to try his luck with the likes of Marcus Brinkman.

"Seven days. You get the cash or you get removed from the equation." He offered a hand to Dante and helped him to his feet. "Oh, and don't make it worse for yourself. Don't take it from her clients and don't step on her interests. Understand?"

Dante nodded.

Marcus tilted his head as if reading his thoughts. "You run, I'll find you. And, Trick, I won't just come after you. I'll hit you where you hurt most." He replaced the pistol and walked out silently, leaving Dante to corral his panic.

Hit him where he hurt most? What did that mean? As far as Dante knew, the Syndicate knew next to nothing about his private life. Was Marcus threatening to burn down the church building? The thought was unpleasant, to say the least, but in the end would be an acceptable loss. If that was it, Dante could run. He could blend in anywhere; that's what he did. And the sooner, the better.

Then something caught his eye, something stacked on the chair where Marcus had been sitting only moments ago. Photos. He scrambled over and snatched them up. With each flip, his stomach sank further.

His mother. His sister. His niece.

He looked around at the almost-worthless piece of real estate—worth less than a third of what he'd paid for it five years earlier, despite all the money he'd sunk into it. Even if he could sell the church in a week, it would barely help. He thought of his savings account and his two cash hordes. They got him nowhere close.

Where would he get half a million dollars?

Chapter 5

The youth group room at Harbor Beach Community Church was the same as every youth group room everywhere. A collection of couches lined the perimeter—either castoffs from church members or picked up from the side of the road by overeager ministry interns. The cinder block walls had been spray-painted with a variety of slogans and patterns by a previous incarnation of the youth group, now all out of college with children of their own. Framed posters and prints captured the essence of decade-old Christian pop culture like some sort of unintentional time capsule.

At the moment, Fletcher was the center of attention. He had just hit the climax of his testimony—the part where he was sitting in a prison cell, reading the Bible, giving his heart to Jesus. He'd kept the presentation short and light on details, as Brad had insisted, and was more than happy to have put this chore behind him.

"The thing is," he said, scanning the mostly blank faces of teens and parents, "Jesus saved me from prison, but he saved you guys from prison too. You were all in bondage to sin and death, and Jesus set you free."

A few parents offered halfhearted amens, which seemed as good an indicator as any that he had reached the end of his talk. He turned back toward a particularly ratty love seat, where the comfy space between his wife and his daughter was beckoning him.

"That's an interesting way to look at it, Fletcher," Brad said. He was perched on a tall stool, looming several feet above the others. "The Bible tells us that all have sinned and fallen short of the glory of God. Some of us just fall . . . further, I guess. Anyone have any questions for Fletcher? Any concerns?"

Courtney Howard raised her hand. She was sitting on the floor, practically at Fletcher's feet, smiling up at him from between two gum-chomping friends, and he could sense that she'd been waiting for a chance to jump in. Exasperation draped itself over him. Courtney was Brad's sixteen-year-old daughter, and she had taken a shine to Fletcher immediately upon meeting him three months earlier. She frequently engaged him in conversation—particularly when her father was around—and always greeted him with a wide, bright-eyed smile full of blindingly white teeth.

Fletcher glanced at her father, hoping for an out. Whatever his beef with Brad, he had no desire to get mixed up in some teenage girl's campaign to irk her overbearing square of a dad. Brad said nothing, just fixed Fletcher with a warning glare.

"Yes, Courtney?"

"So if you're a 'white collar criminal,' what does that even mean? Did you, like, steal people's identities or something?"

Fletcher chuckled. "No. We weren't identity thieves, and we weren't ripping off old people or single moms of their life savings. We only stole from the uberwealthy—the one percent, as they say."

"What difference does that make?" asked Courtney's friend Tracy, an entitled little cheerleader with a perma-sneer.

"It doesn't, I guess. I mean, it's still wrong. But if you could have met some of these people . . . In today's economy, these milquetoasts just keep on piling it up. And I'm not talking about speedboats and Lamborghinis, but stuff they can't even enjoy. Art. Antiquities. One-of-a-kind pieces they only want so that no one else can have them. Most of them didn't even realize what they had. And so my partner and I would simply relieve them of said items."

Noah, an unmedicated guitar hero, piped up, raising his hand three words in, then lowering it immediately. "You stole milk toast? What the heck is milk toast?"

"No, Noah. That's not a— We targeted very old, very significant items and sold them on the black market."

"Did you use a machine gun?"

"I'm a nonviolent—or, I *was* a nonviolent offender, okay?"

"That's what I don't get," chirped Courtney.

Fletcher sighed. His spot on the love seat seemed to be moving further away. "What I did was called grifting. You don't usually just steal something. You let the person convince you to take it."

Blank stares.

"Look, every thief has his choice set of tools. Some prefer guns, others prefer lock picks and safe-cracking equipment. Some use lines of computer code. Then there are guys like me. Or like I was. I know human nature—at its worst and most predictable. That was my area, and when we used that, we weren't even thieves."

"Who's *we?*" Noah asked. "Did you have your own gang?"

"I had a partner. He kind of groomed me for the Life."

"That's hard-core," Noah whispered.

Noah's mother, Carol, sitting behind him and wearing an increasingly concerned expression, asked, "Didn't you say you studied religion in college? How did you wind up being a criminal?"

"I did study the philosophy and history of religion—and I've got the degrees to show for it." Fletcher glanced at Brad. "But I wasn't a Christian back then."

Everyone waited expectantly. They wouldn't be satisfied until they had details.

"Okay, it went like this," he said. "In grad school I got this internship at the metropolitan museum. When it ended I stayed on as a custodian. I figured it would be good to have my foot in the door when I finished my master's degree.

"Well, I got the degree, but I just stayed a janitor. Even when positions opened up, someone with experience would swoop in and fill it. So I started on my PhD. And finished all my course work—still a janitor. Then one day we get this traveling exhibit of priceless Maltese artifacts. At the same time, all the security guards but one get food poisoning—bad meatballs, something. So I traded my mop for a nightstick. Turns out the other guard was planning on stealing a sword that used to belong to the Grand Master of the Knights of Malta. He asked me to help him, said he needed an inside man on the job. And I agreed."

"But why?" Carol asked.

"Pride, really. I was sick of being taken for granted. Andrew offered me a chance to actually use all the knowledge I'd been accruing. Looking back, he played on my disillusionment. He grifted me. He found my peg."

"Fletcher," Brad said with a dollop of disdain, "these kids don't speak Underworld."

"A person's peg is what they want most in the world. If a grifter can spot your peg, he can win

53

you over. What I wanted was respect. And he provided it. And excitement. And lots of money. I paid off my student loans and bought my wife a platinum ring with the money from that first job."

Every head wheeled and gawked at Meg, who stared down at her lap for a moment before rolling her eyes up angrily at Fletcher.

"But that Andrew guy poisoned them, right?" Noah asked.

"Poisoned who?"

"The other security guards. He knew your *peg* or whatever, so he got them out of the way."

Fletcher paused. "Yes. I suppose he did. And I guess I always knew that. But Andrew needed me since he wasn't really an expert on historical artifacts, and then I needed him because I couldn't beat an alarm or a safe and I had no idea how to fence a five-hundred-year-old sword or an antique Bible."

"You stole Bibles?" The question came from more than one direction as teenagers and adults alike gaped at the felon in their midst.

"If you know what to look for, antique Bibles can be very valuable."

"So you stole stuff too, right?" asked a jock in the far corner. "You didn't just trick people."

Fletcher hesitated. "Yes, that's true."

"How many things?"

The truth was that Fletcher had lost count, but he wasn't about to say that.

"I think we're getting off track here," Brad said. "We don't want to glorify what Fletcher did. Why don't you tell us how you got caught?" A smile played at the corners of his mouth.

"Well, it wasn't a grift. It was more like the first job in the museum—a straightforward heist. We were stealing a monstrance. That's like a golden stand that holds the bread for Communion in some churches."

"So you were raiding a church, stealing its priceless relics," Brad said, clearly enjoying himself.

Fletcher felt like he was back on the witness stand, being badgered by that rat-faced prosecutor.

"It wasn't even an active church anymore," he said, trying not to sound defensive. "They just rented it out for weddings and social events and stuff. They had this thing collecting dust in the back."

Brad furrowed his brow. "You almost sound like you're trying to justify your actions, Fletcher. Aren't you sorry?"

Fletcher caught his rage en route between his guts and his tongue. "Yes, Brad," he said, looking him in the eyes. "I'm very sorry for what I've done."

"Might I suggest we leave room for grace?" Pastor Dave had slipped into the back of the room at some point during the discussion. "Fletcher's sins are under the blood of Jesus, just like yours and mine, Brad. And let's not forget how many of the characters in the Bible did time: Joseph, Paul, Peter, even the Lord Jesus."

Brad shrugged. "They were all falsely accused, weren't they?"

"It's getting late," Fletcher said. "And I still need to finish packing."

There was a general murmur of agreement.

"Good idea, Fletcher," Pastor Dave said. "Let's call it a night. I'll see you all back here at seven thirty tomorrow morning. The elders and I will pray you on your way. Take it from me: a mission trip can be a life-changing experience."

Noah shot his hand up and immediately asked, "But what happened to that monster thing?"

"No more caffeine for Noah," Pastor Dave said. "He's not making any sense."

"The thing Fletcher was trying to steal," Noah said, annoyed. "Did you get it?"

"No," Fletcher answered. "By the grace of God, I got caught and left the old life behind. My partner got out, as far as I know. And the monstrance was moved, I think. Probably somewhere with more security."

Noah's hand went up again, but the minister cut him off. "That's enough for tonight," he said. "Get some sleep. I want to see seven chaperones and eighteen youth groupers here at seven thirty sharp tomorrow morning. And don't forget your air mattresses. Twin-size only. You'll be sharing your sleeping quarters with about two hundred other kids."

A groan of complaint rose up from among the youth.

"Not to worry. You're staying at Life Journey Church again this year. We stayed there for service camp a few years back, and it was really nice and plenty roomy. It's not like sleeping in a cell or something."

Every eye went from the pastor to Fletcher and back again.

"Oh, ohhh," Dave blustered. "I'm so sorry, Fletcher. I meant like a monastery cell."

Brad snickered loudly.

Chapter 6

November 8, 1772
Valletta, Malta

Cagliostro rushed down the hall as quickly as his plump legs would carry him, past full suits of armor demarking the beginning and end of brick arches. His green silk coat flapped against the air, causing the design of its gold brocade to shift and morph. He burst into Fonseca's bedchamber and found his friend reclining. The old man was still in full uniform—black cloak and pantaloons, boots, wig—clutching his sword to his chest but breathing shallowly, with a pronounced rattle.

"I have brought more of the Elixir of Life," Cagliostro announced.

"I am in great need of it," the Grand Master said. He accepted a small bottle from his friend's hand, removed the cork with his teeth, and swallowed down its contents. He squeezed his eyes shut for a moment before sitting up with some difficulty. Cagliostro relieved him of his sword and set it down on a small rosewood table. He took a moment to admire its craftsmanship. Where the hilt and handle met there was attached a large, ruby-studded eight-point cross—a Maltese cross.

"They all thought you had taken me for a fool, you know," Fonseca said, "when I took you into my palace and gave you rooms for your laboratories. The treasurers tell me I spent a million lira entertaining you. I've heard them laughing about it. But look at me—ninety-one years old, still lucid and leading my knights. I owe that to you, Cagliostro. But we must move forward with our plans. I fear change is coming."

"It is indeed. And we must ride ahead and cut it off," the younger man replied. "I was in Rome when word of your illness reached me. And I have been in England and France. Your instincts are correct. While you live here in your palace, revolution is spreading across the once-civilized world. It is imminent in America, of course, but also in Europe. On the streets of Paris and even here on Malta, people are embracing the absurd notion that all men have been created of equal estate. Empires that have stood for millennia will fall, Fonseca. And this sovereign order of knights, which has endured for seven centuries, will not last another generation. Mark my words: what the masses do not take, the Protestant nobles will."

"Stop!" Fonseca rasped. "Do you prophesy? Or is this only an opinion?"

"I am . . . not sure."

"You must be wrong. For we did not arrive at this island by chance. It was the Great Architect's design. Look at the evidence! When the Moslems lost the Holy City, our order came to dominate the Christian quarter. To show our faithfulness we kept the infidel at bay, protected Christian pilgrims from their demonic scimitars."

"I know this well, old friend. You need rest now."

Fonseca ignored him. "And when we lost the Holy City, we took Cyprus and Rhodes. Even when the Templars ceased to be, devoured by their own avarice, we carried on with divine protection. For six hundred more years, we have carried on!"

"Please, try to calm down, Fonseca. The elixir takes time."

"We built a navy such as the world had never seen. And castles! Defenses!" He tried to rise out of the bed but flopped back down. "The very mention of our name caused the Turks to wet themselves for fear. When the Moslems again stole our island, we came here, where the Great Architect wills us to be. Here we are the scourge of Barbary pirates and the subject of every Turk's nightmare. They still tell frightful stories of their folly on our shores, when forty thousand Mohammedans attacked us." He raised his hands as if giving a rousing speech to a gathered army. "They nailed the bodies of our dead to crosses and floated them into our harbors. So we fired the heads of their dead from our cannons. Their ships crashed against our great underwater stakes in our harbors and were forever lost."

"Yes, my friend," Cagliostro said soothingly. "You have told me this many times. And two hundred years later, Voltaire still says that 'nothing in the world is better known than the siege of Malta.' "

Fonseca gave his hand a weak squeeze. "This is why I sent for you to begin with, Cagliostro. Do you know what the punishment is for any member of the Sovereign Order of the Knights of Malta who is discovered practicing alchemy? Or funding it? Or even encouraging its use?"

Cagliostro nodded. "Such a man should be condemned to row in the galleys for the rest of his days, as should anyone found working on metal apart from natural methods."

"But you and I know what alchemy truly is, that it is far more than metallurgy. It is boiling a thing down to the essence, whether lead or gold or a man! We can find its essence. And that is why we will continue to thrive beyond these days of treason and treachery.

"When we first met, I saw you examining the tombs of the fallen knights in our conventual church. Do you know why we decorate the tombs of our companions with skulls and bones? We make light of Death because we do not fear him." A coughing jag overcame him for the space of a minute. "You still have it?" he asked.

"Do I have what?"

"The cloth of St. Paul," the Grand Master croaked.

"Of course I still have it."

The old man smiled weakly. "I knew I was right to entrust it to you. Your knowledge, your skills as a pharmacist . . . you will harness its power. The world sees us venerating St. John, but it is St. Paul's cloth that will give us dominion over Death. And if we do not fear Death, how can we fear mere words spoken by peasants in the streets?"

"But, Fonseca, the tides are turning, and not in our favor. The old order stands precariously, like dominoes placed in a line. It is only a matter of time before someone tips them."

"Then you would admit defeat?" A look of

betrayal spilled across the Grand Master's face. "Even you?"

"On the contrary, I believe that we have one good move open to us, and only one." He leaned in close to his friend, who, despite the lemon water he had just drunk, would be dead within three months. "We must tip the dominoes ourselves."

Chapter 7

"I doubt you'll need this dress," Fletcher said, holding up an unzipped garment bag.

"It's a skirt and jacket," Meg said, "not a dress." The tailored suit was one of the few reminders of the brief window when she and Fletcher had been flush. For that reason, she both loved and hated it.

"Either way . . ."

"What if we go to church?" she asked.

"But we're coming home Saturday."

"My mother taught me to always pack something dressy, no matter what. It's best to be prepared. Speaking of which . . ." She walked across the hall into Ivy's room. "How's the packing going in here?"

"Ummm . . ."

"You haven't even started, have you?"

Ivy shook her head. Meg wanted to be angry,

but the sight of her daughter in her pajamas, smiling sheepishly, derailed her plans.

"I'll tell you what," Meg said. "You go downstairs and find a suitcase, and we'll do it together, okay?"

"Thanks, Mom!" The girl bolted from her bedroom, leaving her mother alone to survey the collections of bottles, plastic containers, Styrofoam packaging, and other items that had all been carefully washed, grouped together on the floor, suspended from the ceiling, or perched on shelves —some color-coordinated, some ordered by size, and some apparently grouped randomly.

Meg heard Ivy's steps loudly descend into the basement. In less than a minute her daughter was lugging a rather large suitcase through the door.

Meg laughed. "We could pack *you* in that thing!"

"Should I get a different one?"

"No. We can share this one." She stepped over to Ivy's dresser and started counting out socks and underwear.

Ivy shrieked. "Oh my—what is *this?*"

Meg had heard her daughter raise her voice so rarely that she dropped the armful of clothes and rushed over. "What's the matter?"

Ivy was doubled over in laughter. "Oh, I don't know, Mom. I only opened the suitcase and found this." She held up a purple glittery faux snakeskin fanny pack.

Meg stifled a laugh. "It's called a fanny pack."

"I know what it's called," Ivy gasped, "but why do you have it?"

"Shut up." Meg laughed. She snatched the functional accessory from her daughter and fastened it around her waist. She made a lap around the bedroom, turning each corner like a runway model and drawing howls from her daughter.

"Okay," Meg said, wiping her eyes and regathering her breath. "It's all out in the open now. I had a fanny pack in the midnineties. I used to wear it once in a—a lot. It's good to get that off my chest. Now let's get you packed; it's getting late."

She flipped the suitcase back open to reveal an identical purple pack inside. Ivy let out another squeal. "Two of them? Please don't tell me you and Dad had matching fanny packs!"

Fletcher poked his head into the room. "What's going on in here?"

Ivy held the offending item up next to her deep crimson face. "Explain this," she demanded.

"Oh, yeah—that one's mine," Fletcher said.

"He's kidding, honey," Meg assured her daughter.

"No, I bought that one with my own money. Before I married your mother. Therefore, it belongs to me. In fact, that's how I won her over."

"Don't . . . ," Meg pleaded.

"I think she's old enough to hear this," Fletcher

said, sitting on Ivy's bed and adopting a fatherly posture. "It was those very fanny packs that brought us together. They're why you exist."

Ivy was shaking her head vigorously, as if this would negate the truth of the statement.

"You see, I met your mother in a psychology class our sophomore year of college."

"Philosophy," Meg corrected.

"No, I first noticed you in psychology. Maybe you didn't see *me,* but I noticed this beautiful young woman with big blue eyes and a dazzling purple fanny pack. She was never without that thing. I kept my eye on her that whole semester."

"That's called stalking," Ivy interjected.

"Fair enough. Anyway, I noticed that she would always take it off and carefully hang it on the back of her seat before class. Then, about halfway through, she'd open the zipper pouch and take out one of those cardboard-flavored Little Debbie brownies."

"Oh, this is getting so much worse," Ivy said.

Meg was covering her face but couldn't stop laughing.

"So the next semester we had philosophy together—I made sure of it."

"Stalker," Ivy repeated.

"Right, and I had seen a fanny pack just like your mom's at the mall, so I bought it and stuffed it full of Little Debbie brownies and a note asking if I could take her to a concert. Then I just sat behind her and carefully swapped the two packs. And that is how I won over your mom."

"I actually called him to get my dorm room key and my wallet," Meg said.

"Oh my gosh, I love that story," Ivy said, grinning. "I mean, it's horrible, but I love it."

"The best stories are true stories," Fletcher said, locking eyes with Meg. She gave him exactly the smile he wanted.

"Wait a minute," Ivy said. "I thought you said you rescued Mom from a bridge."

Fletcher laughed. "I can't believe you remember that. No, I rescued her from the other side of the bridge. Because she's Canadian."

Ivy looked from the purple abomination around her mother's waist to the one in her hand and then to her father. "So I guess you were a grifter before you even met Mom."

Meg's laughter stopped. Fletcher's smile faded. An awkward moment passed. Ivy, oblivious, rubbed her eyes and yawned.

Meg broke the silence. "How about I just pack your stuff for you? I think you need to go to sleep."

Ivy nodded.

"That means you take what I pack and don't complain, okay?"

"Okay, Mom." Ivy crawled into bed and pulled the sheet up to her chin.

Fletcher kissed her on the forehead. "Good night, sweetie."

"Good night, Father."

"I love you."

She nodded. "Got it."

He left his wife to say her good nights and plopped down on the living room couch. Meg emerged a moment later, a yellow legal pad full of to-do lists in hand, and seemed about to disappear.

"I was close," Fletcher called.

"Hmm?" She looked up. "What was close?"

"She called me Dad when I wasn't in there. I heard her. It was nice, and it was nice to see her come out of her shell a little bit. Like the old Ivy." He smiled. "Now if I could just phase out this Father stuff once and for all."

"Dad is an earned title," Meg said, "and when you relinquish it, it takes more than three months to earn it back."

Fletcher sat up. "Did I do something wrong, hon?"

Meg looked off into the distance for a moment. "Of course you did, Fletcher. Or they wouldn't have sent you to prison." She paused, shook her head once, and finally looked at her husband. "I'm sorry. That was mean. It's just . . . after all we went through for the past six and a half years, it's hard to have you just roll back in and expect everything to be normal right away."

"What should I do, then?" He was working to keep the edge off his voice. "I've missed out on half her life already. I don't want to miss any more. Why would you want me to?"

Meg sat down next to him and studied her feet. "I don't want you to miss anything. I just want you to remember that she's fragile, okay? We both are. We lost everything. She lost her dad. I lost my partner in life. We suddenly had zero income. She was just coming back out of her shell when we lost our home and everything we knew. An eight-year-old doesn't understand what bankruptcy and foreclosure are."

"I know, Meg. I know what I did to you. I've said I'm sorry at least a hundred times, and I'll say it ten thousand more if you want."

"I don't want you to be sorry. I want you to *get it.* Ivy was at a private school. One-on-one attention, lots of friends, an amazing future. Then suddenly she's in literally the worst public school in the country."

"Don't exaggerate or anything," Fletcher said. "An elementary school?"

"It went up through eighth grade. And the school district was the worst in the country. I'm not exaggerating. It was on a list on the Internet. What does that do to a kid? She's suddenly living in a one-bedroom apartment, hearing gunshots in the night. Then she's dragged out to the suburbs away from everything she knows and she's getting picked on for her jailbird dad. That kind of stuff leaves scars, Fletcher."

"She seems pretty well adjusted to me," Fletcher offered.

"She is. Thank God for Dr. Levi. He's really helped her sort out her feelings."

"Yeah." Fletcher did not like to think about Dr. Levi, a counselor who had been picked out and paid for by Brad Howard. Whenever Meg and Fletcher had a disagreement, there always seemed to appear some unsubstantiated quote from the good doctor.

"You know why he thinks she collects all that junk?"

"What does he shrink?"

Meg rolled her eyes. "He said she's trying to salvage what's left of her childhood. That's why she takes things that have been thrown out and washes them up and keeps them."

"Seriously?" Fletcher laughed. "Wow, that's so incredibly deep. I'm glad I didn't pay for that guy."

"Well, I'm glad we happened to find someone who cared enough to get help for a little girl who isn't even his."

Fletcher stood up. "Are you kidding me? You think Brad did all that out of the kindness of his heart? You think he gave you this place for half the rental value to be nice? He's not nice, Meg. He's a jerk. Which means he had one goal in mind, and it had more to do with your skirt than Ivy's psychological well-being."

"He's not like that. He was going through some hard stuff too, and he was just being kind."

"That's way beyond kind. And if Brad moved here two years ago, why does he even own two houses? Did you ever wonder about that?"

"That's part of what he does for a living. He invests in real estate. And he's not making any money on this place. You might try and remember that."

"Yeah, I'll keep that in mind."

"We owe him so much, Fletcher. How can you not see that? Ivy and I had nothing when we moved here. *Nothing*. One month after filing bankruptcy, and every landlord wanted to run a credit check. I had debts up to my neck and a car that wouldn't go in reverse. Brad had some compassion when no one else did."

"Oh yeah, he just oozes compassion. That and creepiness. You're young enough to be his daughter, for crying out loud!"

"He's not as old as you think," Meg said. Then added, quieter, "He's not even fifty."

"So he's got that distinguished-older-man sexiness going? Is that it?"

"It's not like that, Fletcher! How many times—?" She caught herself and took a deep breath. "He's a nice person." Her voice faltered on the last word, and Fletcher knew he was in danger of eliciting tears. He had to redirect.

"Right, real nice, between his constant reminders

that I'm a convicted felon and his condescending little comments about my job. What an angel, this guy."

Meg moved a few inches farther away. "I admit that he's not very kind to you, but it's only because he's worried you're going to leave us again. He's protective."

"It's my job to protect you. Not his."

"Well, he did protect us when you couldn't. You might try being grateful for that. He helped us feel normal again, got us in a nice enough house, even got me back into the theatre."

Fletcher squeezed his fists. "I can't sit here and listen to how supportive Brad has been of your acting. I let you pursue it full-time. And maybe I wasn't making an honest living, but I wanted you to realize your dreams, and you were getting there. For real. Now this tool gets you hooked up with some dinky community theatre, and he's the one who supports your acting aspirations? Call me nuts, but I think it's enough that I live in his house and go to his church and listen to his crap. Can the guy maybe find his own wife?" He waited for a response. None came.

Fletcher looked down at his wife, bent over on the couch, hugging herself around the abdomen, possibly crying. And he hated himself.

"I'm sorry," he said. "I'm not mad at you. Or even Brad. I'm mad at myself. I'm working on it, okay?"

She nodded, still looking at the floor, and said, "I'm sorry too." She looked up, her eyes red. "And, Fletch, you really are doing a good job with Ivy. She's a different person now that you're back. I know it'll be hard, what with Brad coming too, but let's try and leave all this behind this week, okay? Let's just enjoy some time away as a family."

"That sounds nice," he said. "Some time away will be good."

✠

Across the street, a nondescript gray van was parked at the curb. The driver sat back in the shadows, fiddling with the ring on his finger—a gold ring inlaid with a black Maltese cross. The man had watched Fletcher and Meg fight and make up. He'd also listened to every word through a wireless earpiece. He smiled to himself.

Yeah, some time away will be good.

Chapter 8

The sight of the familiar city skyline reaching up from the horizon brought a sense of pure joy to Fletcher. It was as if part of him—the most important part—had been dead for the better part of a decade and had now been resurrected by simply laying eyes on those familiar buildings. He took it all in: the art deco skyscrapers jutting up in all their geometric diversity, the morning sun glinting off those familiar round glass towers. A wide grin filled his face, and his foot mashed the van's accelerator as he felt the city drawing closer and closer.

Then he remembered the van's twelve teen-aged passengers and eased off a bit. Sure, the circumstances were not ideal, but a return to the city was just what he needed. Time away from the smallness of suburban life—the stupid vending machine job, the stigma of being the convict who'd been hired for the tax breaks, the house he didn't even own. He felt an almost uncontrollable urge to drop these kids off and disappear into the city.

Then he saw his wife and daughter chatting and laughing two rows back, and the desire left him. They were happy. He was happy. What could go wrong?

"Are you okay, Mr. Doyle?" Courtney had called shotgun before Fletcher had been tasked with driving.

"I'm fine. Why?"

"You just, like, stopped talking midsentence. I thought you were having a stroke."

"No, I'm fine. What was I saying?"

"The long con."

"Oh, right." He glanced at Meg in the rearview mirror. He was fairly sure she wouldn't want him regaling Courtney with stories of the Life, but she was preoccupied and he was too amped to control himself. "Grifters either work the short con, which is going for one big take and then disappearing forever, or the long con, which is when you keep milking the same mark for more and more. You send him to friends and family to borrow more money. It's nothing to mess with. I've never really gotten into it."

He suddenly felt Meg looking at him.

"The turn is right up here, Fletcher," she said.

"Thanks." He looked at her face in the mirror, trying to decipher what she might have heard, but came up empty. His emotional high was suddenly losing altitude. He shook his head. A grifter who couldn't read his own wife. Boy, was he out of practice.

"What's this old place?" came a surly adolescent voice from the back of the van. "This isn't Life Journey Church. We're in the ghetto or something!"

"This is the address Brad gave me," Fletcher said, surveying the edifice. The Church of St. John the Baptist was a gorgeous, if ill-preserved, hundred-and-eighty-year-old brick structure with Byzantine influence. Fletcher's smile returned. It had been torture for a man of his interests and education to finally convert to Christianity, only to begin attending a church that met in a drywall and cinder block box built in the early 1980s. He pulled up to the curb and climbed out, craning his neck to admire the buttresses.

Brad emerged from the church bus in front of them and barked, "Unload quickly! *Chop!Chop!* We need to make room for the other church groups coming behind us!"

Courtney sidled up to Fletcher and bumped against him with her hip. "Hey!" she chirped. "You forgot something." She pulled a cell phone out of her pocket and offered it to him.

"Did you steal my phone?"

She laughed. "Pretty good, huh?"

Fletcher glanced up and saw Brad glaring at them.

"I programmed my number in for you," she said with a smile, "in case you ever need to text me."

"Um, thanks. Better get your stuff unloaded." He looked up again. Brad was gone.

"This place is so junky," Noah announced. "I thought we were staying in a new church with a gym!"

"Lower your voice," Brad chided. He addressed the eighteen youth and five adults gathered around him in the vestibule. "Last night a water pipe burst at Life Journey Church, so they're not going to be able to host us. Several churches around the city have been kind enough to take up the slack, including this one. I do not want to hear any complaints, okay, people? They're doing us a favor here. Oh, and the neighborhood is iffy. No one goes outside without an adult. No exceptions."

A priest strode up to the group. He looked to be in his early sixties, with graying hair and olive skin, and was a head shorter than Brad and Fletcher.

"Greetings, and welcome to our historic church," he said. "My name is Father Alexander Katrakis. Most people call me Father Sacha, but I know that might sound weird, so you can call me Father Alex if you like. If you would be so kind as to follow me, I'll show you where you'll be staying."

They all picked up the duffels and suitcases they'd dropped only moments before and followed Father Sacha down a hall into a more recent addition to the church. Probably sixties or seventies, Fletcher thought—somehow even more depressing than the church building back home.

Noah poked up between Fletcher and Brad and pointed at the priest's collar.

"Why do you wear that?" he asked. "My pastor doesn't have one of those."

"There are many reasons," Father Sacha answered, "but personally I like to wear it so that people know they can come to me for help or counsel or prayer. Wherever I am, people know I'm there to show them God's love."

"Does it come off?" Noah asked.

"It does. It's held on by two little buttons called shanks. See?" He pulled up the collar.

"Shank means something different to you, doesn't it, Fletcher?" Brad asked quietly. "Ooh, gotta be on guard in the lunch line." He turned to the priest and said, "Seriously, keep an eye on this guy here." His voice was playful, but he looked back at Fletcher with pure spite.

They arrived at the door of a large, open room, the floor covered with a sea of inflated air mattresses and sleeping bags.

"Here is where the men will sleep," the priest announced. "You're the last church to arrive, but I'm sure you'll find room enough."

"A lot of those mattresses are queen size," Brad observed with no little annoyance.

"Let it go, Brad," Fletcher said as he separated his bags from Ivy's.

"I guess you've slept in worse, right?" Brad said a little louder.

Courtney balled up a fist and belted her father on the arm. "Stop being such a jerk!" An awkward beat passed.

"Uh, if the ladies want to follow me, I'll take you upstairs to your accommodations," Father Sacha said.

The women filed away, and the boys poured into the room, intent on staking out the best of what little real estate remained. Fletcher and Brad lingered, eye to eye.

"We need to talk," Brad said.

"No, we don't." Fletcher rehefted his duffel bag onto his shoulder and made for the door. He felt himself pulled back by Brad's right hand on his upper arm—stronger than he expected.

Fletcher dropped his bags and took a threatening step. "Are we finally gonna do this?"

"Go ahead. Knock my block off. We both know it's just a matter of time before you go back to your cage, Fletcher. You might as well get it over with."

"You're nowhere near worth it." He wanted to spit for some reason, but knew he shouldn't in the church. "You got something to say to me? You've got five seconds."

"I have two things to say. First, don't think I didn't notice the way you looked at this church when we pulled up. Don't get any ideas. Anything valuable disappears, you'll be the only suspect. I don't want to see you skulking around where you're not supposed to be. Just stay with the group."

Fletcher said nothing.

"More importantly, keep away from my daughter. She was kind enough to take Ivy under her wing when they were the new kids in town, but I don't want you influencing her. Got it?"

"I'll make you a deal, Brad. I'll steer clear of your daughter if you stay away from my wife."

Brad shrugged. "I'll do my best, but your wife is a grown woman. She can make her own choices."

"Okay, how about this one? You stay away from my wife or, prison or no prison, I will take you apart."

Chapter 9

Dante had been brainstorming all morning. He had exactly three ideas, all of which were sure to fail. He'd called in every marker and some favors too, which had put him up near thirty large, although he had none of it in hand. Both of his cars were now listed at very attractive prices, which could bring in another fifty if he got what he asked.

He'd also made a list of easy marks, but his lack of an independent team made a large-scale job impossible. There had never been a lucrative one-man grift in the history of the art. By himself, the best he could hope to pull down was a few hundred here or there.

But the real missing factor was time, not targets. Even if he bled every mark dry, it would take months or even years to get where he needed to be. And he had six days. Dante had seen firsthand what Marcus Brinkman did to people who welched on their debts. Excuses were repaid with broken bones, missing fingers, missing people. He thought again about running. Then he thought of the stack of pictures, which reminded him of Brinkman's stipulation that he not cut into Bella Donna's profits. He went down his list of marks and one by one crossed off every single name. Who did he know outside of his connections through the Syndicate? No one.

Except the members of his little congregation. He felt a familiar twinge of guilt at the thought. He could scarcely afford to take any options off the table at this point, but these were faithful people, struggling people, and they were already giving from what little they had to prop up Dante's front of a church. Besides, they were all lower income. They would be no help either.

He pushed his face down into his hands, a posture that had become more and more common over the past twenty-four hours. He had more than enough skill to pull off his own game; if only he'd been less dependent on others in the beginning, he wouldn't be in this impossible situation.

Dante had always been able to play people. It was second nature. Or perhaps it was just nature. Two of his grandparents were white, one was black, and one Cuban. As a result, his skin was lighter than some Caucasians, and a pool of rather Irish-looking freckles hung on either side of his nose. But his hair and facial features were distinctly African.

He learned quickly how to adapt based on where he was and, particularly, who he was with. He could instantly adopt anyone's voice and mannerisms and mirror them back with no effort at all—something that had an immediately disarming effect.

It was in high school that he realized the depth of his talent. He'd been suspended from school for three days for fighting. Knowing he'd be out on his ear if his mother found out, he'd gone directly home, marched up to the attic where his father's old clothes were kept, and found a suit that fit him well. Then he walked right back into the school, up to the very same principal who had suspended him, and pretended to be his own father. The administrator never questioned his identity, and Dante was able to successfully renegotiate the three-day suspension into half a day. He ran home, changed back into his own clothes, and returned after lunch.

That's when his friends started calling him Trick. And Trick could talk. He was everyone's best friend for the remainder of high school. If you were in with Trick, he could get you free basketball tickets, buy you alcohol, or square things with your mom when you came in late.

Then one day, when Dante was nineteen, a good friend of his was sentenced to six months in jail.

"I'm afraid you can't see him," Dante was told when he tried to visit. "Each inmate is allowed six family members and friends on his visitation list," the lobby officer had said, "plus clergy and legal counsel."

"I'm clergy," Dante said without missing a beat. Ordinarily, clergymen were required to provide a valid ordination certificate to be added to the chaplain's list, but again, Trick could talk. He was allowed to see his friend at once and bring in his ordination certificate next time, which he did. It was very official—seal and all—and cost him all of twenty dollars and a few hours of his time.

Once he realized that clergy were not subject to the metal detectors, Dante had promptly tracked down horn-rimmed glasses and a double-breasted suit at local thrift shops, made his cutaway Bible, and begun visiting his friend weekly, bringing in cigarettes, food, and other desirable items. Dante's friend told a few of his most trusted associates in lockup, and before long his client base was established.

It was five years later that new regulations required eligible clergy to list a street address for their house of worship, and that was when Broadmoor Outreach Tabernacle was born. Purchasing the deserted front and retrofitting it as a church took much of Dante's accumulated profits, but it was necessary. And it had attracted the attention of La Bella Donna, who found herself in need of a mechanism for smuggling items in and out of the old county jail. It was certainly a niche service. Prisons were far less problematic. Any prisoner knew which guard could be paid off to slip an odd item into the bottom of his lunch pail and get it to an inmate, but the jail—home to pretrial felons and those serving less than a year—was Dante's domain and his alone.

What a waste. His talents, which had at one time seemed like a sure pass to unfettered success, had dead-ended here—a half million in the hole and six days to pay. He looked down at his three options and made a decision. It was time to launch the city's first Father the Fatherless campaign. He would begin with an initial fund-raising drive. He looked in the mirror and smiled.

"My name is Reverend Dante Watkins, and I'm helping to raise money for fatherless children. Will you help us reach our goal of five hundred thousand dollars?"

"Fletcher, come here a minute." Meg beckoned her husband from the door of the men's sleeping quarters. He leapt his way over air mattresses and duffels until he was face-to-face with her.

"What's up?"

"Ivy forgot her toiletries. It's the only thing I asked her to pack, but somehow she forgot them. Can you find a store and get her some deodorant

—unscented—and a toothbrush. She can share the rest with me. Here, I wrote it down for you."

"No problem." He took the note and gave her a peck on the lips. He made contact, but it was impossible not to notice her involuntarily pulling back. Fletcher looked at the note for a moment and walked out onto the street without another word. He felt like brooding, but it was a gorgeous day—seventy-three degrees with an intermittent breeze—and here he was, back in the city he loved.

Fletcher had been single-mindedly trying not to despise his life in the suburbs. After all, it was better for Ivy. Now that money was tight, the city was no place for a child to grow up. He'd reminded himself of that a thousand times as he tried to find their new town quaint and charming, and he'd almost convinced himself. But now that he was back where he belonged, the truth was all too clear.

Here there was room to wander and explore. Here you could blend in or stick out. This was the city where grifters, con men, and cardsharps had invented the game and honed their craft a century earlier—men like Curley Carter and Big Lawson. He loved the fact that he could walk for half an hour in any direction and he'd still be in the sprawling city. Yeah, he might get shot, but he'd never get bored.

By contrast, the smallness of his life as a

parolee—the menial job, the lack of public art or culture, the smug, small-minded people—was suffocating. It was somehow smaller than life in prison. In a way, it *was* prison. He loved his family and, for their sake, he would continue to do his time. But for the moment, it was nice to be Outside.

He wandered for forty-five minutes before he remembered the task at hand and circled back toward the church. When he was about six blocks away, Fletcher spotted a sign that read PHAR ACY in large neon letters. He opened the door with a jingle and stepped in. Whatever the missing letter had been (Fletcher's money was on an *M*), the store was clearly in the midst of an identity crisis. One wall, running the length of the entire shop, was stocked floor to ceiling with liquor. Three fixed security cameras kept an eye on the merchandise. In the back corner, where the pharmacist had once stood, was a selection of pipes, bongs, and rolling papers.

Sure, this place was grim, but it was still the city. Fletcher could smell cars being manu-factured nearby and feel six-figure deals being closed dozens of stories above his head. He located the slim selection of personal care items and grabbed a toothbrush and some deodorant. Meg had both underlined and circled the words *fragrance-free,* but Fletcher couldn't exactly be choosy here. Perhaps he would come across another store and see if he could find something better. For now, he got in line to pay.

The man in front of him held a bottle of wine in each hand and a copy of the *Free Press* under his arm. Fletcher silently admired the weave of the man's suit and suddenly felt self-conscious about his T-shirt and jeans. The man took a step forward, and the newspaper fluttered down from under his arm. Fletcher knelt and quickly gathered it up.

"Here you go, buddy," he said, extending the newspaper. "You dropped your pa—"

Fletcher froze at the sight of the man's face.

"Andrew?"

"Fletcher!" Andrew wrapped his arms around Fletcher and nearly lifted him up off the ground. "I can't believe it's you. I thought you were still in the pen."

"No, I . . . um . . ." He clamped his eyes shut and reopened them, not at all surprised to find that his mentor and former partner had not vanished into thin air. Andrew Bishop was a couple inches taller than Fletcher and about ten years older. His brown hair and eyes and square jaw made him the grifter's ideal—handsome, but not memorably so. He oozed enthusiasm on everyone he engaged in conversation, but in a way that left them feeling like it was their own.

"Good grief, kid, I haven't seen you in six, seven years? You look great."

"Thanks. You look pretty good too. Doing well for yourself?"

"Yeah, I'm all right. But forget me. How are you? How's Meg? Ivy must be, what, ten years old?"

Fletcher suddenly felt sick. He was violating his parole talking to this man, and he did not like hearing the names of his wife and daughter from Andrew's lips. He stepped back toward the door, instinctively pocketing the toothbrush and deodorant.

"I'm . . . They're fine, Andrew. I have to go."

He backed out the door and almost ran right over an older man who apparently had been just standing there, staring at the door of the PHAR ACY. Fletcher stopped his retreat a moment to gawk. The man was short and ugly and dressed like it was Halloween, wearing a loose-knit robe that dragged on the ground. With both hands he held a long, dirty piece of fabric up to his heart. But what had Fletcher locked in were the man's eyes. At first he thought they were crazy, the eyes of your everyday sidewalk madman, but then he realized that it was the way the man was staring at him, *into* him— almost with a familiarity.

Fletcher backed away slowly, then turned and headed back to the church at a clip. Perhaps the city was not as great a place as he remembered.

Chapter 10

Fletcher's extended errand had caused him to miss lunch, and his stomach growled audibly through a lengthy and dreadfully dull orientation that he could have summed up in nine words: *We break up into teams and go help people.* Brad had nodded vigorously during the entire presentation, which annoyed Fletcher all the more.

He was approaching *hangry* status by the time they formed a winding line in the church's fellowship hall, leading eventually to a makeshift buffet full of grayish meat and mixed vegetables. As he watched both being slopped onto his tray with large metal serving spoons, he couldn't help but note the similarity to the chow line at Jackson.

"Ivy can't use that deodorant," Meg said as they shoveled the tasteless food into their mouths. "She's allergic to the perfumes they use. I told you it had to be fragrance-free."

"Sorry," Fletcher said. He was trying to forget the afternoon rendezvous with Andrew and the creepy old man in the robe.

"How did it take you that long to get two things?" There was an edge to her voice that could have been accusation or something more benign. "There's a Rite Aid, like, three doors down."

"It was nice out," Fletcher said, trying and

failing to identify his meat. "I hadn't been to the city for years, so I took a walk."

"Well, Brad was on the warpath. Be warned. I tried to cover for you, but he was ranting and raving about how we're responsible for these kids and what if we all just wandered off and on and on."

Fletcher thought of Brad's malicious smile and veiled threats. "I don't care. Brad can go—"

Ivy returned to her chair, a large cup of red sugar water in her hand.

"—home if he doesn't like it."

"I was a little worried too," Meg said. "You didn't bring your cell phone. How was I supposed to know if something was wrong?"

"Sorry," he said again.

They ate in silence for a few minutes until a matronly woman and her granddaughter sat down next to Meg and engaged her and Ivy in a tedious conversation that amounted to a simple exchange of everyone's statistical information— age, hometown, general interests. Fletcher thought Facebook had removed the need for these conversations. He wished it had. Then again, the nonstop spouting of pleasantries was one of the only things to set this place apart from dinner in prison. That and all the teenagers staring at their cell phones.

In the distance, beyond the rows of diners, something out in the hall caught his eye.

Movement. Flailing arms and stomping feet. It was a fight. Or rather, an intense argument. The kind that only can take place between a teenage girl and an overbearing parent. The kind that Fletcher was not looking forward to having with his own daughter.

At this distance he couldn't know for sure, but Brad seemed more exasperated than angry. Courtney, on the other hand, was clearly livid, punctuating each word with her index finger, sometimes simply pointing at her father and sometimes jabbing her finger into his chest. All at once she spun around and stalked off out of sight.

Brad collapsed onto a bench, head in his hands. Fletcher felt an unwanted wave of compassion. Yes, the man was obnoxious and judgmental, but he was also doing his best to be the single father of a rather willful teenaged girl. Meg had numerous times recounted Brad's pain at losing his wife to cancer two years earlier and his struggles to be an adequate parent. In the back of his mind, Fletcher had assumed this all to be a ruse on Brad's part—an attempt at creating some solidarity between the "single" parents. But now, looking at Brad's broken form on the bench, he felt ashamed for making such assumptions.

"I'll be right back," he said, leaving his half-empty tray at the table. The closer he drew to Brad, the less sure he was that this was a good idea. But he wanted to make peace. This man had helped his family in so many ways, and yet Fletcher was always ready to snap. It would feel good to lay this to rest.

"You okay, Brad?" he asked, approaching the bench.

Brad looked up, his eyes red. He started to say one thing, then seemed to change his mind and asked, "Where were you at lunch?"

"I had to run out and get some things for Ivy." Fletcher determined that they would not dwell on that subject.

"You just disappeared. Are *you* twelve years old too?"

"No. I'm not twelve years old."

"We've got a responsibility to watch these kids, you know."

"I know. I'll run it by you next time."

"Good." Brad looked in Fletcher's direction, though not directly at him. "Is there something else, Fletcher?"

"Yeah, look. I said some stuff earlier that I didn't mean. And I just wanted to tell you that I really am grateful for what you've done for my family. And if there's ever anything I can do for you and Courtney—"

"You can stay away from Courtney. I already told you that."

"Right, no, but I mean . . . I saw you guys arguing and I know it must be hard trying to raise a daughter by yourself and—"

"You must be kidding me."

"Sorry?"

Brad leaned into a massive scoff. "Are you trying to give me fathering advice?"

"No, that's not—"

"You, the guy who left his family to fend for themselves for six years while he did time in prison? You're going to offer me advice?"

"I was thinking more like encouragement."

Brad stood up, seeming taller than he had when they last stood nose to nose. "Listen to me, convict. I don't need your advice and I don't want your encouragement. Why don't you worry about being there for your own daughter and wife? Because believe me, if you don't step up to the plate soon, somebody else will." He turned and walked down the hall, disappearing into the black.

Fletcher was shaking with rage. He tried to gather the anger in a ball in his chest, as Andrew had taught him, so he could do away with it— change it into something else—but it filled every square inch of him. He thought of how useless all of Andrew's grifter training had proved to be. Then he thought about bumping into Andrew that afternoon, and his rage turned to dread.

So, at least there was that.

"Hello, Officer Roberts. This is Fletcher Doyle, inmate #491632."

"This is my cell phone, Fletcher. You don't need your inmate number. I know who you are."

"Sorry, sir."

"Don't be sorry and don't call me sir. What's up, Fletcher?"

"Just calling to check in."

"We had our appointment two days ago, Fletcher. In person, per regulations. I was happy to give you my cell number, but it's for special circumstances. Is that what we've got here?"

"I don't know. I'm on this mission trip. It just started."

"Oh, right. How's that going?"

"Not awesome. Look, I don't know if you're allowed to talk to me about this stuff or not, but I remembered you used to be a chaplain and a minister, and I'm really just feeling lost right now."

There was a brief pause on the other end. Roberts was either sitting down or switching ears. "Okay. We can have this conversation, Fletcher, off the record. But realize this: I'm not your pastor or your priest. If you confess a parole violation to me, I'm obligated to report it."

"That's fine."

"Okay, then. Tell me why you're feeling lost. Your family is with you, right? Are things going all right with them? Meg and little Abby?"

"Ivy. Yeah, it's going okay with them. Slow, but good."

"So what's wrong?"

Fletcher ran a hand through his hair. "I feel like a fake."

Officer Roberts laughed. "The Department of Corrections agrees with you there, son. You're one of the best con men we've seen in some time. Maybe you're feeling like a fake because you're not being one. Maybe being genuine is foreign to you. Give it some time."

"No, it's . . . I feel like I'm faking this whole Jesus thing. I know a lot of people think they find God Inside and then they get out and God's not there anymore. But with me, I thought it was real."

"And now?"

"Fire's dying down. It's been, what, two years since I got saved, and it's already dying down."

"What do you mean by that? 'Dying down'?"

"At first, I was so intense about it. I wrote my wife letters every day about Jesus and what he was doing in my life and how everything would be different and all this stuff I was finding in the Bible. I mean, you know my academic background; I already knew the Bible better than most pastors, but I was leading Bible studies and finding things for *me* in there. It was awesome.

"I was so excited about it that Meg started taking our daughter to church. And that was a huge turning point for us. I think . . . I think she was planning to divorce me before I got out. I think she was just saving up the money. But once we started this Jesus stuff . . ."

"And now your initial zeal is wearing off. That's normal, Fletcher. This sort of thing comes in seasons. Just stick with it. Don't give up on God."

"It's not just that. I'm afraid I was grifting the whole time. Like, grifting *myself.* You and I both know parole boards love a born-again story, so everybody tries to sprinkle a little of that in. What if I knew I needed to sell this thing so completely that I fooled myself into believing it? What if I'm the grifter *and* the mark here?"

"Well, you wouldn't be the first false convert in the world. But the fact that you're even worried about it makes me think you're the real deal. It was good that you called. Keep reaching out to people, okay? Promise you won't lone-wolf this thing. Keep going to church with your family."

Fletcher felt his eyes growing moist. By sheer instinct he walled off the emotion. "Yeah, that's half the problem. There's this guy, this jerk, who's one of the leaders of the church. He's such a hypocrite, and he's dragging me down with him."

"Maybe try a different church?"

"Wouldn't matter. He's my landlord too."

"Ahhh. Yes, I've talked to that man. He . . . does not like you."

"So what should I do?" Fletcher could hear

someone—a child?—trying to get Officer Roberts's attention on the other end. He knew they were about done.

"Two things. One: do not violate your parole. You're back in the dragon's lair for a week, and there is bound to be some temptation. Add this whole internal struggle with your faith and it could go bad quickly. I'd hate to have to send you back to prison, son."

"And number two?"

"Keep reaching out. Seek out a mentor. Or better yet, a couple of them. Maybe someone older and wiser and someone more your own age. People who've been through some struggles but aren't in the midst of them now. That's my advice. Give me a call back in a couple days and tell me how things are going, okay?"

"Sure. Good-bye, sir."

Fletcher squeezed the phone. He'd called for encouragement and advice, but the only thing he could remember was, *Don't violate your parole . . . send you back to prison.* He thought about bailing on the trip and heading home. But then, he didn't have a car here, and he and Meg didn't even have money for bus fare.

His stomach was gripping the mystery meat with a vengeance. What was going on here? What were the odds that Andrew would just happen to be in that store at that moment? He'd been so sure he was ready to come back, and yet he'd violated the terms of his parole within two hours of crossing the city limits. Could this be any more of a mess?

His phone buzzed, announcing a text message: Hey, can we talk? Courtney

Chapter 11

January 31, 1785
Paris, France

Everyone in Paris knew who lived at No. 30 Rue de St. Claude—at least, everyone of consequence —and they all coveted an invitation. After all, Count Cagliostro was known throughout Europe as the greatest conjurer, psychic, and (as rumor had it) alchemist who had ever lived—not to mention a pharmacist so accomplished that he had served as Benjamin Franklin's personal physician during the American's time in Paris.

But more than that, the count simply knew how to throw a party.

A gaggle of young women jostled their way through the wide gate and up the stone stairs, holding tight to the railing, as the stairway was narrow and they had already indulged in a good deal of wine. Although, at five gold livres, it had not been a "good deal" per se.

Taking up the rear, sandwiched between two particularly busty women in silk dresses, was the man who had paid the five livres, Cardinal Louis de Rohan—a churchman, yes, but also a libertine. He, too, had indulged in much wine that night and, while he was generally marked with regret and self-loathing, the only regret he seemed to have at the moment was that he possessed but two hands.

The entrance hall of the house was decorated at great expense to resemble the ancient halls of an Egyptian temple. Several servants milled about, dressed as Egyptian slaves. At the center of it all was a black marble slab, engraved with the words of Alexander Pope:

> Father of all! in every age,
> In every clime adored,
> By saint, by savage, and by sage,
> Jehovah, Jove, or Lord!

The cardinal and his companions entered the main hall and were met by Count Cagliostro himself, dressed in a black silk robe embroidered with Egyptian hieroglyphs. On his head he wore a gold turban. An emerald-studded chain hung around his neck, from which were suspended several gold scarabs. From a red silk belt hung the sword of the late Grand Master Manuel Pinto da Fonseca.

"My dear friends," he said in a warm but reserved tone. "Welcome." He offered his hand, which they each kissed. Cagliostro's French was flawless, his only accent the one he placed there by design.

"It is so good to see you, Grand Kophta," Cardinal de Rohan said, beaming. "They tell me we are to see a divination of spirits tonight." His eyes were wide with excitement.

Cagliostro drew back. "What! With a cardinal of the Holy Church in attendance? I should think not!"

Cardinal de Rohan giggled, high and effeminate. "He's kidding," he said, first to the woman on his right and then to her leftward counterpart. "Not only does the Grand Kophta know of my interest in divination and sorcery, but he keeps laboratories in my episcopal palace in Strasbourg. In fact, Count Cagliostro lived with me there for several months."

"It was a pleasure," Cagliostro said. "The cardinal has one of the finest libraries of alchemical texts in all of Europe. Now, if you will excuse me, I must prepare for the evening's event."

As soon as Cagliostro was out of sight, a gong sounded through the house and the servants corralled the group into the divination room.

Nobles and friends of Cagliostro were seated in the front. Near the back of the hall, curious onlookers stood on their toes, hoping to catch a glimpse of something incredible. The air was filled with expectancy. Eyes flitted here and there, taking in the Oriental statues, the kabbalistic markings on the wall, and especially the small wooden booth, itself covered in glyphs and occult symbols and closed off with a black velvet curtain.

With a sudden puff of smoke the Grand Kophta appeared before the booth, his arms stretched out at his sides, palms up.

"Tonight you will witness what your modern minds think to be impossible," he said, his voice grave and foreboding. "We will look beyond the sphere of this world and see with more than just our eyes."

He beckoned to a young girl of about eight to come forward from the back of the room.

"To do this, I have selected an innocent spirit to serve as our clairvoyant. She is pure and can see what we cannot." He took the girl by the hand and led her over to the booth. He pointed at the black curtain and, without touching it, caused it to fall to the ground. A few in the crowd gasped. Inside the booth was a small table covered with a black cloth, upon which sat a crucifix, two burning red candles, and a large glass globe filled with water. In front of the table was a short stool.

"Please hold out your hands," he said to the girl. When she obeyed, he poured oil over them. "Now, enter the booth and kneel before the globe."

She knelt and two servants rehung the curtain, hiding her from view.

"And now," said Cagliostro, "we must test our clairvoyant. Who is willing to help me in this?"

Every hand went up. Cagliostro selected a young man in the front row, handed him a card, and instructed him to sign his name on it. The man did so and handed it back to the Grand Kophta, who produced fire from out of thin air, burning the card in a stunning display of first green, then blue, then red flames.

"Dear clairvoyant, can you hear me?"

"Yes," the girl answered from behind the curtain.

The Grand Kophta closed his eyes and pushed his fingers against his temples. "If you look beneath the bench upon which you kneel, you will find a sealed envelope. Tell me, do you see it?"

"I do," the girl replied. The envelope, however, was not sealed at all and was, rather, lying open on the table while she used the flame of one candle to heat the bottom of the other, now extinguished. She heard Cagliostro's voice say, "Give me the envelope," and then saw his arm appear through the slit in the curtain. As they had rehearsed, she quickly reached into the sleeve of his robe and drew the card out from the hidden pocket. With speed and quiet precision, she slipped the card into the envelope, shut the flap, and sealed it closed with the base of the red candle. She pushed the bottom of the crucifix against the wax, leaving an intricate impression behind.

"I have it in my hand!" she heard Cagliostro shout.

She blew lightly against the wax for a moment and handed the envelope to Cagliostro. The moment the envelope touched his fingers he withdrew it back through the slit in the curtain. The whole process had taken no more than two or three seconds.

"Now," Cagliostro announced, "I wonder if the gentleman who wrote his name on the card would be willing to break this seal and tell us what lies within."

"I certainly would," the man said.

"Excellent." Cagliostro held the envelope by its four corners, about four inches from the man's eyes. "But before you do, tell me: What do you see on this seal?"

"It looks like a snake with an apple in its mouth, shot through by an arrow."

"Indeed." He looked around the room. "Do any of you comprehend the meaning?"

There were several murmurs in the affirmative, although no hands went up this time. Cagliostro tapped his finger surreptitiously against the wax seal. Finding it to be dry, he handed it to the young man, who excitedly tore the envelope open, gasped in delight, and held up the card for all to see.

Cagliostro flipped his hand toward the curtain, which again fell to the ground, revealing everything as it had been, the candles both burning and upright and the young girl hunched over the table, gazing into the water-filled globe.

"And now," he announced, "having proven herself, our clairvoyant will receive the spirits that surround the throne of the Divinity and tell us what is happening at this very moment in Vienna, in St. Petersburg, and on the enchanted Island of Malta." Suddenly, the water in the globe churned, and the forms of seven winged creatures came rising up from within.

The Grand Kophta looked down the row of astonished faces nearest him. For a moment he locked eyes with Cardinal de Rohan, who was sure he had just seen something supernatural and who was completely oblivious that he was already Count Cagliostro's mark in the greatest grift of all time.

Chapter 12

Fletcher ignored a total of four texts from Courtney that night. In the first, she had simply asked to talk. Then she needed to talk about her dad. Then she wanted to apologize for her father's behavior. The final message had insisted that she absolutely needed to discuss something "rlly srs," which could have meant "really serious," but by Fletcher's estimation, anything all that serious would have justified the extra half second it would have taken to add vowels.

Although the messages were annoying and a reminder of his confrontation with Brad, Fletcher was almost thankful for the distraction they created—a distraction from bigger problems. The run-in with Andrew. The reminder from his PO that a return trip to prison was a very real possibility. The doubt and uncertainty shrouding his faith.

Lights-out had been announced at 11:00 p.m.—another reminder of incarceration. It was now 11:48 and Fletcher's mind was reeling. Even amidst the chorus of mucus-rattling snores all around him, he felt completely alone as he stared up at exposed ductwork, hardly visible through the dim light of the streetlamps spilling in. All he wanted was to sleep, to let his mind and body rest so he could start tomorrow fresh—just another member of Christian Service Camp, a week-long opportunity for volunteering and helping the less fortunate, something normal people with normal problems and normal families took part in every year.

Then again, he and his problems were anything but normal. He twisted on the air mattress and felt it give. He'd borrowed it from an older couple at church who had only used it once, they kept saying, but it clearly had a leak somewhere. Usually a side sleeper, he'd had to abandon that due to his hip pressing against the wood floor. He chuckled dryly. Yet another aspect of their trip that was slightly less comfortable than a minimum security prison.

If there was one thing he was thankful for, it was a few nights of sleeping alone. There was little Fletcher dreaded more these days than the awkwardness of climbing into bed with his wife, hoping this was the night she would snuggle up to him and fall asleep with her head against his chest like she used to, only to have her click off her lamp, turn her back to him, and doze off. Their bedroom was certainly uneventful, if amicable.

Of course he couldn't blame her; she barely knew him. After his first job with Andrew, the two of them had convinced Meg that Fletcher had been promoted to assistant director at the museum. Andrew, playing the role of Fletcher's boss, had painted a picture of a handsome salary and cosmic potential for advancement. Meg had eaten it up, quitting her job and throwing herself into her acting career. They moved to a new apartment in the Hills and enrolled Ivy in a top-of-the-line school. Fletcher and Andrew had a good thing going.

Until they got caught. Or until Fletcher got caught.

That left Meg to deal with everything all at once. The fact that her husband was a fraud, a thief, and anyone but the man she thought she knew. The sudden lack of income. The eviction. Et cetera. Fletcher knew she'd toughened considerably through the process, and therefore he should not expect her to be the same person she'd been seven years ago. But he often felt like the door was not only closed but barred and booby-trapped. He tried again to collect his troubles and push them out of his head.

His cell phone buzzed again under his pillow. Okay, this was going a little too far. Not to mention that texting after lights-out had been condemned many times over at the orientation they'd all endured. He should probably just turn off his phone for the night. It buzzed again. Not a text. Someone was calling him. He retrieved the phone and checked the display.

CALL FROM THE ALCHEMIST, it read.

Who?

"Hello?" he whispered.

"Hello, Fletcher." The voice was unfamiliar. "Run into some old friends today?"

Fletcher's stomach dropped out from beneath him—odd, considering how close it already was to the floor. Suddenly feeling like he might throw up, he rolled onto his side, causing half of his shoddy air mattress to tip up into the air.

"Who is this?" Fletcher demanded. He wanted to take his phone out into the hall, but the thought of trying to jump over all those teenagers and backpacks and mattresses without landing on anyone was less than ideal. Instead, he pulled his sleeping bag up over his head to muffle the sound, feeling like a five-year-old making a "fort."

"You may call me the Alchemist," the man said. He had a slight accent that Fletcher couldn't quite identify. Something Middle Eastern, he thought. Or Greek?

"Noah?" he asked. "Did you have that other Red Bull?"

"I am not Noah, Mr. Doyle," the Alchemist said. "And I suggest that you pay attention to what I have to say."

"Listen, Al," Fletcher said, "it's late. So either tell me who you really are and what you want or I'm hanging up."

"That's rather rude," the man said. "And after I left you those beautiful pictures."

"Pictures?"

"Look in your bag. The side pocket."

Using the backlight on his phone for guidance, Fletcher wiggled over to his bag, wedged firmly between his mattress and the one next to him. He dislodged it with some difficulty, pulled back the zipper, and found a manila envelope inside. It was sealed shut, but not with the usual lick-and-stick feature of a modern office envelope or even the little metal brad. Rather, it had been fixed with a red wax seal: the letter *S*.

The man on the phone was still talking, but Fletcher couldn't make it out. He retreated again into his sleeping bag and carefully broke the seal and slid the contents from the envelope.

Black-and-white photographs. Of him and Andrew. He slumped back, feeling the floor beneath the mattress, and pushed the phone back to his ear.

"Andrew? You scared the heck out of me. Nice accent, by the way."

"Wrong again."

Fletcher was flipping through the pictures. There were at least thirty of them, taken in quick succession from outside—grainy, but clear enough to see what looked like a covert hand-off between two associates. He felt beads of sweat sprouting on his forehead as he relived the encounter. The newspaper. The hug. Leaving the store while Andrew stayed in line.

The man on the other end was tsk-tsking. "What would your parole officer think?"

Fletcher's heart sounded like a jackhammer. "What do you want?"

"I want you to meet me in the sanctuary in two minutes."

"No. I'm not going anywhere. You've got nothing. You send these anonymously to my PO, out of context, he won't do a thing. They could be from before I went to prison for all he knows."

"Or maybe he'd check the store's security tapes. Five angles of you doing business with a former criminal associate. Not to mention stealing a toothbrush. The store keeps two weeks' worth of archives."

Immediately a plan began forming in Fletcher's mind—a plan to break into the liquor store that thought it was a pharmacy and relieve them of their security tapes. It wouldn't be difficult.

As if reading his mind, the Alchemist said, "I have copies of the video, but if you'd like to add breaking and entering, feel free. Oh, and have a look at the last few pictures."

Fletcher skipped to the end and saw a series of zoomed-in shots. Andrew reaching into the newspaper and pulling out a stack of hundred-dollar bills—the front page of today's *Free Press*, including the date, was clear—and tucking the money into his jacket pocket. In the final picture, Andrew was abandoning the paper and the wine and leaving the store empty-handed, looking off to the side surreptitiously.

Fletcher frowned. One of the smoothest grifters operating today, there was only one reason Andrew Bishop would be so sloppy: he was in on this.

"What, then? I do what you say or you get me thrown back in prison?"

"Don't think of it as do it *or.* Think of it as do it *and.* Do as I say *and* you remain a free man. *And* you can get a break from lugging around boxes full of Fritos. A little taste of the Life. That's what you want, isn't it?"

Fletcher's breath caught in his throat. Whoever this man was, he'd done his homework. "You think you know my peg?" Fletcher asked, trying to sound flippant.

"Oh, I have you pegged."

"Let me talk to Andrew," Fletcher demanded.

"Not yet. Meet me in the sanctuary. Two minutes. And bring your phone."

"No, you let me—"

But the call had ended.

Fletcher found a pair of jeans in his bag and pulled them on over his boxers. He thought about shoes, but decided he could be stealthier without. Besides, if he bumped into someone, stocking feet would support his cover story: just a lost, sleepy guy looking for the bathroom.

He stood quietly and began shuffling his way down the tiny, winding path that led between sleeping teens and chaperones to the door. The phones of a few rebellious souls went dark as Fletcher approached. Twice he had to jump over a mass of luggage, but he managed to reach the hall without stepping on anyone.

At the door, he hesitated. Why would anyone want to meet him somewhere dark and deserted in the middle of the night? He could think of no good reason. But really, what choice did he have?

Starting down the hall, he made several resolutions: He would not leave the church building, no matter what. He would not be seen by anyone. And most importantly, he would not become involved in something that continued on into the light of the next morning. Whatever this was, he would deal with it tonight.

Chapter 13

The church proper was every bit as beautiful as Fletcher had imagined, although his mind had to fill in the details, the only active sources of light being a few illuminated EXIT signs around the perimeter and a single spotlight shining down on the large fixed altar.

He entered the nave, his feet silently padding along the stone floor of the outside aisle. Somewhere between the half-deflated air mattress and the rows of oaken pews, the scales had tipped such that the exhilaration he now felt outweighed his sense of trepidation. It had been a long time since he'd moved stealthily through a dark room, adrenaline churning through his body, and he had not realized just how much he missed it.

A sound to his right caused him to flinch. He froze, eyes searching, muscles tensed. He took three more steps and saw two high schoolers making out in a pew across the nave. He cupped his hands around his mouth and said in his best impression of Brad the Killjoy, "You kids shouldn't be here. Get back to bed." The kids scrambled out of the pew, into the vestibule, and were gone.

Fletcher chuckled. He waited a few more seconds, worried that someone might have heard the commotion, then continued on. He was about to mount the stairs to the chancel when his phone rang again. How did it know to call this guy the Alchemist? It was all beyond weird.

"I'm here," he said into the phone. "Where are you?"

"I'm nearby. Good job clearing out Romeo and his girlfriend, by the way."

Fletcher tried to search the room without moving his head, realizing quickly that with the lights off it was hopeless.

"Now," the Alchemist said, "next to the stairs, right by your feet, you will find a small aerosol can."

Fletcher could hear the man breathing a little heavier, as if walking up steps, and then the unmistakable sound of the night wind whistling against the phone. He considered sprinting out into the street to try and spot this man, maybe get his hands on him. But it would be easy for the Alchemist, whoever he was, to disappear in this neighborhood at this time of night. Besides, at the moment Fletcher's curiosity was in the driver's seat.

"I see it," he said, picking up the small can.

"Do you know what that's for?"

"To spot laser trip wires, I assume, but I'm not going to be needing it tonight."

"No?"

"That's right. I'm not leaving this church. You can do whatever you want with your pictures."

The Alchemist let out a low, dark laugh. "Did I tell you to leave? Now spray the air in front of you."

Fletcher heard a car door on the other end of the call, and anxiety came back to the forefront. The man on the phone, who had been close by just a couple minutes earlier, was putting space between himself and Fletcher. Why?

"What do you see?" the man asked.

Fletcher sprayed the opening in the chancel rail and saw two crisscrossing red lines appear, precisely where he had been about to walk when the Alchemist had called.

"I see it, but I don't get it. This place lets eighty teenagers crash just down the hall. Why would—?"

"Don't overthink it. Just be sure not to trigger anything."

Planting a hand on the rail, Fletcher swung his feet over and landed neatly on the other side.

"Any other security measures?" he asked. "Heat sensors?"

"If there are, I suppose you'll have given yourself away. Which is why you are doing this and not me. Now approach the altar."

Fletcher circled around behind the altar and stopped just short of entering the ring of the spotlight shining from above. "I'm here."

"The Second Council of Nicaea made a ruling about altars. Do you recall what it was?"

"Every altar should have a relic associated with it."

"And these are generally kept in reliquaries built into the altars," the Alchemist said with a leading tone.

"Altar cavities, yes."

"And did you know that these reliquaries are sometimes accessible?"

"Rarely." He looked at the altar in front of him. "I'm guessing this is one of those rare cases."

"You are correct. I need you to access the altar cavity and tell me what's inside. Keep your eyes open for surprises."

"Give me a minute." Fletcher stuffed his phone into his pocket and stared at the altar. He'd seen too many movies not to worry that breaking into the light would send a torrent of poison-tipped darts in his direction from a hundred little holes in a nearby wall. But common sense was a grifter's best friend, he reminded himself, and paranoia among a burglar's worst enemies. Andrew had taught him that.

Crouching low, he crawled into the light and shuffled quickly up to the rear of the altar, almost underneath. He adjusted himself for the best vantage point, sitting on his feet, facing the altar. The spotlight was so bright that he couldn't even see the pews beyond.

His best bet was probably to begin right where he sat, at the rear. Here at least he could work in secret without the danger of exposing himself to an insomniac on a late-night stroll or more teenagers roaming the building, up to no good. He flipped the altar cloth up and tucked it under the large brass altar cross.

The altar was constructed of marble, as he had expected, and along the apron at eye level was an inscription. Ten Greek words. Fletcher translated as he read: "LIONS HONEY SMOKE DIAMONDS WILD BEAST ABYSS JUDGMENT FIRE LOCUSTS."

Okay, *that* made no sense.

He ran his fingers along the engraved letters, discovering nothing out of the ordinary about the inscription but noticing that each word seemed to be etched into its own block of stone, all firmly connected to one another and to the large stone slab above them, upon which the Eucharist was celebrated. He reached up behind the row of engraved stones. Bingo. A line of small levers—one behind each word.

It was some sort of riddle. Pull the right levers, open the secret compartment. He leaned back and reread the words. What did they have in common? Obviously it would be something to do with the Bible or church tradition, given the context, but that hardly narrowed the scope of possibilities.

He closed his eyes and waited for something to gel. His first thought was the story of Sampson in the book of Judges. Sampson had killed a lion and later found honey in its carcass. Or might it have something to do with the book of Revelation? Locusts and smoke came up out of the abyss to torment the earth in one of the more off-putting passages of John's apocalypse. Or did it have to do with St. Paul fighting wild beasts in Ephesus?

All feasible options, but random, with no real antecedent in the altar itself. And who knew what pulling the wrong levers would do? Maybe nothing. Maybe alert the police. Maybe send that torrent of poison-tipped darts.

He needed some perspective here. He mentally backed up a step. If he *did* succeed in opening the altar, what should he expect to find inside? Altar relics were generally fragments of bone from a saint—usually the saint after which the church was named, if possible. He deemed it unlikely that there was a genuine piece of John the Baptist inside, but perhaps he was the key all the same.

Words were jumping out from the altar now. John the Baptist ate locusts and honey while living in the desert. Worth a try.

Hand trembling slightly, he reached up behind the words AKRIDES and MELI—*locusts* and *honey*—and pulled the two levers. Nothing happened. He pulled them again. Still nothing, but nothing was not the worst-case scenario. He let the breath he'd been holding slowly escape.

He whispered the list of words to himself in the original Greek, hoping there might be some kind of rhyme scheme or etymological connection. That's when he remembered. It wasn't just locusts and honey that John the Baptist ate; it was locusts and *wild* honey. He pulled back the word AGRION, then the same two levers as before, stretching his left hand out as far as he could. *Locusts* and *wild honey*.

Still nothing. He punched his thigh in frustration. It did seem a little too simple. Perhaps he needed a more methodical approach. He counted up the words and did some quick mental math. Each lever had two possible positions—on or off—meaning there were just over a thousand possible combinations. If he could try one combination every three seconds, it would take about an hour to cycle through them all—assuming he could reach all the necessary levers with just two hands.

But what if the order in which they were pulled factored in? That would make sense if these levers operated like tumblers in a lock, as Fletcher suspected. It would also increase the number of possibilities exponentially—into the hundreds of millions if multiple levers might be pulled at once. Could it be as simple as reversing the order? In biblical Greek, adjectives usually came after the noun they modified. Fletcher pulled the lever for *locusts* first, then added *honey,* then the modifier *wild.*

There was a click and the sound of a spring releasing somewhere within. And then the word DIAMANTIA connected with Fletcher's forehead, knocking him to the ground. He gave his head a violent shake and pulled himself back to his knees. A compartment—like a small drawer—had opened. It was not empty.

Fletcher freed his phone from his pocket. "You there, Al?"

"Yes. What have you found?"

"Looks like a piece of cloth wrapped around something."

The Alchemist began breathing loudly into the phone.

"Keep it together," Fletcher said. "What do you want me to do?"

"Pick it up carefully."

Fletcher examined the inside of the chamber for any sort of sensor or switch. Seeing none, he snatched the bundle and sat back down on his feet behind the altar, quickly unwrapping the item—a seven-sided shape, about three inches across.

"Looks like a piece of bone, carved into a septangle," Fletcher said. "Common shape in the occult and Freemasonry. Less common in the altars of Catholic churches, I'm thinking." He ran his fingers along the glossy surface. One side was perfectly flat and smooth, save for a smaller septangle carved into the center and a Greek word inscribed at each angle. He flipped the object over. The other side resembled a miniature mountain range. "On second thought, I don't think it is bone. At least not human. It's too big. And not porous enough. Maybe ivory?"

"What about the cloth?" the Alchemist asked, impatient.

"Um, it's beige, I guess. Buff colored? It's just a cloth."

"Does it have a stain on it? Dark spots?"

"Nope." Fletcher examined both sides. "Pretty clean."

"How old is it?"

"I have no idea. Looks like a cotton-poly blend, maybe." He brought the cloth out into the circle of harsh light and studied the fibers. "If I had to guess, I'd say thirty years."

The Alchemist swore. "Put it back," he said. "Put it all back how you found it and get out of there. I'll be in touch."

Fletcher pocketed his phone and began rewrapping the item, doing his best to approximate its original state. He stuffed it into the small compartment, which he was about to close when he paused. On a whim, he quickly exposed the septangle again and, wrenching his phone from his pocket, snapped a picture. Then another from higher up, getting the altar in the shot as well. He then quickly flipped the cloth back over the artifact and pushed the little drawer back in. He had to throw his hip into it, but it finally clicked shut.

After replacing the altar cloth, he grabbed the aerosol can, swung over the chancel rail, and quickly padded his way back out through the vestibule and into the connecting hallway. The harsh fluorescent lights seemed to reintroduce a measure of reality to the situation. Fletcher doubled his pace. Fifty more feet and he'd be back at his sleeping bag and slowly deflating air mattress. He felt an unexpected sense of pure exhilaration.

"Hello?" The word came from behind him.

Fletcher stopped in his tracks and turned to see Father Sacha approaching.

"Oh! Hello to you," Fletcher said, rubbing his eyes and forcing a yawn.

"Can I help you with something?" the priest asked. He was still wearing his clericals at nearly 1:00 a.m. and seemed as bright and chipper as he had been that morning.

"Just using the bathroom," Fletcher said, lying to a priest.

"I see. What's that?" He pointed to the can in Fletcher's hand.

"Oh, this is just . . ." He looked at the label. "Hairspray. One of the girls must have left it behind. I didn't know if you guys had a lost-and-found or . . ."

"What happened to your head?"

Fletcher's hand went up to discover that his forehead was hot to the touch and, he assumed, red where the chamber had struck him.

"I tripped on some luggage trying to get out of that room. Really nowhere to walk in there."

"I'm supposed to keep my eye on you," the priest said.

"I'm sorry, what?"

"Your friend. The one who hides his sadness with discourtesy. He told me to keep an eye on you, remember?"

Fletcher faked a laugh. "Oh, that's Brad. Always joking around."

"There's a restroom just outside the men's sleeping quarters, by the way. That should be more convenient for you in the future."

"Right. Sorry, I'm a little groggy."

The priest looked at him again, his eyes penetrating Fletcher's, then trailing down to the hairspray in his hand. "I see," he said. His eyes narrowed. "Well, you won't find what you're looking for here."

"Excuse me?"

"The lost-and-found. It's in the church office. I can take that for you." He held out his hand.

"Oh, sure. Here you go." Fletcher gave him the can. "I guess I better go get some sleep. Big day tomorrow. Good night, Father."

"Good night."

Fletcher practically ran to the sleeping quarters and retraced the maze back to his air mattress, now nearly empty. There was no way to fill it back up without waking the whole room, so he just lay on top of his sleeping bag, feeling the cold floor beneath.

He pulled his phone from his pocket and brought up the first picture he'd taken. What was that thing? He zoomed in on the words in each of the seven corners: *White, Red, Black, Pale, Martyrs, Earthquake, Silence.* These were the seven seals in the book of Revelation. Fascinating, but clearly not what the Alchemist had wanted it to be. Closing his eyes, he was surprised to find his mind at ease—something he had not felt in a long, long time.

He'd been wrong. The city wasn't freedom; the grift was.

I'll be in touch, the Alchemist had said. The last thought Fletcher had before drifting off to sleep was, *I hope so.*

Chapter 14

A morning chill edged the air as the participants of the week's Christian Service Camp lined up at the curb. Fletcher and his family were in Group B, headed to a live-in drug rehab center where they would prepare and serve lunch to the residents, then help lug boxes in from a truck. Tomorrow they'd be doing a similar task at a local soup kitchen.

The prospect failed to thrill Fletcher. Still, he was looking forward to spending time with Ivy and Meg and happy they would see him in action, doing something selfless. If the passion for prepping and serving lunch did not materialize, he would fake it. That was his area of expertise, after all, and for the past three months he'd overlooked no opportunity to prove to his family that he was a new man, distancing himself from his identity as a thief and a fake as often as possible.

"Line it up, people. Straighten up." Brad came tromping up to the curb, addressing the group as a whole as if he were in charge. He jostled his way to the front of Row A, right next to Fletcher. He was dressed as always: pleated khakis, a polo, and penny loafers. But today he had added a brand-new canvas tool belt, stiff and unused, laden with a variety of tools that also bore no signs of wear.

"I'm jealous." Fletcher laughed. "Our group isn't time-traveling."

Brad drew down his brow, calling on a ready network of furrow lines across his forehead. "What's that supposed to mean?"

"Well, based on that getup, I have to assume your group is going back to 1991 to model for the JCPenney spring catalog. Right?" A spattering of laughter rose up behind him. Even Meg chortled a bit.

"I'll have you know our group is rehabbing a house for a needy family," Brad said. His head wagged a bit as he spoke. "You may think you know me, Fletcher, but I promise you: I can swing a hammer when I need to."

"I'm sure you'll fit right in," Fletcher said. "Most guys at construction sites have tassels on their shoes."

Fletcher heard Noah repeat the word *tassels* behind him at least twice, spreading news of the burn laterally to other lines.

Brad glared for a beat before halfheartedly joining in the laughter. "Aren't you in the wrong group?" he asked. It was a public question, though directed at Fletcher.

"Nope. We're Group B." Fletcher held up the lanyard around his neck.

"Oh, they didn't tell you." Brad lowered his

voice in a way that drew in his audience. "I talked with the director last night, and we agreed that it really wouldn't be fair to send you in with all those drug addicts, considering your past. We're moving you to Group F for today."

"Hilarious, Brad."

"I'm not kidding. It's just best for everybody."

Fletcher looked around as if searching for hidden cameras on a prank television show. "That makes no sense. I've never been addicted to anything in my life."

"Still, though."

"I don't even drink, Brad. Unlike some people."

Brad laughed through his nose. "This isn't about me. These addicts are trying to better themselves, Fletcher. We don't need them hearing your stories glorifying crime and prison. It might be a real stumbling block to them."

Fletcher stepped closer. "Let me tell you something, you—"

Meg interceded. "It's okay, hon. We can all move to Group F today." She tugged her husband's hand, pulling him back a step. "All three of us."

"That's not the point. This guy is just being an—"

"I know," she said, fixing Brad with a firm look. "He sure is. But it's not worth making a scene." She tipped her head and rolled her eyes back toward the pack of kids enjoying the show.

"Fine," Fletcher said, and stalked fifteen feet down the curb to where a fake-baked young woman in a sorority T-shirt was holding a large letter *F* at the top of a pole.

"I guess we're supposed to join your group today," he mumbled, tasting the resentment.

"Oh, I'm sorry," she said, stretching out all three words. "We only have room for one more in our group."

"Let me talk to Brad," Meg said.

"Forget it," Fletcher said. "No big deal. We'll be together tomorrow."

"Any other business before we close?" asked the Rev. Dr. Andre Foreman with a level of gravitas far exceeding the pragmatic question. He was the chairman of the Clergy Forum, a group of city ministers who met each month for fellowship and to discuss possible collaborations and opportunities to serve the community.

"I've got something," Dante said.

"Reverend Watkins from Broadmoor Outreach," Dr. Foreman said for the benefit of the other thirty men seated around the table. "It's good to have you here this month, by the way. We'd like to see more of you."

"Thank you. And I'm sure you will. We're trying to put the *outreach* back in Broadmoor Outreach Tabernacle these days." He smiled, bringing a knowing chuckle from several of his colleagues.

"To that end, I have an opportunity I'd like to share with you." He pulled a stack of leaflets from his briefcase and passed them to his left.

"This is information about a new initiative I'm helping organize. It's called the Father the Fatherless campaign. As you know, many of our young men simply have no positive male role models in their lives. If you've done jail and prison ministry as I have, you've seen where that road too often ends. We're starting a major fund-raising effort to launch a ministry that will provide mentoring opportunities and community centers where young men will have a place to get off the street and spend time doing what kids should be doing."

A man across the table spoke up. "Reverend Watkins, this sounds great. But I suggest you take some time to learn about our existing efforts to provide mentoring and after-school alternative programs."

"That's a good suggestion," said another man. "What you're describing has really been the main focus of the Clergy Forum for several years, and we've built up a pretty decent network. We've all been doing prison ministry—especially Dr. Foreman. And no offense to your vision, but I think we're all in agreement that the real pressing need is more godly men willing to volunteer their time, not more money." There were a few grunts of agreement.

Dante's chest tightened. "I know there are a lot of piecemeal services being offered, but my dream is to put it all under one roof, a clearinghouse for all sorts of ministries. Centralized."

"You say you've got a fund-raising drive underway," Dr. Foreman said. "What's your goal?"

"Five hundred thousand dollars."

All the other men at the table gawked at Dante for several seconds.

"I'm, uh . . . sure we'll all have a look at your information," Dr. Foreman said, shaking the leaflet in his hand. "Now, who would be willing to close us in prayer?"

Dante looked around at all these men of God and hated them.

Chapter 15

The Orangelawn Shelter for Women and Children had once been a high school—the kind that popped up all over the country after the War, filled with wide stairways and named after presidents. It still smelled like a school to Fletcher.

Inside, though, the conversion had been extensive. Classrooms were now dorms for the nightly homeless, abused, and disabused. An entire wing had been gutted and turned into more permanent suites for women enrolled in the center's year-long Life Transformation program. The library and music room were now play areas for toddlers and grade-school kids.

The gym was still a gym. And that's where Fletcher was playing Frisbee with two little red-headed brothers. This was the job that every male in the group had been given upon entering the facility: find some boys and just have fun. Shoot hoops, throw the pigskin, chase each other up and down the halls. Fletcher thought about the rest of Group B, sweating over vats of powdered potatoes and lugging boxes from a truck. *Thanks, Brad. You actually did me a solid.*

Still, after two hours Fletcher was beat. He had never been overly athletic, and these kids seemed to have limitless energy—running, jumping, and laughing with abandon. Knowing he wouldn't last the full forty-five minutes till lunch, Fletcher excused himself from the horseplay and plopped down on a stack of mats in the corner. The two boys followed him.

"Are you coming back tomorrow?" Kyle asked.

"No, not tomorrow." Their faces fell. He mentally cycled through the days. "Thursday I'll be back," he said cheerily, "and my wife and daughter will be with me."

"You have a wife?"

"Yeah. You'll love her. She's better at throwing a Frisbee than me."

The boys exchanged a disappointed look.

"We're gonna go play basketball," Kyle said, and they disappeared.

Mark Walker, the center's director, had been standing nearby.

"Don't feel too bad," he said. "Their mother's not even allowed to date until she completes the program next year."

Fletcher smiled. "This place is awesome. You do great work."

"It's challenging, but certainly rewarding," Mark said. "And we really do appreciate men like you willing to get in there with the kids. Trust me, it's time well spent. A lot of these kids are in their most formative years with no fathers to speak of. Some of the dads are in prison. Others were never part of the picture." He shook his head sadly.

Fletcher's fatigue seemed to grow heavier. "Which years are the most formative?"

"About six to thirteen," Mark answered matter-of-factly. "That's when kids really learn their values and cement family relationships."

Fletcher felt a stab of guilt. No wonder he was having such a hard time getting traction with Ivy. Then again, she had one more formative year left, according to Mark. Maybe there was still a chance to graduate from Father back to Dad.

The director rushed off across the gym floor, bellowing something about lacrosse equipment and fencing, and Fletcher lay back and closed his eyes. Between his leaky mattress, racing thoughts, and covert mission, he'd only gotten about four hours of sleep. And the mats were far more comfortable than his mattress at St. John's.

He was startled from a shallow doze by a deep and resonant voice asking, "Don't I know you?"

The man towering over him was tall, well built, and nearly bald. His eyes were kind and a deep chestnut brown that matched his skin.

Fletcher shook the grogginess from his head and pulled himself to his feet.

"Yeah. You do," he said. "I know you, anyway. You're the preacher from Jackson." He held out his hand, which was immediately enveloped in a firm grip and given two precise pumps. "It's great to see you, Dr. Foreman."

"You can call me Andre . . . Fletcher, right? We talked a few times after chapel."

"That's right." Fletcher realized he was wearing an enormous grin. "You saved my life, Andre."

"I don't know about that."

"No, you did. Two years ago I was in the darkest place I'd ever been. My marriage was pretty much over. My daughter didn't want to visit me anymore. I had no prospects for when I got out. I didn't even *want* to get out. And then I heard you preach about redemption. And it's crazy because I'd been studying the Bible for years, but you made it actually click for me.

How God comes when we're broken and empty-handed and leads us to the cross to receive life. I never put that together on my own."

"Because you were an identity thief."

"No—what? Why does everyone think that?"

"We all were, Fletcher. God gives us our identity, our purpose for existing: to glorify him and enjoy him forever. Then we come in and try and jack the whole process. But Jesus told us that if we find our lives, we'll lose them. But if we lose our lives for his sake, we'll find them. People give up everything trying to find themselves and reinvent themselves and make something of themselves, and they wind up losing their identity. I'm glad to hear you're finding yours again."

Fletcher was silent for a moment. The smile had left his face.

"Walk with me, son," Andre said.

They left the gym, crossed through the atrium, and entered a sparsely decorated chapel containing a pulpit at the back and about eighty chairs lined up in rows. Dr. Foreman deposited his leather attaché on the wooden platform up against the lectern and sat down next to it.

"How long you been out?" he asked.

"Three months."

"And you're hitting the wall?"

Fletcher wavered for a moment. "You could say that."

"Happens to everybody. You feel like you're faking it, don't you?"

Fletcher perked up. "Exactly."

"That's the big question," Dr. Foreman said. "Which you is the real you? The one leading the study groups in the cellblock? The one who fell at the foot of the cross empty-handed that night in Jackson? Or the one who finds his identity in doin' dirt and stealing from people?"

"I don't—"

"Don't tell me, son," he said, folding his palms out. "And don't tell him either. You need to *ask* him. That's how identity works. And when you do, you'll find . . ." He trailed off.

Something had caught his attention across the way from the chapel. He pulled his glasses from his breast pocket and put them on. The preacher's bright eyes slowly darkened, concern etched into his face.

Fletcher cranked his head around, trying to follow the preacher's gaze, and found himself looking across the atrium into the director's office. Through the window he could see Mark Walker talking to a well-dressed man about Fletcher's age.

"Excuse me a moment," Andre said, crossing to the office in long, quick strides.

Seeing no reason to sit in the empty chapel, Fletcher followed him out, looking around for Kyle and his brother.

"What are you doing here, Reverend Watkins?" Dr. Foreman's deep preacher voice carried from inside the office like a foghorn across a harbor.

Fletcher involuntarily took a few steps back, cocked his ear toward the slightly open door, and pretended to fiddle with his phone.

"Same as you, I imagine," the man answered. His voice was less stately, but just as refined.

"I'm here to preach the Word and encourage these women and children," Dr. Foreman said. "And you're handing out more of these? Trust me, there's no half million dollars in this place. If there were, we'd use it to finish the back wing."

"I thought you'd appreciate what I'm trying to do here," the other man said.

"I've heard of some of the things you do, Dante. The kind of things you hear once and dismiss. But you hear them ten times and you start to wonder. What does this man want, Mark?"

Fletcher closed his eyes. He had trained himself to listen in on hard-to-hear conversations. It was an effective way to learn about a mark. Or, in this case, Mark.

"Same thing he wanted yesterday," the director said. "A copy of our donor list. I told him we have a privacy policy."

"Why don't you head back to your own church?" Dr. Foreman said, more a demand than a question.

"You'll see how wrong you are when we're up

and running," Dante vowed. He stormed out of the office and past Fletcher, then caught himself and doubled back.

"Do you work here?" he asked.

"Just volunteering today."

Dante peeled one of the flyers off the stack and handed it to Fletcher. "This place has insanely high overhead," he said, gesturing up at the high ceiling. "You know anyone who really wants to help fatherless kids, have them call me. Ninety-three cents of every dollar goes directly to those kids." He pointed at the flyer, which featured a stock photo of some boys who looked just the right combination of dangerous, lost, and adorable.

"Um, okay," Fletcher said, watching Dante disappear into the sun.

His phone, still lodged in his hand, vibrated. MESSAGE FROM THE ALCHEMIST, it read. Fletcher pocketed the flyer and opened the message.

Meet me in Romeo's pew. Thirty minutes.

Chapter 16

Fletcher had to put the cab ride on Meg's credit card, which didn't sit well with him, particularly after using Meg as an excuse to vacate early.

"Hey, Tiffany, I've gotta run. My wife needs

me," he'd told their college-aged group leader, holding up his phone as if it corroborated his story. She'd made a pouty face for a few seconds and then waved at him with one finger, like one would wave at a child.

He instructed the cabbie to drop him off two blocks from the church. The last thing he wanted was to bump into Father Sacha again while skulking around inside. He fell in behind two older women on their way up to the church's large double doors. He quickened his pace and held the door for them, smiling with the old charm.

"Thank you, young man," they said, nearly in unison.

"My pleasure." He walked close to the plumper of the two, bending down and inspecting the large red hat on her head, one eye searching for the curious little priest who had grilled him the night before. It was hideous—the hat—covered in some sort of decorative tulle and an assortment of pins and brooches.

"I really like your hat," Fletcher said. "I wonder whatever happened to women wearing hats to church. It's just so classy." They smiled widely at each other, then at Fletcher. "Do you think the priest is in there?" he asked, pointing through the doors to the church proper.

"No, he's meeting with our women's mission group in—" She looked at her watch. "Oh! We're late! Come on, Hazel."

While they bustled away, Fletcher walked halfway up the center aisle of the church and sat down in the very spot where the teenagers had been entangled the night before. He opened the text from the Alchemist and replied I'm here. Looking around, he was slightly disappointed that the murals and plasterwork had not been nearly as well maintained as they seemed in the dim light of the previous night.

His phone juttered against the pew beside him, drawing sharp looks from two devouts praying a few rows ahead of him.

Look under your seat.

Reaching between his legs, he found another manila envelope taped in place. He wrenched it free and pulled it up close to his chest. It was sealed shut with the same symbol as the envelope from last night, currently buried at the bottom of his bag. In the light of day, he could see much more detail in the wax seal. The *S* was actually a snake, impaled with an arrow and holding an apple in its mouth.

Fletcher's heart lagged for a moment. It was the Seal of Cagliostro. This made zero sense. He put a pin in the stream of thoughts that was about to erupt and cracked the envelope. Inside he found a stack of papers held together with a paper clip. On the top were three hundred-dollar bills—grease money, he assumed. Under that was another print of him and Andrew, eye to eye, yesterday's newspaper featured prominently. The last three pages were full of single-spaced text. His phone began to ring, and he walked back out into the vestibule.

"I've got the information," Fletcher said.

"Good. To your right, there is a men's room. The door is locked. Go inside."

Fletcher surveyed the door in question. Both the door and the lock were flimsy, and Meg's credit card again came in handy, providing access to the small restroom. Hanging on a garment hook on the wall were a white Borrelli shirt and a tailored Brooks Brothers suit. On a plastic chair next to the sink were a pair of dress socks and shoes and a necktie. He felt a prickle of excitement. Without having made a single decision in that direction, Fletcher Doyle was going back on the grift.

"I understand you usually work the outside," the Alchemist said. "But I need a fresh face on the inside. Is that a problem?"

"I can do it," Fletcher said, pulling off his jeans.

"Good. Get dressed and catch a cab to the drop point listed in the packet. The mark will meet you there at one fifteen. You can review the details en route. This should take only an hour or two. Let me know when it's done." The line went dead.

Fletcher dumped the phone on the chair and got dressed, not at all surprised that every item fit him perfectly. After all, Andrew was in the mix—

somehow—and he had frequently procured a variety of outfits for the two of them to wear when pulling off jobs. In fact, Andrew had kept a storage space filled with every conceivable wardrobe and uniform that a grifter might need, in both his size and Fletcher's.

Glancing in the mirror, Fletcher felt another large chunk of his confidence fall back into place. He hadn't worn a suit since his trial and, *man,* could Fletcher wear a suit. He tightened his tie and checked the time on his phone: it was only twelve thirty. He had plenty of room to take care of this and get back before Meg and Ivy returned.

He twisted his own clothes up into a tight roll, walking out of the bathroom and down the hall into the church's new addition, the envelope and his street shoes under one arm. To his right, down a short flight of stairs, a fire exit caught his eye—wedged back among a small city of file drawers. Seeing no alarm, he decided this was his best way out and, later, back in.

He filed his clothes under *C* in the nearest file drawer, then forced the heavy door, which clearly hadn't been opened in years. He propped it with his hip while carefully pulling away the remnants of duct tape that had held the envelope to the pew. He shoved some tape into the catch in the doorjamb, filling it up, then covered it over with a flat piece of tape along the latch plate.

The fire exit was now an entrance.

Stepping outside, he found himself in a small, rather derelict garden and followed a stone walk up to the street, opposite the way he'd come in. As he cleared the church property, he glanced back over his shoulder and found his eyes drawn up to a third-story window and a man gazing out in Fletcher's direction. He and Father Sacha made eye contact for just a moment before Fletcher disappeared from view.

It took a few minutes to find a cab. Once inside, he relayed the address of the coffee shop where the drop was to take place and settled in to review the particulars. It was a grift that he and Andrew had pulled a number of times to raise capital between big jobs—a digital upgrade of a classic that grifters used to call the Wire. He and Andrew called it the Wireless.

The Outside Man had roped the mark earlier, dropping hints about his friend—portrayed by the Inside Man—who had a surefire way to make money on the stock market. He'd seen it in action, he would say. It was all very technical, but the way he understood it, this guy had a job working at a major Internet server hub, giving him access to incoming data a full second before it arrived at the end user. In the space of that second, an algorithm would analyze the data and determine which stocks to buy and which to dump, resulting in a huge profit for the friend. The catch, of course, was that the Inside Man could not be directly involved without arousing suspicion, given his employer. And the Outside Man had now placed so many successful transactions on his behalf that he was in danger of himself gaining unwanted attention.

That's why they needed the mark. He could take over making the Inside Man's trades for him and, as payment, invest some of his own money as well and walk away that much richer, risk-free. The mark would even be allowed to see it in action on a laptop computer in a coffee shop or some other neutral place, and then would be permitted to participate with a few small, but ever-increasing, amounts. Each time he would see a significant payoff, serving only to whet his appetite for more.

Then, when the mark had gathered, cashed out, and borrowed as much money as he could scrape together, and handed it over to the Inside Man, the server would conveniently go down at just the wrong moment, while the mark's money was tied up in a worthless, tanking stock, causing an enormous loss. The mark always freaked out, of course, but he couldn't exactly go to the police and complain that the illegal stock scam he signed up for hadn't worked out. Best-case scenario: the mark begged for a second go at it and scrounged up more cash, which was also lost, before the mark was cooled and cut loose.

This had all been done already—with Andrew as the Inside Man, Fletcher guessed. Fletcher would be coming in as the Fixer. In some cases, it wasn't money that a grifter wanted from his mark. In those situations, it was best to get the mark heavily indebted, then bring in a fresh face posing as the guy who could make it all go away if the mark will just provide a little money— generally enough to recoup the job's expenses— and X. In most cases, X was information or an introduction, which would then be leveraged into a more lucrative grift with a bigger fish as the mark.

The profile provided by the Alchemist was short on details. Fletcher would have to take it on faith that the mark was providing what had been agreed upon. All he knew was that it would come in a briefcase. And apart from a name and a basic physical description, he knew nothing of the mark's identity. But this kind of drop was child's play for an experienced grifter. Besides, that the mark was a mark at all told Fletcher what he needed to know. It meant the man was greedy and looking for a shortcut. That would make him easy to manipulate.

Fletcher was able to pay cash for the cab this time, which felt good, and he arrived twenty minutes early. Stepping out onto the street, he remembered to remove his wedding ring. Never a good idea to broadcast a weak spot like a wife or child. He'd gained a bit of weight since coming back home and had a hard time wrenching the gold band off.

D-Town Bean was a self-consciously hip coffee shop with semi-arty framed photographs covering the walls and about two dozen tables spread across a spacious dining area. Mediocre indie rock blared from above, drowning out any nearby conversation. It was a good place for a drop. Fletcher would have chosen it himself.

He surveyed the clientele. There weren't many open tables, and he quickly found what he needed: a burly, bearded man with neck tattoos and a lip ring sitting in the corner, reading a magazine and drinking something thick and black. Fletcher walked over and sat down across from him.

"How would you like to make two hundred dollars in the next half hour without having to get up from your chair?" he asked. The man shot him a quick menacing look and turned back to his reading. Fletcher set one of the hundred-dollar bills on the table and slid it over to him.

"Here's half now," he said. "I'm not asking you to do anything weird. Or really anything at all. I'm going to be meeting someone right there," he said, pointing to an adjacent table, "and I just want you to sit here and glare at the guy. Anything makes you uncomfortable, go ahead and leave and keep that." He pointed at the bill.

"Otherwise, just lock onto him with an intimidating kind of a—yeah, just like that. Just your natural sort of . . . vibe."

The man nodded, almost imperceptibly, and palmed the bill.

Fletcher ordered a six-dollar coffee drink—more milk and hot air than coffee—and chose a seat with a peripheral view of the door. He sat upright, staring straight ahead, his expression unreadable. It was imperative that a grifter be in character before making contact with a mark. Those who got cocky, who thought they could turn it on and off at will without any method or preparation, usually saw things go south quickly.

From the corner of his eye, he saw the door open and a very tall man in a very cheap suit walk in holding a briefcase. That would be the mark, Mr. Paul Mason. Fletcher felt his guts twist a little at the sight of a telltale lump in the man's suit coat—waist level, about four o'clock.

That would be a handgun.

Chapter 17

The mark's gaze slowly panned the coffee shop, landing on the prearranged signal: the word *Ultima* on the side of a coffee cup—scrawled there twenty minutes earlier by Fletcher's barista. The lanky man approached cautiously.

"Are you the guy?" he asked nervously, holding the briefcase close to his body with one hand and fiddling with his watch with the other.

"No," Fletcher answered. "There just happens to be a man named Ultima enjoying a latte in this particular café at this exact time. Sit down."

"All right," Paul said. He pulled back the chair opposite Fletcher and awkwardly wedged himself into it. He set the briefcase down on the floor, unconsciously crouching his body to the right in an attempt to cover it up. "I could get fired for this, you know."

Fletcher looked right through him. "You don't pay these people and looking for work will be the least of your worries. I was brought in because I can make this whole thing go away. But I'm going to need what you've got in there."

Paul brought the briefcase up onto the table, but didn't release his grip when Fletcher tried to receive it.

"Mr. Mason, I'm not sure what kind of options you think you have here, or why you brought that piece to a business transaction, but let me assure you of something: I'm your last chance to walk out of this intact." He sat back and smiled a thin, cold smile. "I didn't bring a gun. Never do. Instead, I bring the Crusher."

"The what?"

"The Crusher. To your left." Fletcher kept his eyes on his mark. "About two hundred and fifty pounds, backward baseball cap, big beard. You see him?"

Paul's prominent Adam's apple made a slow run up and down his neck. "Yes," he said quietly.

"His parents called him Dwight, but the guys in his cellblock decided that Crusher better suited him. You've got five seconds to give me this case or you're going to find out why, firsthand."

Paul released his grip.

"Good," Fletcher said. "And don't worry about this coming back to you. That's the last thing my people want." He tapped the briefcase, having no idea what was inside of it. "Trust me; we'll use this wisely." He slid the latte over to Paul. "Here, I didn't touch it. It's salted caramel. I want you to stay in that seat until you've finished every drop. Then you walk out of here and forget we ever met."

"What about the other thing?" Paul asked.

Fletcher was thrown momentarily off-balance. "Uh, yeah, we'll expect you to follow through on that too," he said, walking away from the table, case in hand. He paid his accomplice before stepping swiftly down a back hall, past the restrooms, and into the alley behind the café. The moment the door clicked shut behind him, his phone buzzed.

MESSAGE FROM UNKNOWN, it read.

He opened the text. Grand River Ave. Get in the black Impala. —Andrew

Fletcher trekked up to Grand River. He spotted the classic car and climbed into the passenger seat. The air-conditioning was on full blast. Andrew liked it cold.

"Great work, kid!" Andrew said, happily receiving the briefcase and giving Fletcher's shoulder a firm shake.

Fletcher felt the battle raging in his guts. Part of him could see the path ahead of him, replaying the past: sitting in the freezing car with Andrew, counting the take. Sitting in the back of a squad car. Courtroom. Prison. But part of him could not hide the pleasure of being back in the saddle. Other visions crowded out the first. A never-ending backlog of vending machines waiting to be filled. Brad pulling coat hooks out of the wall and dressing Fletcher down for not asking before he punctured the sacred drywall of his house.

"Where's that smile, kid? You pulled it off."

"I'm supposed to be happy I dropped the wolf on some stooge at the back end of the Wireless? Give me something hard to do."

"You serious?" Andrew asked.

"I don't know. The way you did this whole thing—the pictures, the weirdo on the phone, all that stuff . . . that doesn't exactly fill me with a nostalgic itch to go back on the grift with you. If I'm your mark, then I'm not your partner."

Andrew shrank back, a hurt expression washing over his face. "You think I'm behind this? I got pulled into it just like you, kid. I had no choice. It's the Alchemist here. What am I gonna say, no?"

Fletcher was skeptical. "Who's the Alchemist? I've never heard of him."

"Of course you haven't. This guy's below the radar," Andrew said, his voice dropping as if someone in the backseat might hear. "A world-class thief, but that's not all. Fixer, fence, long con, short con, muscle—he's the whole thing. And you do not want to cross this guy. I've heard things."

An annoying and repetitive samba beat came leaking out of a tinny speaker in Andrew's pocket. He pulled out his phone and glanced at the display. "Speak of the devil," he said. "Hello?" Andrew's jovial air quickly deflated as he listened. "Uh huh. He's right here. You got it." He held the phone out to Fletcher. "He wants to talk to you."

"Yeah," Fletcher said into the phone.

"Well done," the Alchemist said. "Andrew assured me we could count on you. You salvaged the job. Now we can move forward."

"That's great news," Fletcher said. "You kids have fun. I've got to get to church."

"Not just yet. I have an errand for you to run."

Andrew put the car in gear and they began to move.

"Where are we going?" Fletcher asked him.

The Alchemist answered, "Back toward the

church, Fletcher, as you wanted. But I need you to pick up a few things for me before you rejoin your fellow humanitarians. I'll send the list to this phone, which I want you to keep on your person at all times. And hang on to the briefcase as well. You'll need it."

Dante would be dead soon. Of this, he was increasingly sure.

He left the office of his final prospect and walked aimlessly for blocks before flopping down on a bus stop bench. He pulled up the spreadsheet on his phone and added the final total. All other things being equal, he'd be extremely proud of what he had achieved in the last forty-eight hours. Between his own substantial initial deposit and the funds he'd been able to raise, his newly designated Father the Fatherless bank account held $46,516—nearly 10 percent of what he owed La Bella Donna, and he still had four days left. But he was spent. In every way.

He hadn't slept more than a few hours since the visit from Marcus Brinkman. He'd burned through every associate, acquaintance, and institution he could think of—and he'd spent hours thinking. Almost every church and ministry had told him the same thing: it sounded like a good cause, but the city was full of good causes. Lost causes. In a sense, *it* was a lost cause.

If he was to have a prayer at raising the rest, he'd need a new strategy entirely. He snickered. *A prayer.* He was a preacher, at least to most people who knew of him, but he hadn't prayed in twenty years. Not since the day after his dad left. Praying was for suckers. Preaching was for suckers. Throwing money at a church, hoping for points in the afterlife, was for suckers. And that was fine; suckers were Dante's bread and butter. But now the suckers had all been used up.

The idea of applying for some kind of business loan had occurred to him the night before. Sure, the economy was a mess and such loans were about as common as a payout in Greektown, but Trick had skills, swagger, charm. A bit of late-night research had blown the whole thing apart, though. Business plans would have to be assembled, permits pulled, studies and background checks conducted, references checked.

Despair was closing in on him. Trick wanted to keep grifting, try and hit 100K, try and work out a deal with La Bella Donna. Trick could talk. But he had seen Marcus make examples of people who tried such things. Early on he'd been instructed to assist Mr. Brinkman on an errand that turned out to be horrifying. He assumed this was a sort of initiation that everyone underwent upon joining up with the Syndicate. It certainly put things in perspective.

Dante rubbed his eyes. Midafternoon always

hit him like a fistful of Benadryl, and it was many times worse today. He studied his feet and thought about running. Maybe taking his family with him. No, that was a stupid idea.

What about going to the cops? Could they all be relocated in witness protection? But then, what did he really know? Marcus had been right when he called him a cog in the machine. Dante only knew what he himself had done. Each week the old ledgers were collected and new ones started. Only in the past two years had Dante started keeping his own scans week to week, and what did those prove? Nothing. It would be his word against the machine. Besides, he'd be dead before the first warrant was issued.

All at once Dante felt something disconcerting. He looked up, across the street, and saw a large city bus placarded with an ad for a TV show that had been canceled a month ago. It pulled away from the curb, and Dante saw him. The old man from the jail.

Dante stood up from the bench and began crossing the street. Cars skidded to a stop to avoid a collision. Drivers honked and yelled. But no one noticed the old man clutching that piece of cloth. No one gave his bizarre clothing a second glance, although here in the city, Dante wouldn't expect anyone to stop and take inventory of the latest homeless fashions.

But that was just it; the man didn't look

homeless. His robe was worn, but clean. His eyes probing, but clear and sane. A car buzzed Dante at forty miles an hour, just a couple feet away. He could feel the vibrations in his clothing. By reflex he turned to shout an epithet at the motorist, who was already disappearing over the horizon and never heard it.

Dante looked back at the old man. But he was gone.

Chapter 18

"You about done with this Jesus stuff?" Andrew asked. They had pulled to a stop a few blocks from the church. "I'd hate to see that get in the way of what we need to do here."

"Leave it alone." Fletcher felt the same brand of violated as he had when Andrew asked about Meg and Ivy. He didn't want to discuss his conversion with this man. These two worlds needed to remain separate.

"I get it," Andrew said. "You needed a little bump for the parole board so you put on a born-again act. And naturally, a gifted grifter like yourself is going to commit, do your research, play the part. But, kid, you're out. You can take it off now."

"Why don't you worry about your own soul, and I'll worry about mine," Fletcher said. He was in fact worried about it, but he hadn't meant to disclose this to his once and current partner. The phone from the Alchemist emitted an annoying beep.

"This must be my shopping list," Fletcher said, skimming the text. "What is this, a joke? A jar of peanut butter? A porcelain dish? Car Jack 9? What the heck is Car Jack 9?"

"It's a video game," Andrew answered. "And you need precisely that one. Don't come back with Car Jack 8, because we can't use it."

"Whatever." Fletcher stepped out of the car, back into the warmth of the sun.

"Don't forget your briefcase," Andrew called out after him. "Boss wants you to hang on to it tonight. Besides, there's five grand from our buddy Paul in there. That'll more than cover expenses."

"Fine." Fletcher grabbed the case and gave the door a healthy *whump*. As he walked back toward the Church of St. John the Baptist, he read through the shopping list more closely. A candle, sleeping pills, a talking greeting card, ammonia, starch powder . . . Why would the Alchemist send him to buy all this crap?

And if the Alchemist persona was just misdirection on Andrew's part—an idea that seemed increasingly viable—what could Andrew be trying to prove? That Fletcher was expendable, the intern who could be thrown menial tasks? He thought about the hundreds of vending machines he'd filled in the past three months and felt his blood run hot.

Or did the Alchemist want to hammer home that he had Fletcher under his complete control, even to the point of sending him to buy a random list of—

Wait. Fletcher's mind was making connections. Candle, starch powder, porcelain coaster, makeup compact with brush. The rest began to fall into place. This list was not random. These were supplies for a bigger job, something on a whole different scale from the drop that afternoon. That's why the Alchemist, whoever he ultimately was, wanted Fletcher to do the shopping. Fletcher would have the supplies, the case, the grease money. He would have it, he would keep it safe, and he would have to get it to them somehow. And that would all reinforce one message: *This isn't over. It's just getting started.*

✠

Dante didn't bother locking the door of Broadmoor Outreach Tabernacle. For the first time since receiving the keys, he didn't care about protecting this veneer of legitimacy. What did it matter? Someone off the street could come in and kill him for the contents of his wallet and the copper pipes running through the walls, and they'd just be saving Marcus Brinkman the bullet.

He looked around the meeting hall. The altar and pulpit had come from a church that was folding nearby, as had the majority of the religious items in the room. Its members had been delighted at the idea of another church carrying on their use. Dante had struggled a bit with the guilt of accepting them, but these pangs grew duller and less frequent over the years. The pile of money in his newly opened bank account had barely registered a blip on his conscience.

After all, Dante's father hadn't been there for him, and neither had anyone else. So what? He was doing just fine. At least he had been, right up until he started relying on other people. Perhaps the greatest gift one could give those kids was to show them that they need to fend for themselves, that they can't trust anyone. Dante had learned that lesson decades earlier and was now having to relearn it the hard way. The hardest way.

Sitting there in that folding chair, right where Marcus had held a gun to his head two days earlier, Dante knew he had two choices: give up or double down. The first made no sense—not with four days left—but it was oddly appealing. He looked up at the large wooden cross on the back wall. He used to stare at the cross when his mother brought him to church as a boy. The music did nothing for him, and the emotional railing of the preacher struck Dante as disingenuous.

But the cross captivated him. Two lines intersecting, the simplest thing, and yet compelling people to weep, to rant and rave, to kill or be killed. He used to wonder what it was about this symbol, apart from all others, that could so easily motivate people. Grifters talked about a peg, an ultimate desire—usually sex, money, power, or revenge—that could be exploited in order to manipulate a mark. Is that what it was? He leaned forward in his seat, transfixed by the two pieces of wood. Any simpler, and the shape would literally be one-dimensional.

Like most church crosses, this one was usually stark and bare, then draped with a purple pall during Lent, black on Good Friday, then white on Easter morning—the most trivial alteration, eliciting massive changes in mood among otherwise intelligent people. Easter had been a month and a half ago, but the white cloth remained. It looked good up there, and Dante was hardly a stickler for religious convention. Besides, he liked the effect it had on his faithful flock—a little souvenir of the Big Day to hold them over to the next one. If the cross was a peg, the ultimate long con, then it was worth studying, contemplating. But if it wasn't, then perhaps there was a third option for Dante. Perhaps this simple shape had such an effect on people because it meant a way out when there seemed to be none.

Dante stood quickly, tipping the chair behind him, and took five long strides up to the cross. He grabbed a fistful of the white cloth and yanked it down. Pulling the Communion table back, he riffled through a battered cardboard box beneath it, quickly finding what he was looking for. He had to jump a bit to loop the black pall over the cross, and he missed the first time. He took two steps back and surveyed the icon, draped in black. *That's better.*

What now—pray? How? Prayer was a gimmick Dante employed to feed instructions to inmates. The last time he had spoken directly to the Almighty had been twenty years earlier, and had ended abruptly with the realization that he was talking to himself. But praying is what men did when they were about to die. And really, what did he have to lose?

Dante dropped to his knees. If he was going to do this, he would go all out.

✠

Fletcher guessed he had close to two hours before the service groups began arriving back at the church. He probably should start shopping. This would be difficult to time properly. Arrive late and he'd have to explain himself to Brad or Meg, or both. Arrive too early and face another awkward run-in with Father Sacha.

What he didn't want was time alone with his thoughts, which despite Fletcher's best efforts were crowded around Dr. Foreman's question: *Which you is the real you?* The grifter? The convict? The scholar? The father? Fletcher wished he had bags of Fritos and Cheez-Bombs to count. Such tasks had kept these questions from filling his mind for the past three months. But he'd known all along that it was only a matter of time before they would have to be addressed.

He had just rounded a corner, eyes peeled for a convenience store, when he saw him again. The robed man. He was forty feet away, standing on the sidewalk and staring Fletcher in the eye as if he'd been waiting there for him. After a moment the man broke his gaze and disappeared into one of the storefronts. Fletcher felt compelled to follow. He wanted to see a clerk or waitress react to the weird little man, the way no one had on the street the day before.

It was impossible to tell where the robed man had gone, but it didn't matter. As he drew closer, Fletcher found that about half of the storefronts were empty. Another was a barbershop—currently closed—and another a hole-in-the wall church. Most likely, the poor guy lived in one of the abandoned units. Fletcher walked slowly by, looking through the cracked windows, but he saw no one.

He picked up his pace, suddenly feeling very exposed. Here he was in one of the more criminally inclined parts of the city, carrying a briefcase that contained five thousand dollars in cash and who knew what else.

A few more steps and he was standing at the door of the church. BROADMOOR OUTREACH TABERNACLE, the sign read. A cartoon dove poked its beak down between the first two words. Fletcher smiled. This place was the very opposite of what he'd looked for in a church—as a student, as a grifter, even as an ex-con. But at least it was authentic. It lacked the IKEA ethos of the suburban "worship centers" back home. The furnishings were a mixture of old junk and genuine antiques, somehow creating an eclecticism that hit Fletcher just right.

As if to complete the look, a man was up on the dais, kneeling in prayer. Officer Roberts's words filled Fletcher's head. *Seek out a mentor. Someone who's been through some troubles.*

Why not? He pulled the door handle, found it unlocked, and entered the air-conditioned building. Unsure how to interrupt a praying man, Fletcher approached slowly and quietly until he was just a few feet behind him.

The man stiffened, clearly aware he had company. "I hadn't really started yet," he said, "so I don't suppose you're the answer to my prayers." He let out a weak laugh, tinged with desperation.

"I was hoping it might work the other way around," Fletcher said.

The man laughed again, this time more robustly. "You came in here looking for some hope?" he asked, still kneeling, his back to Fletcher. "You see that Bible on the chair next to you?"

"Yeah. Nineteenth century. Not bad."

"Open it."

Fletcher hefted the old book and parted the pages, revealing the void within. "I don't get it," he said.

"That's the kind of place you just walked into. It's all misdirection. No hope here. Got the black cloth goin' now."

Fletcher glanced up at the cross. "That's out of season."

"Not for me." Dante finally stood and turned. Recognition spilled across his face. "Oh." He snickered, again laced with despondence. "You want the list back."

"What list? Aren't you the guy from—?"

Dante was pulling a stack of papers from a briefcase. "Can't use it anyway," he said, extending the pages toward Fletcher. "Just a lot of foundations and grants and stuff. I don't have time for that."

Fletcher pushed the papers back. "I'm not here for that. I just wanted some . . . guidance or something, I guess."

"It'll cost you five hundred thousand dollars."

Fletcher patted his pockets. "Other pants."

Dante laughed again, a bit more genuine, and a weak smile remained on his face like a shadow. "You want advice?" He raised his bloodshot eyes to Fletcher's. "I've learned only one thing in my whole life worth sharing: Don't get comfortable with people. Don't trust anyone. I should have run my own game." He seemed to be talking to himself more than to Fletcher. "You let anyone else call the shots, you wind up stuck."

The smile disappeared and, in the process, the man seemed to age twenty years. "That's all I got, man. Sorry." And he disappeared down a narrow hall, leaving Fletcher standing alone.

"I've learned that one too," he said to no one in particular.

Chapter 19

Lugging the briefcase in one hand and a gym bag he'd purchased to hold the fruits of his supply run in the other, Fletcher entered the Church of St. John the Baptist the same way he'd left, making as little noise as possible. He quickly changed back into his own clothes. His wedding ring was stuck at the first knuckle and his finger was already turning a deep crimson.

Checking the time, he picked up the pace. It was 5:32 and, according to the Xeroxed schedule they'd all received at orientation, the service groups would return to the church between 5:00 and 5:15 each day, with dinner following at 6:00. He could already hear laughing and shouting above as teenagers poured in.

The shopping list had been eclectic, necessitating visits to half a dozen stores. Many items were still a mystery to him. The roll of duct tape made sense. The suction cup shaving mirror and the MP3 travel speaker, not so much.

He carefully folded the suit and button-down and shoved them, along with the dress shoes, into his new gym bag before taking a moment to assess his storage options. Only one of the cabinets was large enough to accommodate the bag and the case—a wide, concrete-reinforced job. There had been a lock at one point, but the entire mechanism was now missing. Fletcher pulled open the bottom drawer and resisted the urge to carefully examine an antique leather-bound book, instead placing the briefcase carefully atop it and shoving the gym bag into the next drawer up.

The chore of shopping for supplies had given him some time to clear his head. He'd tried seeking out a mentor, and what had it gotten him? He wasn't entirely sure. A fellow grifter? Fletcher had never come across the praying man before, but that didn't mean much; his circle of criminal associates was limited to Andrew's preferred collaborators. At any rate, the man who had handed him a flyer at the women and children's shelter carried a trick Bible and had stolen the donor list from at least one charity.

But Officer Roberts had suggested an older mentor as well. Fletcher's thoughts turned to the resident clergyman-in-charge, whose church contained hidden compartments guarded by laser alarms. He wasn't sure about God, but it did seem like the universe might be trying to tell him something.

Fletcher took a moment to mentally prepare himself for the inevitable confrontations that lay ahead, and was surprised to find that they seemed small and easily manageable. He thought of Brad, huffing and shouting and calling him "convict." Nothing. No queasy feeling, no nerves. Was it because he had much bigger problems at the moment? No, that wasn't it. He smiled. Brad was the easiest mark in the world. His peg was obvious: he wanted to feel big and important, as if every aspect of his little life was of tremendous consequence. How had Fletcher failed to exploit that?

It was his pride. The same shortcoming that made Fletcher Andrew's mark back at the museum had kept him from playing Brad. Well, no more. He allowed himself one more thought of the contents of the gym bag and the impending job, feeling a little rush in return, then stepped up the stairs, blending into a throng of kids wielding Nerf guns. He moved through their midst, following the flow of traffic down into the fellowship hall for dinner.

He spotted Brad from a distance and planned his move. He needed this to go down where no one else would see. Brad was looking over the heads of the kids around him, eyes searching. Then he found Fletcher's gaze, and the two locked eyes.

Fletcher turned on his heels and headed down a side hall, into a small classroom. The smell of chalk and slate brought him back almost twenty years to high school. He pushed the memories and all the other thoughts out of his head. If he was going to keep all of this from blowing up, he needed Brad off his back. *You're a grifter*, he told himself. *Grift*.

A moment later Brad burst into the room, golf shirt billowing around him. The sight of him filled Fletcher with a growing rage. He collected it in his chest and found himself able to transform it into what he needed it to be. There it was. He'd just been out of practice.

"Why do I hear that you left your post today?" Brad demanded like a wartime officer about to drag a truant guard to the stockade.

Fletcher looked him in the eye, then let his gaze drop to the floor, an act of submission among all primates. "I'm sorry," he said. "I kind of had a crisis."

"What's that supposed to mean?" Brad asked. His words were still loud, but the edge had left them.

"We were working with all these kids whose fathers had left them," he said, letting his voice crack, "and I couldn't help but think, *I'm just like these deadbeats*. You know? I'm no different."

"You don't have to be," Brad said, adopting a fatherly tone, albeit a father midlecture. "Get your act together, Doyle. It's not too late to step up."

Fletcher sniffled and wiped his hand against his nose. He winced; his ring was still stuck, and the finger stung like the victim of a hundred little needles.

"I just needed some time alone. It won't happen again." He glanced up at Brad as vulnerably as he could. "You're not going to tell the director, are you?"

"I suppose we can let this one slide. But get it together, okay, Doyle?" Brad whacked him on the shoulder, a little harder than the average friendly gesture, but confirming for Fletcher that he'd pulled it off, and walked out of the room.

Fletcher waited half a minute and walked out into the hall, practically colliding with Meg and Ivy on their way to the fellowship hall.

"Hi, Father!" Ivy waved, grinning.

"Hey, kiddo."

Meg's face bore signs of concern. "Brad was

looking for you again. He looked really mad." Her voice dropped to a near whisper. "Promise me you're not going to mix it up with him again."

"Ivy, can you go ahead and grab us a place in line?" Fletcher asked. "I need to talk to your mom a minute."

"Got it," she said, and half ran into the fellowship hall.

"Come here a minute," Fletcher said, leading his wife back into the same classroom he'd just left. She crossed her arms, a barrier of protection against what news she might receive. "I think I smoothed things over with Brad. It's not fair, the position I've put you in with him and the house and everything."

Meg's hands moved down to her stomach.

"I apologized and he accepted," Fletcher said. "Not that everything's going to be great with the guy, but I'll make it work." He didn't want to be turning his wife's peg with such expertise, but he was in the zone and he almost had no choice.

Meg smiled. That smile.

Fletcher realized that at some point he'd pushed his wedding ring the rest of the way on. He gave it an absent-minded turn and looked at his wife. He'd tried timidity—hanging back, giving her space, letting time work its magic. It had gotten him nowhere. He grabbed her around the waist, yanked her in close, and planted a kiss on her, the very opposite of timid. She hesitated for just a moment before returning the kiss—their first in seven years. She wrapped her arms around his neck and pressed into him, right there in the church basement.

Amazing what a little confidence could accomplish.

Chapter 20

January 31, 1785
Paris, France

The séance had concluded with the girl in the booth, through convulsions and the grinding of teeth, channeling the recently deceased Voltaire and the would-be assassin Robert-François Damiens. The girl, who would be paid a few coppers for her troubles, was led away, ostensibly to recover from the ravages of prolonged divination. Count Cagliostro bowed deeply and bid his guests adieu.

Cardinal de Rohan, bouncing and giggling with all the foppishness he could muster, was practically dragged from the hall amid the sea of spectators, waving wildly at Cagliostro with both arms and promising to visit again soon.

Cagliostro withdrew to his laboratory, a converted parlor, where three large furnaces covered the back wall, surrounded by fine cabinets filled with the tools of metallurgy and alchemy. A man of medium height and build was bent over one of the furnaces, examining a crucible. He wore the black cloak and white cross that had so enthralled Cagliostro some years earlier. It was a simple symbol, but meant so much more to the men who wore it, who battled the Moslems and hunted Barbary pirates under its standards.

The man, hearing the count approach, turned to face him. His wig was flawlessly placed, his nose long and Romanesque, and his mouth pulled into a wry smirk.

"I see the secrets of alchemy unfolding before me," he said.

"You should not be in this room," Cagliostro said.

"Yes, your lackey told me the same thing," the Grand Master said. "It did not go well for him." He opened the hinged lid of the crucible. "I open this side, and I see lead." He flipped the crucible over. "But look! A little time in the furnace and we have gold," he said, tipping open the other side.

The man was Emmanuel de Rohan, a distant relative of the cardinal of Strasbourg—now boarding his carriage outside—and the current Grand Master of the Knights of Malta. He was fifteen hundred miles from Valletta, and that had everything to do with Cagliostro.

"It's in the wrist," the count answered. "I keep

the light low in the laboratory and stand hunched such that my Masonic apron obscures the move." He bent his knees. "Like so."

"I see." The Grand Master studied Cagliostro's outfit, from the turban down. "Why do you have the Grand Master's sword in your possession?" He pointed a gloved finger at the blade hanging from the count's belt.

"Your predecessor bequeathed it to me."

"It was not his to give." Grand Master de Rohan replaced the crucible and took a step toward him.

"I see that you have replaced it with an even finer sword," Cagliostro said. "I hope you have not traveled all this way for a duel. I am no swordsman."

Grand Master de Rohan laughed, his age showing around the eyes. "No, I am here because of the letters you sent me and because I would like to continue the plans you began with Grand Master da Fonseca."

"I am happy to hear it."

"Before we move forward, however, I must tell you that I share neither my predecessor's belief in the occult nor his gullibility."

"All the better," Cagliostro said.

"I do share his desire to keep my position and wealth in a world that is sliding headlong into chaos."

The Grand Kophta removed his turban and smoothed his hair back. "I have anticipated your visit and have already set everything in motion for the next act of our unfolding drama. Your kinsman is just now leaving with his buxom ecclesial escorts. He is more willing than ever to do whatever I advise in order to reenter the queen's favor."

"I assume that the good cardinal has seen this transmutation of lead into gold?"

Cagliostro smiled darkly. "Mercury into gold, which is harder to accomplish but far more impressive. Not here, but in my larger laboratories, which I keep in his episcopal palace. Unlike you, Cardinal de Rohan shares both Fonseca's gullibility and penchant for the occult. While I lived in his palace, he lavished me with every gift and luxury."

The Grand Master snuffed derisively. "Sadly, the House of Rohan has become a breeding ground for naiveté and superstition, particularly the Guémené branch. When I think that such a man is both a prince and a cardinal of the Holy Church, I almost begin to sympathize with the revolutionaries on the streets and in the Bastille."

"He aspires to even more power. The end goal of all Cardinal de Rohan's machinations is that he attain the position of prime minister, to which he thinks he is uniquely suited."

The Grand Master grimaced.

"But remember," Cagliostro said, "that you are a prince and a cardinal as well. And you must protect what the Great Architect has entrusted to you."

De Rohan nodded. "Tell me where things stand," he said.

"I have spoken with the Monsieurs Böhmer and Bassange."

"The jewelers?"

"The finest in all Paris. Perhaps all of France. They work their craft in an extraordinary and ostentatious mansion on the Avenue des Champs-Élysées. But what few know is that these men are broken in spirit and very nearly ruined financially." He sat down on a bench, smoothing his skirts around him. "The source of their grief is a necklace. A diamond necklace commissioned by King Louis's late father for his mistress—a gaudy and impractical piece of jewelry, composed of hundreds of diamonds and costing far more than one million livres. They bring it out on occasion in their showroom, and many have seen its opulence, although few know the full story."

The Grand Master sat on an adjacent bench, facing Cagliostro and leaning forward attentively.

"Before the transaction could be completed, the king died and his mistress was banished. This left the fine jewelers in a horrible position. Without payment for the necklace, they were crippled with debt, unable even to keep up with the interest they owed."

"And who could afford to buy such a lavish piece?"

Cagliostro nodded. "They have twice tried to sell it to His Majesty, as a gift for the queen."

The Grand Master smirked. "It is hard to imagine that Marie Antoinette would pass up such an ornament."

"But she did. Twice. She wants nothing to do with a necklace crafted for another man's mistress. Besides, she knows what great public outcry would result if she were to spend so much from the royal treasury on a piece of jewelry. With the political climate as it is, such a transaction could prove the final provocation."

De Rohan rubbed his chin. "I am beginning to see how this fits into the scheme you laid out in your letters."

"And you see the potential?" Cagliostro asked.

"As if it has already happened and we are looking back."

Chapter 21

The Orangelawn Shelter for Women and Children went cold as Kyle and his brother were introduced to Meg, whom they apparently assumed to be the only obstacle standing between them and domestic stability wrapped in a white picket fence. It took her all of three minutes to thaw the ice and win them over entirely. Their latent plans to replace her with their mother moved quickly to the back burner and then out the back door as she chased them up and down the gym floor, unleashing dodgeballs in their direction. Ivy, meanwhile, had quickly connected with an awkward loner of a nine-year-old girl, and the two were discussing some television show about a post-apocalyptic high school. Fletcher just sat back and smiled.

He'd been wrong in figuring the groups' rotation and was elated to find their van pulling up to the converted school that morning. His high spirits were further boosted by the fact that there were four of them crammed into the backseat of the van, squeezing Fletcher up against his wife, who had taken his hand and tipped her head against his shoulder, leaving it there the whole ride. Fletcher suspected that the thirteen-year-old boy two seats up was in a similarly good mood for almost exactly the same reason. Nothing like a weeklong church mission trip to kindle some fires.

"You worried me yesterday," came a deep, resonant voice.

"Oh, hello, Dr. Foreman," Fletcher said. "Sorry about the quick exodus; I had to go take care of something. But I worked it out so I could come back again today."

"Is she your wife?" Dr. Foreman asked, gesturing

at Meg, who was currently caught between the two boys in a raucous game of monkey in the middle.

"Yeah. My daughter is around here somewhere too."

"You're a lucky man."

They watched the kids play in silence for a moment before Fletcher asked, "That guy yesterday—the one you were chewing out—who is he?"

The minister frowned. "I fear that he is in very deep trouble. And I wish I could help him. That's all I'm going to say."

They were enveloped in sudden chaos as Meg rushed over and ducked behind Fletcher, using him as a shield against a torrent of foam balls. Before he could introduce his wife to his old friend, he found himself literally pulled into a game of two-on-two basketball. Meg had played in high school and had Fletcher easily outclassed, but he didn't argue when accused of going easy on his wife. Halfway through their game, Ivy and her new friend wandered into the gym and were cajoled with some difficulty into turning the game of two-on-two into three-on-three.

Game over, they lined up at the drinking fountain. Fletcher felt like he'd never stop smiling. Until that annoying beep from his pocket jarred him back to reality.

Meg raised her eyebrows and warned, "You better turn that thing off. I heard they confiscate phones here."

"Yeah, let me just see who it is," he answered, withdrawing a dozen paces. He'd stuffed his own cell phone into his left pocket that morning and, against his better judgment, placed the burner phone from the Alchemist in the right.

Since no one else even knew the phone existed, Fletcher was not surprised to see 1 MESSAGE FROM THE ALCHEMIST on the display, although he was disappointed. The temporary high from yesterday's exploits was fading in comparison to the domestic bliss he was soaking up today. He brought up the message. **Corner of Ashland & Central. 45 minutes. Bring everything.**

Fletcher made up his mind to ignore the message. He'd tell the Alchemist that he forgot the phone. Or it ran out of battery. Or the director had confiscated it, as Meg suggested. He returned it, now far heavier, to his pocket and rejoined the group, all of whom were now talking about lunch. The flow of traffic brought him into the cafeteria, where the universal smell of lunch line food filled the air. Fletcher, Meg, Ivy, and their three new friends settled in around a small table.

Dr. Foreman launched into a prayer of blessing, the sound of his voice bringing about instant silence. "Heavenly Father, we thank you for the food we are about to receive and for the good friends—both old and new—who surround us. Amen." The din of conversation returned to the room as the hungry were released, table by table, to go through the line.

"Why does he say that?" asked Keisha, Ivy's new companion.

"Why's he say what, hon?" Meg asked.

"Heavenly Father." She traced a pattern on the table with her finger. "My dad's in prison," she added.

Ivy stretched an arm around her. "My dad was too," she said. "It stinks, I know."

Keisha's eyes snapped onto Fletcher. "What did you do?" she asked.

"He stole stuff from churches," Ivy said.

The girl's jaw dropped. The burner chirped again from Fletcher's pocket. Then again, two more times. He felt every eye at the table boring into him, but no one spoke. A volunteer rescued him with the news that it was their turn.

Fletcher grabbed two trays and handed one to his daughter. "You know that's not really who I am, right?" he asked her quietly. "That was something I did because I thought I had to, but it's not really me." They accrued silverware and napkins as they slid their way down a metal track.

"Why?"

"Because I wanted to provide for you and your mom. I wanted you to have the best things, and I lost sight of right and wrong."

Ivy took half a dozen coffee creamers—

undoubtedly to add the containers to the collection in her room, Fletcher thought.

"I'd have rather had a janitor for a dad than no dad." It wasn't an accusation, just a statement of fact.

"I know," Fletcher said, then added, "I love you," because he didn't know what else to say.

"Got it," Ivy answered, and walked off to the sparse salad bar. Fletcher's pocket beeped again. Plate heavy-laden with hot tuna noodle casserole and watery green beans, he returned to the table, his appetite quickly evaporating. Despite Meg's efforts to rope him into the conversation, he ate in silence, offering only the occasional syllable or two in response to direct questions.

"Are you okay, Fletcher?" she finally asked.

"Yeah," he answered. "I just don't feel great."

"Who keeps texting you?" Her words were laced with suspicion—understandable, since Fletcher rarely communicated by phone with anyone outside of his family.

"I think it's this new program I downloaded," he lied. "Sends baseball scores to my inbox. I'll turn it off." He stood. "Just let me hit the bathroom."

Once in the privacy of a stall, Fletcher turned his attention to his eleven messages. Their tone grew increasingly annoyed at the radio silence. The last four were picture messages: a choice shot of Fletcher and Andrew in the convenience store, a couple of the drop at the coffeehouse, and Fletcher surreptitiously removing cash from the briefcase. Someone had followed him at a distance and snapped these with a telephoto lens. Someone good.

Fletcher checked the time. The initial forty-five minutes had come and gone. Another message beeped in: **Last chance.**

He hit Reply. **On my way.**

Chapter 22

The van parked at the corner of Ashland and Central was nothing special. None of the people trudging by paid it any notice. But the very sight of the old vehicle tapped into a well of memories locked deep inside Fletcher. He'd spent many nights climbing in and out of that old van— planning, prepping, monitoring. The flood of emotions twisted his stomach a bit—mostly in anticipation.

The tuna casserole—lying in his stomach like a heap of wet rags—was a small comfort, as it meant he hadn't lied to Meg outright; he did feel a bit ill. When he had hobbled up to her, bent tightly at the waist, and announced the impending emergency exit of his lunch, she had squinted at him with a combination of concern and distrust before offering to take him back to the church.

Fletcher insisted that she and Ivy stay behind while he take the bus. After all, he'd reasoned, why should the women and children of the shelter be deprived of their company because Fletcher had ingested something that didn't agree with him? She finally relented, admitting that leaving would be unfair to Ivy. Besides, she and Fletcher had always been rather private about illness, generally giving a wide berth to all things projectile.

Fletcher had caught a cab back to the church and, with no little luck, slunk in unseen. After grabbing a couple things from his luggage, he returned to the file cabinet, where he changed into the suit, stuffed his own clothes into the gym bag, and emerged back out into the garden. He followed the stone path, head down, not daring to glance back up toward the window where Father Sacha had spotted him the day before.

The side door of the van rolled open now as he approached, and a familiar boyish face grinned at him from beneath a shock of red hair.

"Fletch lives," the guy said, reaching out his hand—first in greeting and then by way of helping Fletcher and his bags up into the monster of a van. All but the driver and passenger seat had been removed, and in their place were a couple of swiveling captain's chairs, a small table, and two counter tops—one on either side of the van—covered in monitors, computers, tools, and surveillance equipment. The smell of cigarettes permeated everything. The first time he'd seen the setup, Fletcher had laughed, thinking it looked more like a cartoon than anything professionals would really use.

"Happy," Fletcher said, feeling his anger recede as the word left his mouth. "How did I not see this coming?"

"No one sees me coming," Happy replied. "That's the point."

"Never thought I'd climb into this bucket of bolts again."

"And you don't deserve to." Happy slid the door shut with more force than he needed.

Fletcher chortled. "Don't tell me you're still mad about that stupid vanity plate."

"Stupid van—?" Happy swiped at the air. "You don't take a van's plate, Fletcher. That's her identity. That was her heart and soul!"

"Happy, it literally said 'nondescript.' That defeats the whole purpose of driving a nondescript vehicle."

"It didn't say 'nondescript,' " Happy mumbled. "There were no vowels."

Fletcher shrugged. "Sorry, man. What can I say?"

"You know what?" Happy said, his face softening. "Let's put all that behind us. Because that's what friends do." He paused. "Oh, and unrelated: I may have been the guy who took the recent incriminating pictures of you." He traced an *X* over his heart. "I had no idea you would be involved until it was too late." He slapped his hands against his knees. "So we're good, then? All is forgiven?"

"You I forgive," Fletcher answered.

"I see how it is," Andrew called from the driver's seat. "You don't forgive me."

"You didn't ask me to."

"And I won't either. Remember how Cagliostro began his treatise: 'Men who live by the art of misdirection must never apologize nor implicate themselves in any scheme or falsehood unless it is required to further the deception.' "

Happy groaned. "You been away for years. He still won't shut up about Count Whatsisname."

"And that gives him away," Fletcher said, leaning up between the front seats. "The envelopes you left me—both of them had Cagliostro's seal."

"I told you," Andrew said. "It's not me."

"Yeah, I know. It's some other guy who just happens to share a penchant for the same semi-obscure historical figure. Look, I don't know why you think you need to make me your mark to get my help on a job, but don't insult my intelligence."

Andrew shook his head. "There's a whole school of grifters who look to Cagliostro as the ultimate con. That's why I had you read his memoirs when you were coming up. It's why I study his work so intensely. Because at any given moment he was exactly who he needed to be to get what he was after." He started the van's engine, which turned over on the third try. "And speaking of which, let's head out. We're already late."

Fletcher eased back into the chair next to Happy, the familiar feeling of the vinyl and duct tape striking a chord of nostalgia. "So what's the job?"

Happy whacked him on the arm. "Don't worry, we'll brief you. But first, did you bring the video game?"

"Got it right here." Fletcher rummaged through the gym bag.

"Aha!" Happy inspected the item, almost giddy. "This right here is the most shoplifted piece of merchandise in America today. It's a 3D first-person video game about this guy named Jack who steals cars and kills people. Really popular among tweens." He ripped open the shrink-wrap. "Seriously, dude. Our generation is, like, the worst parents yet."

Fletcher anchored his mind, kept his thoughts from tipping toward Ivy.

"But what I need is not the game itself," Happy said, pulling a small metallic sticker from the inside cover of the case. "It's this: next-gen RFID tag."

"What's it do?"

They hit a bump on the road, and everything in the van bounced a little and slid.

"You know those sensors at the mall that buzz if you try and leave a store with unpaid merchandise? Well, those go off when they pick up a radio frequency from a passive tag in a product. But those tags are only good for a few feet. These little babies, however," he said, holding up the sticker with a pair of tweezers, "can track the product around the store and out into the parking lot. Range of two hundred yards or more. Not widely used yet, but perfect for what we need."

He turned his attention to a business card, one corner of which had been carefully split into two thinner pieces. Despite the van's worn shocks and the sad state of the city streets, Happy placed the tag inside the card with a surgeon's precision and carefully glued the edge back together. He blew on it for a few seconds before placing it in a sleek metal case atop several other identical cards and handing the whole thing to Fletcher.

"Remember, the top one goes to the head of security, not the old man."

Fletcher pocketed the case. "What old man?"

"William Belltower," Andrew answered. "Millionaire auto executive turned capital investor and currently in possession of something we need."

"Belltower?" Fletcher laughed. "You're making that up."

"No, I'm not." Andrew adopted an exaggerated accent. "He's of noble birth."

"Guy's like two hundred years old," Happy said. "Total gomer, easy mark. Didn't you look through this?" he asked, pulling the file folder from the briefcase Fletcher had collected the day before.

Fletcher shook his head. "Financial information?"

"Nah, Ultima Insurance Company's file on old Belltower," he said, leafing through the pages. "We've got room-by-room inventories, insurance values, an overview of his home's security, the works."

"Not bad," Fletcher said, settling back into his role in the group. "What's his peg?"

"What do all gomers want?" Happy said. "Dinner by four thirty, then right to bed."

Andrew chuckled. "Don't worry about Belltower. He's the mark, but he's not really the mark. He does whatever's expected of him. The guy we need to grift is his head of security, Julian Faust."

Happy dropped a much thinner folder on Fletcher's lap. "Also a senior citizen, but younger than his boss and plenty dangerous. Have a look; formerly British Special Forces, knows three hundred ways to kill a man using only his pinky finger, that kind of thing."

Fletcher opened the folder and saw a picture of a severe man in his midseventies. His receding hair was black, tinged with silver, his eyes a metallic blue. "And what are we after?"

"Just need to set the table for tonight—a house call."

"Tonight? I don't know." Fletcher's stomach churned and dropped as they hit another pothole. With each successive absence, Meg's suspicion was rising exponentially. Denial would only keep her from drawing the obvious conclusion for so long.

"Yes, tonight," Andrew said. "You've got what you need to fade out of there, but let's keep our focus on the job at hand. Step one: we drop in on Belltower and Faust at their office. You follow my lead and get him that card. And hopefully Mason will come through."

"Paul Mason?" Fletcher asked. "The guy from the coffee shop?"

"That's him," Happy said. "He's a midlevel IT drone for Ultima. I gave him a patch to run on their phone system. Nothing he can't handle." He handed Fletcher a clip-on name badge. "And you are Jordan Lyons, an art appraiser contracted by Ultima Insurance. Congratulations."

Chapter 23

"I have nothing in the appointment book," the receptionist said, peering over her glasses as if reprimanding a child. She wore a bulky headset that reminded Fletcher of the nineties but somehow still seemed to add to her air of authority.

"Of course you don't," Andrew raged. "We left three messages, and my colleague here is only in town today. You tell Mr. Belltower that if he wants the insurance coverage on his two Renoirs to continue past midnight tonight, he will see us right now." He punctuated the last two words with his knuckles against her desk, then glanced at his watch impatiently.

The receptionist disappeared for a moment, ostensibly into Belltower's office, then returned accompanied by Julian Faust, a thin but solid man who was far more imposing in person than on paper.

"Gentlemen," Faust said, his accent pleasant and crisp. "I am afraid there's been something of a mix-up with the scheduling. Mr. Belltower is unavailable, but perhaps I can help you."

Fletcher let out an exasperated sigh. "Let me just call the Art Gallery of Ontario and tell them that I'll be another day late because 'Mr. Belltower is unavailable.' "

"Excuse me?"

"If you keep playing these games, your coverage will expire. And not just on the Renoirs—on everything." His voice was rising steadily.

Faust thought for a moment, his eyes moving between Andrew and Fletcher, before saying, "Why don't you two gentlemen step into Mr.

Belltower's office? I trust we can deal with this matter quickly."

Entering the spacious office, Fletcher had to fight down a sense of awe. It was all oak and mahogany, antiques and leather-bound volumes, with a panoramic view of the city. William Belltower sat at a ship of a desk, smiling at his visitors as if they were the first people he'd seen in some time. His unruly white hair stood up from his head in several spikes, like a hand reaching for the ceiling.

"Hello," he said, standing with some difficulty and reaching out over the end of his desk.

Andrew shook his hand, firm and a little curt, and said, "It's good to meet you, Mr. Belltower. Now, when can we have a look at your home?"

"My home?" He turned to Faust. "What is this young man talking about?"

"I have no idea, but I'm going to find out." He flipped through a Rolodex at the edge of the desk, then punched the speaker button on the desktop phone and dialed. Fletcher noticed that there was no computer on the desk, nor digital devices of any kind.

"Whom are you calling?" Belltower asked.

"The insurance company." Faust fixed Andrew with a stern look. "They've never dropped by unannounced before." He rested his right hand on his hip, causing his jacket to ride up and offering a glimpse of a handgun in a black leather holster.

"Ultima Insurance," crackled a voice from the muffled speaker. Fletcher immediately recognized it as Paul Mason. "How may I direct your call?"

"This is Julian Faust, calling on behalf of William Belltower. There are currently two men here in our offices claiming to be agents of your company and acting rather rudely." He paused. There was no response. "Are you still there?"

"Uh, yes, sir. Do you know who—?"

"The question is, do *you* know who William Belltower is? He's your second-largest client. So why don't you connect me with someone else— someone with some authority? I don't have time to waste chatting with a trained monkey in a cubicle."

Fletcher smiled inwardly. He loved grifting jerks. Faust was exactly the kind of pretentious gasbag he and Andrew had sought out in the early days. And Andrew's plan—if it was Andrew's— was the kind they'd perfected. Their initial mark had not only supplied useful information, but he was also establishing their cover as insurance company employees, something no one would pretend to be if they were not.

"I'm sorry for the wait, Mr. Faust," Paul was saying through the speaker phone. "Let me connect you with Ms. Vischer. She's in charge of our corporate division."

"No," Faust said, "this isn't—"

There was a beep and click, and a moment later a woman's voice filled the room. "This is Caroline Vischer. How may I help you?" Her voice was familiar to Fletcher, but he couldn't quite place it. She sounded educated, pleasant, and attractive.

"There are two men here demanding to see some of Mr. Belltower's valuables. They showed up unannounced a few minutes ago. Please explain."

They heard a few keystrokes coming from the other end. "It says here," she said, tapping more keys, "that our intern Hunter has left three messages over the past week, trying to set up a meeting while our appraiser is in town."

"We did not receive any calls from your office in the past week," Faust said sourly, "and Mr. Belltower has not acquired any new art in the past five years."

Fletcher spoke up. "It's nothing new." He retrieved the inventory from a green file folder tucked under his arm and handed it to Faust. Two lines were highlighted in yellow. "You have these two Renoirs insured for a combined 3.5 million dollars, but I have reason to doubt their authenticity."

"This is preposterous," Faust said, punching a button on the phone and hanging up on the woman. "Mr. Belltower has a professional art buyer on retainer. There is no chance that he has forgeries in his collection. But if you'd like, you can send someone out this weekend to—"

"This weekend?" Fletcher wheeled to face Andrew. "I have to be in Toronto tomorrow!"

"I know," Andrew said, his voice low and calming.

"You *know?* Well, know this: if I don't lay eyes on these Renoirs tonight, I'm opening an investigation on the whole collection. And that's on you, Jenkins." He pushed a finger into Andrew's chest, then turned his attention to Faust. "Here's my contact information," he said, pulling the modified business card from its case. "Give me a call if you decide to stop playing games."

Faust glanced at the card for just a moment before slipping it into his inside jacket pocket. "I think we can accommodate you tonight," he said, forcing a smile. He turned to Belltower and asked, "Are you planning on staying in this evening?"

The old man smiled pleasantly. "We've nothing at the lodge, so yes. Feel free to stop by. Not too late; I turn in rather early."

"How's eight o'clock?" Andrew asked.

"Sounds delightful," the old man said, clasping his hands together.

"Fine," Fletcher said. "We'll see you then."

They were halfway to the door when Faust called after them, "Mr. Lyons, if you don't mind my asking, how long have you been with Ultima Insurance?"

Fletcher took a half step back into the office. "I don't work for Ultima directly. I've been contracting with them as a freelance appraiser for four years now." He noticed that Faust had Happy's phony business card in his hand once again and was studying it.

"You don't mind if I check up on you a bit, do you?" he asked, cocking an eyebrow.

Fletcher smiled politely. "I'd expect nothing less."

"Don't worry about that," Happy assured the others, back in the van. "I set up the usual background stuff: An account on LinkUp with connections to a bunch of people in the industry. Jordan Lyons's name shows up on the archives of a variety of university and art museum websites and publications. Just what you'd expect of an appraiser starting to build his name."

Fletcher leaned against the computer-laden counter, his weight causing it to sag. "We've got our invite," he said. "So what's the objective?"

Andrew handed him a rolled-up blueprint of a sprawling Georgian-style house, which Fletcher unfurled on the counter, pushing aside a soldering iron and a collection of cell phones.

"Here is where the art is stored," Andrew said, pointing with an ink pen. "You'll keep Faust and Belltower busy there while I enter here, directly into the library, and access a safe hidden there."

Happy giggled. "Who has a *library?*"

"Rich people," Fletcher said. "But the question is, what do they hide in the library?"

Andrew shrugged. "He called it a satchel."

"Like a book bag, with a strap?" Happy asked.

"No strap. It's a leather case, a little smaller than that." He gestured at Happy's laptop. "That's all I know. The Alchemist wants it, so we need it. Happy will keep in contact with eyes on the house from this vantage point in the woods, just the other side of the property line. We've been set up there for two weeks without being discovered."

"How many on his home security staff?" Fletcher asked, studying the plans.

"Four," Andrew answered. "But there's a brief window in the evening when only Faust is on-site. We'll be in and out before that window closes."

Fletcher traced his finger along the natural routes and ran through the basic plan in his head. "This leaves too much to chance. What if Faust leaves during my appraisal and does the rounds?"

"It's your job to keep him by your side. Besides, guy's a control freak. He won't leave you alone with the old man, let alone with all that priceless art."

"I don't know," Fletcher said. "I think we need another player. Someone to run an Uncle Billy if things get dicey."

Andrew pursed his lips. "Now that's not a bad idea. How much cash you got left in the briefcase?"

"Almost four grand."

"That'll get us our choice of cast members. How about the Trilby kid? He could run an Uncle Billy in his sleep and then pop around the back and help me with the safe."

"No way," Fletcher said. "I'm breaking my parole by talking to you guys, by being in this stupid van. Every person from my past we add to the roster increases my chances of going back to prison. It's got to be a stranger."

"What about Mad Mike?" Happy offered. "You ever worked with him?"

"Yeah, that check-cashing thing. Andrew, you've got to know somebody from before my time."

"Guys are spread all over. New York, Indy, LA. It's not like there's a job board to keep track of who's in town." Andrew rubbed the back of his neck. "I think we might be stuck making this work with the three of us."

Fletcher felt his hand instinctively go for his pocket, as if it remembered the folded piece of paper before he did. "I've got it," he said.

"Someone you met on the Inside?"

"Someone I met yesterday." He climbed up over the console into the passenger seat. "Head up to Broadmoor. We're going to church."

Chapter 24

Happy was nervously plotting their surroundings, assessing potential danger, his trademark paranoia operating in the vicinity of threat level orange. "Hurry up, Fletcher," he said. "This is not a great neighborhood. And look at us. We're like a violent criminal's coupon over here. Three for one. Like a triple-scoop sundae for muggers, and I'm the cherry on top."

"You mean the carrot on top?" Fletcher asked.

Andrew chortled. "The carrottop."

"Carrottops are green, moron."

Fletcher pounded again on the metal accordion gate stretched over the front door of Broadmoor Outreach Tabernacle. He could see a light on inside, back where the preacher had disappeared the day before, but no other signs of life.

He pulled out the flyer once again, along with his phone. He had two more texts from Meg, both asking how he was doing. "Hang on a second," he said, quickly responding to his wife.

Still sick, he wrote, resting. Before he'd finished dialing the number on the flyer, another message popped up from Meg.

So U R at the church then?

He paused, unsure how to answer. What if she had returned to the church herself and this was some kind of a trap to catch him in a lie? He decided to put it off. He could always claim that the necessities of illness and bodily functions had kept him from responding. She wouldn't push for details there. He closed the message and dialed the contact number for the Father the Fatherless campaign.

After two rings a scratchy voice answered. "It's a blest day at Broadmoor Outreach Tabernacle. How may I help you?"

"Hey, this is Fletcher. We met yesterday."

Nothing.

"You showed me your Bible, remember?"

"Right. What do you want?"

"I'm standing outside your church. You want to let me in?" He could almost feel Dante's irritated sigh blowing out through the earpiece of the phone. "Look, I know you don't trust anybody, so I brought payment up front. It's not half a mil, but it's better than nothing."

"I'll be right down."

A moment later Dante appeared, unlocking the gate and waving them in.

"What are we talking about here?" he asked. Every muscle in his face was drawn back, taut. "I don't have time to play around."

"I'm going to be straight with you," Fletcher said. "You're on the grift. So are we. My name's

Fletcher. These are my partners, Happy Ganton and Andrew Bishop."

Dante pointed at Andrew. "You, I've heard of."

"We're not talking long con here," Fletcher said. "We're talking one night. We need a fourth, somebody on standby for an Uncle Billy, maybe help keep an eye on the big picture. Pays two grand."

"Three," Dante countered.

"Two point five," Andrew said, his tone closing negotiations.

"Okay," Dante nodded. "I'll accept twenty-five hundred tonight and a line on another job tomorrow. Take it or leave it."

"You got it," Andrew said, reaching out his hand.

Dante's brow crumpled. "Grifters don't shake on a deal."

"Just checking," Andrew said with a smile. "So what's your name?"

"Call me Trick."

"Gun it! Take a left here." Fletcher ducked down in the passenger seat.

"What is it?" Andrew asked.

"Meg and Ivy are getting out of that van back there. They'll be in the church in a second. Pull me around to the other side. Quick! Yeah, pull over here."

Andrew squealed to a stop. Fletcher jumped down to the curb. "See you guys in an hour," he said.

"Wait." Happy thrust a plastic bottle and a small plastic bag out the window. "Don't forget your upset stomach."

"Right."

Fletcher was halfway up the stone walkway when he remembered his clothes, rolled up and stuffed into the gym bag in the back of Happy's van. *Idiot.* Why hadn't he changed in the van on the way back? He broke into an awkward run, encumbered by the dress shoes.

The church would already be full of kids and chaperones; he would have no way of getting to his luggage in the sleeping quarters without answering a hundred questions about the suit and wingtips. Time to improvise. He burst in through the emergency exit and mounted the first few stairs up to the hallway. He could hear no one in the immediate vicinity, but Ivy's laugh wafted in from a distance. She was getting closer. And she was far from alone.

Taking a chance, he rushed up the stairs, then turned 180 degrees and raced up another floor, unsure what he'd find there. The area had been skipped during the initial tour and deemed off-limits to the youth groups temporarily calling the church home.

A woman looked up at Fletcher from behind an

old steel desk. Her matronly face formed a warm smile.

"You must be Dr. Simonetti," she said. "Let me tell Father Sacha you're here."

"No," he practically yelled. "Don't—"

"He's been waiting for you," she insisted, pushing a button on her desk intercom. "Dr. Simonetti is here," she chirped.

"I need a bathroom," Fletcher said, trying to convey urgency.

"There's one just off Father Sacha's office."

He could hear the priest's footsteps approaching from around a corner beyond the secretary's desk.

"No, I'm . . . I'm kind of sick." He put a hand on his stomach. "I need some privacy."

The woman's smile turned to concern and empathy and froze there for the space of at least three footsteps. Fletcher's phone began to ring in his pocket, a stupid TV theme song that had seemed cute when he'd downloaded it two months earlier. He willed the phone to shut up and the woman to speak.

"Through those doors behind you and to the left," she finally said. "I'll tell Father Sacha you'll be a few more minutes."

Fletcher turned and bolted, seeing the reflection of the priest rounding the corner behind him in the glass door as he yanked it open. He left scuff marks on the floor and threw himself into the small unisex bathroom, locking the door behind him. He pulled out his still-ringing phone and hit Ignore.

His sense of panic at being cornered here quickly downgraded itself to simple concern when he saw the double-hung window, providing a view of the garden below. By Fletcher's estimation, he was almost directly beneath the third-story room from which the priest had spotted him the day before. His phone chirped again, the tone itself seeming to grow more urgent with each unanswered call and message.

Where R U??? it demanded. Fletcher flinched. Neither he nor Meg had texted when he was first arrested and imprisoned almost seven years earlier. While he was locked up, his wife—despite being an otherwise intelligent and educated woman—had picked up the same annoying shorthand their twelve-year-old daughter used.

He closed the toilet lid and sat down. **Bathroom on the second floor,** he wrote. **Still feeling sick.**

Off-limits 2nd floor? she replied.

Yes. Needed some privacy. He was getting some mileage out of that one.

B right there. She must have been thumb-typing while climbing the stairs as the message arrived almost concurrent with her knocking on the door, calling, "Fletcher? Are you in there?"

"Yeah, I'm here," he said, affecting a pained voice.

"You okay?"

"Not really, hon. Must have been that junk they fed us last night. Worse than prison food. I'm feeling pretty torn up."

"Well, they're taking us out for pizza tonight," she said brightly. "It's a surprise for the kids."

"You go ahead," Fletcher said, remembering the bottle and small bag in his hand. "If I so much as smell pizza, I'm through." He stood and opened the window, looking down two stories at the ground below. If he hung by his fingertips, it would only be about an eight-foot drop into some yew bushes.

"That's a shame," Meg said. "It's going to be fun. Ivy's ecstatic. It's Reno's East. Remember that place? You took me there for our second date. Or maybe our third."

Fletcher was uh-huhing as she talked and unscrewing the top from the twenty-ounce bottle. He needed its contents because he was not really sick, although his stomach was clenching all the same—clenching in regret that he had to miss a chance at some real family time; clenching in anger at the Alchemist and Andrew for their endless demands and total disregard for any collateral damage in Fletcher's life; and clenching in guilt, because he knew deep down that he'd rather be heading to William Belltower's estate to empty that safe than to Reno's East with his wife and daughter.

"That sounds great, hon," he said. "I really wish I could go."

The smell from the bottle choked Fletcher a bit. The evening before, upon returning from his shopping trip, he'd dropped two dozen match heads into a cup of ammonia and screwed the top back on tightly. They had been reacting for twenty-four hours, forming ammonium sulfide, the same chemical that gave rotten eggs their distinctive smell.

"Are you sure you don't want to try and come?" Meg asked, the disappointment in her voice palpable. "You don't have to eat; you could just sit with us."

"I'd just be uncomfortable, and I'd ruin the fun for you guys."

"I'll stay with you, then," she said.

"No, please don't," Fletcher said, pulling the pack of Glisten teeth-whitening strips from the bag and stuffing several strips into the mouth of the bottle. He needed more of that foul smell. Tightening the cap again, he shook the bottle vigorously.

"Sickness and in health," Meg sang. "Let me take care of you, okay?"

The bottle was getting warmer in Fletcher's hand—a good sign. The bleaching agent was acting as a catalyst to speed up the chemical reaction. Fletcher cracked the bottle and the fumes just about knocked him over. He poured a little of the mixture into the sink, reminding himself that breathing too much could be fatal. His stomach turned further at the smell.

This was not the impression Fletcher wanted to make on his wife, especially considering their recently rekindled physical relationship, but he knew there was no better way to override someone's principles than to overwhelm their senses. Whether for good or ill, people could only handle so much input.

"No, really, I can stay," Meg said, her voice now free of conviction. Fletcher could hear her talking through her hand. He couldn't blame her. The stench was thick.

Andrew had taught him the trick of clearing a room with ammonium sulfide years earlier, and this was far from the first time it had come in handy. It may seem juvenile, Andrew had explained, but the US government had spent millions developing what they called a Standard Bathroom Malodor spray, which they used to disperse crowds almost instantly without the inherent dangers of tear gas or rubber bullets. If you can't read your opponent's peg, you can always create one—like the need to retreat from a horrible smell.

He poured a little more into the sink and closed the bottle. His eyes were watering. "Really, hon. I'd just like some privacy," he said, the words edged with embarrassment. "Promise me you won't check on me tonight, okay? Have fun, and I'll see you in the morning."

"Okay." She was another ten feet away, Fletcher could tell—backing up, probably involuntarily. "But answer my texts, all right? I want to know how you're doing."

"I promise," Fletcher said. "I love you."

"I love you too." He heard her footsteps descending the stairs.

Fletcher slumped back onto the toilet. The first time his wife had said "I love you" in years, and it was through a bathroom door amidst a fog of lies and the rotten-egg stench of a homemade stink bomb.

Chapter 25

August 7, 1784
Palace of Versailles, France

The queen met her lovers by night in the garden of the Chateau de Versailles. Many people knew this, but few thought about it as frequently or as vividly as Cardinal de Rohan. He had read her invitation to meet there at least a hundred times over, pausing every few readings to reread their former correspondence. Marie Antoinette's language had grown increasingly more familiar, more amorous, more leading.

And the last letter had led him here, to the

garden. Rohan's insides were a clenched fist of anxiety. He thought of the years of disfavor, the iron ceiling halting his upward social and political movement. The cardinal had badly miscalculated in what he had written to the queen's mother, Empress Maria Theresa, years earlier, then again in the rumors he had drunkenly repeated about the empress to women with loose morals and looser lips—the former being a preference of the cardinal, and the latter having been his downfall on more than one occasion.

But now he had all but mended the breach, and in the process the queen had fallen in love with him and vice versa. While he thought himself above such sentimentality, Rohan could not deny that his desire to attain the position of prime minister had now been overshadowed by his desire to attain other positions with the queen herself.

He hadn't brought the letter with him, as he was sure the queen would see doing so as a foolish indiscretion, but he did not need to have the letter in hand to read it. Every word, every stroke of the pen, was locked in his mind, easily accessible. He thought of the last sentence again and felt his confidence rise. The letter was certainly genuine, Cagliostro had assured him. That or it was the work of the greatest forger in all of Europe.

———

A short distance away, enveloped in the darkness and partially obscured by honey locust trees, sat

Count Cagliostro, the greatest forger in all of Europe. To his left sat Madame de LaMotte. She called herself the Countess de LaMotte, but she was no more a countess than Cagliostro was a count. He had sought her out after hearing of her tireless bids for a place at court. A woman who wanted something so singularly could be easily manipulated.

It had been Cagliostro who had suggested to the jewelers Böhmer and Bassange that they might approach the Countess de LaMotte, who was, after all, very close to the queen, and offer her a commission should she be able to facilitate the sale of the necklace. The dupes had agreed, not knowing that this would mean paying de LaMotte to steal their own prized necklace. It had also been Cagliostro who had, during a divination session, introduced to Cardinal de Rohan's mind the idea that the same de LaMotte might be the key to his reentering the queen's good graces.

The meeting tonight was a bit of a risk, granted, but if it went well, all doubt would be banished from the cardinal's mind and Cagliostro's design could move forward unfettered. As the tone of the letters grew more heated, Cardinal de Rohan had insisted with increasing fervor that de LaMotte orchestrate a personal meeting between himself and the queen, until his fervor had quite literally knocked her to the ground, leaving her left shoulder blade badly bruised.

News of the altercation had gotten little rise out of de LaMotte's husband, who would be playing the role of the queen's valet tonight and, if things went well, again when the necklace was purchased.

The queen herself would be a streetwalker and actress. Or, rather, a streetwalker would be queen. Cagliostro had seen the woman performing as Marie Antoinette on a corner in Paris and was immediately intrigued by the resemblance she bore to Her Highness. With the addition of a veil and illuminated only by the dim light of the quarter moon, she was the exact image of the monarch as she emerged from the shadows wearing a replica of the lawn dress in which the queen had been famously painted the year before and holding in her dainty hands a single rose.

From their place in the garden, where to any passersby they appeared to be two lovers enjoying the night, the self-identified count and countess could see immediately that the rendezvous would go as planned. At the sight of the prostitute queen, Rohan began shifting his weight back and forth between his feet in the sort of jig one would expect from a child. He would believe her to be the queen. He would believe her when she told him all was forgiven. And he would believe her when she said that she secretly coveted the necklace.

Chapter 26

"I also will have the hippy hash," Happy said gleefully, "and a cup of the strongest coffee you've got. In fact, you'd better brew another pot just for us. Thick."

The waitress drew down the corners of her mouth for a moment before reading back the order: "I've got three hippy hash breakfasts and four cups of coffee. You sure you don't want anything to eat?" she asked Dante.

The three of them cranked their heads toward the newcomer.

"Trick? No hippy hash?" Andrew asked. "It's kind of a ritual with us."

"No thanks. Just the coffee."

The waitress turned on her heels and wordlessly couriered their order to the kitchen window.

"Why do the girls here wear scrubs now?" Happy asked, watching the waitress disappear. "That's kinda gross if you think about it. What are they, hooking up IVs and cleaning bedpans between orders? I don't want to think about that when I'm eating."

"That's where you draw the line?" Dante asked. "Scrubs? This whole place is disgusting." He sat straight, his back not touching the seat behind him. "And that van. Unsanitary, man. Worse than the county jail."

Fletcher frowned. "Like the man said, this is our ritual. We come here and eat this particular slop and talk through the job before we carry it out. Join the team, Trick."

"I've got no use for superstitious grifters," Dante said. "And if we're going to talk through the job, let's get started before you jokers are stuffing your gobs with whatever you call that junk."

"Hippy hash," the three chorused.

They were situated in a remote corner booth at the Olympic Diner—*their* booth—bathed in orange sunlight and out of earshot of any other diners.

"Trick's right," Andrew said. "Let's get to it." He passed out photocopies of the floor plan, each bearing the Ultima Insurance Company logo in the lower right corner.

"So you grifted someone at the insurance company?" Dante asked.

"Yep."

"Why not go right to the security firm so you know you've got the latest information?"

Andrew leaned back in the booth. "You new at this or something, Trick? The kind of low-level peon you can rope on the fly and squeeze for information wouldn't have access to alarm schematics of multimillion dollar homes—not at a security firm. But insurance companies are far more lax. Any cube jockey can bring up a client's file, especially a guy who works in IT and holds all the passwords. Belltower's file was a click away for our mark—including a list of security measures in the home. Without that, no one would insure him for millions in art."

"Sure," Dante said, "but it might not be complete."

"I'm confident that it is," Andrew said, annoyance bleeding through the words. "That's the good news. But let's run the bad news first, because there's a whole lot of it.

"I'm going to be approaching from the east, out of these woods." He pointed at his map with a felt-tip marker. "Happy's set up at a high point in the same woods, right about here, where he'll have a panoramic view. The property is isolated, surrounded by a barbed wire fence and equipped with proximity alarms. Anything bigger than a squirrel approaches and alarms go off inside, accompanied by a closed-circuit video feed of the intruder.

"The exterior of the house is also retrofitted with a variety of cameras, but the real danger is being ripped to pieces by the pack of very unfriendly dogs roaming the yard."

His three partners mapped out the plan and scribbled notes on their own copies.

"Assuming I get past all that, in addition to

the security lock on the side door, there are three independent alarm systems to deal with—meaning we can't knock them all out at once.

"First, there's a keypad at the door that controls the electronic dead bolt and triggers an internal alarm if it's tampered with. The code changes every day. Inside the house we've got motion sensors and sound sensors, both expertly calibrated. If we succeed in taking those out, then I just need to locate the safe, crack it, and get the contents back to Happy's position without being seen or tripping any of the aforementioned alarms. And all within half an hour, so we don't bump into the night security guy clocking in."

Fletcher let out a low whistle. "That's a lot of bad news."

"And again," Dante said, "you're assuming the insurance company's file is comprehensive. There could be more."

"No, that's all they've got," Happy assured him. "Every three years Faust renews the guy's policy, and every three years he submits pretty much the same thing. Two minor upgrades in two decades."

"Answer me this, Andrew," Dante said. "The thing we're there to steal—is it listed on an inventory in that folder?"

"No."

"Then what makes you think all his security's listed there?"

Anger welled up visibly around Andrew's jaw, then melted away.

"That brings us to the good news," he said. "Trick wants to know why we didn't go to the security firm. How about this? There isn't one. This whole thing was designed and implemented by Julian Faust, and it's all run by him. Here's what we know about the guy: He's got a military and intelligence background, full of decorations and accolades. He led scores of men into battle against enemies who outnumbered them and always came out on top. The buck stops with him as far as he's concerned, so he's learned to rely entirely on himself and his instincts. That's his weakness. He doesn't trust technology. He doesn't trust law enforcement. Not one of these alarm systems makes a call out; it's all internal, all designed to alert Faust so *he* can deal with the intruder. Or one of his little clones; he only hires ex-military guys with a similar skill set."

"So, wait," Fletcher said, "the good news is that we're dealing with a group of hard-core commandos and killers who would rather take care of us on the spot than call the police. That's comforting."

"Think about it, Fletch. What's the peg here? Money's no object, and yet this guy almost never updates the security system. That tells us something. Faust trusts his senses to a fault. He doesn't want more sensors and alarms because he values human instinct and intel. But he's getting older, and his instincts are getting duller."

Dante nodded. "Intuition can be a good backup. Bailing on a bad feeling has saved my hide more than once, but it's stupid to lead with instincts. We can exploit that."

"You're breaking your own rule here, Bishop," Fletcher said. "You're the one who taught me that there're only two breeds of security guard: RoboCop and—"

"Barney Fife," Andrew finished. "I know. Always wait for the Barney. But in this case they're all RoboCops. So we hit them quick and get out of there while there's only one on-site. And that's our real edge. We've got a team, working together. There's only one of him." He circled a room on the east wall of the house. "This is the security hub. Happy's guessing, what, eight monitors?"

"At least."

"Have you been inside?" Fletcher asked.

"No," Happy admitted, "but there's a fist-sized reinforced steel conduit going through the wall, and according to my readings, almost a quarter of the house's electricity is consumed in that little room."

"So as long as Faust is in there, he's got eyes on everything," Fletcher said.

"Yeah." Andrew stared at the plan sketched out before him for a few seconds, his confidence apparently falling, before he snapped back. "Timing's everything here," he said. "Faust and the old man usually arrive home at about six. Faust walks the perimeter while the day shift sits on the monitors. Then at eight Mr. Day Shift punches out, leaving Faust to monitor everything himself, which he does for about half an hour before the overnight guy shows up. At about nine Faust does one final sweep and then heads home."

Dante expelled a breath. "Is that all?"

"Nope," Andrew said. "The security guys come and go through the same door I'll be working on." He tapped it with his pen a few more times, adding to the already extensive collection of black dots on and around the door. "Third shift shows up early or anybody takes an unexpected smoke break, and the whole thing is in danger of going tires up. That's where you come in, Trick. Anything goes off-script and you pull the Uncle Billy. Anything unforeseen, Fletcher and I will be tied up, it's on you two"—he pointed at Happy and Dante—"to improvise and keep the ball in play. We screw this up, we could all end up mounted in Julian Faust's trophy room."

Andrew pulled the van slowly up into the woods adjacent to Belltower's house, headlights off, and killed the engine. Here they diverged, Fletcher heading down the road toward the house and the others feeling their way up through the woods in the twilight, slowly climbing to the perch over-looking the estate where Happy's equipment had been covered over with a dark-green tarp.

"I hate the woods," Dante said. He angrily slapped at his arm and then the back of his neck. "Stupid mosquitos." He was wearing the standard outfit of an Uncle Billy—tattered suit, shirt half-unbuttoned, tie pulled loose—and he'd snagged his clothes on at least a dozen twigs and branches getting there.

Happy yanked back the tarp as if unveiling a work of art and flipped a toggle switch on a small power pack. A number of screens and devices came to life, slightly illuminating Happy's face with a diffused light. He lay down on his stomach on the incline like a sniper settling into his nest.

"Batteries are good." He peered through a spotting scope mounted on a low tripod. "And I've got visual. How about coms? You hear me, Bishop?"

"Loud and clear," came the response from Andrew, who was slowly working his way down the hillside toward the fence that marked the property line. He pulled his headset mic another inch back from his mouth. "How about you, Fletch?"

"Yeah, this stupid thing is working," Fletcher said in the direction of his lapel pin, itself concealing a mic, as was the obnoxious cell phone earpiece in his left ear. He had argued that Jordan Lyons was not the kind of man who would wear a Bluetooth headset, but Happy had insisted that a trained eye like Faust's might spot a high-tech listening device tucked back into the ear canal, but he would simply scoff at the blinking contraption protruding from Fletcher's head. At any rate, Fletcher was a grifter and so he would sell it.

———

"What is that? A ray gun or something?" Dante asked, his face and tone betraying fresh doubts about his new accomplices.

"No, man—radio waves," Happy said. "Let's hope Jules is still carrying our business card." He directed the device, which did bear a resemblance to some sort of sci-fi weapon, toward the middle of the house where he expected to find Faust. He slowly scanned until a red light came on, dull at first and then at full luster. "Bingo," he said. "Our boy is watching the feed. Hold your positions. The moment he steps away from that room we are *go*."

Chapter 27

Three hours earlier the hippy hash had arrived at the grifters' table to much fanfare. Fletcher's mouth had watered at the familiar sight and smell.

"What's in that garbage?" Dante asked.

Fletcher held up his plate like a contestant on a Food Network show. "It's a base of hash browns and chopped broccoli, mushrooms, and onions, covered in feta cheese and best served topped with a fried egg and absolutely slathered in Red Hot Sauce."

Dante poured three creamers into his coffee, eyeing the water spots on his spoon suspiciously before plunging it in. "So what we doing about the dogs?" he asked.

Andrew tried to answer with his mouth full, half gagged, and held up a finger until he'd swallowed. "I've got the usual canine-repellant pepper spray stuff, like joggers carry, but I won't need it. I've got my own method. Hand me the hot sauce, would you?"

"What's your secret?" Dante asked, passing the bottle with two fingers.

"Peanut butter."

"Peanut butter?"

"That's right. People train dogs to ignore kibble and treats, maybe even a thirty-dollar New York strip, but peanut butter is in a league all its own when it comes to canines. They completely forget everything else. They forget who they are. A tablespoon will keep a dog busy for twenty minutes. He'll lick away every trace and then sit there licking his own fur for another ten."

"You really want to wager everything on peanut butter?" Dante asked.

"Meh, high-end professional trainers might not leave us that window, but we've been watching these dogs for weeks—undisciplined, lazy. They're purebred Neapolitan mastiffs, so they're huge and imposing, but more of a status symbol than a serious guard dog these days. Trust me, these pooches are an afterthought. Anyway, I've always got the pepper spray, but that's risky and noisy—almost guaranteed to draw attention."

Fletcher's phone vibrated against the table, heralding the arrival of yet another text.

"The wife again?" Happy asked.

"Yeah."

How are you feeling?

Fletcher looked down at his heaping plate of hippy hash, hot sauce overflowing from the peak like lava from a volcano, and answered, A little better. Thanks.

"Leave that phone in the van when we get there," Andrew ordered.

"This isn't my first job, Mom."

"You seem a little rusty, is all."

"Do you think maybe that's because you got me—?"

"Guys," Happy interrupted. "You want to quit it? You two need to be exactly in sync for this to work." He pushed his own copy of the floor plan into the middle of the table. "Proximity alarm will go off when Andrew gets about eight feet from the fence right here."

"You can't disable that?" Fletcher asked.

"Won't need to. I've sacrificed the last two weeks' worth of evenings crouched in the woods laying the groundwork, running a Petrovich on our buddy Faust. Every time someone walks up to the front door, I trip the front east sensor. And they've been getting a lot of drop-ins since we listed Belltower's address on Craigslist under 'free puppies after 7 pm.' " Happy snickered.

Dante folded his arms against his chest. "You think that's going to work with someone like Faust?"

"It's classical conditioning: stimulus and response. Works on everyone. When he hears the alarm go off, his heart rate and breathing will increase, his pupils will dilate, and he'll be ready for action. A moment later he'll hear the doorbell ring and he'll suddenly feel calm and relieved, if a little annoyed about the whole puppy thing. Rather than rush to the security hub, where he'd see Andrew climbing the fence up on the monitor, my money is on Faust answering the door."

Andrew nodded. "Not just your money. We're all banking on it. The key is, we don't move until Faust steps away from the hub for a bathroom break, cognac refill, whatever. Then me and Fletcher approach the house simultaneously."

Now Fletcher was huddled behind an ash tree, waiting for the signal.

"What am I wearing here?" Andrew asked through the headset. "Is this a fanny pack?"

"That's not on me," Happy replied. "Fletcher bought it yesterday."

"On the contrary," Fletcher said, "that's from my personal collection. So you be careful with that, Andrew. That's genuine faux snakeskin right there."

He smiled to himself. The shopping list from the Alchemist had called for a "small tactical field bag," and Fletcher's first instinct had been to check an army surplus store. But considering his annoyance at the time and knowing that Andrew would be the one to wear it, he'd brought in one of the storied fanny packs instead. He had packed it with his own things three nights earlier, thinking he might break it out to make Meg laugh, recreate the spark. Instead, he had become a literal stench in her nostrils.

"I have another one too," Fletcher said, "if you

need more room next time. You could always wear one on each hip. Start a trend."

"I won't forget this," Andrew said. "Thing's purple. Is Faust still at the security desk?"

"Yeah," Happy said, "he's . . . Wait, he's moving. He's headed toward the front of the house. Go! Go! Go!"

Andrew rushed down from the cover of the woods, the van's two floor mats rolled up under his arm. He unfurled them as he approached the fence and leapt up onto the chain link, grabbing on with one hand and swinging first one mat, then the other, over the four strands of barbed wire, overlapping them by several inches. He flipped over the top and dropped seven feet, rolling as he landed.

A small bulb lit up in front of Happy. "That tripped the alarm, Fletch. Pick up the pace."

Fletcher was power walking up toward the front door. He needed to get there fast, but couldn't afford to be winded when he greeted Faust. He had about sixty feet to go—more than he'd estimated—and he knew Faust was a fraction of that from the image of Andrew breaching the perimeter. He doubled his speed, chastising himself for not picking a closer spot to wait.

"Hurry, Fletcher," Happy urged. "You need to

ring that bell. Faust is turning back toward the security hub. He's fifteen feet away. Ten." Fletcher began to run at a full sprint.

"We're toast," Happy said. "Andrew, he's gonna see you! Abort! Abort, you guys!"

Fletcher threw himself onto the porch, all of his momentum going through his index finger into the doorbell, sounding an obnoxious recording of chimes.

"He's at the security hub!" Happy was saying. "He's gonna make us. Fletch, get out of there."

Fletcher was frozen in place. He knew they would not get another shot at this house. Once someone like Julian Faust sensed a threat, security would tighten like a python. What would be the price of failure? He looked up at the reinforced steel door, adorned with decorative fiberglass panels—an attempt to disguise its utilitarian nature. It wanted to keep them out, but Fletcher would be invited right in. He could feel his heart slamming against his rib cage. He told himself it was the running, not the stress. A grifter had to stay cool.

"Wait," Happy said. "He's on the move again. He's getting the door."

Fletcher took a deep breath, in then slowly out, and straightened his tie.

———

"Yeah, baby!" Happy shouted, holding his fist out toward Dante expectantly.

"Nope," Dante said.

"Fine."

———

It took the dogs a good twenty seconds to find Andrew, which gave him time to pull the large Ziploc bag from his vest pocket and retrieve three sticks of Buddy Bac'n—long, stiff dog treats, the consistency of cardboard. Each treat had been caked in peanut butter, into which a number of small blue pills had been pressed. They looked to Andrew like twisted little Christmas cookies.

The first dog closed in, baring its teeth. Andrew was momentarily thrown by the sheer size and girth of the thing. It skidded to a stop five feet away and leaned into him, barking savagely, spit flying, eyes wild. Andrew tossed a treat at the dog's feet. It looked down and back up, still growling, then began sniffing the peanut butter. Three more dogs bounded in, not as angry as their brother but all of them bigger.

Andrew threw two more treats, then went back into the bag for more. By the time they were all delivered, the first dog had finished his and was looking up at Andrew eagerly, a bit of a snarl brewing. Andrew reached back into the bag and withdrew a small, bone-shaped rawhide treat, also covered in sticky peanut butter. He distributed one to each dog, all the while making his way closer and closer to the house, entering its long shadow. He could see two cameras mounted beneath the eaves and had to remind himself that Faust was currently occupied and that the dogs wandering freely throughout the yard ruled out the possibility of motion-activated video recording.

He crouched at the side door, the largest of the dogs happily licking away about twenty feet from him, and studied the lock. He was inside the proximity sensors now and directly beneath the cameras, no longer subject to their constant reporting. He could relax and take his time, as long as the night guard didn't decide to show up early. He looked up the stone walkway, ending at a locked gate in the fence, about five feet from the house. This is where the security guard would enter. *Security guard . . .* right. This would be a professional with an impressive military background and all kinds of expertise. And even if everything went according to plan, Andrew had twenty-four minutes and counting to find and recover the Alchemist's trophy.

✠

"Okay, walk me through the breach of the door, just so I have a feel for the timing," Fletcher said, pushing the remains of his hippy hash away from him. It had reminded him of Little Domino's prison creations, keeping him from fully enjoying it as he had hoped.

"Keypad's the easy part," Happy said. "The code rolls over every night at midnight, halfway

223

through the night watchman's shift. So you know what he does?"

"Writes it down?" Fletcher guessed.

"On his hand," Andrew said, laughing, "like Sarah Palin. I followed him into McDonald's this morning, and when they handed him his Egg McMuffin I snapped this." He held up his phone, which bore a photo of the number 6904 written in pen on a man's hand.

"What about the sound sensors? We've never dealt with those."

Happy grinned. Clearly he'd been waiting for this subject to come up. He reached into a bag at his feet and pulled out a small device—a few batteries wrapped in electrical tape with a wire running from them, culminating at a large suction cup. Fletcher recognized several components from the items he'd purchased the night before.

"Did you make that thing yourself?" Dante asked.

"Yeah," Happy nodded, beaming with pride.

"I'd like to be paid in advance if you don't mind."

Andrew chuckled and pulled out a small stack of cash, which he plopped on Dante's lap. "Half now, half when the job's done," he said. "Don't worry; Happy goes the MacGyver route as a source of pride, not because we're a low-rent operation."

"Not pride," Happy said. "It's control. If I make

it, I know it works. Do you want to rely on some poor sweatshop laborer on the other side of the world making two bucks a week? Besides, my stuff's off the grid. No serial number, no digital paper trail."

"So what is that thing?" Fletcher asked, nodding at the handmade gadget.

"It emits a high-pitched squeal—outside the frequency range that trips the alarm but loud enough to drown out light footsteps, quiet movements, that sort of thing," he explained. He looked at Andrew. "But you knock over a vase or something and we're made."

Dante folded his arms, dubious. "So, what, you stick that on the outside of the window? And that little speaker is strong enough to blare right through the glass?"

Happy shook his head. "No, the glass *is* the speaker. That's the beauty of it."

"And they won't hear the squeal inside?"

"Nobody over five years old can hear this tone. It's too high."

"What about the manual lock?" Dante asked. "You got a gizmo for that?"

"No, something better. We've got Andrew Bishop."

Andrew smiled.

Chapter 28

"I hate to be a bother," Fletcher said, panting in the foyer of Belltower's house, "but could I have a bottle of water or something? Spring water, not distilled. I just need to rehydrate and calm down."

Faust gave him the dead-eyes for a moment before answering, "Yes, of course."

Fletcher smiled. *Rusty,* Andrew had said. *Getting rusty.* Could a rusty grifter have gotten to the door in time to save Andrew's butt, then turned around and used the fact that he was sweaty and wheezing to the group's advantage? Unlikely.

When Julian Faust had answered the door, Fletcher was ranting up into the air, "Eight! Eight o'clock you said!" He'd held a finger up at his would-be host, standing baffled in the doorway, and barked, "I need to be rested tomorrow morning when I get on that plane. You have exactly fifteen minutes to arrive or I do this without you, Jenkins." With that he'd touched the Bluetooth earpiece, as if disconnecting a call, pulled his fingers together in front of his face and drew them down as if calming himself, and extended a hand to Julian Faust.

And now he was using his flushed cheeks to further the plan one more step. He unzipped his leather folio and flipped through a series of papers.

"Pardon me, Mr. Lyons," Faust said as he wedged himself between Fletcher and a numbered keypad on the wall.

Fletcher took a step away to accommodate, making sure the lens on the back of his cell phone—gripped against the cover of the folio—was angled just right.

———

"What's this card reader above the keypad?" Andrew asked. "You didn't mention that." He was carefully affixing the suction cup near the center of the security-filmed window.

"That's just an override for the guards when they arrive so they don't trip the motion detector on their way in. Or the sound sensors. Don't worry about that. Worry about beating that lock."

But Andrew wasn't the least bit worried about beating the lock. Just as he thought, it was a Grade 2 mechanism—a challenge, but nothing too difficult. Happy had snapped dozens of photos of the thing with a telephoto lens and Andrew had narrowed it down to two picks, which he slipped along with a torque wrench from the zippered pouch in the purple fanny pack.

This particular lock had been marketed as

impervious to picking, drilling, and sawing, but Andrew knew that with enough skill almost any cylinder lock could be picked. Ironically, as a grifter he felt a bit like a fraud every time he did. After all, he should be able to get himself invited inside, even trusted with his own key and security code.

He shrugged off the thought and refocused on the task at hand. It took a great deal of finesse to maintain exactly the right amount of pressure on the torque wrench. Too little and the pins would fall back to where they'd started; too much and they wouldn't budge. As he felt the last pin stack reach the shear line, he coaxed the side pin into place and the lock rolled over.

"One down," he said into his headset.

✠

Happy tipped back his head and drained what was either his sixth or seventh cup of coffee—Fletcher had lost count.

The redhead was speaking at a mile a minute. "Now, while Andrew is neutralizing the lock, Fletch, you need to be taking out the motion sensors."

"I thought I was keeping Faust and Belltower occupied," he said.

"You're multitasking. Here's what we've got: the place is broken up into six zones, so the system is versatile. If no one's home, you activate all six. If you've got a houseful of guests, you turn them all off. Or if you don't want anyone wandering upstairs, you might leave those on. If you've got an art appraiser looking at your multi-million dollar collection, you lock everything down except that one zone."

"So I need to somehow turn off all the zones."

"That's right. It's called single sector mode—half an hour with all motion sensors deactivated."

"Well, we've got the code, right? 6904. Shouldn't be too hard."

"Nah, that would be too easy," Andrew said. "Remember, these are entirely separate systems. The good news is that this code doesn't change every day. The bad news is we've got no line of sight and no helping hand from Mr. Egg McMuffin, so we're going to have to get it the sneaky way."

Happy smirked. "Luckily, that's our specialty."

✠

Andrew flipped the switch on the battery pack leading up to the suction cup speaker. Gingerly, he turned the volume knob up. Happy had insisted that the sound could not trip the alarm, and yet he had warned him to ease into it—just to be safe. Of course, Andrew had no way of knowing if the device was even making a noise. He gave the knob a twist from two to six.

The dogs all snapped to attention, heads up, eyes locked on Andrew. He felt his heart phone in a couple of beats. Yep, it was making noise. The nearest dog—the largest of the group—popped up to its feet and began moving in Andrew's direction.

The moment Faust was out of sight, Fletcher plopped the folio on an end table and dashed to the keypad on the wall. He yanked the small compact from his pocket and flipped it open. The tray of pressed powder foundation had been removed and replaced with a darker substance, composed of starch powder and soot from a candle left burning against a piece of porcelain.

Fletcher roughly dabbed the makeup brush into the powder and dusted it onto the keypad. "Okay," he whispered, "four, two, seven, zero." He pulled a handkerchief from his suit coat and wiped the powder away. "This model takes a five-digit code, so you've got a repeater."

Up in the woods, Happy and Dante were watching the cell phone video of Faust punching in the numbers—watching it on a loop. He had blocked the keypad itself, but the movement of his arm was still visible. Happy zoomed in on the image of his elbow, moving almost imperceptibly down, then left, then back up, then down again. He looked at his cell phone keypad and mapped the numbers in his mind.

"Okay, it's got to be 2–0–4–7–4," he said, his voice betraying his uncertainty.

"No good," Fletcher said a moment later. "How many tries do we get before it locks down?"

Happy didn't answer him. The truth was that two more incorrect codes would fill the house with a shrieking alarm. He watched Faust's elbow on the video again.

Andrew pulled the pepper spray from his belt, pushed aside the safety tab, and rested his thumb on the trigger button. The words *Dog-B-Gone* and a badly drawn attack dog looked back at him. The mastiff was closing in, teeth clenched, an angry growl emanating from its throat. Andrew did not want to hurt the dog, but it looked like he would have no choice. As a Hail Mary, he wrenched the Ziploc bag—half full of treats and peanut butter—from his pocket, turned it inside out with a flick of his wrist, and tossed it toward the hulking dog, which turned its attention toward the unclaimed spoils for just a moment before resuming its advance.

"Am I clear to enter the house?" he said into his headset mic.

"Not yet," Happy said. "Fletcher, try 2–0–4–7–2."

Andrew didn't know how far the pepper spray would shoot, but guessed that it would be most effective at close range. Two more dogs came

231

rushing up behind the first, converging on the plastic bag, the larger one snapping at the smaller, reestablishing dominance.

―――――

"Did that work?" Happy asked, glancing over at Dante, who was locked into the video loop on the iPad's screen, seemingly zoned out.

"No," Fletcher answered, exasperated. "It's still not . . . hold on . . ." They heard movement through their headsets and then, "Thank you so much, Mr. Faust, but could I trouble you for a glass with some ice? I should have mentioned that before, I know. It's just—I can't drink it directly from the bottle. That's my own thing."

Happy couldn't make out Faust's response, but the tone was clear enough.

"Look," Fletcher droned, "I want to get out of your hair as badly as you want me gone, but I can either spend the next forty-five minutes recovering from a fainting spell on your lovely settee over there or you can bring me some ice. Or I can get it for myself. I'm not helpless. Where's the kitchen?"

They heard Faust's voice again, fading into the distance. "Okay, now what?" Fletcher whispered, his voice tinged with panic.

"Okay," Happy said, "try 2–0—"

"No," Dante said. "Don't! It's 7–0–2–4–2. I'm certain."

"Wait . . . 7 . . . ?"

"7–0–2–4–2."

They heard Fletcher breathing heavily for a moment and the faint click of buttons. "That worked," he said. "System's unlocked. Now what?"

Happy let out a sigh of relief. "Hit Mode," he said. "Now arrow down twice and hit Select. Now arrow down to Single Sector and choose that. We're good now." He muted his mic and turned to Dante. "How did . . . ?"

"It's an older system," Dante said. "The numbers on the keypad go from one at the bottom up to nine, not vice versa like on a phone."

Happy held his fist out toward Dante again. "Come on, man," he said.

Dante smiled and gave it a bump.

———

The lumbering mastiff turned back once more, its attention on the smaller dogs squabbling over the remaining peanut butter and ever-more-shredded bag.

"You're good to go, Andrew," Happy's voice said through the headset.

About time. Andrew wiped the residual peanut butter from his gloves onto his pants, punched in the code from the guard's hand, and heard a click from the electronic dead bolt. The three embattled dogs looked up at Andrew. He gave them a little salute, backed into the house, and shut the door firmly but quietly.

"Sleeping pills better work," he whispered to Happy. "I'm fresh out of peanut butter."

"Will Mr. Belltower be joining us?" Fletcher asked, a bit concerned by the unknown whereabouts of the old man. Worst-case scenario, Belltower was wandering into the library now, catching Andrew in the act of cracking his safe. He didn't want to think about what Andrew might do in that situation.

"He's resting," Faust said. "I will call for him when you're ready to begin. Are we still waiting on your associate?"

Fletcher looked at his watch. "I'll give him two more minutes and then I'll have to begin without him." The two men looked at each other in awkward silence for a moment.

"So," Fletcher said, "what do you do for fun?"

Chapter 29

It took a moment for Andrew's eyes to adjust to the dim light of the library. A few lamps shone on end tables around the room, revealing the swirling dust that Andrew's every move kicked up. The smell of cedar filled the air, although Andrew could see nothing made of the stuff.

He had been hoping for darkness and had

come equipped for it, but this would be fine, assuming Fletcher did his job and kept the home's occupants well away from the library. He took three steps into the middle of the open room and came to a sudden stop.

Sitting on a leather couch, leafing through an old issue of *The Wine Interlocutor*, was William Belltower. He smiled up at Andrew.

"Are you new?" he asked.

Andrew looked down at his outfit—black long-sleeve T, black vest, black Dockers, purple faux snakeskin fanny pack—and said, "Yes. Just started today," in a quiet voice.

"Are you a doctor?" the old man asked, pointing at the stethoscope wrapped around the waistband of the fanny pack.

"I dabble," he said.

Belltower nodded. "My sons are both doctors."

"Who are you talking to in there?" It was Happy's voice in the headset.

"Mr. Belltower," Andrew said, "it's my first day, and I'm not supposed to be in here. Could you maybe not tell on me?"

Belltower raised his eyebrows and pushed a finger to his lips. "Your secret is safe with me," he said.

Andrew forced a smile of gratitude. He hated that this confused old man was involved. Real grifters didn't target the old and senile.

"William!" The voice came from the front of

the house. "We need you up here. Time to look at the paintings."

"I have to go," Belltower said to Andrew. "It was lovely to meet you."

"Likewise." When he was alone, Andrew let his eyes drift around the spacious room from wall to wall, analyzing each piece of art and furniture, looking for a hint of where the safe might be. He mentally chastised himself for not asking the old man outright. But then it didn't matter because he spotted the old gramophone.

The Victrola was easily the least expensive piece in the library, and not by a small margin. That made it stand out to Andrew's keen eye. And then he noticed the steel reinforcements on the legs; there was extra weight involved here. He scrambled over to the piece and plopped down in front of it, remembering halfway there that he was supposed to be quiet during all of this. But then, he wasn't sure if that still applied, considering the fact that Belltower had just been back here.

"Another new friend," Belltower announced, wrapping both of his hands around Fletcher's and giving it a squeeze. "How nice."

"What do you mean, 'another one'?" Faust asked.

"Oh, nothing." The old man winked at Fletcher and asked him, "Do I know you? You look familiar." His eyes brightened. "Have you been to the lodge?"

"Let's get this over with," Faust said. "The paintings are down the hall to the left. Give me just a moment." He returned to the keypad on the wall and pushed a few buttons. "Why is this—?" He punched a few more keys with more force than he needed, muttering a few *bloodies* and other assorted curse words and then the word *reset*.

Fletcher scratched his scalp, pulling his lapel as close to his mouth as possible and whispering into his microphone, "He just reset the alarm system. I think Andrew is stuck in there."

Andrew froze, gripping the sides of the Victrola. "Stuck?" he asked, trying to speak without moving his lips. "Happy, can you override it?"

"No, somebody needs to get to that central control unit by the front door and switch it back to single sector. You hear me, Fletcher?"

"Yes, yes, I see," came Fletcher's voice. "So you keep all the art down here in the gallery."

"In the meantime," Happy said, "tell me what we're looking at. Where in the room are you?"

"I'm crouched down—really uncomfortably, I might add—at the safe," Andrew said. "Middle of the south wall. It's inside an old phonograph."

"Okay. Here's the deal: the alarm system uses passive infrared sensors. They go off when they detect changes in temperature caused by the radiation you emit."

"I'm actually not radioactive," Andrew dead-panned. "So maybe we're okay."

"We all are, man, to some degree. The sensors are probably installed on the wall closest to the security hub, which would be the south wall. If it were me, I'd direct one sensor at the outside door and put one in the corner, about seven or eight feet off the ground, to cover the rest of the room. Can you roll your eyes in that direction and see if there's anything solid between you and that wall?"

Andrew turned his head as little and as slowly as possible, cranking his eyes in their sockets. "Yeah, there's a big leather armchair right behind me."

"So no line of sight between you and the far wall?"

"Not really. I can see the very top, where it meets the ceiling, but I don't see any motion detectors."

Happy sighed. "Well, you're stuck there for now, but you can go ahead and crack the safe while you wait."

"Nice," Andrew said. "I'm taking my ears off for a minute. When I put them back on, I want to hear good news." He removed the headset and set it on the floor in front of him, then slipped the stethoscope around his neck.

The Victrola was about a hundred years old and had clearly been refinished, a fact that made Andrew wince. He pulled open the cabinet doors and instantly began to deflate. Lined up neatly inside the cabinet were about twenty-five old 78s. Not what Andrew was after. Could the safe be hidden up inside the resonance chamber? That would make this a much more difficult process—probably not one that could be undertaken from his present position, sheltered by the armchair. Though perhaps he could access it from beneath?

He grabbed at a few albums, intent on quietly moving the stack down to the floor, only to find that the records were a veneer—the face of one album glued to the spines of many more, all lying over a small safe, hiding it from view. The façade folded sharply in two and clattered to the floor. Andrew cursed to himself. He was still unsure as to whether the sound sensors were active or how much cover Happy's squealer device provided him.

Sweat was crowding Andrew's eyes, and he wiped it onto his sleeve. Crouched as he was, his legs were falling asleep, but he dared not move despite the discomfort. Even worse was the pain of the .38 snub-nosed revolver, clipped into a holster in his waistband and digging into his side. That pain, at least, he deserved. Real grifters didn't carry guns on a job unless it was part of a character they were filling out. But this was no ordinary job, the Alchemist was no ordinary client, and Julian Faust was no ordinary mark. True, Andrew did have the Dog-B-Gone, but he knew that Special Forces training often involved building up a tolerance to pepper spray to the point where one could use it like potpourri to spice up a stale room.

Andrew inserted the ends of the stethoscope into his ears and held the diaphragm up to the safe. He spun the dial five times to the left, while simultaneously pulling out a folded piece of graph paper and a pencil from the sparkly fanny pack, which he found even less funny given his current predicament.

He closed his eyes and gave the dial another spin. It was happening automatically now, the result of innumerable practice runs. The drive pin made contact with the first wheel and he had his first number. His left hand spun while his right wrote down the contact points.

This was more like it. A safe had secrets, just like a man had secrets, and Andrew Bishop could con either into giving them up.

———

"And here are the Renoirs," Faust said. "I believe these are the two in question. Here are the authenticating documents, and I trust you will find everything to your satisfaction."

The gallery was just slightly smaller than

Fletcher's entire house. Make that Brad's house. Dozens of framed paintings adorned the walls, accented with tasteful directed lighting. Small sculptures, distributed throughout, broke the room into a variety of natural lateral paths.

"Hurry it up, Fletcher," Happy chided through the earpiece, "Andrew is pinned down and night security will arrive in about ten minutes. Or sooner. You need to get to that central control and punch in the code."

Fletcher pulled on a white cotton glove and took a step toward the painting. He studied the scrawled signature and reached up toward the canvas, suddenly going wobbly at the knees. Standing straight, he said, "I forgot my water by the door. Let me go grab it a minute."

"I can get it," Belltower said helpfully.

"Oh no, sir, I can—"

"No. Let him get it," Faust said, his eyes hard and demanding.

———

"I think we need you in the equation," Happy said to Dante. Plans were forming as he spoke. "Time for the Uncle Billy, but sober him up a little bit. Ring the bell and tell them you're there for a free puppy. Force your way in the front door and draw their attention away from the keypad while Fletcher switches the mode. Stall until Andrew is out the door, then you leave when he trips the proximity alarm." He ran it through his head again and nodded. "It's doable."

"Have you been tripping the alarm whenever someone walks away from the house?"

Happy thought for a moment. "No. Only when they approach."

"Then we're going to arouse suspicion. Let's do this instead: I make a distraction for Fletcher. Then you show up to claim your own free puppy right when Andrew trips the alarm. Then we all clear out as fast as we can."

Happy shook his head adamantly. "I'm the worst grifter you've ever met. They don't let me near the action."

"No choice, man. This is the only way we get Andrew out of that room without a squad car involved. Or worse."

———

Andrew had repeated the process three times over—once for each wheel—and written down all four contact points. In the movies, this would be where he spun the handle triumphantly and opened the safe. If only.

He flipped over the graph paper and began to chart the data he'd collected. This part was not automatic, and Andrew always found it a challenge to overcome the adrenaline clouding his mind and think analytically. It was the kind of math that had prompted him as a child to raise his hand and demand, "When will I use this in real life?" Only his teachers had never answered,

"Thirty years from now, when you're cracking safes in the libraries of wealthy capital investors."

He pulled the headset back on. "Almost done," he said. "Give me some good news."

"We're coming down," Dante said.

"*We?* No, no, we don't let Happy interact with the mark. He's a bundle of tells."

"There's no other way," Happy said. "I can do this."

Andrew circled the combination several times. "Hang on just a second. Don't do anything crazy. Let me make sure I've got what I need." He carefully dialed in the combination. The safe door released and swung open easily.

"I've got it," he said, grabbing the old leather satchel. "Just one more thing." He pulled a small device from Fletcher's fanny pack and placed it in the safe before shutting it securely and carefully replacing the album façade. He checked his watch. "Whatever we're gonna do, we need to do it right now."

———

"Just a second!" Happy grabbed Dante's sleeve, delaying his descent from their lookout point. He held on tight and took a deep breath. "Let me get into character a minute."

"Into character?"

"What's my backstory?"

"You're a guy who wants a free puppy."

"But what's my motivation?"

Dante yanked his sleeve free. "Puppies. Come on!"

Happy leaned over his knees, feeling like he might hyperventilate. A sound grabbed his attention from down near the house. The sound of a gate closing against a chain link fence.

"Oh no, we've got a big problem here." He pointed down at the night security guard arriving early, milling about the yard, finishing a smoke.

"No," Dante said. "I think we've got the solution to our problem."

Chapter 30

Andrew's voice came through the headset, bordering on anger. "Tell me what's going on."

"Overnight guard is here," Dante said. "I think he's your way out."

"What? How?"

"He's going to swipe a card on that reader, right? That shuts down motion sensors between the door and the security hub." He glanced over at Happy. "For how long?"

Happy shrugged. "Thirty seconds? How long does it take to walk through the room? Just stay out of sight, Andrew."

"Doesn't matter," Andrew said. "He'll see the suction cup deal on the window and raise the alarm. We're made."

"Maybe not," Dante said. "I'm heading down."

The guard was texting now and smoking. Happy held his breath as he watched the security guard approach the door. According to the dossier Andrew had compiled, this man had kept it together in the thick of the action in Afghanistan, earning practically every medal there was, and had been known for his ability to spot the enemy in a crowded urban setting. But he wasn't a soldier in the heat of battle right now. He was a guy killing a few minutes before his shift started.

The guard laughed at the words on the little screen, pocketed his cell phone, flicked the cigarette down next to the door, and swiped his card.

"My man didn't find much on you," Faust said. "Seems a bit odd, them sending you here with such a sparse résumé."

Fletcher smiled. "What can I say? It's a good time to specialize in Impressionism. Five of the eight leading experts have either died or retired in the last few years, leaving the field wide open, and I've really been establishing myself." He leaned in, as if to disclose a secret. "I'm eccentric. The art world loves that."

"Mm-hmm," Faust said slowly. "Tell me, what do you think of Sisley's work?"

Fletcher cocked his head. "*Lane of Poplars* is a nice piece, I suppose. He was more quantity than quality, though—probably the reason he never made it out of Monet's shadow." He returned his attention to the Renoir.

―――――

Andrew heard a click from the electronic dead bolt, followed by the scrape of a key sliding into the door lock. He pulled himself into a tight ball behind the chair and closed his eyes. He was reasonably sure he could not be seen from the door. Well, maybe that was less reason and more hope.

He heard the man's heavy footsteps move through the room and then round the corner toward the security hub.

"If he settles in at the monitors, he'll see you leaving," Happy said. "Fletcher, you need to draw this guy away."

―――――

Fletcher stepped back from the second painting and took them both in for a moment before raising his arms above his head and emitting an ear-splitting "Aaaarrrrrrghh!" He fell to his knees and slammed his fists against the floor. "Why?" he shouted.

Faust took a step back from him while Belltower hurried to his side.

"There's a doctor in the library," the old man said. "I'll go get him."

"Stay here," Faust ordered. A young man in his twenties with a muscled physique came rushing up from the back of the house, his hand inside his jacket.

Belltower frowned at him. "You're not the doctor."

"Is everything all right, sir?" the young man asked Faust.

Fletcher stood. "I apologize," he said, straightening his tie. "Like I said, I'm eccentric. And I can't believe they flew me up here for *this*." He pointed at the place where the artist had signed each of the paintings. "Near the end of his life, Renoir's signature changed significantly. Everyone knows this, but some overeager student intern at Ultima flagged it as an irregularity. Probably trying to impress the brass. Moron."

He turned to Belltower, who was visibly shaken, and smiled. "Sir, your home is lovely and your paintings are, of course, genuine. I'm sorry we've wasted your time."

Andrew gently pulled the door closed and felt the cooler night air setting in around him. The sun was setting behind the house, and it was difficult to see anything in the yard stretched out before him. He thought of the peanut butter rubbed into his pants, beckoning the pack of dogs, and he readied the Dog-B-Gone again. But he immediately realized he wouldn't need it. The sound of the snoring mastiffs rose up from various locations around the yard. Andrew spotted the meanest of the bunch sleeping a few yards away from him and resisted the urge to scratch the thing behind the ears.

He quickly made his way across the grass and up over the fence, pulling the floor mats with him as he dropped to the ground. He quickly rolled them up and tucked them under his arm. From forty feet away he could barely make out the top of Happy's head protruding from his perch.

"Let me know when to pass under the proximity sensors," he said.

"Just one second," Happy answered. Andrew could hear multiple people breathing heavily into open mics. "Now!"

A bass-heavy *who-ap-who-ap-who-ap* sounded all around the men in the gallery. Faust and his underling locked eyes, their faces stern but guarded. A moment later the fake chime of the doorbell followed it up.

"Get that," Faust spat, then turned to Fletcher. "Any papers we need to fill out?"

"No, I'll close the file tomorrow morning," Fletcher said, heading back up the hallway. "And don't worry, your coverage will continue. Again, I apologize for this whole mess."

They arrived back at the front door.

"I already told you, we don't have any puppies," the night guard was shouting. "You're trespassing on private property and you're publicly intoxicated. You have five seconds to get out of here."

"The Internets told me," Dante slurred, "you had puppies." He gasped and clamped a hand to his mouth. "Are you hurting the puppies?"

The bigger man gave him a hard shove. "Leave."

"Fiiiiiiiiine," Dante said, stretching his hands out at his sides. "I'm leaving." He stumbled away into the growing darkness.

"I'm leaving too," Fletcher said. "You mind if I take this with me?" He held up the plastic bottle of water. Having wiped the glass of his prints, it was the only physical trace of his identity that remained.

"Feel free." Faust locked his eyes onto Fletcher's. "What do you suppose happened to your colleague from earlier. Where was he?"

Fletcher knew what Faust was trying to do, and it almost worked. He felt the unconscious pull—his eyes wanted to flick toward the back of the house where Andrew had been, but he overrode it. "No idea," he said. "But I'll be lodging a formal complaint with Ultima about him, and I suggest you do the same thing."

Chapter 31

"Are you hurting the puppies?" Happy recited from behind the wheel. "No, wait! The Internets!" The van erupted in laughter, the four of them high as they were on adrenaline and the thrill of a successful job.

"I thought we were toast when you walked in on Belltower," Dante said, shaking his head. "I had my doubts about you guys, but you really came through."

Andrew handed Dante another bundle of cash. "There's an extra five hundred."

"Appreciate it," Dante said, pocketing the money without counting it.

"You earned it. But that squares us." It was suddenly silent, save for the constant squeak of the van.

"After the job tomorrow," Dante said.

Andrew's smile remained on his lips but faded from his eyes. "There's an extra five hundred there. For all you know, tomorrow's job would have only paid four hundred. Let's just call it quits, huh?"

Dante pulled the cash back out and counted off five hundred dollars, tossing each bill to the floor as he went. "I'll take my chances," he said.

He and Andrew glared at each other for a

moment before Happy chimed in with, "So what did you pull from that safe?"

The smile returned to Andrew's face. "This," he said, holding up the half-inch-thick satchel. The leather was slightly cracked at the bottom, and the whole thing was wrapped many times over with a leather cord.

"So what's in it?" Fletcher asked from the passenger seat.

"No clue." He reached past Dante and handed the package to Fletcher. "Boss said I was to send the take back with you, Fletcher, and that you should be the one to look inside. Said you'd need it for tomorrow."

"Guys, I don't know," Fletcher said. "I mean, this was fun, but there's no way I can disappear another night without major consequences. I think I'm out."

Dante leaned up and reached for the satchel. "He's out and I'm in," he declared.

Andrew grabbed him by the shoulders of his jacket and jerked Dante back into the captain's chair. He landed hard, causing the chair to spin.

Dante went with the momentum and grabbed two fistfuls of Andrew's shirt. "If you ever touch me again . . ."

"Guys!" Happy shouted. "Guys! Knock it off." The two released each other and sagged their weight in their seats like pouting children. He dressed them down like an angry father on a family vacation. "Trick, we can't give you the package. We do what the Alchemist says, and he says we give it to Fletch. Andrew, you know Trick fits our team like a pair of yoga pants, and he's in on the take tomorrow. We're gonna need him." He turned his attention to his right. "And, Fletcher, if you try and back out now, you'll wish you hadn't. We're all in deep here. Walking away isn't an option."

✠

Fletcher was relieved to find the duct tape still holding at the emergency exit. He had changed back into his street clothes in the van and was carrying only the satchel with him. Everything else—the briefcase, the suit, the gym bag full of supplies—he left in the van. Fletcher was unsure whether he should stash the take from tonight's score in the file cabinet or keep it on his person. What he *had* decided was not to look inside. He had an enormous decision ahead of him, and looking at the contents of the leather case would make impartiality an impossibility.

Using his cell phone as a flashlight, he crept over to the fireproof file cabinet and opened the bottom drawer. His pulse picked up. The leather-bound book he'd seen before was still there, but it had been turned upside down—or rather, right side up, so that Fletcher could read the words on the cover. *Catalogue of Relics and Holy Vessels*, the title read, over a red Maltese cross.

He carefully hefted the book and opened the cover. Each page bore a number, the name of an item, and an ink drawing. Number 1 was a sword. Fletcher felt his knees go weak. He and Andrew had stolen that very sword, which had once belonged to Manuel Pinto da Fonseca, the Grand Master of the Knights of Malta. The buyer—someone Andrew had lined up—had paid eighty thousand dollars for it. The information listed in the book was sparse; Fletcher already knew far more, having studied the object at great length before stealing it. He turned the page.

Number 2 was a monstrance. Fletcher looked all around, not feeling anyone watching him but convinced that someone must be. His neck suddenly felt hot and prickly. This was the Valletta Monstrance—the one he and Andrew had been trying to steal when Fletcher was caught, convicted, and locked away. Again, he knew the object only too well. Numbers 3 and 4 were also items that he and Andrew had stolen—a piece of gold that had allegedly been transmuted from lead in the Grand Master's palace in Valletta and a four-hundred-year-old Greek New Testament.

He flipped another page. Number 5 was the object he'd found in the altar two nights earlier. Finally, something he could learn about. "Sacred Septangle," it was labeled. The only explanatory note read, "Auxiliary for the Great and Holy

Relic and, with the sacred trowel, the key to obtaining same."

Could this get any weirder? He turned the page. It was blank. He turned again. And again. The rest of the book was empty, aged pages waiting to be filled in. Fletcher took a couple minutes to photograph the first seven pages with his cell phone, then stuffed the satchel into his waistband at the small of his back and let his T-shirt hang down over it. He needed time to process all this.

He checked his watch. The forty-five-minute drive, plus the stop for gas and snacks, had added up. It was after ten, meaning the kids would all be brushing their teeth and preparing for another night on the sea of air mattresses. With any luck Fletcher could fall right in, answer a few questions about how he was feeling, crawl into bed, and reply to Meg's slowly amassing mountain of texts.

Quickly and quietly Fletcher mounted the steps and made his way down the hall, ready at any moment to hear Father Sacha's voice, somehow comforting and accusatory at the same time. Or worse, an ambush by Brad, realizing he'd been conned and having reestablished his crosshairs on Fletcher. But he made it down the wide hall and around the corner without incident. He was going to make it. A dozen boys were coming and going from the men's sleeping quarters, toiletries in tow. He greeted a boy from his service group with a friendly nod.

And then he saw Meg, sitting in a heap outside the door, eyes red and puffy, resting her head against a balled-up pair of sweatpants. She looked up at Fletcher, her eyes oddly empty, and said, "I'm glad you're okay." She rose and set off down the hall, back toward the old part of the church.

Fletcher followed. "Meg, what's the matter?" he asked. He had to work to keep up. "Will you talk to me? Look, I'm sorry I didn't answer your texts. It was just—"

"Do you really want to do this, Fletcher?" They were in the vestibule, apparently a satisfactory distance from the mass of teenagers for Meg to raise her voice. "Because I was planning on going in there"—she pointed into the church proper—"and praying about whether or not I can even keep this up. It's clear to me that I don't even know you. You're still conning me, aren't you?"

"Honey, no!"

"No? I went up to check on you when we got back from Reno's and—"

"I told you not to do that."

"Well, I wanted to, because I love you and that's what normal people do when they really love someone. And you know what I found?" He hadn't noticed the bottle in her hand until now. "I found this in the trash, covered over with some paper towels." She sloshed the contents around.

"Some kind of stink juice or something. What are you, ten years old?"

Contempt flashed over Fletcher's face for a moment. He hated hearing Brad's words from Meg's lips.

"Look, this is not something I chose, okay? I need you to trust me."

"Trust you?" She laughed a hollow laugh and tossed him the bottle, which he caught and retightened, just in case. "That looks like it took some planning, Fletcher. That's not a white lie; that's a con."

"This is not a con," he said, trying not to sound condescending.

"I think we need to go home." She was looking past him. "Things were starting to go so well, but now everything's falling apart, just like this trashy town. I should have known we couldn't come back here. Let's just go home, okay?"

"I can't," he said. "But maybe you two should."

Meg took a step back, a sense of betrayal in her eyes. "If we leave you here, that's it," she said.

Fletcher slumped at the shoulders. "I just don't want anything to happen to you."

"What have you gotten yourself into, Fletcher?"

"Nothing! I didn't do it! I didn't choose it." He heard his voice echoing off the stone walls and suddenly remembered his earlier success. Why did he keep letting his emotions get in the way?

He gathered the angst in his chest and transformed it into charm. A familiar calm washed over him. If that move had a name, it would be called The Fletcher, he thought.

"Look, honey," he said, smiling.

"Don't." He could hear the prelude to angry tears balling up in her throat. "I don't want to see that stupid dimple."

"What?"

"You don't even know? When you smile for real, there's no dimple. When you're lying—when you're *faking*—it appears. I hate that stupid dimple and I hate your lying and I hate this city."

"I'm so sorry, Meg. I—"

"Just go to bed, Fletcher." She disappeared through the double doors of the church, leaving him standing in the vestibule.

"Look out for laser trip wires," he said under his breath.

Chapter 32

April 3, 1785
Paris, France

Cardinal de Rohan had not slept in two days when he turned up at Cagliostro's door. His wig was disheveled, his clothes and nerves ragged, and his thoughts full of ruin, exile, and the Red Widow—that merciless machine that had separated the heads from a mounting number of bodies and seemed to be only growing in appetite over the past few years. He knew all too well that neither his nobility nor his position in the church would protect him from her falling blade.

The cardinal sipped the elixir his friend offered him, seeing the effects of his shaking hand in the liquid's surface. He had arrived at Cagliostro's home on Rue de St. Claude before five that morning, only to find the alchemist apparently on his way out, carrying a bundle of letters and dressed in a very fine iron-gray coat trimmed with gold lace, brilliant-red breeches, and a fine ruffled hat on which perched a long white feather.

"My dear Louis," Cagliostro had said, setting down his papers and guiding the cardinal to a chair. "Sit, please! I will fetch something for your nerves."

He had returned with the elixir, a balm for the cardinal's hands, and a great deal of apparent concern.

"What has happened to you?" he asked.

"I fear I have been played for a fool," de Rohan answered.

"By whom?"

"The Countess de LaMotte. She has been acting as an intermediary between the queen and my own person, carrying our letters back and forth. It was she who arranged our meeting in Versailles last year. Oh, how could I be so dense?"

"What has she done?" Cagliostro leaned forward, his face full of empathy.

"Some months back she informed me of the queen's desire for a certain necklace, one worth two million livres. But the queen, she said, was hesitant to buy such a luxurious item during a time of need. And so I volunteered to carry out its purchase and to obtain the piece for Her Majesty, which I did."

"But do you have that much gold at your disposal?"

"Not even a fraction! I arranged for payment to be made in five installments, the first of which was due a week ago. But the queen has not paid. The jewelers have been harassing me, threatening to go to Her Majesty, moaning that I have ruined them. The older man has twice threatened to end his own life at the gate of my palace."

The count pursed his lips in thought before saying, "It would seem the queen did not want the necklace after all," as if this were some hidden kernel of knowledge that he had managed to divine. "Can you simply return it?"

"If only I could! I gave it to the queen's valet the day I signed surety for it. And now neither he nor the Countess de LaMotte is anywhere to be found, and I am done for."

Cagliostro placed a firm hand on the cardinal's shoulder. "It sounds as though you have only one course of action open to you, my friend," he said. "You must go to the queen, remind her of the intimate letters the two of you have traded, and insist that she abide by the terms of your agreement."

Rohan looked up at Cagliostro, his mouth agape. "I value your advice, old friend, but do you really think that would be wise?"

Count Cagliostro smiled. "You've said yourself that the queen no longer bears you any ill will. This seems to be a simple misunderstanding. So tell me, what trouble could possibly come from an honest and forthright approach?"

Chapter 33

The burner phone awakened Fletcher early the next morning. Another text from the Alchemist. **The van. Broadmoor and Willow. 30 minutes.** Fletcher slammed the stupid phone against the ground. The battery had been on the verge of dying yesterday until Happy had helpfully charged it back up during their trip to the Hills. Fletcher gave it another, harder rap against the floor and assessed the damage. A small crack bisected the screen, but to his disappointment the display still worked, informing Fletcher that it was 6:40 a.m. That explained the messy rows of sleeping teenaged boys all around him. The wake-up bell wouldn't sound for another twenty minutes.

Fletcher had slept maybe four hours, and that fitfully. He was sagging on the air mattress, although not as much, as a fellow chaperone had loaned him a vinyl repair kit the night before. Still, he knew there was no more sleep to be had this morning so he rose and grabbed his bag. May as well get a shower in before the morning rush, he reasoned. He worried what damage the steam from the unventilated shower area might inflict on the satchel and its contents, but he was not about to let it out of his sight. Once in the bathroom, he zipped his bag shut, wrapped it in a towel, and stuffed it under the bench outside his shower stall.

Clean, clean-shaven, and wearing fresh clothes, Fletcher emerged from the men's locker room feeling something of a separation between last night's angry encounter and the day that lay ahead of him. Somewhere in scrubbing away the remnants of yesterday's failures, Fletcher had determined to put an end to his involvement in the Alchemist's schemes. They had Trick now, who was talented and eager to be involved; having replaced himself in the dynamic of the group, Fletcher would take his leave one way or another.

In addition to severing ties with his criminal associates, Fletcher had determined to repair his relationship with his wife and reconnect with his God. He'd almost said a prayer in the shower to that end, but it seemed somehow foolish to take such a major step with a scalp full of shampoo when he could wait a few minutes and offer a proper prayer on a kneeler surrounded by sacred art and architecture.

"Look up there. Is that a ladder?"

Fletcher came to a stop. The voice came bouncing down a flight of stairs. It belonged to Courtney, and it came from an area of the church that had been deemed both off-limits and dangerous. He thought about calling her down from there and giving her a lecture on respecting the church and following the rules. Then again, that would make him a bit of a hypocrite, wouldn't it? Besides, he'd managed to avoid interacting with Courtney since ignoring her texts, and he had no desire to land back on Brad's list. He took another step toward the main sanctuary, then stopped again.

"I bet there are bats." It was Ivy's voice. "No way I'm going up there."

Fletcher headed up the stairs quietly.

"Good place to go with a guy, though," Courtney was saying. "Nobody would find you up there." She laughed. Ivy laughed with her, halfheartedly.

Fletcher reached the landing and saw the two of them peering up through a trapdoor in the ceiling, which Courtney was pushing open with a broom handle. He guessed it was the access for either the bell tower or an attic.

Three quick steps and he was standing between the girls. "Is this what your dad meant when he said you've been 'mentoring' Ivy?" he asked, his best combination of severe, disappointed, and hurt.

Courtney tried to mask her surprise and embarrassment with a snarky smile. "Maybe if you'd answer my messages, I wouldn't have so much time on my hands," she said. "Idle thumbs are the devil's playthings."

Ivy was studying the floor, biting her lip. Fletcher gently took her hand and led her back toward the stairs. "Come on, hon. I'll buy you breakfast in the social hall," he said.

"Breakfast is free." She laughed, descending the stairs.

"That's good, because I don't have any money."

She giggled, then said, "Sorry I was up there. I didn't know what to say to her."

"Don't worry about it. Listen, we've got half an hour before breakfast; I was about to go find a pew and pray. You want to come with me?"

She pointed down at her clothes. "I'm in my pajamas, Dad."

"Oh, right." Fletcher smiled at his little girl. He found it hard to believe that she only had one formative year left, but he would make every day of it count. "How about you go get changed and come on back?"

"Okay." She disappeared down the hall toward the new addition. It wasn't until she was out of sight that Fletcher realized it—she had called him Dad.

He entered the main sanctuary, a grin dominating his face. The smell of matches recently struck hung in the air. He walked up the aisle, his eyes on the massive cross hanging over the chancel.

"You look like you're feeling better." Andre Foreman sat in a pew near the aisle, a battered old Bible open on his lap.

"Dr. Foreman, hi!" Fletcher leaned against the pew in front of him. "Yeah, I'm feeling great today."

"I understand you had quite a bug. Hopefully nothing you caught at the shelter."

"Oh, right." He felt the impulse to generate a smile despite the fact that he was already smiling. Then he felt the dimple appear. "No, I'm fine," he said.

The preacher nodded slowly. "I come here every Thursday to pray and read the Scriptures," he said, "before I lead a workshop on inner-city ministry. I do love it here."

"It's beautiful," Fletcher agreed.

"How's your search coming?"

"What?" Fletcher felt his face flush. "What search?"

"For the real you. You told me everyone finds Jesus in prison. But did he find you?"

"Oh, right. I'm still trying to figure that one out, but things are looking good."

"You're a good grifter, are you?"

"Well, I did get caught." Fletcher laughed.

"But you know you can't grift Jesus. You can grift yourself, but never him."

Fletcher's smile melted away.

"I was just thinking about you while I read my Bible," Andre said. "Are you familiar with Second Corinthians chapter seven?"

"Sure. St. Paul tells the Corinthians how pleased he is that they're sorry for their sins."

"Not just that they're sorry. Remember, he says there're two kinds of sorrow—godly sorrow, which brings repentance and leads to salvation without regret, and worldly sorrow, which brings death."

"So the question is, which kind did I experience in prison?" Fletcher said.

Dr. Foreman nodded again. "It sure looked like godly sorrow to me. You read your Bible voraciously. I remember you telling me that all your academic studies of the Scriptures were coming alive now that you were born again."

"Yeah, but still . . ." Fletcher shifted.

"What?"

"I used to catch myself thinking how easy it would be to grift Barnabas or Lydia or any of the early Christians."

"I don't know about that," the preacher said, smiling. "Ananias and Sapphira tried grifting the church and got zapped dead by the Holy Spirit."

"So how do I know which kind of sorrow I have?"

"Godly sorrow leads to repentance. A change in direction. Newness of life. It doesn't mean the old you never comes to the surface, but it's not *you* anymore. You're new. That's why the apostle Paul talks about our fight against the Old Man— the old self, who's constantly trying to take the wheel. We have to keep putting him out of his misery because we're becoming a new creation."

"I lied to my wife last night," Fletcher said. "I feel awful about it—*some* kind of sorrow—but I don't feel new. And I don't feel saved."

"Pshh!" Andre waved a meaty hand. "You think Noah and his family felt like they were saved inside that ark for months on end—more and more claustrophobic, sick of the animals, the smell, worried they'd never see dry land again? The point is they *were* saved, whether they felt it or not. Let me ask you this, son: What's your next move?"

Fletcher looked up at the ornate ceiling for a moment. "I guess I see if Jesus takes me back a second time," he said.

"There's your answer. It's like Peter and Judas. They both betrayed Jesus on the same night. They were both sorry. They both wept. Judas tried to return the money and Peter followed along to see if he could help Jesus. But at the end of the day, Judas didn't look for forgiveness. His was worldly sorrow and it led to death. Hung himself, the joker. Peter's was godly sorrow, and look what God did with him.

"Or take St. Paul. Jesus found him on the road to Damascus and knocked him right down, turned his whole life around. Godly sorrow. And yet he's the one who wrote, 'I do not understand what I do. For what I want to do I do not do, but what I hate, that I do. Wretched man am I!' "

Fletcher heard footsteps behind him and then Father Sacha's voice, pleasantly calling, "Andre, how are you this morning?" He reached past Fletcher and shook the preacher's hand. "Oh, it's you," he said, glancing up at Fletcher. "Going casual today, I see."

"Yeah." Fletcher laughed. He needed to separate these two men of the cloth. He had lied twice to one of them about his urgent need to leave, only to be seen dressed in a suit by the other a short while later.

"I'm supposed to keep my eye on him," the priest said, gesturing at Fletcher. "He's making it easy. Late at night, early in the morning, middle of the day—I find him in here."

Fletcher was trying to think of a clever reply, something that would belie the rapidly growing sense that he was caught in a trap. His tongue seemed on the verge of delivering when the double doors opened and Happy tromped in.

"Hey, Fletch," he called out, filling the acoustics of the church, "there you are."

"Happy," Fletcher said. "I'm surprised they let you . . . out."

Happy bounded up the aisle, announcing, "I just got chewed out, man. This dorky guy in a tool belt had the biggest stick up his—"

Father Sacha turned to look at Happy.

"Oh." The volume of his voice dropped by half. "Hi, Father." He bowed awkwardly, noticing Andre in the process. "And, Father?"

"Pastor," Andre said.

"Right." He pointed at Fletcher. "Anyway, we really need you for the, uh . . . thing for the . . . orphans. Outside. Right now."

Fletcher checked the time. The thirty minutes the Alchemist had given him had come and gone almost twice now. He sighed. Better to deal with this now than let it hang over him. "Okay," he said. "But let's make it fast. I've got a breakfast date."

Happy bowed again, rigidly, once at each of the clergymen, offering each a "Sorry."

Fletcher's phone beeped as they walked. A message from Ivy. Courtney is outside talking 2 older guys. Not cool. He rolled his eyes. How could that girl get into so much trouble before breakfast?

He replied, Tell her get in here now or I'll send her dad after her.

They cleared the vestibule and stepped out into the morning sun, Happy prodding Fletcher along. "The boss is pissed," he said. "Let's go."

Another text from Ivy. Will you tell her? Creepy out here. Sketchy guys.

He hit Reply. Just go back in the church. Happy led him to the van, a block and a half away. Andrew was smoking and pacing the curb next to it.

"Finally!" he announced, pulling open the van's back door. "Come on, Boss wants us to call him."

✠

Manny sat in the driver's seat of the delivery truck, waiting. He'd prepared everything the night before, and all that was missing now was the girl. A clipboard bearing a picture of her lay in his lap, a carry-over from when he had been a sniper in the first Gulf War. It was hard to confuse your target if you had a photo a flick of the eyes away—even if the target was blended into a sea of white and red turbans. Or teenage girls in spaghetti-strap tops.

How they would lure her to the mouth of the alley at eight in the morning, he had no idea. But he would be ready. He absent-mindedly fingered the long scar on his right cheek, his eyes and ears taking in everything around him. Movement. He snapped to attention and looked down at his

269

clipboard, pen in hand as if checking a list of deliveries. Not her. Wait, there she was. Two of them. He hit the speed dial on his phone.

The Alchemist answered. "Yes?"

"I've got the girl in sight, but she's not alone."

"How many?"

"Just the two."

"Grab them both."

"Yes, sir." He grabbed the zip ties and the duct tape and climbed through the back of the truck.

Chapter 34

Dante had risen early and done his usual regimen of two hundred push-ups for the first time in almost a week. He could feel the sloth and despair burning away.

Since Brinkman's visit, he'd taken to sleeping on a cot in the bare room above the church. Despite being in a far worse neighborhood than his apartment, it was more defensible, logistically speaking. No large windows inviting bricks or bullets from people whose deals had fallen through by the running of his mouth. No witnesses to dial 911 should he have to take care of someone skulking around. He kept the Glock close at hand.

But now maybe his luck was changing. Upon arriving back at the church last night, he'd found a check for ten thousand dollars from a donor who had seemed a long shot the day before and who had continually fiddled with his iPhone during their meeting. Then he saw the e-mail from a dealership in town offering twenty-five large for the Infiniti, assuming it matched his description. Add in the two thousand from the job in the Hills, and he was closing in on ninety grand of the five hundred he owed. Sure, half the sand was through the hourglass, but he had another job lined up with Bishop and his people today, and he was confident he could negotiate a bigger piece of the pie. They needed his skill set and they knew it.

But the strongest lift to Dante's spirits had been one word uttered by the nervous little tech guy the night before. He'd referred to their boss as the Alchemist. Dante had heard that name spoken before, always with the same sort of fear and reverence that adorned the name La Bella Donna. Perhaps he could leverage this into a major payday —Trick could talk, after all—or perhaps he could roll over on the Syndicate, offer the Alchemist some valuable information and find protection with a new organization. If he could play one against the other, he might come out with his head intact. The important thing was that more parties—more variables—meant more options.

He updated his spreadsheet and slurped up a spoonful of cereal. Would a hundred grand be enough to buy his way in with the Alchemist? Better to try and hit one fifty—a reasonable goal—and then make an offer.

The church's landline rang.

"It's a blest day at Broadmoor Outreach Tabernacle. How may I help you?"

"Is this the guy with the hollow Bible?" The voice was scratchy and flat, and Dante didn't recognize it.

"I think you have the wrong number," he said. He picked up the Glock from next to his cereal bowl and quietly chambered a round.

"You're the guy. You got my brother thrown in the hole last month."

Dante ran through the deals he'd made over the last few weeks. Nothing jumped out at him. Then again, he'd probably seen a hundred inmates in the past month.

"You're confused. I make pastoral visits and file reports. That's all. Anything involving retribution is above my pay grade."

"No, Brinkman told me it's you," the man said. "You're gonna pay. Ten large. Or you'll find out what retribution really looks like."

Dial tone.

Dante hung up the phone and set the gun down next to it. Marcus Brinkman was sending a message—a small reminder of the cloudburst of pain and destruction that would be falling on Dante's head if the Syndicate removed its umbrella of protection. He looked at his spread-sheet again. Seventeen percent. It seemed smaller now. If he was going to make a play, he had to do it soon.

✠

Happy sagged his weight on the console between the van's front seats and dialed the Alchemist. He looked from Andrew to Fletcher. Both were silent, glaring at each other, waiting. The sound of the phone ringing, wired into the van's sound system, filled the space.

Immediately upon entering the vehicle, Fletcher had pulled the satchel from the small of his back and tried to hand it off to Andrew. He was out, he said. But Andrew would have none of it. If Fletcher was going to quit, he'd have to do it firsthand.

"You have many talents, Mr. Doyle," the Alchemist said in his now-familiar accent, "but punctuality is not among them. You really want to stop disappointing me."

"Oh, I'm a big disappointment," Fletcher said. "And add this: I'm out. To smooth things over, I found you a guy who's as good as me, more of a go-getter, and he's willing to take my place. Andrew has his number. I suggest you tie him down before he gets a better offer."

The Alchemist laughed. "You're not out. You're in deeper than ever. Now, the next job is an easy one. It—"

"Are you deaf? I'm out. I've done everything you asked up to this point, but if you push me any further you'll be in danger of making a new enemy, and who needs that? How about we just part amicably?"

There was silence on the line for a few seconds and then a click. For a moment, Fletcher thought the Alchemist had hung up. "Hello?" he said.

Then the Alchemist was back. "You will hear me out," he said, "and if you decide you still don't want the job, we go our separate ways."

Fletcher plopped down in one of the swivel chairs. "Fine," he said.

"Can I assume you looked through the prize from last night?"

"Nope. Not interested."

"What self-control. Open it now."

Fletcher couldn't deny a bit of excitement as he unwound the leather cord, opened the satchel, and pulled out a stack of very old pages—perhaps thirty of them—wrapped in bubble paper, which Fletcher quickly discarded.

"Uncool," Happy said, popping a bubble with his thumb. "Why not just store them in acid?"

Fletcher thumbed through the old papers quickly. "Looks like letters," he said. "Late eighteenth or early nineteenth century. All in French."

"That's correct. Your next task is to provide translations of these."

"You got the wrong guy, Al," Fletcher said. "What little French I ever knew is pretty much gone."

"Ah, but your lovely French-Canadian wife speaks it fluently. It's time we activate her. And let's bring in your would-be replacement as well."

Fletcher felt the blood pounding in his temples. "Dream on, Al. I'm not about to bring my wife into this."

"You will if you care about what I have in my possession and what I do with it."

"Yeah, yeah, you've got a pile of incriminating photos and footage. That's old news. And you haven't thought this through." His phone bleeped in his right pocket. A text from Meg, as if she knew they were talking about her. "The only reason I even care about my parole and your stupid pictures is because I don't want to lose my family. I tell Meg about all this and I lose them anyway. So go ahead and make your play."

"I already have," the Alchemist said, laughing again.

Fletcher opened the message from Meg. Ivy with U? Not @ breakfast. Another message popped up. Courtney missing 2. Brad ir8. Prank?

"I repeat," the Alchemist was saying, "you'll do this job if you care about what I've got in my possession and what I do with it. Or rather, with *her.*"

The burner phone buzzed in Fletcher's other

pocket. It felt like it weighed five pounds as he lugged it out and opened the message: a picture of Ivy on a chair in a white room, her mouth taped, hands bound behind her back.

Fletcher dropped the phone.

"What is it?" Happy asked.

Fletcher looked at Andrew, sitting across from him, trying to hide the guilt spilling across his face. Rage was growing in Fletcher's chest. By instinct, he gathered it together there. Then he consciously uncaged it. His left hand found Andrew's throat and clamped down, feeling the flesh compacting. He slammed his old partner against a mounted LCD monitor, spider-webbing the screen. His other hand groped on the counter for something sharp, coming up with a flathead screwdriver. He pushed it up to Andrew's left eye, where it met the bridge of his nose.

Five expletives in, Fletcher realized he was wasting words. "You're a dead man, Bishop," he said.

"Come on, Fletcher," Happy pleaded. "We're all friends here. Use your words."

"Shut up!" Fletcher ordered. "Tell me where she is, Andrew. Or you will die right here in this stupid van."

"I don't know."

"Dead. And that's not a figure of speech. I'm talking *dead*-dead. You know, like when you've finished a long day of letting your friends go to jail in your place and destroying their families and you roll into that depressing basement apartment of yours and flip on the TV. And there's a news story about some poor sap who got stabbed to death on the street, and his heart is no longer beating and he's just a bag of meat, lying on a slab at the morgue, slowly assuming room temperature. That's you if you don't tell me: Where is she?"

Fletcher could see Happy in his periphery, frozen there, eyes wide, squeezing two fistfuls of his red hair. He could hear the Alchemist trying to talk him down over the phone. But he didn't care. Andrew was behind this. All of it. Fletcher had known it from the beginning, but he'd let himself be fooled because he missed the grift. But this . . . He slid the screwdriver another millimeter, pushing against the soft tissue of Andrew's eye.

"It's not me!" Andrew tried to shout. His voice ground against the meat of Fletcher's hand, causing him to feel the words more than he heard them.

"What do you think it'll be like when the cold metal goes into your brain?" Fletcher asked. "Will it hurt or just—*lights out?*"

He saw Andrew's fingers inching toward the gun in his waistband.

"Go ahead and pull," he said. "Let's see who dies first. You're pathetic, you know that? Grifter with a gun."

The space was suddenly full of sunlight and road noise. Fletcher squinted at the man who stood framed in the now-open door at the rear of the van. He wore a gray jumpsuit with the name *Dale* embroidered on a patch over his heart and held a long-barreled revolver in his hand, trained on Fletcher. He said nothing, just stared with dead gray eyes, pointing that enormous gun.

Fletcher released Andrew and let the screwdriver clatter to the floor. He looked at the man with the gun again as his eyes adjusted to the light, locking that face down into his memory. He focused on the man's dead eyes, not the prominent scar on his cheek. Scars or tattoos could be faked. Andrew had taught him that—draw your mark's attention away with a distinctive trait, only to erase said trait as soon as you're out of sight, leaving your mark describing a ghost. But eyes were eyes. Even if one employed colored contact lenses, a good grifter could memorize a set of eyes and know them anywhere.

The man in the jumpsuit looked over at Andrew —a look of warning—and then to Happy and then shut the door, leaving them once again in the artificial light of the van's dome lamp.

"Have you finished your tantrum?" the Alchemist asked.

Fletcher said nothing.

"It's not me," Andrew croaked again, rubbing his throat.

"Right," Fletcher said. "How *could* it be? You're here. The Alchemist is on the phone. So I guess I keep my attention on him, right? Classic misdirection. Just a guy with a script and a phony accent." He pointed at the back door. "Or maybe it's our friend Dale in the jumpsuit."

Andrew shrugged.

"You forget where I learned my craft," Fletcher said. "One of the first things you taught me: make your mark look at the empty hand while you slip his coins into your pocket with the other." He spoke up louder. "Are you the empty hand, Mr. Alchemist?"

"I'm the hand that holds your entire life in its grip," he answered. "All I have to do is squeeze and everything goes *pop*. The 'do it *and*' portion of this job is over, Mr. Doyle. You will do as I say *or* I will blind your daughter."

Fletcher felt the panic growing in his chest. There was too much to gather together.

"Do I have you pegged now?"

Chapter 35

"Oh, there you are!" Meg's face relaxed a bit at the sight of Fletcher approaching through the narrow hallway, then resumed its deep furrows as he drew closer. "She's not with you?"

"No," he said. "We need to talk."

Meg took a long step back, fear settling onto her face.

"Come in here." He beckoned her to follow him into the same room where he had kissed her two days earlier. She hung outside the door for a moment, instinctively savoring the last few seconds before Fletcher's words changed everything. Then she entered, slowly rubbing her bare arms despite the stifling temperature.

Fletcher couldn't meet her eyes. Not without grifting. He fished the burner phone from his pocket and tapped his way to the pictures.

"That first day," he mumbled, "when I went out for Ivy's toothbrush . . . I ran into Andrew." He held the phone up toward her and began slowly thumbing through the record of the encounter. "He'd been following me."

Meg's face darkened at the sight of the man who had corrupted her husband, driven a wedge between them, and eventually stolen the better part of a decade from her family—all while visiting regularly, rocking Ivy to sleep, bringing her gifts, calling her Jumpin' Bean.

"He says it's not him calling the shots," Fletcher said, "but I don't know. Anyway, a man blackmailed me with these pictures, got me to do another job. Then he held that one over my head to get me to do another." He flipped forward to the picture of him slipping money from the briefcase. "I tried to cut it off today," he said. "It was getting out of hand. I knew if I lost you, it didn't matter if I was in prison or not. But—"

Meg's face had gone white and she stumbled backward, falling hard onto a metal folding chair. The last picture on the phone was of Ivy, mouth taped shut. Even in the low resolution of the tiny screen, the fear in her wide eyes was clear. Meg's shoulders went up and down a few times, then she began pawing through her purse.

"What are you doing?" Fletcher asked.

"I'm calling the police."

"No, you're not."

"Oh, but I am." She was punching keys. Fletcher prayed he could reason with her. She'd always been good in a crisis—better than he was—but this was different.

"He said he'll blind her, Meg."

She stopped.

"We have to do what this man says." He was silent a minute, waiting for it to sink in.

Meg dropped her phone back into her purse and stood. "How do we know they won't just—"

"This man is a grifter. He doesn't follow the code to the letter, but he's not going to hurt anyone he doesn't have to hurt. Trust me." He regretted the last two words before he'd even gotten them out.

Meg grabbed up her purse and took a few quick steps, pausing at the door. "Well? Are you coming?"

Fletcher couldn't read her. Not in the least. "Where?"

"To talk to Brad."

After a fruitless search of the lunchroom and men's quarters, they found Brad sitting on the front steps of the church, staring blankly at his cell phone. When he saw Meg approaching, he quickly rubbed his sleeve across his eyes. He stood, the contents of his tool belt clattering together.

"Have you found them?" he asked, a bit of hope in his voice.

"Ivy, yes," Meg said, "but not Courtney. I left her three voicemails."

"Not again," Brad mumbled. "She promised she'd never do this to me again."

Fletcher thought of Ivy's text about Courtney and the "sketchy guys." Without thinking, he redirected. "Do what?" he asked.

"When her mom died, Courtney ran away. I didn't see her for three weeks. A fourteen-year-old girl sleeping on friends' couches and who knows where else."

"But why would she—?"

"We've been fighting." He glanced up at Fletcher. "I didn't know she was this upset, though." He squeezed his eyes shut, fighting back the tears. A few eluded him and trickled down his cheeks. "This city," he said. "The abandoned houses. The gangs and drugs and . . ."

He shook his head violently and again wiped his face. "Fletcher, I know we've had our differences, but if you can help . . . If you know someone who can find people or, I don't know . . . I wouldn't tell your parole officer."

Meg put her hand on Brad's cheek and locked her eyes onto his. "I'm sorry, but we can't stay. You were right; being around all this is just too much reality too soon."

He nodded.

"I'll keep trying Courtney," she said. "She'll come back." She wrapped her arms around his neck and squeezed. Fletcher was surprised by his desire to separate the two of them with a blow to Brad's head and by the fact that their current situation, both of them chasing after missing children, did nothing to mitigate this desire.

"I miss Karen," Brad said into Meg's neck.

"I know."

"We've got to go," Fletcher said, pulling on Meg's arm. It took the third tug to pry her away from Brad's embrace.

Fletcher fed Meg the best version of events he could concoct during the three-block hike to the van, careful not to leave a window in his words large enough for Meg to jump in. As the van came into view, Fletcher hit a wall of dread. The thought of bringing his wife into the heart of his secret world sickened him. The thought of the

Alchemist addressing her directly, by name, the fact that he seemed to know a good deal about her—it was almost enough to turn him back. They could call the police, show them the picture. Perhaps the burner phone could be traced back to its source somehow.

But the Alchemist was always several moves ahead, wasn't he? And the dwindling police force of the struggling city was not exactly swimming in resources at the moment. He doubted they would even bother looking for Courtney.

He took the last few strides to the back of the van and pulled open the door. Andrew was exactly where Fletcher had left him, sitting in the captain's chair, his head in his hands.

"Hello, Meg," he said without looking up.

Fletcher could feel her tense and, for a moment, he feared she might scramble up into the van and pick up where he'd left off. But Meg closed her eyes, pressed her fingertips together, and pushed them to her mouth. At first he thought she was praying, but then he recognized the gesture. This is what she did backstage before a performance, in the car before auditions. Emptying her mind of all her own motivations, she had explained, and replacing them with those of her character.

"Hello, Andrew," she said politely, and stepped up into the van.

Chapter 36

"I just don't understand why we need him," Andrew said.

"For a start, because this van is too small for the four of us," Fletcher said. "We need somewhere to plan, somewhere to crash for a few nights. You want us staying at your place? I don't see that working out. And remember, you'd have been kibble and bits if it weren't for him."

"Anyway," Happy piped up, "the Alchemist said to bring him in. So we bring him in."

They were pulling into a derelict pay lot in Broadmoor. Happy had tried to engage Meg in conversation at least three times during the drive, but after three monosyllabic replies he got the hint and let her stare out the window in peace.

"Where exactly are we?" she finally asked.

"It's a church," Andrew said, "but not really. The preacher's a grifter, kind of low-level. He goes into jails and does a little supply-and-demand action." He raised his eyebrows at Fletcher. "Maybe that's why everyone finds Jesus inside, huh?"

Meg narrowed her eyes at her husband.

"No, hon," he said. "Trick works the jails, not prisons. I only met him this week."

Happy hopped down from the driver's seat.

"Either way, it'll be nice to have a decent work space. I love my van, but it's hard to keep the equipment organized."

Fletcher called Dante's number as they crossed the street, and the metal gate was open by the time the group reached the church. The moment they were inside, Dante locked the gate back down, followed by the door. He was holding something behind his back. Tupac was playing from a stereo inside at a lowish volume.

"We got a job?" he asked hopefully.

"Yeah," Andrew said, bustling past him. "We're about to call the boss for the details. Turn off this jungle music."

Dante stepped toward him, bringing the Glock into view. "What's that?"

Andrew smirked and pulled back the jacket of his Italian suit, revealing the grip of the Colt Detective Special. "You want to go out in the street and count off ten paces, or you want to work?"

Fletcher stepped between them. "What happened to the professional grifters I worked with last night? Who cares if you like each other? You're supposed to fake it. That's your job. Now let's call the boss and find out what kind of snipe hunt he's sending us on." He considered taking a moment to fill Trick in on recent developments, but decided against it, simply offering, "Trick, this is Meg. Meg, Trick," as he brought up the

Alchemist's number and hit Send. He set the phone on a chair, and the five of them huddled around it.

"I was beginning to think you'd forgotten about little old me," the Alchemist said, not masking his annoyance. "Tell me where you are and who is present."

"We're at our new headquarters in Broadmoor," Andrew said, locking eyes with Dante, "and it's our crew from last night plus Fletcher's wife, just like you wanted."

"Hello, Meg," the Alchemist said. "It's nice to finally speak with you."

"Hello," she said. She felt her arms begin to shake a bit and pushed her fingertips together again until she regained control.

"And the hero of last night's adventures," the Alchemist said. "What is your name?"

Fletcher shot Andrew a sidelong glance, trying to read his reaction. Somehow the Alchemist knew details of last night's job.

"They call me Trick."

"That's not what I asked."

"Name's Dante. Dante Watkins."

"Well, then," the Alchemist said, "let's get down to business. The task that—"

"I want to talk to Ivy," Meg blurted.

The Alchemist sighed into the phone. They heard footsteps, then a muffled scuffing, then a door squeaking open, then, "Mom?"

Meg began to cry. "Sweet pea! Are you all right? Did they hurt you?"

"I'm okay," she said. "We had Subway. And they've got cable."

Meg laughed through the tears. "You're gonna be okay, sweetie. I promise."

"I know," Ivy said. "The man told me Dad owes him money. From before he went to prison. He said I was his collateral, which is pretty creepy, but ya know . . . They tied us up in the truck, but they've been pretty nice since we got here."

"Who's us?" Meg asked.

Again the sound of the door—closing this time —and the scuff of shoes on concrete.

"Satisfied?" the Alchemist asked.

"Who's us?" Meg asked again.

"They've got Courtney too," Fletcher said. "Don't you?"

"I do," he answered. "She saw my men and began raising hysterics. They had no choice."

"Let her go," Fletcher said. "She couldn't be further removed from all this." Besides, Fletcher thought he had a decent chance of tracing the Alchemist's location if he could just play twenty questions with Courtney.

"I was considering it. She is what you might call a handful—not nearly as docile as your Ivy. But now that I know you care for her, I think we'll just add her to the pot. Bring me my prize and you will have them back safely; you have my word. But drag your feet, cross me, call the authorities, or try to turn the grift back on me in any way, and I will fill that phone with horrific pictures that will haunt you all for the rest of your lives."

Meg let out an involuntary sob and buried her face in her hands. Fletcher rubbed her back gently. She neither pulled away nor leaned into him for comfort.

"After we translate the letters," Fletcher said, "what's next?"

"That's for you to determine," the Alchemist said. "I'm through holding your hand. It's time for you to impress me by doing what you do best."

"We're listening," Andrew said.

"The letters you took from Belltower's safe speak of an object of immense value. The five of you are going to find it for me. And you're going to steal it for me."

"Okay," Fletcher said. "Where should we—"

"Call's ended," Happy said.

"What are these letters he's talking about?" Meg asked.

Fletcher opened the satchel and handed her the stack of old pages. "They're a few hundred years old; can you translate them?"

She swallowed back some tears and pressed her palms to her face, taking a moment of semi-solitude before coming out from between her hands, seemingly collected, and perusing the first page. "Sure. It's not much different from modern French. Kind of like reading the Declaration of Independence." She pulled a small notepad from her purse, propped it up on her lap, and com-menced scrawling.

"I've got a better question," Dante said. "What was that all about?" He nodded at the phone on the chair.

"Right," Fletcher said, and cleared his throat. "Remember our conversation on the way home last night? Well, I tried to walk away. Apparently the Alchemist, whoever he is"—he glared at Andrew—"anticipated this and had my twelve-year-old daughter kidnapped."

"Guys," Meg shouted. They all went silent, eyes glued on her. "Sorry," she said. "I'm trying to concentrate." She returned to her pad, writing frantically, stopping every minute or so to reread her work and check it against the page in her hand.

Fletcher leaned in and spoke quietly. "Look, I'm sorry, Trick—Dante. You didn't ask to get pulled into this. If you want, we'll find some-where else to go. You could leave town for a while until this blows over."

Dante rubbed his face for a moment. "No. I'm in," he said. "Whatever this thing is, I'm guessing there's a significant back end."

"I can't imagine he'd go to all this trouble

unless the thing was priceless," Fletcher agreed.

"Okay," Meg said. "The first letter is short. A page and a half. The rest are longer. But they're all from the same guy: Alessandro."

Fletcher and Andrew locked eyes. As far as they were concerned, there was only one Alessandro in France in the late 1700s whose letters would be locked up in a secret safe.

Alessandro Cagliostro.

Chapter 37

"How much money do you think your dad owes these guys?" Courtney asked.

They were lying on a rug in the middle of a bare room. The walls were white and unadorned, save for the old tube TV hanging in the corner. They'd been blindfolded before leaving the truck and led into what seemed to be an abandoned office building. The girls had needed to use the bathroom twenty minutes earlier and were again blindfolded before the man with the scar paraded them down a hall and into a dank men's room. He'd given them two minutes and then banged on the door and demanded they come out.

"I don't know," Ivy said. "We don't have any money, though. I hear my parents talking about it all the time. Fighting about it."

"At least you have both your parents,"

Courtney said. She was changing channels with the remote, but the TV was muted and she was going too fast for the shows to even register. "I'd give anything to have my mom back. I'd love to hear them fighting."

Ivy patted her arm. "I'm sorry," she said. They were both quiet for a couple minutes, Courtney flipping the channels and Ivy studying the exposed ductwork of the ceiling.

"They weren't supposed to have any kids," Courtney said abruptly. "That's why my dad is so much older than yours. And I think it's why he's so protective. The doctor said they were infertile, so they gave up on the idea. Then I showed up." She stopped clicking the button. "I bet he wishes he could trade me for her."

"Your dad loves you," Ivy said. She pinched her lips together in thought, as if internally fact-checking the statement, and then gave a deliberate nod of confirmation.

"Not like he loved her. When she died, he didn't leave the house for, like, six weeks, because everything reminded him of Mom. Our church, the grocery store, even our house. That's why we moved to Harbor Beach."

Ivy closed her eyes. "You didn't have a mom, and I didn't have a dad. I feel bad about it now, but when my father was in prison I kind of wished your dad and my mom would get together. Then I'd have a dad and a sister."

Courtney squeezed her hand. Then the door swung open, and the man with the scar took three quick steps into the room and yanked Courtney to her feet by her wrist. She yelped in protest, then shrieked as he pulled a bag over her head and dragged her from the room.

Ivy heard the door slam shut, then the lock slide into place.

"Who's it addressed to?" Fletcher asked.

"Someone named Fonseca. So is the next one." Meg saw Fletcher and Andrew gaping back at her. "Do you know who that is?"

"He was the Grand Master of the Knights of Malta," Fletcher answered.

"Knights?" Dante asked. "The 1700s seems a little late for knights."

"What's the first letter about?" Andrew asked, ignoring the comment.

"It's some plan that they're hatching together—Alessandro and Fonseca. Here: 'Today I saw children playing dominoes, lining them up and toppling them as children do, and I thought to myself how marvelous our plan is. We continue to hone our grand design, biding our time for the moment to topple them.' It goes on like that for a couple more paragraphs, pretty vague."

"There's no date?" Fletcher asked.

"Nope."

"What about the next one?"

She picked up the second letter, reading in little bursts as she translated a phrase at a time. " 'It was the Great Architect who revealed to me the Elixir of Life and the secrets of . . .' ummm . . . 'alchimie'? I don't know that word."

"Alchemy, right?" Dante said. "Like your boss, the Alchemist."

"Who's that?" Meg asked.

"The guy on the phone."

"Oh." She was quiet for a moment, reminded of her daughter's captivity, then snapped to. "Whoever this Great Architect guy is—"

"That's how they talk about God," Fletcher said.

"I see. Well, apparently God has shown him, 'the means of achieving our goals in the person of a rotten little vicar here in Vienna. He flaunts his women and his sin and makes a game of offending the empress. And yet he wants more than anything to rise in status and power. Despite his wicked life, he is almost sure to become the bishop of Strasbourg because of his position in the most prominent family of Brittany. He will be the first domino we tip. I need only to nudge him into position.

" 'Now as to your illness, please remember' . . . blah, blah, 'Elixir of Life,' blah, blah . . . okay, he goes on for a while about this Fonseca's illness. 'We will meet again, of that I am sure. Either in Malta or elsewhere. Your friend and physician,

Alessandro.' So this Alessandro is sort of a grifter?"

"No," Andrew said. "Not *a* grifter. *The* grifter. What Elvis is to rock 'n' roll and Bob Ross is to happy trees, Cagliostro is to the grift."

"The memoir you had me read mentions that he used all of his friendships to his advantage," Fletcher said, "but it doesn't specify what he and Fonseca were up to."

"Wait," Dante said. "You've both read this guy's memoirs?"

"So did I," Happy said. "Andrew insisted. Only it's more a textbook on grifting than an autobiography."

"And you don't find it odd that the Alchemist now has you reading the guy's mail? That would be one big coincidence." He eyed Andrew.

"My own mentor made me read it when I was coming up," Andrew said. "There's a whole school of grifting that looks to Cagliostro as the gold standard of long and short cons."

"It wasn't even authentic," Fletcher said. "Somebody just put together some lessons from Cagliostro's life and slapped his name on it."

"How do you know?" Dante asked.

"Well, unlike these letters, each entry is actually dated, and the last one is from 1798."

"So?"

"Cagliostro died in prison in 1795."

Andrew shook his head. "That's what he wanted the world to believe."

Dante was jotting down notes, trying to keep up with the back-and-forth. "So these guys were French?" he asked.

"No," Fletcher said. "Fonseca was Portuguese and Cagliostro was Sicilian."

"Then why are they writing to each other in French?"

"Everyone did. That's where we get the term *lingua franca*."

"But who were these knights?" Meg asked, cutting short the tangent.

"The Knights of Malta," Andrew answered. "Cagliostro showed up at their capital in 1765. He knew it was the best place for him to cut his teeth. Just like him, the Knights became whatever they needed to be in a given moment to stay on top."

"How so?" Dante asked.

"Well, they started out as a little band of monks a thousand years ago, running hospitals and defending poor Christians on pilgrimage. Then they started battling Muslim forces in the Crusades. Five hundred years later they were hunting down pirates and amassing treasure. They morphed whenever they needed to, bounced from place to place just like Cagliostro, even changed their name like Cagliostro did. At first they were the Most Venerable Order of St. John of Jerusalem, then the Knights Hospitalers, then the Knights of Cyprus and Rhodes, and finally the Knights of Malta."

"More reinventions than Madonna," Happy said.

Dante flipped to a fresh page in his notebook. "The pilgrimage stuff reminds me of a documentary I saw on the Knights Templar. They started out the same way."

Andrew and Fletcher shared a knowing, unamused look.

"I got this one," Andrew said. "Write this down, Trick: The Templars were amateurs. They came on the scene after Fonseca's predecessors and they barely lasted two hundred years before they disbanded. And when they ceased to exist, guess who got all their treasures and land and everything."

"Must have been satisfying," Fletcher said. "The two groups went beyond friendly competition, even skirmished a few times. But in the end, the Knights of the Temple couldn't adapt like the Knights of Malta."

Andrew nodded. "Maybe that's why everyone's so enamored with the Templars these days—they haven't existed in seven hundred years, so they seem mysterious, magical, the stuff of legend. A few Renaissance Fair nerds meet together in lodges here and there, claiming some connection to them, but it's just fantasy. Meanwhile, the

Knights of Malta run fund-raisers and provide first aid at soccer games. Not very mysterious or romantic. They have a website, for crying out loud."

Happy scoffed. "The website sucks, though. Not even compatible with BlueScript 9.0."

"You're serious?" Dante said. "They're still around today?"

"Yep," Fletcher said. "They still exist, and membership is still closed to anyone who can't trace a noble bloodline back a couple hundred years."

"I take it our boy Belltower is a member in good standing?" Happy asked.

"For sure," Andrew said. "He has a plaque on the wall of his library. And as a millionaire, he fits right in. They're not as prominent as they were, but they're as powerful as ever. They've even got a special seat at the UN."

"So they're a country?" Meg asked.

"No, that's the scary part. They've got independent sovereign status under international law, but we're talking about ten thousand people spread throughout the world, mostly high up in industry and government—including ours. But their ultimate allegiance is to the Grand Master. He's their head of state and a cardinal in the Catholic Church."

Dante gave up and tossed the notebook in frustration. "Why do you guys know all this?"

Fletcher shrugged. "We've helped ourselves to a number of their artifacts over the years. In fact, the first job Andrew and I did together was Fonseca's sword from the Metropolitan Museum."

"One of you is lying, then," Dante said. He looked from Fletcher to Andrew to Happy. "I can buy one coincidence, but we've got a two-hundred-and-some-year-old letter from one dead guy I never heard of to another, and you three just happen to have a connection to both? That's too much."

"Kind of what I was thinking," Fletcher said, turning to Andrew.

The four of them stared him down expectantly.

"Okay. It's not a coincidence," Andrew finally said, taking a deep breath. "I had Fletcher read Cagliostro's memoirs because my mentor made me read them."

"You already told us that," Dante said.

Fletcher's eyes darkened. "But you never told us your mentor was the Alchemist."

Chapter 38

"Yeah, right." Happy laughed. "Tell 'em that's not true, Andrew . . . Andrew?"

"This is what he told me," Andrew said. "The Alchemist—or Charles Farrington, as I knew him—was a member of the Knights of Malta.

He'd been part of some kind of internal dispute, going back centuries. His faction was trying to take over."

"For what?" Dante asked.

"I guess it started with Fonseca. He brought in new ideas—heretical by popular opinion—and all sorts of forbidden occult practices."

Fletcher nodded. "Like kabbalah, necromancy, alchemy . . ."

"Right. Fonseca wanted to change with the times, but the more conservative knights resisted, which makes sense when you consider that the order goes back a thousand years, riding the white martyrdom craze."

"The what now?" Happy asked.

"The white martyrdom," Fletcher said. "When Christianity was legalized in Rome, the faithful could no longer show their devotion by spilling their blood to the lions or the sword—what they called the red martyrdom. The *white* martyrdom meant giving up your life and fortune to go and join a monastery.

"But the Crusades changed everything. The pope told nobles and knights that they could get the same sort of points for the afterlife without all that poverty and chastity stuff if they went off and fought for Christendom."

"That's how the Knights of Malta got their start?" Meg asked. She was half listening while skimming through the last few letters.

"Not exactly," Andrew said. "And that's the real source of the conflict. They started out as legitimate monks and priests during the First Crusade, traveling behind the Crusaders, caring for the wounded. When the fighting stopped for a time, they turned their attention to protecting groups of Christians on pilgrimage. Then they grew larger and more powerful. Their hospitals took up more and more land. Then came castles. Then the knights began to outnumber the priests, and they became a full-on military order, fighting for the Holy Land. Fast-forward a couple hundred years and they're privateering, amassing wealth. At that point, it was no longer faith or principle fueling the movement, but ruthless entrepreneur-ship."

Dante shook his head. "Organized religion and organized crime—thin line. So I take it Fonseca brought the conflict to a head; like forcing the issue of 'Who are we really? Are we monks or a world power?' "

"And the power side has been gaining traction," Andrew said. "You ever hear of the Rat Lines?"

"The Nazi thing?" Meg asked.

"Dozens of top-ranking Nazis disappeared all at once at the end of the war. And who issued the passports?"

"No way," Dante said.

"A faction within the order got even richer off

of that," Andrew said. "That's what's at stake in this conflict."

"And I think we can agree which side the Alchemist is on," Fletcher said. "So what are we supposed to steal to help further their evil plans?"

Meg finished skimming the last letter, then grabbed up the whole stack and began shuffling through them, a little more roughly than Fletcher would have liked.

"Unless I missed something, the only mention of a treasure would be here in this last letter, and it's vague." She ran her finger down the margin. "This one's written to 'Your Eminent Highness, Grand Master de Rohan.' The whole thing's a lot more formal than the others. It says, 'The priceless treasure to which I alluded in my former correspondence is now safely in my possession, hidden away where no man will find it. I am currently under much' . . . um, *scrutiny*, I guess, 'but anticipate that I will be bringing the item to you within a matter of months—to you, continued power, and to us both, a true elixir of life.' "

Fletcher squinted in thought. "Aren't there extant letters between Cagliostro and Emmanuel de Rohan? Happy, can you find scans of those?"

"On it," Happy said, pulling a laptop from his messenger bag.

Fletcher snagged the letter from Meg and

looked it over, unable to decipher more than a few words. "This is pretty thin," he said. "Why would the Alchemist have us break into Belltower's place, risk us getting caught, risk losing our help, tipping the wrong people off, for *this?*"

Andrew stared at his shoes. "He was hoping this would be the big clue that led him to whatever he's looking for. You're not going to want to hear this, Fletcher, but almost every relic and artifact you and I stole together was supposed to be the Big Clue. You always wondered how I could move all those rare ecclesiastical antiquities when I hardly knew a thing about them? The Alchemist was my fence. I wriggled out from under his thumb, but we still did business."

Fletcher felt his head swim. "The sword from the museum?"

"That was for him."

"And the monstrance?"

Andrew nodded. "While you were in prison he tried to pursue it on his own, got mixed up with a few other disgruntled academics—but none of them had your encyclopedic knowledge and puzzle-solving skills. So as soon as you got out he was ready to pounce. Spent the last two years cooking up his end game."

"So it was a long con?" The rage was calcifying in Fletcher. "The whole thing?"

"No, kid, it was business. We didn't con you any more than the Alchemist conned me."

"And yet here we all are."

There was a moment of tense silence, filled only with the sound of Happy tapping frantically on the keys of his laptop.

"Okay," Happy said. "The bad news is the letters aren't digitized. The good news is that they're nearby. The library of Castille College. What's that, about a half-hour drive?"

"Makes sense." Fletcher thought of the leather-bound catalog of Maltese relics and the Holy Septangle. "Think about it—in the late seventeen hundreds, this city was a burgeoning French settlement. If someone in the Old World wanted to spirit away an item of tremendous value and importance, they'd bring it here, where they could blend right in. Besides, there's a reason the Alchemist came here to begin with."

"It's a promising basket," Happy said, "but we've got five of us eggs here. Let's diversify."

"Agreed," Andrew said. "I'm going to check in on Belltower again. He's cute and all, but he's got to be mixed up in this. Why else would he have those letters locked away? We might want to work the inside with him."

"How?" Dante asked. "What if he's discovered his empty safe?"

Happy snickered. "Andrew left him a little present in there: a bank-grade explosive dye pack. Anyone who opens that safe will be red in the face." He paused and looked around at his companions expectantly. "Eh? Caught red-handed . . . Seriously? Nothing? Hold on, I've got one more—"

"Anyway, you can't just wash that stuff off," Andrew said. "One look and I'll know if he's on to us. And somebody can go get a look at those letters."

"Road trip," Dante said. "Happy, you could pass for a student. Why don't you go snap us some pictures?"

"I already told you," Andrew said, "we keep Happy away from the mark. Bad things happen when he's off his leash."

Happy shrugged. "Andrew's right. Anyway, it's not going to be that easy. The catalog number has an RC at the front."

"What's that mean?" Meg asked.

"Reserve collection. You can't just waltz in and look at these letters; you need academic credentials. Maybe it's time to get some honest work out of that PhD, huh, Fletcher?"

Fletcher cleared his throat. "Actually, uh . . . I never finished the PhD."

"Yes, you did," Meg said.

"I finished the course work and submitted my dissertation, but I never actually got around to defending it."

She stared at him, mouth agape. "But we had a party."

"I know. It's just—you were so excited when I

said I was done and you kept going on about how nice it would be to have me around for Ivy's milestones and everything . . . I didn't have the heart to tell you there was more to the process."

"I'm glad your family was such a priority," she said quietly. "Really panned out."

"I'm sorry, Meg. I was—"

"I don't care," she said. "I just want to get Ivy back. So how do we get these letters?"

"Probably have to wait till dark," Andrew said. "I'd guess security is lax at a midsized private college."

"Forget that," Fletcher said. "You ever been to one of these snooty college libraries with their little restricted areas?"

"Can't say that I have."

"Well, I have, and I guarantee the only thing standing between us and these letters is some egghead college junior trapped behind a circulation desk while his classmates come and go, laughing and making plans. How do you *think* we get in?"

"You mean we pull a Coletto," Andrew said. They all looked at Meg. "You think she's got it in her?"

Chapter 39

"Honestly, the last thing I want is to eat," Meg said. "My stomach is in knots."

"Get some toast then," Fletcher said. "You'll need fuel if you're going to pull this off."

Andrew scoffed. "This isn't the Louvre. It's a college library." He snapped his fingers at a passing waitress. "Dear, we're ready to order. Bring us a pot of coffee, some toast, and three hippy hash breakfasts."

"Ah, what the heck," Dante said. "Make it four." Happy grabbed his shoulders and shook him excitedly.

Andrew was straightening and restraightening his silverware—an annoying habit. "I suppose this is sort of an initiation, though, isn't it?" he said, giving Meg an appraising look. "I mean, if you're going to be on our team, we need to make sure you're up to the challenge."

Meg stewed for a moment, opening her mouth just as the waitress arrived with the coffee. A flurry of activity followed as cups were filled and packets torn.

When all was calm again, Fletcher said, "Look, hon, you already know how to do this. It's just like theatre. A good grift involves all the same elements as a play. You've got the audience—

that's your mark. You've got costumes, makeup. A grifter needs to know his character's motivation and backstory. You have to make it so real that people don't notice any of what's going on behind the scenes. And you have to sell your performance. That's why they used to call grifters 'confidence men'—you have to truly believe that you are this person in this situation or your mark won't believe it."

"Just like theatre," Meg repeated.

"I actually picked up a lot from watching you practice and perform."

"Lovely," Meg said, stirring her coffee. "But we don't have time to put together a real show. That takes months."

"You're right. And that's okay. I mean, some of the greatest grifts have had a huge scope, like a Broadway production—workshopping, full cast and crew, dress rehearsals. They involved a complex web of coordinated grifts, perfectly synchronized to create a smoke screen. But we've got a skeleton crew here and almost no budget."

"That's how we roll," Happy said.

Andrew tipped back in his chair. "Those large-scale classic cons were built around what they used to call the Big Store. It was a semipermanent setup, made to look like a well-established operation. Maybe a bookmaker's office, maybe a bank. The illusion of permanence set the mark's mind at ease. It's like Dante's place. Looks like a church, all the trappings of a church. Why would anyone think it wasn't a church?"

Dante stared into his coffee cup.

"But we play the mark against the wall," Andrew said. He refilled his coffee as he spoke, topping it off until the meniscus was visible above the brim of the cup. "No Big Store, no permanent location. The best grifters change with the times, just like Cagliostro. Back in the twenties a grifter had to part with a chunk of his profits to hire solid shills—those are like the extras who posed as bankers and telegraph men." He carefully slurped some coffee from his overfilled mug. "But not anymore. Today people walk up to an ATM or type a password on their laptop and then believe whatever the screen tells them. And what makes up the information on the screen? Little glowing dots. Did you know that little glowing dots work for free? We only need to pay their supervisor." He slapped Happy on the shoulder. "And glowing dots never get greedy or drop the ball or quit at the last minute. A skeleton crew is an asset these days if you do it right. And it all comes down to one thing."

Meg shrugged impatiently. "What?"

"This." Andrew tipped his coffee cup over in her direction. She gasped and scrambled halfway up onto Fletcher's lap.

"Oops. Nothing in the cup," Andrew said,

smiling. "But you knew for a fact that there was. That's object permanence. It separates infants from toddlers, and we couldn't get along without it, but a grifter can use it to his advantage. That's why we always say 'show, don't tell.' If your mark's peg is money, you show money. It's no good to just talk about it. Talk might stir up a little interest, but people lose all rationality when they actually see it or, better yet, feel it. Even in the age of glowing dots, nothing beats fat stacks of cash.

"The old confidence men would have a safe in the wall at the Big Store with a trick panel in the back. The mark would see money changing hands all around him and stacks and stacks of it deposited in the safe. What he didn't know is that it was the same stacks going in again and again, then coming around from the next room and back into the pockets of the shills. In the mark's mind, the total is growing in that safe. That's object permanence."

"We think it works better without the Big Store," Fletcher said. "People see no room for sleight of hand. What's in that briefcase I just handed you? If you've seen the inside of an identical briefcase a minute ago, your mind will fill it in." He nudged her with his elbow. "Or what's in that fanny pack on the back of your desk chair?"

Meg kept her eyes locked on Andrew. "So how

would I use that at the college? I'm not offering the librarian money."

"It's all misdirection," Andrew said. "You create an event over there—something complex, something outrageous—while you're helping yourself over here."

The waitress arrived, precariously balancing the many plates on a single tray.

Fletcher felt his stomach twist at the sight of the hippy hash in front of him. He scraped it away and slid the egg out from beneath. "The goal is always the same," he said. "Get your mark chomping on the bit to convince you of your own grift. Never be overeager, never try to close the deal. That's the mark's job. You just find his peg—money, power, pleasure, whatever—and twist it."

"Cupidity is your friend," Andrew agreed.

"Cupidity?" Meg asked.

"It's an old grifter word. It's like greed, but deeper."

"The Bible calls it covetousness," Fletcher said.

Andrew shook his head. "I like cupidity better. Rhymes with stupidity, which works because people are at their stupidest when they want more and more."

"Like the platinum ring you gave me," Meg said, turning toward Fletcher. "You knew I wanted it, and it made me stupid enough to miss what was really going on with you guys."

"No—"

"Exactly," Andrew said.

"What do you think of the hash?" Happy asked Dante.

"I could see it growing on me."

Happy laughed. "I could see it growing on something."

Meg pushed her plate away and rested her head on her hand. "I can't believe you had this whole other life and I was oblivious to it."

Andrew reached across the table and squeezed her elbow. "Hey, anybody we grifted was trying to get something he didn't deserve. They should have listened when their parents told them 'if it sounds too good to be true, it probably ain't.' "

"*Is,*" Meg said.

"Hmm?"

"If it sounds too good to be true, it probably *is.*"

"Not how I heard it," Andrew said. "It's good, but it isn't true."

Happy shook his head. "No, Meg's right. It's true, but it isn't good."

"Either way," Fletcher said, "it's cupidity, and that's key. Because you can't grift an honest man . . ."

"And there are no honest men!" the four veteran grifters thundered, followed by a smattering of laughter around the table.

Fletcher felt Meg glaring at him and locked eyes with her. His smile froze, then faded.

312

Chapter 40

"Undo one more button," Happy said. "What? I'm not being creepy, that's just—"

"He's right," Fletcher said from behind the wheel of the van. "Misdirection." He changed lanes to avoid a pothole.

"I'm not that kind of actress," Meg said. "The button stays."

They had stopped briefly by St. John the Baptist, where Meg had run in and retrieved luggage and air mattresses from the women's sleeping quarters. She had been planning to grab Fletcher's as well, but she heard a number of male voices coming from the men's quarters and thought better of it. What if Brad was there? Or someone else from their group? Better not to have to explain her presence.

"And to think you didn't want me to pack this," Meg said, indicating her suit. She had changed en route in the back of the van while Happy covered his eyes, and Fletcher became suddenly preoccupied with checking the rearview mirror every few seconds. She was now trying to straighten her twisted shirt.

"Come here a minute," Happy said, leaning off his chair and pinning an ugly old turquoise brooch to her lapel. He then plugged an audio connector to the back of it, inside the jacket. "Run this wire around to the small of your back and clip this on your waist," he said, handing her a bulky plastic casing. "That way we can listen in. If you get in trouble, Fletch'll save the day. Always does."

Meg twisted in her chair and felt the telltale bulge in her coat. "This is pretty obvious," she said. "Do people still wear an actual wire? I thought that was just an expression. Can't they fit everything into the pin itself?"

"You can buy that stuff, but I make all our gadgets, custom. And hiding a bug in a watch or a cufflink is pretty much impossible. You've got a bunch of components—mic, power source, transmitter—that all have to fit in a tight spot without being obvious."

"What if you have to bug someone without them knowing?"

"Well, a cell phone already has a mic and a battery and the capacity to broadcast sound as a digital signal. All that's missing is for somebody like me to hack the device, reprogram it to transmit all the time, and you've got a steady stream of audio wherever they go. They'll even recharge the bug for me every night."

Meg crinkled her brow. "Really? I've been pocket-dialed before. You can't understand what people are saying."

Happy waved a hand dismissively. "The right

software can filter out most of that rustling and isolate the voice. Plus, people rarely let their phones leave their hands anymore."

Meg turned her attention to the items on the shelf behind her. "What's this thing?" she asked.

Fletcher had seen this brand of curiosity before; Meg dealt with nerves or stress by asking an endless stream of questions and focusing on minutiae.

"That's a squib vest," Happy answered proudly. "This little bulb here is from a blood pressure cuff. You squeeze it and blood squirts out of your chest. Fake blood. It's for pinching the gizzard."

" 'Pinching the'—I'm sorry?"

"In the old days, if a mark got too curious, the Outside Man would put a little rubber pouch full of chicken blood in his mouth. Then the Inside Man would shoot him with a blank and he'd bite down on it and blood would pour down his chin."

"That's disgusting."

"It works, though," Fletcher said. "You overwhelm someone's senses like that, they'll disappear."

"What about this?" Meg asked, picking up a short node at the end of a thick wire.

"Don't touch that!"

Meg yanked her hand back.

"Sorry. I call that the Happy Zapper. Far superior to your standard police Taser. Except you have to lug this battery pack around, so it's not very stealthy."

"About five minutes and we'll be there," Fletcher said.

Meg closed her eyes and pushed her fingertips to her mouth.

"You'll do fine," Happy said. "Remember, cupidity leads to stupidity. Find your mark's peg and his snare."

Meg opened her eyes. "Snare? What's that?"

"Doesn't matter. Never mind."

"No, tell me. It'll keep my mind off—you know."

"The snare is something shameful or illegal—so forbidden that your mark would rather swallow his losses than admit what he's done. If he was trying to skirt the law himself or he was trying to cheat the grifter, then he can't really go to the cops without incriminating himself. Or if he's a family man and he was after another woman, or he's a politician and he was promising favors—he's actually swindled himself and then he gags himself. That's your back end, your insurance."

"Like blackmail," Meg said.

They pulled into a drive and past a large sign that read CASTILLE COLLEGE, surrounded by immaculately pruned Old Garden roses.

"Self-blackmail," Happy said. "Anyway, no need for all that here. All you'll need to cool this mark is to give him your phone number before you leave. And you really should undo one more button."

Fletcher pulled into a parking spot. "Looks like that's the library just past the fountain there. Remember, as many pics as you can get."

Meg hopped out the side door and walked around to the driver's window. "Any last words of advice?" she asked.

"Yeah. If you think you're made, just smile," Fletcher said. "Or better yet, laugh. Nothing makes you look guilty faster than trying to look serious. And make sure your eyes crinkle when you smile."

"Should I try and fake a dimple too?"

✠

Courtney had been thrust back into the bare room two hours after being taken. She'd been sobbing but wouldn't say why. Ivy rubbed her back and said, "Shhh shhhh" like her mother always did when she was upset.

"You should splash some cold water on your face," she said, walking over to the door and banging on it. "Excuse me," she called out. "We need to use the bathroom! Hello?"

A moment later the door opened a few inches. Ivy took an involuntary step back at the sight of the man with the scar. "You just went a few hours ago," he said gruffly.

"Girls have to go more than boys."

He entered the room and ordered them both to turn around before again blindfolding them and leading them the thirty paces to the men's room. Once inside he pulled off the blindfolds, ordered, "Make it quick," and left the room.

Courtney splashed some water on her face while Ivy—again channeling Meg—ran some paper towels under the faucet, wrung out the excess water, and placed them on the back of Courtney's neck. She rubbed the older girl's back again for a minute before Courtney announced, "I actually have to go" and disappeared into the bathroom's lone stall.

Ivy plopped to the floor and opened the cabinet beneath the sink, pawing through the dirty space. There was an aerosol can of disinfectant, a mostly empty plastic tub of liquid soap, and two small bottles made of amber glass. She pulled out the two glass bottles and tipped them toward the sink. Empty. They were only about four inches tall and looked very old and very interesting. She turned on the water and began rinsing them out.

The toilet flushed and Courtney emerged, far more composed. Squeezing up next to Ivy, she pumped some soap onto her hands and ran them under the water.

"You're still doing that thing with the bottles, huh?" she asked.

Ivy said nothing, just dried them off and

placed one in each of her shorts pockets. "We're all done," she bellowed.

The man with the scar reblindfolded them and led them back to their room, where he—or someone—had spread out two sleeping bags while they were away.

"Thank you," Ivy said. The man grunted and shut the door. She looked at Courtney and noticed that the whole side of her face had begun turning a deep blue. Leaning in close, she wrapped her arms around her friend's neck and whispered in her ear, "I could see out the side of my blindfold on the way to the bathroom. There's a door and a window."

"So?" Courtney whispered.

"There's only one of him and two of us. And there's some chemical cleaner under the sink. The next time he takes us to the bathroom, one of us can spray him in the eyes and we can run for the door."

Courtney shook her head violently. "No. We can't." Her calm was receding as fast as it had settled in. "We need to just do what they say."

"Don't you watch TV?" Ivy asked. "Kidnappers never let you go. They always kill you."

Chapter 41

Meg looked at her reflection in the glass doors as she approached the library, trying to gauge the effect she would have on a stranger. She paused. Maybe she *should* unbutton one more. No, she would not follow Fletcher's script. Look where it had gotten him. She would help get Ivy back from these monsters, integrity intact.

The library was larger than Meg expected, with low light and walls of finished dark wood and framed art. She approached the circulation desk, tentatively at first, then remembered that it was all about confidence. She straightened her spine and walked with quick, purposeful steps up to the desk. There was nobody there. She rang the little bell, wincing at how loud it was in the otherwise silent room. Hearing someone approach from behind, she panicked and undid another button.

"Are you ready to check out?" came a pleasant voice.

Meg turned and found herself face-to-face with a young woman who could have easily been her sister. "Sorry?" She laughed. "Oh, no. I'm actually a professor. Adjunct."

The girl looked back at her, waiting. In addition to being female, the young woman was pleasant and smartly dressed—the very antithesis of the socially awkward nerd Fletcher had predicted. Meg thought about going back to the van and sending him and his dimple in to do the heavy lifting. No. She wouldn't give him the satisfaction.

"Okay," the librarian said. "How can I help you?"

Meg handed her the little slip of paper with the catalog number on it. "I need to see these letters. They're in the rare books and papers room, I guess."

"No problem. I just need your faculty ID."

"That's the thing," Meg said, smiling apologetically. "My purse was stolen last night, all my credit cards, IDs. Everything. I've spent the whole morning on the phone."

"What a nightmare."

"I know, right?" Meg said. "Look, I don't need to check the letters out or anything—just need to write down a few passages."

"I'm sorry." The girl frowned. "They're just really strict about that. The head of security, Mr. Vilhena, he can be really mean. Can't you just have them make you another ID?"

"I could, but it's the second one I've lost," Meg said. "And Mr. Vilhena was so nasty to me last time. So condescending."

"Did he say 'strike one'? He said that to me yesterday."

"Yes! And he called me 'darling,' but, like, in a

derogatory way. I really don't want strike two."

"I know what you mean." The girl chewed her lip for a moment. "I'm Melanie, by the way," she said, extending her hand.

"Tabitha," Meg said, firmly shaking. Her childhood cat had been named Tabitha.

The librarian's eyes darted this way and that, and then she said, "Come on, follow me."

She led Meg through a door labeled LEGACY ROOM and into a lavishly decorated parlor full of high-back leather chairs, antique furniture, and soft lighting.

"Have a seat and I'll bring you the letters," Melanie said. "But can you make it quick? We don't want you-know-who coming in here. You'd think it was the Pentagon for how often he asks to see IDs."

"I just need three minutes," Meg said.

Melanie stepped out, and Meg let her eyes drift around the room. It reminded her of the country club she and Fletcher had belonged to during their few years of plenty. Indeed, ignorance had been bliss. The thought of their former life brought a pang of longing, followed by a deeper pang of regret.

The sound of the door opening dragged her back into the present. "Here they are," Melanie said, handing her an archival folder and a pair of white cotton gloves. "I'm sure I don't need to remind you that these are as old as our country."

"I'll be very careful. And very quick."

"Great," Melanie said. "Call me if you need anything. Oh, and you've come unbuttoned." She pointed at Meg's shirt, hanging open.

"Oops!" Meg said, blushing. "Thanks."

"Don't get so close," Andrew said.

Dante shot him a look. "I know how to tail a car."

"This is different. We've got the GPS on them; we've got their position here." He gestured at the iPad on his lap. "And this car may as well have a big NOTICE ME sign in the windshield."

"It's a classic Mustang," Dante said. "If you don't love this car, you're not an American."

"The car's fine. It's the driver. Hey, they're getting off the next exit. Looks like we're going uptown."

"Tabitha," Melanie whispered. *"Psst!"*

It took Meg a moment to remember that she was Tabitha and tear herself from the project at hand.

"Yes?"

"He's coming. You need to go or he'll ask for your ID. He always checks in here first."

"Okay." Meg snapped one more picture and stuffed the last letter back into its plastic sleeve.

"Here," she said, handing the folder and gloves to Melanie. "Thank you so much."

She stepped out the door and nearly collided with a broad-shouldered man with silver hair and a black suit. A name badge clipped to his jacket pocket identified him as ANTHONY VILHENA, HEAD OF SECURITY.

"Pardon me, miss. May I ask what you were doing in the Legacy Room?"

Behind him, Melanie's face was a frozen mask of horror.

"Mr. Vilhena. Just the man I want to see. I had to duck into that room because a student has been stalking me, and I didn't want him to see me."

He drew down his brow. "What's his name?"

"David," she said. "David St. Hubbins."

Vilhena nodded slowly. "I think I've heard of him. Why don't we go fill out a formal complaint?"

"I'm sorry," Meg said. "I'm late for an appointment. I'll be happy to set up a meeting with you. This has to stop."

"Of course." He handed her an off-white business card. "My campus extension is here. I'm sorry for this trouble, and believe me, we'll get to the bottom of it." As Meg made for the door, she heard the man say, "The door to the Legacy Room is to be locked at all times. That's strike two for you, young lady."

Meg power walked back to the van as quickly as her three-inch heels would allow, climbed in, and threw the sliding door shut behind her.

"Where's Happy?" she asked.

"He's in the library," Fletcher answered. "Said he may as well use the time to research. I just texted him. Sounds like you did pretty well?"

She held up her phone. "They had six letters. I got shots of all of them."

"Front and back?"

"There was nothing written on the back."

Fletcher fought down a pained expression.

Meg sighed. "You want me to go back in?"

"No, that's okay. You did good in there. Kept it together."

"I've learned how to handle a crisis, Fletcher. The hard way."

They were both silent for a moment. Then Fletcher asked, "Isn't David St. Hubbins the lead singer of Spinal Tap?"

Meg shrugged. "First name that popped into my head."

The side door slid open again and Happy came flopping in, three heavy tomes in tow.

"Can you believe I had to sign up to audit a class just to get a library card?" he asked, incredulous. "I'm taking step aerobics. Tuesdays and Thursdays."

Fletcher started the engine. "What have you got there?"

"Some decent stuff. *The Knights Hospitalers*, *Monks of War*, and I've been reading this one: *Secret Societies and the French Revolution*. May be useful." He mopped the sweat from his brow and fought to catch his breath.

"Look at you." Fletcher pulled out onto the street. "You wouldn't make it through ten minutes of step aerobics."

Chapter 42

May 30, 1786
Paris, France

Cagliostro was called before La Parlement of Île-de-France in the early afternoon. He took to the witness seat like a peacock, wearing a coat of green silk embroidered with gold, his hair divided into tresses that met in the back and fell to his shoulders.

The attorney for the crown approached him with little attempt to mask his contempt. "Who are you and whence do you come?"

Cagliostro pursed his lips, as if he had never considered this question before, and answered in a bombastic voice, "I am an illustrious traveler."

The assemblage burst into laughter. Some cheered.

"What do you mean by this?" the attorney demanded.

"You do not truly wish to know the answer to your query, nor could you understand it. What the court will learn about me is that I have lately been a dupe of this woman, Madame de LaMotte. A convenient scapegoat. And why? Because I sought to help my friend the good cardinal avoid falling prey to her machinations. For that crime, a commissaire and a horde of policemen burst into my home last August the twenty-third, dragged me from my bedchamber, and helped themselves to many of my priceless elixirs, balms, and precious liquors. For this same crime I have been detained in the Bastille without a hearing for nine months, like a babe in the womb of injustice, before now being birthed to this place, where I will receive my freedom in the sight of all."

More cheering rose up from the gallery.

"Have you been listening to the testimony of those who came before you?"

"I have," said Cagliostro.

"You are aware, then, of the order of events presented to the court. You know that, when Cardinal de Rohan could not pay the first installment for the necklace, the jewelers Böhmer and Bassange sent an appeal to the queen."

"Indeed."

"And you heard Madame de LaMotte describe how you promised to use alchemy to multiply the diamonds so that each of you had the equivalent of the entire necklace?"

Cagliostro rolled his eyes. "Yes."

"Do you deny that you appear to be at the center of all of these events?"

"I do deny it, for you miss a simple and fundamental fact of the case. I did not arrive in Paris until January thirtieth of last year, at nine in the evening. There are many who can bear witness to this. However, the cardinal, by his own testimony, had already treated with the jewelers on the twenty-ninth of January."

The attorney opened his mouth to speak, but his words seemed to flee.

"You asked who I am and whence I come," Cagliostro said. "Perhaps I should start at the beginning." He leaned forward in his seat and spoke in a solemn tone. "I was born to Christian nobility and abandoned on the shores of the enchanted Island of Malta . . ."

Chapter 43

"Trick drives like an amateur," Andrew said.

"You mean I drive like a man, not a grandma?"

They were gathered back in the main auditorium of Broadmoor Outreach Tabernacle. Having cleared away the neat rows, they sat on folding chairs arranged in a circle like some sort of support group for grifters. Only in reverse.

"At any rate," Andrew said, "Belltower and Faust spent the whole morning in the Lodge of the Egyptian Mystery Rites."

"Cagliostro's sect," Fletcher said. "I'd like to be a fly on the wall in those meetings."

"Well, no luck there," Dante said. "Andrew Bishop, the famous grifter, was unable to talk his way into a senior citizens' clubhouse."

"You need a password. Why was I the one trying to get in anyway? Faust already knows my face."

"Have you seen *my* face?" Dante asked. "Ironically, it's not the right color for the Egyptian Mystery Rites."

"Tell me you had better luck than us," Andrew said.

"Meg came through," Fletcher said. "Got six letters and translated most of it on the way back."

"Hit us with the highlights," Andrew said.

Meg flipped through her notepad. "Well, something that comes up several times is a group of 647 allies. Is that how many Knights there were?"

Fletcher shook his head. "Anything more specific?"

"Twice he calls them *alliés chatoyantes*."

Fletcher felt his blood pump a little harder. Nothing was sexier than his wife speaking French. A look at Andrew's face told him he wasn't alone in this assessment. Fletcher gave him a hard glare. "What's that mean?" he asked.

"Oh, sorry. It's like, shimmering allies."

"Look that up for us, Happy," Fletcher said.

"Six hundred forty-seven shimmering allies."

Happy typed at his laptop for a few seconds. "Oh, there's a band called that. In fact, they're playing the Fox Theater tonight."

"Really?"

"No. Zero results."

"Money, maybe?" Andrew mused. "Gold coins?"

"Wait," Fletcher said. "*Diamantia.*"

"Come again?"

"When the Alchemist sent me to look in the altar at St. John the Baptist's, there were all these Greek words along the back. The one that opened up, popped me in the head, was *diamantia*. But all the others were Bible words. *Locusts, lions, judgment.* I don't think the word *diamonds* even occurs in the Scriptures."

Happy typed in a search on his laptop and announced, "Nope. Not in eight different translations."

"Then why would that be on the face of the altar cavity? Unless, at one time, there were diamonds in there. Try looking up *647 diamonds.*"

"Whoa," Happy said. "Now we've got some hits. Lots of them. They're all pretty much about the same thing: the Affair of the Diamond Necklace. Wait a minute." He pushed his laptop aside and began flipping through the books he'd checked out, muttering. "Here it is: when the Knights had to abandon the Island of Malta in 1798, they were only allowed to bring the skull of St. John. 'Witnesses claimed that an old cloth with a distinctive stain could be seen protruding from the eyes—a cloth rumored to contain innumerable diamonds.' "

"When I was at the altar," Fletcher said, "the Alchemist asked me more about the cloth than the septangle inside of it—especially how old it was. The original cloth could indicate the necklace nearby."

"Am I the only one here who doesn't know anything about this necklace?" Dante asked.

"It's not what you think of when you hear 'diamond necklace,' " Happy said. "It was like five necklaces in one, with diamond tassels hanging off it. This thing would put Mr. T to shame." He dumped the book and picked up his laptop. "Six hundred and forty-seven diamonds, 2,800 karats. Here's a replica." He turned the screen toward the others.

"That is ugly," Meg said.

"That's what Marie Antoinette thought," Fletcher agreed. "But even apart from the historical value, the diamonds alone would be worth a hundred million today, easy."

"Whatever happened to it?" Meg asked.

"No one knows for sure. The main grifter involved was a woman named Jeanne de LaMotte. It's assumed that she sent her husband to England to break down the necklace and sell the diamonds individually."

Andrew nodded. "A couple dozen of the scallops did turn up in London. But none of the real big rocks was ever seen again."

"I've always thought of that whole grift as kind of a mess," Fletcher said. "But if Cagliostro was the mastermind, we have to assume he meant for it to fall apart like that."

"Fall apart how?" Meg asked.

"It sort of caused the French Revolution. Even Napoleon said so."

Andrew rubbed his stubble. "But Cagliostro was no revolutionary."

"No," Fletcher agreed. "But what if it was all misdirection? You steal something that big and you need an epic distraction."

Andrew furrowed his brow for a moment. "If we zoom out, it does have all the pieces of a solid grift. Each player has a peg. De LaMotte wanted money, the jewelers wanted to unload the necklace. The cardinal wanted more power."

"What cardinal?" Dante asked.

"Prince Louis de Rohan."

"How could he be a cardinal and a prince?" Meg asked.

Happy laughed. "How could he not?"

"You've got the snare too," Andrew said. "I mean, what could the cardinal say in his defense —'Sorry, Your Highness, but I thought I was having an affair with your wife?' The guy even burned the supposed letters from the queen, even though they were the only possible evidence to get him off the hook."

"But what about the fix?" Fletcher asked. "Cagliostro's accomplices all turned on him. De LaMotte accused him of masterminding the whole thing, along with alchemy and blasphemy. He was locked in the Bastille for close to a year."

"Further stoking revolutionary sentiments," Andrew pointed out. "It made the king look like a bully. People loved Cagliostro. He was at the height of his rock-star fame when all this went down."

"And don't forget he was acquitted," Happy said.

Fletcher and Andrew wheeled.

"What?" Happy shrugged. "I read the Cagliostro memoir. I just thought it was bogus."

"So maybe he wanted to be tried," Andrew said, "so he could be completely exonerated. There are even apologists today who insist *he* was the victim of a long con, rather than a criminal mastermind. Just shows how good he was."

"Any object permanence?" Meg asked.

"Absolutely," Fletcher said. "They had a woman dress up as the queen and meet with the cardinal one night, and they made sure he saw de LaMotte's husband acting as the queen's valet, which fixed his place in the cardinal's mind. That's probably why he felt so good about handing the guy a hundred-million-dollar necklace."

Andrew slapped his knees. "This is the same game every grifter is working today and the same cons they were running in the twenties. It's Newman and Redford a hundred and fifty years earlier."

"Butch and Sundance?" Meg asked.

"No, *The Sting*. All the elements are the same: the Roper, the Inside Man, the cast—only Cagliostro is all of them and everyone else is a mark. And a fall guy. Think about that; at the end of the day, everyone but Cagliostro paid the price. The cardinal lost his titles and was banished; de LaMotte was sentenced to life in prison and her husband to life in the galleys. Marie Antoinette was beheaded. The whole country was plunged into chaos, and Cagliostro got to sail away from it all while throngs of admirers cheered and wished him well. What does this tell us?"

"That people get hurt," Meg said. "There's always collateral damage."

Andrew balked. "I was thinking more like: Cagliostro got his hands on the necklace and then disposed of everyone else."

"Agreed," Fletcher said. "But we need something solid to go on. Some direction for our next step."

"How about a name?" Meg underlined a word on her notepad and turned it toward the group. "He said he had entrusted the location of the shimmering allies to José Pinto da Fonseca. Whoever that is. And he gave the Grand Master the key to identify it."

"A literal key?" Happy asked.

"No, a number: 19.12."

Chapter 44

Ivy was sitting on the floor behind Courtney, braiding her hair and whispering seeds of dissent in her ear.

"A lot of girls at my old school had moms in jail," she said. "Did you know you can make a knife out of a toothbrush? Maybe we can get that guy to give us each a toothbrush."

Courtney twisted around and asked, "How do you make it into a knife?"

"I think you just sharpen it against a brick or something."

"Do you have a brick with you?"

"No," Ivy said, and returned to braiding.

"Just forget that stuff, okay? We can't escape. Whatever these guys want from your dad, I'm sure he'll give it to them and they'll just let us go."

"I doubt it," Ivy said. "My dad hasn't really been there for me much."

"Well, I'm not picking a fight with that guy out there. You don't know what they did to me. And there's not just one of them. There's, like, three, and the other two are even bigger and meaner."

"There's only one now," Ivy said. "And if you don't want them to hurt you again, we need to get away. You can stay behind if you want, but I'm getting out next chance I see. He talks to me like I'm a baby because I'm small. But I'm going to surprise him. I'm tough. I went to the worst school in America when I lived here."

Courtney scoffed. "Was it a nursery school?"

Ivy's brow sharpened. "No. And I saw some really bad—"

Both girls jumped at the sound of the door opening. The man dumped a McDonald's bag on the floor.

"Got you some hamburgers."

"Am I going to be able to brush my teeth?" Ivy asked sweetly.

"Nope," he answered. "And you get one more visit to the bathroom tonight, so you better wait until you've really got to go. Now watch your shows and eat your burgers." He disappeared from view for a moment and then reappeared, rolling two bottles of water toward them. "Keep behaving," he said, "and you'll get out of this alive."

✠

Fletcher was filling up Ivy's air mattress, upon which he would be trying to sleep, when he heard his wife's phone ring. He killed the little electric pump and listened.

"Oh, hi," she said. "No, not yet. I've been praying, though, and I have a good feeling. Courtney's a smart girl. She'll turn up." Meg met Fletcher's eyes, and he suddenly realized that he was glaring. Covering the mouthpiece with her hand, she retreated to a corner of the building for a more private conversation.

Fletcher knew he couldn't justify the rage he was feeling. How could anyone blame Brad for following up on every possible lead in finding his daughter, in seeking out anyone who might bring him comfort in all the uncertainty? He turned the pump back on. Another segment of the mattress opened up, revealing a tattered picture of their family, taken the Christmas before he'd been arrested. Fletcher had noticed the photo taped to the wall next to Ivy's bed upon first arriving home from prison.

He wanted to cry, but he knew he couldn't. If he broke down now, Meg would too. Then neither of them would be any use.

A few hours earlier they had ordered in dirt-cheap pizza, which tasted predictably like dirt, and continued fleshing out their theory. For her part, Meg had done a more comprehensive translation of all the letters, and the whole group had gone through them word by word. And still, their only leads were that name, José Pinto da Fonseca, and that number, 19.12. The Internet had identified the man as Grand Master Manuel da Fonseca's illegitimate son, but there was little information available beyond that. Midevening, Happy had lost faith in the information super-highway for the fifth time that week and gone old-school, combing through his books, pen in hand.

The first signs of fatigue had manifested themselves in Fletcher's mind and body at about ten and, knowing he needed to be well-rested in order to be effective, he had suggested they ready their bedding. Meg had reacted harshly, intimating that she would not sleep at all until Ivy was safe in her arms again. Fletcher had not pursued the debate.

Meg walked back into sight, pocketing her phone and rubbing at her eyes. Fletcher screwed the valve cover into place on the air mattress and walked over to his wife, reaching out to comfort her. She slipped to the side and said, "Don't."

✠

Courtney held firm in her principles through dinner and the hour that followed, while Ivy turned up the volume on *Spongebob Squarepants* and, in a complete reversal of roles, delivered an unbroken stream of whispered peer pressure to her older friend. Only instead of suggesting clandestine trips to the church attic with a boy, Ivy was lobbying for an uprising.

Now in the bathroom, having stalled as long as she could—the toilets all flushed, hands and faces washed and rewashed—Courtney had apparently realized she could not sway her young friend.

"Okay," she whispered, "but let me be the one to spray him."

"Are you sure?"

"I'm taller," she said. "I'll get him in the eyes and you run to the door and see if it's locked from the inside. I'll kick him where it really counts."

Ivy grabbed both of Courtney's hands, stood on her tiptoes, and pushed her forehead against Courtney's.

"What are you doing?" Courtney whispered.

"Dear Jesus, help us escape right now. Help Courtney's aim be good and let the door be unlocked. Or else, please help my dad come through so we can go home. And forgive us for our sins. I love you, Jesus. Amen."

She dropped Courtney's hands, handed her the aerosol can, and knocked on the door. "We're all done," she called.

✠

Several years earlier Dante had transformed the roof of the church into a rather nice patio, complete with furniture and fire pit, which was of course illegal, but the police response threshold in the neighborhood had long since passed from zoning infractions to *shots fired*.

The grifters felt the cool night air revive them. Meg had tried calling the Alchemist on the burner phone ten times, intent on speaking with Ivy, but was met each time with a recording informing her that the voicemail box had not been set up.

The discussion on the roof turned back to William Belltower and how he might be wrapped up in all this.

"That lodge could be the key," Fletcher said. "A point where Cagliostro reaches through the centuries to connect with the very guy the Alchemist had us grift."

Dante sipped on a bottle of mineral water and asked, "You think maybe the lodge is the secret society Cagliostro and Fonseca started?"

"No, the lodges were just a way to generate capital and create an enduring network for his grifts. Brilliant scam; he claimed to be 'restoring' Egyptian Freemasonry, but he was just making it up as he went."

Andrew took a puff on his cigar. "And it might have aided the diamond heist—if the revolution really was a bit of misdirection that spun out of control. A lot of revolutionary thought was fomented and fermented in those lodges."

Fletcher nodded. "The count knew how to read the times. It was the Enlightenment, and all the long-held doctrines of the church were falling away, which left people chomping at the bit for anything supernatural. Not unlike today, really. Look at the titles on the bestseller list: New Age stuff, spiritualism, build-your-own god . . . odd for a 'secular' society."

Andrew grinned. "My man found the peg of all Western society and turned it. Egyptian Freemasonry, séances, phantasmagoria . . ."

"What's that?" Dante asked.

"You've heard the expression 'smoke and mirrors'?" Happy said. "That's phantasmagoria —the art of creating ghosts and phantoms by projecting images into smoke using a mirror and lenses. Overwhelm the senses, and the mark is yours. Same thing with alchemy. It was all misdirection."

Andrew examined the embers at the end of his cigar. "Cagliostro knew his marks. I mean, if you or I see a candle melted onto a human skull, we think cartoons, bad tattoos . . . but not in the eighteenth century."

Meg, who had been staring silently into the light-polluted sky, spoke up. "Why does he call himself the Alchemist if people aren't falling for smoke and mirrors anymore?"

"It's not about wizards in a laboratory trying to mix magic with science," Andrew said, exhaling smoke. "Sure, most dabblers in alchemy were just trying to turn common metals into gold. As a short con, you could do worse. I mean, no one really wins, but no one really wins three-card monte either, and that's still around.

"But alchemy grew in prominence for more than a thousand years. That's not a fad; that's not a get-rich-quick scheme. At its deepest levels, alchemy is about distilling a thing down to its essence."

Happy nodded. "And some brilliant people have been into it. Isaac Newton, Queen Elizabeth, Carl Jung, half the Manhattan Project . . ."

"But to Cagliostro, it was just a grift," Fletcher said. "That's what set his Egyptian Rite apart from all the other forms of Masonry: the promise that by the time you reach master Mason, you would have mastered alchemy too—meaning the ability to create gold from other substances and home-brew the Elixir of Life."

"And he had a ready supply of marks," Andrew said. "He'd find guys who had hit the ceiling in the Scottish Rite or York Rite, and offer them a chance to attain something higher, purer, and more mysterious. That's a strong peg."

"I'm really starting to hate this guy," Meg said.

Andrew snuffed out his cigar. "Don't hate the grifter; hate the grift."

✠

The bathroom door opened and the man with the scar walked in. When he was just two feet away, Ivy leapt to the side. She looked back and saw Courtney raise the bottle up toward his face and punch the nozzle. The disinfectant came shooting back in her eyes. Courtney screamed.

Ivy's first thought was about blondes and cheerleaders and how stupid they could be, but then the bottle came rolling in her direction. She nabbed it up and unleashed a stream of cleaner into the man's face. He shielded his eyes with his hand while closing the gap between them, knocked the bottle from her grasp, and threw her six feet into the bathroom door.

The impact knocked the breath from her lungs. The kick that came next hurt more than anything she'd ever experienced—physically, at least. Dazed and defeated, she slumped to the ground. The sound of water running and furious splashing let her know that at least she'd managed to hurt the man. Courtney's sobbing just confirmed for her what she should have already known: Courtney was unreliable.

Next time Ivy would escape on her own.

She felt the man grab her up roughly with wet hands. He carried her with impatient strides to the door of the room that had become her cell and ejected her onto the sleeping bags. The door slammed and the lock turned behind him.

Ivy sat up and gingerly felt the back of her head. There would be a bump there, but it would be worth it. No blindfold this time. She now had the lay of the land between this room and the bathroom. She had seen the way out.

Then she heard Courtney's muffled screaming.

Chapter 45

While Andrew and Fletcher were turning in, Dante slipped out, mumbling something about an errand. He made the fifteen-minute drive to the Warehouse in less than ten, parked on the street, and locked his Glock in the glove box.

A thick-necked nondescript in a black suit met him at the door and told him to wait there.

A minute later Marcus Brinkman emerged, barking, "Give me your phone. Arms up."

Dante complied, and a moment later he was allowed to enter the Warehouse.

"You got a lot of nerve asking for this sit-down, being five hundred large in the hole," Marcus said. "I know you can talk, Trick, but there's no talking your way out of this."

Dante nodded.

"Follow me, then," Marcus said. He led him to the middle of the vast building where a large free-standing room had been erected. From without, it was a big ugly cube covered in metal beams, conduit, and insulation. Dante had only been here once before. It was neutral ground. Nothing illicit was permitted, which made it a safe place to meet without fear that one party would pull a double cross and tip off the cops. The steel frame and wire mesh on the outside contained any signal from a cell phone or informant's wire.

But the inside was dry-walled, carpeted, and outfitted like the kind of swanky boardroom you might find near the top of the Renaissance Center. Marcus opened the door and motioned for Dante to enter.

"Three minutes." He closed the door.

Sitting at the head of the table, hands folded before her, was the most beautiful woman Dante had ever seen.

"Hello, Mr. Watkins," she said. "It's good to finally meet you in person after all these years." Her tone was professionally distant but nowhere near hostile.

Dante opened his mouth but found no words in the chamber. All of his dealings with Bella Donna had been through Marcus. None of his criminal colleagues had ever seen her either. He'd heard occasional vague tales of her beauty, but they hadn't prepared him for this.

For the first time in memory, Trick couldn't talk.

Dante had expected Bella Donna to be Italian, with dark hair, chestnut eyes, and olive skin—the female equivalent of a Mafia don. But she was blond, blue-eyed, and fair-skinned. Her long, shiny hair looked like it had been carefully put up that morning but was now just beginning to fall. He guessed her to be somewhere between forty-five and fifty.

Finally finding his voice, Dante said, "I, uh, wanted to talk to you about the money I owe you."

Bella Donna leaned back and crossed her legs, her shiny stockings glistening under the fluorescent lights, derailing Dante's line of thought again.

"Five hundred thousand dollars," she said. "Do you have it?"

"I have some of it," he said, cringing as her eyes darkened. "But I'm gaining momentum. I have two new lines of income going—neither steps on your interests and both are very lucrative."

"How much do you have?" she asked, half interested.

"About a hundred."

"Do I strike you as someone who would accept twenty percent of what you owe me?"

"No, ma'am, not normally. But I've been a lucrative player in the organization for some time, and I just figured you'd rather have the money and my continued services, rather than neither."

A smile bit at the corner of her mouth. "What is this new enterprise?" she asked.

"It's a fund-raiser. Very vague, very hard to confirm, but easy to sell. You know me; I can *talk*. If you want, I'll gladly resume my ordinary duties and also work this angle. And I wouldn't even ask for a cut. I'll do it indefinitely until you think I've made up for my mistakes."

"Mr. Watkins, do you know what I hate in a man?"

"No."

"Desperation."

Dante felt like he'd been punched in the stomach again. "I'm, uh, sorry if I come across as—"

"A better question: Do you know why they call me Bella Donna?"

He wet his lips. "Because you're, uh, a beautiful lady."

"No. In fact, it's the name of a plant. It was used to dilate the pupils of young ladies because they thought this made them more beautiful and seductive. For years women did this, assuming it to be safe, harmless—and in small doses, it can be. But when used carelessly, belladonna is a deadly poison. Do you understand?"

"I think so."

"Do you think I'm beautiful?"

Dante nodded.

"Do you think I'm harmless?"

"No."

"Good. Now, if you don't have something more impressive to offer me, I'm afraid this sit-down has cost you one day off your grace period. The full five hundred thousand dollars will be due Saturday night at six."

"I understand." Dante pushed himself up from the chair. He paused for a moment and sat again.

"You know what? I *do* have something more impressive."

Bella Donna sighed. "Well, what is it?"

"Do you like diamonds?"

Chapter 46

Fletcher awoke just before six, feeling ragged but oddly alert. He went up to the roof with a notion to watch the sunrise and pray. His thoughts kept him preoccupied, though, and he reentered the building twenty minutes later without having spoken to the Great Architect.

He found Happy buzzing around, plugging his laptop into a projector in the sanctuary, and Dante brewing a pot of coffee in the back. Against the wall, Meg was asleep on her air mattress, one of Happy's library books hugged to her chest, another next to her, and her Bible wedged under her shoulder. Fletcher chuckled. He'd found Ivy in a similar state of entanglement with her own books on more than one morning.

He reached down and carefully extracted the Bible, which fell open, ejecting a vast collection of sermon notes, bookmarks, and the like. Fletcher knelt and began gathering the items. Something caught his eye. It was a small greeting card, lying open and signed with a big "Love, Brad."

Fletcher knew he should just pile it together with the rest and put it all back in the well-loved Bible, but instead he pocketed it and set the Bible next to the mattress. Relocating to the small unisex bathroom, he retrieved the card and examined it. The front was teal with a big cartoon heart in the middle and read "You Are Loved."

He opened the card. "Gorgeous, I know you feel completely abandoned, but I hope you know there's someone who will never abandon you. Love, Brad."

Fletcher read the card twice, then slid it back into his pocket.

"Are we gonna talk all day or are we gonna do something?" Happy asked, standing at the lectern and bouncing with all the enthusiasm of a motivational speaker.

"Did you sleep at all?" Fletcher asked.

"No, no, no," he said quickly. "But I had two of those little bottles of 8-Hour Gusto. Eight and eight makes sixteen. Next question, please."

Andrew picked up one of the empties from the floor by Happy's feet. "It says, 'Not a substitute for sleep' right on it."

"Yeah, but then it has the little winky-face emoticon."

Andrew took a seat facing Happy. "What have you got for us?"

"So glad you asked." He slapped the back of

his hand against his palm three times in rapid succession. "Meg and I were up all night reading and researching—you're welcome—and we have a plan to determine the whereabouts of the necklace."

Fletcher and Andrew groaned.

"What's the problem?" Meg asked.

"We don't let Happy plan out jobs," Fletcher said.

"Why not? He's a genius."

"A genius at logistics? Yes. A computer genius? Sure. Genius with big-picture stuff? Not so much." He shifted toward Happy. "Do you want to tell her about the Canadian quarter scheme or shall I?"

Happy flushed. "It would work," he said, pounding the pulpit. "If you would just give it a chance."

"Okay then, run us through it," Fletcher said. "If Meg thinks it holds water, we'll follow your lead today."

"Fine." Happy sat on the edge of the platform, his feet hanging down. "As a fellow Canadian, you'll appreciate this, Meg." He took a tug off a Watt Energy Drink and cracked his neck. "My first month in the Great Lakes State, I noticed that sometimes when I'd buy something with cash, there would be a Canadian coin in my change— usually pennies and nickels, but occasionally a quarter. I would then spend those coins along with American currency, and no one thought anything of it. The people of this city consider a Canadian quarter to be worth twenty-five cents. Only it's worth more like twenty-three cents.

"So I had this idea. A vision, really. We take, like, fifty thousand dollars to Canada, convert it to Canadian currency. Go to a few banks and exchange the notes for quarters, then bring them back."

"Bring them back, how?" Fletcher interrupted.

"In a . . . dump truck. Anyway, you slowly launder the quarters through a chain of restaurants or convenience stores or something, giving out a Canadian quarter for every few American quarters and you wind up almost five thousand bucks ahead at the end of the day."

"Minus the cost of the dump truck," Andrew said.

"Eh, you could use a U-Haul and just make multiple trips."

"And do you know someone who owns a chain of restaurants who would launder your Canadian money for free?" Fletcher asked.

"Shut up."

Andrew snorted. "How about you stick to the gadgets and let me and Fletcher plan the scores, huh?"

Meg sighed. "We were up most of the night working on this. Are you going to listen or not?"

"Sorry," Fletcher said. "Proceed."

"Okay, hang on." Happy jumped to his feet and raced back to the podium. He pressed a button on his laptop, and the projection screen behind them filled with an image of Cagliostro.

"Oh boy, there's a slide show," Andrew droned. "Super."

Happy ignored him. "The secret society that Fonseca and Cagliostro founded has never really been identified." He glanced down at his notes and found his place. "In his novels, Alexandre Dumas portrayed Cagliostro as the head of the Illuminati, a nefarious international cabal." He clicked to the next slide, a collage of graphics from conspiracy websites. "While this is not entirely untrue, it's based in exaggerated tales. This was no central conspiracy designed to rule the world—just a plan by a few people with a lot of power to hang on to it for a bit longer. They saw the winds of change coming and decided to be proactive—kind of the opposite of an IPO."

Andrew raised his hand. "I thought you said we weren't going to talk all morning."

"Let him get to the point," Dante said.

"Thank you. It seems to Meg and me that this group, drawing its resources from the Egyptian Mystery lodges, was very powerful during the French Revolution and for a while afterward, but quickly lost steam in the nineteenth century. By 1820, even the trail of rumors seems to disappear."

"So how does that help?" Andrew asked.

"We think the group still exists, after a fashion," Meg said. "Show them the picture."

Happy clicked to the next slide—one of the letters from the college library.

"Now look here," he said, pointing off to the side of the screen. Next to the letter sat the acid-free plastic sleeve in which the page was kept. "Do you see what it says?" Happy asked. They could all make it out: "This letter on loan from Fonseca, Intl."

Happy clicked again to the next slide, this one a screenshot from the website for Fonseca, International, featuring an impressive upward-angled shot of a six-story office building. "We need to get into that place."

"*That's* Cagliostro's secret society?" Andrew asked.

"Yeah, but they're a lot less secret these days. Multinational holdings are their bag, along with enough philanthropy to make them look benevolent. And their world headquarters are on Telegraph Road, in this building."

Fletcher snuffed. "Times are tough. Even the Illuminati has had to downsize."

"It doesn't live up to the old rumors, sure, but if anyone still knows how Cagliostro gave José Pinto da Fonseca the location of the necklace or what the heck 19.12 means, it's them."

Fletcher crossed his arms. "But if this is the group lobbying for the Knights to carry on in the footsteps of Fonseca, wouldn't the Alchemist be part of it?"

"No way," Happy said. "If he were, he wouldn't need us. He'd already have access. I'm convinced that our best chance to find the necklace is to make a copy of all their files and run a search algorithm for anything involving Cagliostro, either Rohan, or either Fonseca."

"You can hack into their computers, then?" Dante asked.

Happy fiddled with his notes. "I'm afraid that's impossible. I was poking around the Deep Web last night, and it turns out Fonseca's famous among hackers for their inaccessible network. You absolutely cannot get in from an outside connection. And their redundant backups are all on-site as well—some ultra-innovative system, probably heavy encryption, mixed with some sort of old-school backup system. They don't want to risk someone like me finding a back door in."

"So what, then?" Dante asked.

Happy grinned. "I think I can stroll right in the front door and make us a copy."

"You?" Andrew practically shouted.

"Hear me out—"

"No," Fletcher said. "Bad things happen when you leave the van."

"But I won't be *myself*. I'll be Scott Sprague, their IT manager." Happy flipped to the next slide: a screenshot of Scott Sprague's LinkUp page, the sight of which was met by an initial wall of silence.

Finally Fletcher said, "Uh, Happy . . . that guy's Korean."

"Yeah, I'll dye my hair black. I'm committed, man."

"Umm . . ."

"Show them his profile pictures," Meg said.

Happy began flipping through candid photos of Scott. "See? He's always got that Tigers cap pulled down over his eyes. Same thick-framed glasses and denim jacket every day. At home"—he clicked from picture to picture—"out about town. This one's at work, setting up in a conference room. And look: always face-deep in that smartphone."

"Object permanence, right?" Meg said. "The mind fills in the rest."

"The network, the backup—it's all on-site," Happy said. "But if I can get into that server room, I can upload a virus and make their computer think the latest backup has been corrupted. With any luck, it'll wipe the hard drive and begin restoring from the second newest full backup, decrypting and reencrypting as it copies, and I'll be there, siphoning the ones and zeroes onto this." He held up a large external hard drive.

"Still seems like a lot of risk for a long shot," Andrew said.

"Long shot?" Happy bounced on his toes a few

times. "Let's look a little closer at this picture, shall we?" He zoomed in on a framed document, partially visible on the conference room wall behind Scott Sprague. It was aged and yellowed, but they could all make out two Greek letters in the lower right corner, followed by the number 19.12.

"That's our map," Andrew said.

Dante stood and walked right up to the screen, craning his neck as if another angle would allow him to see the rest of the document. "But how are we going to find that room?" he asked, examining the image. "Walk up and down every hall on all six floors?"

Happy smiled and shook his head. "No need. This picture was taken with a smartphone, which means it's geocoded." He clicked back to the slide of the office building. "The coordinates are right here on the east side of the building. Also embedded in the image are the date and time it was taken, which, along with the angle of the shadows from the sun, gave me the room's elevation." He rose up on his tiptoes and pointed at a window. "Here's our target. Get me down to that server, and I think I can disable the alarms."

Andrew was perking up. "Finally, a real grift."

"There's just one more thing," Happy said, clicking back to the picture of the conference room. He zoomed back out and panned to the right. There in a niche in the wall, lit from above and covered over by glass, was the Valletta Monstrance.

Andrew, too, was on his feet now, approaching the screen. Only Meg and Fletcher remained in their seats.

"If you're making another grab for the monstrance, I can't be anywhere near this," Fletcher said. "My parole officer knows I'm in the city. I did six years for trying to steal that thing."

Andrew scratched his neck. "So Fletcher's in the van and Happy's going in. What could possibly go wrong?"

"You serious?" Dante said. "Everything could go wrong here! There are people you do not grift: syndicate bosses, mob lieutenants, guys with a long reach and an even longer memory. Guys you can never give the fix because they own all the action. You cross them, and the whole city is dead to you. You'd have to pick up and move. But these guys"—he pointed at the screen—"you say they're worldwide, positioned high up in every government. You don't grift the Illuminati! Am I outta line here?"

"What choice do we have?" Andrew asked.

"How are you even going to get in there?"

"Building codes," Happy answered.

"What?"

"They've gone legit—on the grid. At least this aspect of their organization. They're not meeting in underground secret lairs anymore. They have to let the fire inspector in."

Fletcher tipped back in his chair. "Dante, you're the only one here the police haven't grilled about that monstrance. You think you can talk your way past the front desk?"

"Don't worry about me; I can talk."

Fletcher was dubious. "And Happy's going to be Scott the IT guy? Are we really doing this?"

Andrew smirked. "We're both going to be Scott the IT guy."

Chapter 47

April 1, 1789
Rome

The inn was crowded and filled with the din of talking, dining, and occasional bursts of laughter, which suited Cagliostro's purposes. The two men who sat with him were well dressed and well collected, their cloaks and swords of the finest quality. They listened carefully to the count's practiced invitation.

Upon his release from the Bastille, Cagliostro had set sail first for England, then Naples, Turin, and finally Rome. He had hoped to arrive in Rome much sooner, but every element in his Great Design had to be in place, and some were beyond his control. So he waited.

"And I, the Grand Kophta and High Priest of Egypt, offer you far more than fraternity, position, and enlightenment," he said. "I offer you a path to restore your primitive state of innocence, which was lost by original sin. Our symbols include not only the compass and square but the septangle, death's head, the wooden bridge, and the phoenix. Through these we rise beyond mere mortality.

"Our art is an ancient one. Through the ages, the Secret Superiors of our order have included Moses, Elijah, and Christ himself. Their powers have come down to me, and I am likewise able to transmit my powers to the master of each lodge. If you wish to confirm my claims, there are scores in France, England, Sicily, the Netherlands, and even America who can bear witness. When I first spoke publicly of the secrets I possess, it was in The Hague before hundreds who, upon hearing my words, were caught up in such a state of heavenly bliss that many of them became like statues and did not move for more than a day."

"What think you of the Scottish Rite?" asked one of the men.

Cagliostro scoffed. "Many have attained the highest degrees of Masonry in the Scottish Rite and yet remain as base and earthly in their thoughts as the uninitiated. What I offer is as much purer than the Scottish Rite as the crisp, clear waters of the Nile are clearer than what runs through the sewers of Paris."

"It took us nearly a decade to rise to the status of Master Mason in the Scottish Rite," said the other man. "We have no desire to start over from the first."

Cagliostro bobbed his head and looked at the men as if considering the purchase of a new coat. "Considering your foundation in the concepts of Masonry, I believe I can offer you an expedited journey to the highest ranks of the pure and primitive lodge."

"How much expedited?"

"If you renounce your former lodge and devote yourself to the Egyptian Mysteries, within a year you will be Master Masons again."

The men nodded happily. In truth, they were not Masons at all, but spies of the Inquisition. And within a year, they would see the great Cagliostro arrested, imprisoned, and condemned to death.

Chapter 48

"He checks in here with his 4Corners account every morning at about seven forty-five," Andrew scoffed. "How can you be a yuppie and a hippy at the same time?"

"That's been a thing for, like, a decade," Happy said. "He's a hipster. Sort of."

They were in the parking lot of EnerJuice Boost!, an organic smoothie shop squeezed in between a medical marijuana dispensary and a health food store.

"That's him," Meg said from the passenger seat. "Let's go."

She and Andrew left the van, staggering their approach so that Scott Sprague, who barely even looked up from his phone to slip through the door, was sandwiched between them in line.

Standing behind him, Meg reprised a bimbo she'd played in a production a few years back, wearing little denim shorts and a tank top that had been in a bin with a number of similar garments in Andrew's storage space and that he had not wanted to discuss.

"Berry-pomegranate Pep," she read from the menu, mispronouncing pomegranate. "Pacific Passion Probiotic Blend?" She put her hand softly on Scott's shoulder. "What do you get here?"

He looked up from his phone, annoyance all over his face until he saw Meg's—her eyes wide and heavily painted with glittery makeup, modeled after a character from a sci-fi show to whom the IT professional before her was engaged to be married, if one was to believe his online profile.

"I, uh, get the Whole Fruit Pre-boost Mango with an extra post-boost," he answered.

The woman at the counter called, "Next!" and

Andrew approached, quietly ordering Scott's regular while Meg giggled and asked him, "Say that again? That's a mouthful!"

Scott pocketed his phone and repeated the drink name, waiting after each word for Meg to echo it back to him. She got tongue-twisted again and burst into laughter.

"Next!" called the woman behind the counter. Scott excused himself, ordered his drink, then pointed toward Meg and said, "I've got hers too."

"I guess I'll have the Karamel Karma Ice Mocha," she said, feeling a pang of guilt. She'd gotten the girl in the library reprimanded—one strike closer to who-knows-what—and now she was going to break this poor guy's heart and use his ID to help her husband's old criminal cohort carry out the very crime that had landed Fletcher in jail. Things were escalating quickly. She saw Andrew receiving his drink at the counter and furtively mixing in a cocktail of fast-acting tranquilizers, which Happy had dubbed the Happy Napper and described as "GHB on GHB."

Then she thought of Ivy and refocused on the plan and her character. Andrew had left his smoothie on the counter and taken a phone call from no one.

"No! A verbal contract is still a contract," he said, swiping at the air. "I'm at the smoothie place! Keep him there."

"Oh my gosh. Don't look at that guy," Meg whispered.

"Order for Scott!"

Meg leaned up to Scott's ear. "Wait a second," she said. "He's staring at you."

"What? Why?"

"I don't know. He's just—wait, no, he's leaving." She gestured at the two drinks on the counter. "It's a nice morning to have a smoothie outside. Or are you in a hurry to get to work?"

"I make my own hours," Scott said.

"I think you should at least tape his wrists," Andrew said. They were now six in the van—five of them conscious—and it was getting crowded.

"That's a little serial killer, isn't it?" Fletcher said.

"Right, and we're kidnappers," Meg said. "Oh my gosh, I'm a kidnapper. I'm just like them."

"He's not a kid," Happy said. "And by the time he wakes up, he'll be back in his car. Now help me get his jacket off."

"And then we tape his wrists," Andrew repeated.

"He'll be out for at least four hours. We only need two."

"I say we let Fletcher decide. He's the one staying in the van with him the whole time."

Fletcher glanced over at Meg and said, "We're not kidnappers and we're not taping his hands.

We're just borrowing some stuff." He took the denim jacket from Happy and compared it to the three they'd found in the storage space, deciding on the closest match. "This one," he said, rolling it up tight and handing it to Andrew. "And these glasses. Almost exactly the same frames."

"We may have a problem here," Happy announced. He was extracting the contents of Scott's wallet and lining it all up on the counter. "I can't find a key card or a fob or anything that might get us in the door at Fonseca."

"Biometrics?" Andrew asked. "Maybe his thumbprint?"

"I can probably copy that. Let's scan him first, though."

Meg was covering her nose and mouth with both hands. "Am I the only one who feels bad for him?"

"This is your plan, Meg," Andrew answered.

"I know, but he seems like a nice guy. What if he loses his job over this?"

"What if he does?" Fletcher said. "Whether he knows it or not, Scott here works for an evil corporation whose unwritten mission statement is to sway a thousand-year-old religious organization away from caring for the poor and back toward global conquest. The guy should thank us."

Andrew put a hand on Meg's shoulder. "It's no big deal," he assured her. "I slipped a little something into his drink. Think of it as a prank."

"Like you did at the Metro Museum?" Fletcher asked.

"Huh?"

"Your fellow security guards—you give them food poisoning so I'd have to fill in?"

Andrew shrugged. "Well, yeah. I dosed them with Happy's salmonella-E. coli frap. I assumed you knew that."

"Broke the water main too, didn't you? At that megachurch? Made sure we'd wind up at the place with the laser trip wires and the book full of Maltese treasures."

Andrew looked away.

"Yeah, I thought so."

"Keep it down," Happy said. "I'm working here."

"What is that thing?" Meg asked, pointing at a bulky wand in Happy's hand. He had run it over the contents of Scott's wallet and was now making a slow run over his prone form.

"I call it the Happy Scanner," he said. "It'll find any kind of passive tag or chip. Also useful when sweeping a room for bugs." The device squealed, low and quiet at first, and then louder and higher as it approached Scott's hat.

"Clever," Dante said. "I guess that's why he never takes it off."

"We'll need two," Andrew said. "Can you clone the chip?"

"Maybe," Happy said. "Cousin to the chip

Fletcher gave Julian Faust in the business card. I have the equipment; it just takes awhile."

"In the meantime," Andrew said, shaking a bottle of black spray-in hair dye, "we've got other preparations to make."

———

The foyer of Fonseca's international headquarters smelled of chlorine due to the elaborate fountain shooting several arcs of water up past the mezzanine. On the far wall, large block letters spelled out the words LAYING THE GROUND-WORK FOR AN ORDERED WORLD.

Happy held the door for Dante as they entered and fell in a step behind him, staring down at Scott Sprague's phone but seeing only a fuzzy mess through the thick lenses of another man's prescription. He'd been wearing them for less than two minutes and already felt a headache setting in.

Dante broke off toward the front desk, and Happy made a beeline for the men's room, rehefting the brown leather messenger bag onto his shoulder. He could feel the sticky hair dye on the back of his ears, and he wanted to check how badly it was running. His case for a real dye job had been unanimously overruled. There simply wasn't time.

Approaching the tall, circular desk, Dante offered a friendly "Good morning" to the man behind it. "My name is Pat Crosby, and I'm here to follow up with Mr. Tanner about a grant application."

"Do you have an appointment?" the man asked.

"No, but I just need five minutes of his time to clarify a couple things," Dante said.

"We have an appointment-only policy here. Let me give you an e-mail address where you can—"

"Look," Dante said, leaning on the desk. "We're busy men, aren't we? I've got about thirty minutes until my next appointment with a donor, and let me tell you, whoever funds this inner-city laptop initiative is looking at a lot of good press. I can guarantee Channel 3's Hometown Hero award. You can't buy that kind of good will—especially not for fifteen thousand dollars."

"Our philanthropic arm just built two new wells in Uganda," the man said. "We're not worried about publicity."

"Could you just get Mr. Tanner on the phone so I can ask him?"

Chapter 49

In the van, Andrew was carefully applying a thick moustache to his upper lip with spirit gum. The color nearly matched his newly sprayed black hair.

"Remember," he said to Meg. "You love me, and you're sure there's another woman in the mix. Jealousy all over the place."

"Got it," Meg said.

Fletcher nodded. "Jealousy's a powerful motivator." He could feel the card from Brad in his pocket. His phone buzzed in the other. "Dante's in," he said, reading the text.

Andrew double-checked his moustache and donned a pair of big tinted lenses. "Start the clock when I hit the front door," he said to Meg. "Three minutes."

He circled around the side of the parking lot and approached the office building from the west. There were two men in suits waiting in the foyer and a man standing at a reception desk.

"Excuse me," Andrew said, approaching the desk. "I was supposed to meet a man here about ten minutes ago. His name is Pat Crosby. Black guy, about yea tall."

"Ah, yes. He's in a meeting with one of our public relations managers. I don't imagine it will take long. Why don't you have a seat?"

———

"Right in here," Wesley Tanner said. The short, round man opened the door to a small meeting room and fumbled for the light switch.

"I appreciate you taking this meeting on such short notice," Dante said.

"Well, I only have a couple minutes, but you're a very persuasive man." He took a chair and invited Dante to do the same. "I have to admit that we're a little behind in processing grant requests, Mr. Crosby. So if you could give me the elevator pitch . . ."

"We're trying to help fatherless kids," Dante said. "I need about four hundred thousand dollars and I need it by tomorrow night at six, or I'm a dead man."

Meg stalked into the foyer, eyes smoldering and scanning, streaks of mascara running down her cheeks. She spotted Andrew and extended an accusatory finger at him.

"I knew it!" she shrieked. Every eye locked onto her.

Happy slipped out of the men's room and moved quickly down a short hall. As he approached a heavy door at the end of the hall, he heard the lock click off.

He felt like a Jedi.

Mr. Tanner laughed. Dante didn't.

"Four hundred thousand. You're joking, right?"

"I'm afraid not, Tanner. I heard your company has deep pockets and low standards. Did I hear wrong?"

The stocky man sputtered in frustration. "Yes, you heard wrong, and I'm afraid you're wasting your time as well as mine." He stood, his jowls quivering. "I'll show you out, sir."

Andrew stood. "Jeanine? What you doing here?"

"I'm on to you!" Meg shouted. "Where is she?"

"Who?"

"The woman you're here to meet!"

The man at the desk was speaking quietly into the phone while a growing audience gathered from nowhere to watch the show, whispering among themselves.

"I'm here to meet Pat Crosby," Andrew said.

"Is she prettier than me?"

"Pat's a man; he runs a charity for orphans!"

———

Pat Crosby—his charity's request soundly denied —was following the unamused Mr. Tanner down the hall toward the elevator when he suddenly stopped, put his hand to the wall, and gasped.

"Charlie horse!" he cried. "In my calf! Owww!"

Wesley Tanner turned slowly and looked up the six inches to meet Dante's eyes. "Are you quite done?" he asked, hiking up his pants.

"I'm serious," Dante said. "Maybe we could revisit the issue of the four hundred grand while you massage it out? Just a thought."

"Do you want to follow me now or shall I call security?"

"All right," Dante said, pulling his hand away from the fire alarm. The expanding foam pack he had pushed into it would begin swelling immediately. They had maybe twenty minutes before the alarm went off.

———

Happy had passed through two more doors and down a flight of stairs. His years of experience designing computer networks had given him something of a sixth sense in locating a network's hub, and he knew he was close. He moved quickly down another flight of stairs and came face-to-face with a fire door that did not submit to his Jedi-like powers or the chip in Scott's hat. A keypad mounted on the wall announced ENTER ACCESS CODE on a backlit digital display.

Swapping Scott's phone for his own and plugging a headset in, he called Fletcher. "Time to up the domestic dispute to Threat Level Crazy," he said.

"A man?" Meg shouted. "Yeah, right! Does he wear lipstick? Because there was red lipstick on the cuff of your pant leg last night."

"What? How would that even—?"

"Is she younger than me?"

Andrew squeezed his fists at his side. "No, he's a— You know what? That's it, Jeanine. We're through!"

"You'll never get rid of me," Meg vowed. "Wherever you go, I'll be there."

"What, you're going to follow me?"

"If I have to."

Andrew turned and stalked over to the men's room door. "Are you going to follow me in here? Ya psycho?" He disappeared into the restroom.

"You can't stay in there forever!" Meg shouted. She turned toward her audience and screeched,

"What are you all gawking at?" Two dozen onlookers quickly busied themselves with their phones or some manner of convenient paperwork while two large and imposing men closed in on her.

"Excuse me, miss," the taller one said, his Adam's apple looking as if it might burst through the skin at any moment. "I'm afraid we're going to have to ask you to leave."

"Security's on Meg," Fletcher reported. "You've got your window."

"Awesome," Happy whispered, dumping his leather bag to the floor and unzipping it. "Okay, Fletch," he said into his headset, "you've got an electromagnetic lock with fifteen hundred pounds of holding power. No way to hack the keypad; how do you get in?"

"I don't know, cut the power?"

"Wrong-o," Happy said, pulling a long slotted screwdriver and a small cylinder of gas from his bag. "There's a twelve-hour battery backup. Try again."

"Spike the power?"

"No can do," Happy said, wiggling the end of the screwdriver under the rubber door-sweep. "Suppression circuit."

"What then?"

"Like I said: fire codes." Happy was unrolling a flat, shiny object. "Code dictates that any magnetic lock have a safety release wired up to a motion detector inside. You know, so people don't find themselves locked inside a burning building."

"I see where you're going."

"I bet you do. By the way, is our guest still sound asleep?"

"You can't hear the snoring? Forget about him. How are you going to trip the motion sensor?"

Happy smirked. "Did you know that nearly 10 percent of all false burglar alarms are caused by helium-filled balloons? It's true. The Mylar ones especially reflect thermal radiation real nicely and blow around at the slightest breeze. And they conduct heat all right too. I've been keeping this one real warm, right by my—"

"Happy!" Fletcher said.

"Okay." Prying up gently with the screwdriver, Happy slid the deflated foil balloon—which featured a cartoon frog dressed as a nurse—under the door until only the mouth remained. He then hooked up the nozzle of a small helium tank and began inflating the balloon. Half a minute later he clamped it off and released it into the room.

He didn't breathe for a moment, waiting. Nothing was happening. Perhaps it was stuck somewhere. Perhaps he'd miscalculated. Perhaps Fonseca's security team regularly disabled their motion sensor the moment the fire marshal left the building. Just when he was scrambling for some sort of plan B, Happy heard the magnetic lock release with a buzz.

"Am I doing something wrong?" Meg asked, suddenly calm.

"You're making a disturbance, ma'am."

Ten feet away, a door swung open and Mr. Tanner angrily bustled Dante out.

"Oh, good," the red-faced little man said upon seeing the head of security. "Would you please escort Mr. Crosby here off the premises?"

"Crosby?" Meg said. "Pat Crosby?"

"Yes, that's me."

"Well then, who is my husband sleeping with?" she shouted.

"That's it, let's go. Both of you."

Fifteen seconds later Meg and Dante were standing outside, having been warned never to return. And Andrew had emerged from the restroom, his moustache gone, his blazer now balled up in his bag, swapped for a denim jacket, and his eyes obscured by thick-rimmed glasses and a Tigers ball cap. He walked quickly toward the door and heard the lock click open as he approached. The elevator was just up ahead.

Chapter 50

Down in the bowels of the building, Happy had plugged his laptop into the server and was busy accessing the facility's internal security.

"Okay, we're going to a party line," he said. "Andrew, you there?"

"Talk to me," Andrew answered quietly, six floors up.

"They've got hidden cameras all over the building." Happy flipped from one video feed to the next. "Are you at the conference room?"

"I think this is it . . ."

"Room number?"

"Six twenty-four."

Happy tapped at his keyboard. "Yep, that's the one. Fish-eye lens covering the room and a second camera right on top of the monstrance. Hang on." His fingers flew over the keys for another minute. "Okay, the cameras are no longer live, but we have to do this quick. No time to sub in a video loop, so I just froze a single frame— won't fool anyone if they look close enough."

"Alarms?" Andrew asked.

"Hold on, I'm getting there."

"Well, hurry up. I'm feeling exposed out here in the hallway."

Then Happy heard another voice over the

phone. "Scott," the voice said. "Scott, come help me with this a minute."

———

Dante stepped over the unconscious man curled up by the van door and sank into a captain's chair. A moment later the passenger door opened and Meg climbed in the front.

"How's it going in there?" she asked.

"So far, so good," Fletcher said, eyes fixed on the building. The Bluetooth headset was again blinking in his ear.

"I hate all this," she said.

"We'll get her back," Fletcher assured her, his eyes glued to the building.

Meg shook her head. "No, that's not what I mean. I can't even think about . . ." Her voice trailed off.

"Sorry," Fletcher said. He could relate. Walling off the fear and uncertainty around Ivy and focusing on a point just this side of the wall was the only way to stay sane.

"I meant that I hate all this lying and cheating and stealing," Meg said.

Fletcher emitted a weak chuckle. "Right, because no one lies in perfect Harbor Beach."

"This is different. This whole city is depressing."

Fletcher sniffed a laugh. "You know what's depressing to me? Those silk-screened banners at your church with the stock photos of a guy silhouetted on a mountaintop and some vapid inspirational quote written in half a dozen fonts—those make me want to cut my wrists."

"Apples and oranges."

"A legitimate comparison," Fletcher said. "I mean, they're both fruits, so why wouldn't you compare them?"

"Are you trying to start an argument?"

"No. I'm just saying—even in Harbor Beach, people lie and steal. Some people even lie to their tenants and try to steal their wives. It happens."

"Okay, tell me what's going on, Fletcher."

———

"I said *now*, Scott," the man was saying. "Let's go."

In his peripheral vision Andrew could see a man with long gray hair, wearing a vest but no jacket, approaching him from the right. He did his best to block his face with the phone and held up a finger at arm's length in the man's direction. "Hurry it up, Happy," he mumbled.

"You got something more important going on?" the long-haired man asked.

Andrew reiterated the index finger, then began power walking down the hall, away from the man.

"Don't you turn your back on me," the man said, anger bleeding into his voice. "You report to me. Scott? Scott!"

Andrew turned a corner and broke into a run,

holding the bulky messenger bag against his side. At the end of the hall, he took another right and, spotting a janitor's closet, ducked inside. He was not sure whether he'd been made, but going back down that hall was definitely a risk.

The silver-haired man had come within ten feet of him, but only for a moment. Still, Andrew was the wrong build, age, and race to pass for Scott Sprague, and he was fairly sure that the spray-on hair dye was bleeding onto the collar of his jacket. Object permanence aside, at some point the mind stopped filling in details and asked for a closer look.

Andrew lifted the flap on his bag and reached inside, feeling the handle of the .38. If the angry supervisor stalking the halls discovered him, he could always produce the gun, poke it into the man's back, and walk him calmly out the front door. But then who would get the monstrance? Happy? Andrew cursed under his breath. Cornering himself in this closet was the height of stupidity.

"Okay, here it is," Happy was saying. "They've got infrared sensors in that conference room."

"Not surprising, given its contents," Andrew said. "Can you kill them?"

"Not outright. But I think I have a work-around. There's kind of a grid of invisible beams on the ground. You break one and the alarm goes off. But there're actually two grids, staggered, laid down on top of each other. They avoid false alarms that way. I'm going to give one of these grids"—he could hear Happy typing a hundred miles an hour—"a two-second delay . . . There! You'll need to take tiny steps—more of a slow shuffle really—but I think that should do it."

———

Fletcher pulled the headset from his ear and dumped it on the console. "If you must know, this fell out of your Bible this morning," he said, bringing the card out of his pocket and tossing it onto Meg's lap.

"This just happened to fall out?"

"I wasn't going through your *Bible,* if that's what you're implying."

Meg read the card to herself. "It's just a note of encouragement."

"There's one person who 'cares for you'?"

"He's talking about God," Meg said.

"And I suppose it's also God calling you Gorgeous."

Dante cleared his throat. "Um . . . I'm gonna go . . . smoke?" He stepped back over Scott and out of the van.

"Why would you keep that?" Fletcher demanded.

Meg seemed to realize that she was clutching the card up to her chest and consciously put it back on her knees. "Father's Day, last year," she said quietly. "Pastor Dave was preaching about what a blessing it is to have a godly father in the house. I lost it halfway through the sermon and ran into the foyer, crying. No one followed me. No one came out to see if I was okay. Except Brad. He let me cry on his shoulder—literally. I got tears and snot all over his suit jacket and he just told me not to worry about it. He was there for me!"

Fletcher snatched the card back from her. "This is not Brad being there *for* you. This is Brad wanting to be *with* you. And you held on to it."

"Fletcher, you on?" Happy said. "Fletcher? Hey!" He glanced at his phone—still had a connection. "Dante? Are you up there? It's me, Margaret." Nothing. "Well, if anyone is listening, I'm accessing the backups now." He clicked his mouse a few times and paused. "This is weird, you guys. I've never seen anything like this."

Happy needed to upload his virus, but something was off. The backup could be opened, but that was all. "Here goes nothing," he said, and double-clicked.

Suddenly the floor fell out from beneath him and the room was filled with a huge rumbling sound. Happy shouted and flailed, falling hard against the concrete. It took him a moment to get his bearings and realize that the floor hadn't actually moved; rather, eight wide horizontal file cabinets had come thundering up from somewhere underground.

He sat up. "Whoa. That *is* an old-school backup system."

Andrew made it back to Room 624 without encountering the man in the vest with the silver hair. He walked quickly up to the door and pushed down on the handle—locked. Great. A cursory look at the mechanism told him it would take fifteen minutes to pick, minimum. It was similar to the one at Belltower's house, only three or four generations newer. And how was he supposed to do that kind of work, crouched in a hallway, without arousing suspicion?

He thought about Scott Sprague's keys, which he had seen earlier, sitting on the counter in the van and now in Happy's pocket—although he had insisted they were unnecessary. After all, Happy had reasoned, any place as high-tech as Fonseca's headquarters would not employ archaic lock-and-key technology.

Trying to look both busy and nonchalant, Andrew ran over his options. He could try to get the keys from Happy, although that would almost certainly involve two semi-convincing, ball cap–wearing IT managers in one place, which was begging for trouble. And even if they managed a hand-off, Andrew had his doubts as to whether the key was even on Scott's ring, which bore only four keys. No, picking the lock as quickly as possible was his best option. He was fishing for his lock pick set when he heard a familiar voice behind him.

"There you are, Sprague. Who do you think you are, walking away from me?" It was the man with the silver mane. And he was standing right behind him.

———

"You lied to Courtney, you know," Meg said.

"What? Who's talking about Courtney? I'm talking about *us*."

"So am I. You told her you've never pulled a long con. That's not true; you ran one for years. And I fell for it." She chuckled darkly. "The illusion of permanence set my mind at ease, and I never let myself see the truth. Our whole marriage was one big grift to you."

Fletcher was silent.

"Don't feel too bad," Meg said. "For me, it was just another role."

Fletcher grabbed the headset and popped it back into his ear. "Where are we, Happy?" he asked.

Chapter 51

"Oh, nice of you to join us," Happy said. "I've got good news and bad news and they're both the same news: I've accessed the backups and they're in some kind of antique steel lateral files.

Oh, and one of the keys on Sprague's ring opens them all."

"How is that bad news?"

"I can't make copies of all this. I'd need a Xerox machine and a bunch of boxes. And that would take twenty hours. We've got, like, ten minutes, tops, until the fire alarm goes off."

———

Andrew stood frozen, not out of fear or even indecision, but because it seemed like his best option. The grifter's quick read of the silver-haired man suggested someone who rarely made eye contact with underlings. That might come in handy.

The man reached past him and inserted a key into the lock of door 624.

"My presentation is at one," he said. "I want everything ready. None of the glitches we had last time. Understand?"

Andrew nodded slightly and slipped into the room.

"I'll be back in ten minutes," the man called.

———

"You'll just have to be selective about what you take," Fletcher said. "How are they organized?" He could feel Meg staring at him from the passenger seat, but resisted the urge to look in her direction.

In the back, Scott Sprague rolled over, mumbled something, and lifted his head for just a moment before curling back up in the fetal position.

"Looks like the first cabinet is files on principals, high rollers—lots of stuff in here going back to the eighteenth and nineteenth centuries. The others seem to be general files and corporate personnel."

"So grab José Pinto da Fonseca for starters."

"What's that under, *F? D? P?*"

"I don't know. Try *F,*" Fletcher said.

"Let's see . . . *E* . . . *F* . . ." Happy stopped. "Oh, man. Whoa . . ."

"What?"

"You will never guess who has his very own folder here."

"Why would you make me guess, Happy? Just—"

"Julian Faust."

———

Andrew took little steps over to the framed document on the wall and looked closely at the inscription in the corner: the Greek letters pi and alpha, followed by the number 19.12. It was a map of the island of Malta—rather detailed and aesthetically pleasing. Even apart from their present quest, Andrew thought he might have stolen it anyway, just by reflex, given half a chance.

He inspected the frame, particularly where it made contact with the wall. He'd come prepared for a standard art alarm, comprised of a cable, affixed to the back of the frame and loosely plugged into another cable running into the wall. In such a case, removing the framed item would break the connection and trip the alarm. There were a dozen ways around that.

What he was less prepared for was a frame that was built directly into the wall, apparently welded to the beams behind it and plastered into place. He carefully made his way over to the monstrance and saw that the cover over the small niche had been similarly constructed. These items would both take time to properly steal. But Scott Sprague's pushy boss said he would be back in ten minutes.

Andrew checked his watch. Make that eight minutes.

He patched back in to Fletcher and Happy. "I'm in the conference room," he said. "I can't even figure how they got the things in there. Looks like they built the whole place around them. You getting what you need, Happy?"

"Sort of," Happy answered, mopping his forehead. He had in hand the files for Julian Faust and José Pinto da Fonseca (which he had found filed under *D*) and was now looking for Cagliostro. "I've got Cadelmo and then Caulfield," he said. "No Cagliostro."

"Look under *B*," Andrew said. "Remember, his real name was Giuseppe Balsamo."

Happy walked his fingers through a dozen folders. "Balsamo! Here it is," he said.

Then the fire alarm went off.

Happy rushed to his computer and hit the Enter key, executing the script. "Go time, guys. I'm deleting today's video surveillance files as we speak. Andrew, you want to be out of the building by the time it finishes."

"Fire alarm?" Fletcher asked.

"Yeah," Andrew said. "I'm hanging up now. I'll see you guys at the rendezvous with the map and the monstrance."

"Leave the monstrance!" Fletcher yelled, but it was too late.

Happy lingered by the computer, watching the progress bar inch along. He looked down at the three files in his hands and began flipping through Julian Faust's. There were medical records, military documents, photos. He felt a sudden spike of adrenaline, stopped flipping, and thumbed his way back to a picture of some men standing in a courtyard. The person next to Julian—that was someone Happy recognized.

———

Out of options, Andrew tried the only thing he could: the Rescue Hammer. It was a gimmick, meant to be stowed in a car in case one wound up trapped inside at the bottom of a lake. The light plastic hammer contained a weighted metal spike at its head and could shatter safety glass that might otherwise survive a seventy-mile-per-hour collision with a deer.

He pulled the plastic hammer from his bag and struck the center of the map. The glass spider-webbed, and a second shrill alarm filled the building, largely drowned out by the fire alarm. He swung it again, and a thousand little pieces of glass came pouring down off the wall.

"Fletcher, you still there?" Happy asked. The clanging of the alarms made everything else seem quieter.

"Yeah, but we need to hurry. Our Happy Napper is waking up over here."

"Dante can deal with that," he said. "I need to talk to you. Privately. Like, *now*. You know that place a few blocks away that used to have those thirty-nine-cent tacos?"

"Yeah?"

"Meet me there in ten minutes," Happy said. "Just you."

"What's up?"

"I know who the Alchemist is."

Chapter 52

"Where are you going?" Meg demanded. They could hear Scott stirring in the back.

"Looking for Dante," Fletcher said, punching a memory button on his phone. He stood up on the van's running board and peered into the pool of people gathered near the building, slowly growing as more trickled out. The sound of the alarms seemed to be driving the group incrementally farther out into the parking lot.

Scanning the crowd, he saw one of the decoy Scott Spragues exit the building and head toward the north rendezvous. At this distance, he couldn't tell them apart. Dante's voicemail picked up.

"I'll be right back," Fletcher said, heading for the crowd. He wasn't supposed to be interacting with the marks here, and he wasn't the least bit prepared. Andrew had taught him a ritual to prepare for this sort of thing: he would stare into his own reflection without showing a bit of recognition. This was great practice for interacting with a partner midgrift. Fletcher felt a little naked for having skipped it, but at the end of the day, staring at his face in the mirror was a useless exercise. He didn't know that guy anymore anyway.

Entering the outskirts of the crowd, Fletcher was struck with just how normal it all was. Then again, the majority of these people had no idea who they were really working for. He felt a hand on his shoulder and spun, his guard up.

"It's me," Dante said. "Sorry. I should have stayed close. I just thought . . ." He trailed off, his eyes drawn to something in the distance. Or someone.

Fletcher followed his gaze and felt his chest tighten. There, milling about with the displaced accountants and HR coordinators, was the old man in the robe. He was looking at them—at Dante and Fletcher—rocking back and forth slowly. For some reason, Fletcher could only think of the words of St. Paul in Scripture: *Godly sorrow brings repentance that leads to salvation and leaves no regret, but worldly sorrow brings death.*

"You can see him too," Dante said.

"Of course I see him. This is the third or fourth time."

"Look around," Dante said. "No one else does."

Fletcher looked back at the place where the man had been, but as before, he had vanished. He suddenly remembered Happy's message and the bar three blocks away. "Get back to the van," he said. "You guys pick up Andrew, then wait for my call."

Dante shrugged and jogged back to the van,

sliding in behind the wheel. He circled around and pulled up to Andrew, who slid the door open and found himself face-to-face with a groggy Scott Sprague, sitting up and rubbing his eyes.

"Dude. I'm tripping," he slurred. "Are you, like . . . I mean, am I you?"

Andrew dragged him from the van by the shoulders of his shirt and sat him down against a tree on a parking lot island.

"Here's your jacket," he said, tossing it on Scott's lap. "Sorry about all this."

"Don't mention it, man," Scott mumbled. "My treat."

Andrew pulled the van door shut as they squealed away.

"Did you get it?" Dante asked.

Andrew reached into his bag and withdrew a bulky object wrapped in a hand towel. With a shake of his wrist, he revealed the monstrance. It was gold with a round base and three small feet. A sunburst pattern reached out from the center where a round hollow—about two inches in diameter—would house the bread of Holy Communion. He carefully handed it to Meg and went back into his bag, producing a long cardboard tube.

"Two for two," he said.

———

Fletcher ran the three blocks to the Equinox, a defunct bar that looked no more defunct than when he and Happy had frequented it a decade earlier. He rushed around the back, where an overhang in the alley had once protected employees and patrons alike from rain while they smoked. Hundreds of bleached cigarette butts remained.

Happy was hunched up against the wall, nervously tapping his hand against his leg.

Fletcher slowed to a walk and tried to catch his breath. "What's the problem?" he asked, clutching his side.

"Look who's got his arm around Julian Faust," Happy said, offering a file folder in his outstretched hand. He suddenly jerked, pitched forward, and landed hard on the ground, the folder still clutched in his hand. A gaping red hole the size of a fifty-cent piece was gurgling blood from his forehead onto the cracked concrete.

Fletcher couldn't move. He'd never seen anyone die before, much less the violent snuffing out of a close friend right before his eyes. He stood frozen, panicked, trying not to look at Happy's lifeless body or the brain matter on the filthy back wall of the bar. Then he saw movement to his left and heard someone—no, two people—approaching. They were dressed in all black, like Navy Seals, complete with face masks that covered everything but their eyes. On their chests were emblazoned red Maltese crosses.

The bigger of the two stood six feet from

Fletcher, gun trained on him, while the other one—much slighter—quickly wrenched the folder from Happy's hand and took a quick look at its contents before disappearing around the corner of the building.

"On your knees," the man ordered. His voice sounded like two cinder blocks being dragged against each other.

Fletcher complied. He could hear the blood pounding through his head. On the continuum of fight or flight he was somewhere near lie down and die. He thought of his daughter, locked up who-knew-where, of his last words with his wife—angry words—and the prayer he never had got around to praying.

"Stay there and count to two hundred," the man said.

It wasn't until he reached one hundred and twenty that Fletcher realized he had seen the man before. The scar may have been covered by the mask, but there was no mistaking those eyes.

Fletcher had only managed a few words upon returning to the van, but they—along with the blood on his hands and shirt—were enough to convey that Happy was gone.

Back at Broadmoor Outreach Tabernacle, the shock was wearing off and the rage was building up.

"The guy Dale with the gun," he said. "The

guy in the jumpsuit. Is he the Alchemist?"

Andrew shook his head. "No, he's hired muscle. Name's Manny or Manly or something. The Alchemist brought him on after I left."

"He killed Happy. Or the other guy did. Wiry little guy." He thought for a moment. "Might have been a woman." The familiar female voice on the phone in Belltower's office suddenly came to his mind.

"The Alchemist does have a woman he works with," Andrew said. "He calls her Lorenza."

"Cagliostro's wife. How cute."

"I didn't tell you why I broke it off with him. He was getting crazy, claimed to be Cagliostro. Literally."

Dante was sitting backward on a wooden chair, leaning on the backrest. "Any idea what was in the folder they took?" he asked.

"It was a file on Julian Faust," Fletcher said. "But there was something else inside, something the Alchemist was willing to kill to protect."

"But they covered their faces," Dante said. "Tried to grift you into thinking they were assassins for the Knights of Malta."

"We're being grifted all the way around," Fletcher said. "And I think William Belltower is too. Guy's like a charter member of the Order, and his head of security belongs to a group trying to usurp their power? I think Faust wants the necklace."

"Speaking of the necklace," Andrew said, "did Happy get anything useful?"

They all looked to Meg, who had been sifting through the Fonseca and Balsamo files. After counting to two hundred behind the bar, Fletcher had managed to summon the will to unclip the shoulder strap from Happy's bag and slide it out from under his body.

Meg looked up, eyes lifeless and red from crying. "I don't know," she said. "José Fonseca's file is just a will—nothing jumps out at me. Cagliostro's has the opposite problem. There's, like, two hundred and fifty pages. Nothing specific. The first entry is dated June 15, 1789. Listen to this: 'Men who live by the art of misdirection should never apologize.' " She dropped the page onto the others. "Why does that not surprise me?"

Fletcher and Andrew exchanged a look.

"It's real?" Fletcher asked.

"What's real?"

"Meg, can you compare the handwriting with the letters to Fonseca and Rohan? Is it the same?"

She shuffled through a stack of papers until she found the right ones. "Looks about the same."

"When is the last entry dated?" Andrew asked.

"June 13, 1798. But I thought Cagliostro died in 1795."

"I told you," Andrew said. "Faking his death

and swapping out a corpse is child's play for the world's greatest grifter."

"What's the last entry say?" Dante asked.

" 'I conclude these pages of instruction as I prepare to vanish into the ocean mist, having carried out the greatest ruse the world has ever seen and having acquired the greatest treasure ever amassed.' " She flipped the page over and found the other side blank. "That's the end. But that's thirteen years after the necklace went missing, so what's he talking about? What happened on June 13, 1798?"

Dante grabbed up Happy's notepad and found the time line he'd sketched from his library books. "Here. 'June 13, 1798, Napoleon Bonaparte seizes the island of Malta and expels the Knights.' "

"No way," Fletcher said, rising to his feet. "The ship?" He began to pace.

"What ship?" Meg asked, her voice devoid of curiosity.

"What if the French Revolution wasn't some misdirection-gone-out-of-control? What if Cagliostro and the Grand Masters were actually setting it up on their terms, trying to keep their wealth even after the whole system went down?"

"I don't get it," Dante said. "What's the angle?"

Fletcher resumed his seat. "The Knights didn't come out of the Revolution in very good shape," he said. "They'd thrown in with the throne—wrong side of history and all that—and the people were really starting to hate them. In 1798, Napoleon showed up on the shores of Malta in force, and all the French knights refused to fight him, which was a pretty good chunk of the total number.

"Napoleon allowed the Knights to leave and take the hand of St. John with them. But the rest of their treasure—all the church art, relics of the crusades, all the wealth amassed over the centuries—was carried onto one of Napoleon's ships, eventually destined for Paris. But the English fleet got the jump on them not long after, and it all went to the bottom of the sea. To this day, nothing more than a few coins has ever been recovered."

"Could have pulled a switch," Andrew said. "Definitely would qualify for 'the greatest ruse the world has ever seen and the greatest treasure ever amassed.' That's seven hundred years' worth of accrued wealth: gold, silver, captured pirate treasure, spoils from the crusades, prizes from Jerusalem, Egypt, Cyprus, Algiers, Tripoli—all sunk to the bottom of the Aboukir Bay. Or not." He looked at Meg. "Object permanence."

"How does this help me get my daughter back?" she asked.

Andrew cracked his neck. "Let me tell you what I know from my time with the Alchemist. The Republic of Malta gave the Knights the Castel Sant'Angelo back in 1999. That same year, my mentor's passing interest in Cagliostro turned into a full-blown obsession. He caught wind of something they found hidden in the walls of the castle—a clue to a long-lost treasure. I've heard and overheard enough to piece things together. I know why he wants the necklace so bad."

"Because it's worth a hundred million dollars," Dante said.

"It's more than that. It's the key to finding the take from the greatest heist in history." Skepticism ruled the room. "Here, I'll prove it to you." He opened the cardboard tube, carefully pulled out the map, and unrolled it. "You guys think I just took the monstrance because I don't like losing, but there's a better reason." He unwrapped the monstrance and set it on the map. The three ornate feet fit perfectly into three outlines drawn on the map.

"The key is pi alpha 19.12, right? I'm no Greek expert, but I've been doing some research. It could stand for *proelthen astrape* . . . Am I saying that right, Fletcher?"

"No."

"Well, it means for a shaft of light to move along a particular path."

"Not quite," Fletcher said. "And that's pretty awkward Greek. It means 'lightning came forth.' "

"Whatever. This is what the Alchemist expected. It's why he sent us after the monstrance. One of the diamonds paid out to LaMotte was replaced with a crystal replica, which will fit into the monstrance, right in the middle. Then we shine light through it at 19.12 degrees, or maybe nineteen degrees, twelve minutes, and it will show us where on the Island of Malta the treasure is hidden."

"That's Indiana Jones," Dante said.

"I know. Amazing, isn't it?"

"No, that actually happens in *Raiders of the Lost Ark*."

"Haven't seen it," Andrew said.

Dante shook his head. "First you don't like my Mustang, now you haven't seen Indiana Jones. Back me up here, Fletcher."

"That is pretty sad. Nobody tell Happy. He'd have a—" He remembered and swallowed back some tears. "Dante's right; seems pretty far-fetched."

"Either way, it fits," Andrew said, gesturing at the map. "You can see that. If we locate the treasure before he does—"

"Listen to yourself," Fletcher interrupted. "You're in a fantasy world! Even if I wanted to, I can't go to Malta. I can't go to Paris. I can't go to *Cleveland* without permission. I'm on parole."

"We wouldn't come back," Andrew said. "You get Ivy, we all go, we all get rich, we start over."

"Sounds good to me," Dante said.

"We are not getting sidetracked," Fletcher said. "Happy's dead; my daughter is not going to be next. We find this necklace, we give it to the Alchemist, we get Ivy, we go home, and I get back to filling my vending machines. Comprende?"

Fletcher's phone rang, and he checked the display. "It's my parole officer," he said, color fleeing from his face. "He must have heard about the monstrance getting pinched. He's going to want an alibi from me, and I've got nothing."

"I'd answer it, man," Dante said. "Don't dodge your PO."

"Hello?" Fletcher said, suddenly sunny. He stood and walked off toward the far wall. "Oh, yeah, going great, going great . . . Nope, haven't seen any of my old associates. Still praying, still reading the Bible, absolutely . . . I tell you what, Officer Roberts, we're in the middle of a team-building activity here; can I call you back a little later? Thanks. Okay, good-bye." He pocketed the phone and addressed the group. "He was just seeing how I was holding up."

"You really think these people would file a police report?" Dante said. "No way. They will find us. That's why you don't grift the Illuminati. Mark my words: if they're not on their way here, they will be soon."

"Shhh," Andrew said, holding up a hand. "Did you hear that?"

"Shut up," Dante said.

"I'm serious." His eyes traced the ceiling from corner to corner. They heard the sound of breaking glass above them. Then footsteps. Someone was upstairs.

Chapter 53

Dante's hand disappeared into his jacket and came out gripping his Glock. He ran to the stairway, raised the gun, planted his feet. Fletcher instinctively moved between his wife and the threat. He glanced over at Andrew, who was eyeing the exit.

"Andrew," Fletcher hissed. He nodded at the revolver in his partner's waistband.

The deafening blast of a gunshot grabbed their attention, and they looked up to see Dante blown back onto the wood floor, his skull bouncing once and then landing hard. The gun clattered from his hand.

Three men charged into the church. The first held a pump shotgun, smoke chugging from the barrel. The others brandished bats.

"Nobody moves," the gunman said. He wore sagging pants and a baseball jersey. He looked down at Dante. "Can you talk, homes?"

Dante grunted.

"You shot him!" Meg shouted. "Of course he can't talk."

The man sneered. "First one was a beanbag. A riot round." He racked the pump. "Gets your attention. The rest are slugs. I told you I was coming for my ten large. Not for me, for my brother. He spent two nights in the hole, charges five large per night." He walked up between Dante's splayed legs and took aim at his chest.

"Don't have my money?" he asked.

Dante wheezed.

"That's what I thought." He nodded at his two companions, who went to work—one smashing a display case with his bat and the other knocking photos from the wall. Dante squeezed his eyes shut, forcing a cascade of tears to run down his temples.

Fletcher knew they were going for maximum sound and chaos. Shattering glass was disorienting and had the power to quickly change a person's disposition. He glanced at the monstrance, sitting unassumingly on a card table near the back wall between a stack of Happy's books and a bulky backpack. The man with the black do-rag would reach it in a moment at his present rate. Fletcher could only imagine what an attractive target it would make. The sunburst design looked a bit like it was already in the process of exploding.

Apparently Meg had also noticed its impending destruction. She stepped out from behind Fletcher and approached the demolition man.

"Excuse me," she said. "Excuse me!"

The man stopped swinging.

"What you're doing makes no sense. How is this helping you?" From the other end of the room, they could hear splintering of the Communion rail, section by section.

"You got something to offer?" the man said, letting his bat hang at his side and taking a step toward Meg. "Yeah, I bet you do." He touched her cheek with the back of his hand.

Fletcher tasted rage and bile. He began to gather it in his chest. With Dante out of commission, it would be up to him to talk them out of this. Then he realized he couldn't corral his anger. He would have to use it.

"Hey! What are you doing?" the man with the shotgun yelled up toward the chancel, where a brass cross and chalice lay bent and crumpled on the floor. "That's sacrilegious, man!"

The fat man squeezed his bat and murmured, "Sorry."

Flat on his back, Dante caught Fletcher's eye and nodded. It was almost imperceptible, but the message came across: *Now. Do it now, while the focus is over there.*

Fletcher snatched the revolver from Andrew's waistband and smashed it into the bridge of the lanky gangster's nose. The bat bounced to the floor and rolled away. He swung again, connecting with the man's temple. Dante kicked the legs out from under the leader, sending the shotgun sailing, and the two grappled for Dante's hand-gun, just out of reach.

Andrew shoved the lanky man to the ground and kept him there with a kick to the abdomen.

The big guy was rushing down to the aid of his boss, who was beginning to overpower the injured Dante when another earsplitting blast from the shotgun instantly quelled the room. Meg cycled the action, ejecting the spent cartridge, and leveled the gun at the approaching man and his bat. Fletcher took three long strides up to the leader of the intruders, sprawled on the ground, and aimed the .38 at him. He slowly pulled back the hammer, savoring the *chik-chik-chik* of the wheel advancing.

Dante rose to his knees, recovered his gun, and stood with some effort.

Andrew, the only one in their group not holding a firearm, took charge. "You three, on your stomachs right here." He turned to Fletcher. "We need the monstrance, the map, and the letters," he said. "And take everything you want to keep. We're never coming back to this place again."

The man in the jersey forced another sneer. "We'll find you," he said. "I—"

Meg cycled the shotgun again, sending an unspent round flying across the room. "Shut up."

"The gentle art of the grift, you called it," Fletcher spat. He was driving them north on 75 at eighty miles an hour. "Now Happy's dead, Dante's busted up, we're all fighting and shooting guns. But nobody gets hurt, right, Andrew?"

Andrew sat silently in Happy's chair. The sun was setting, and a warm orange glow filled the cargo hold.

"I think we should ditch the van," Dante said, unbuttoning his shirt and examining his bruised chest. "If those punks aren't looking for it, the police will be as soon as they find the body."

"No," Andrew said, fiddling with a soldering gun. "It's registered to me. Won it from Happy in a card game a couple years ago."

Dante touched his side experimentally, wincing at the pain. "I'm sorry about that whole mess," he said.

"That's the weakness of the Big Score," Andrew said. "Angry mark can come back and catch you with your pants down."

"We need to get somewhere no one knows about," Meg said. "How about a hotel?"

"No way. I've lost track of how many people are hunting us. No credit cards, no IDs, no maids or clerks."

Dante nodded. "Somewhere private, but untraceable."

"I think I know a place," Meg said.

✠

Ivy hadn't heard Courtney's voice in at least two hours when the door opened again. The man with the scar dropped a five-gallon bucket to the floor and kicked it toward Ivy. Inside was a roll of toilet paper, a box of Triscuits, and a gallon of water.

"You better hope Daddy Dearest brings us what we've got coming before that runs out," he said.

"Where's Courtney?" Ivy asked, but he was already shutting the door. "Where's Courtney?"

She heard the lock turn. Courtney might be dead, she realized, and if she was alive, she was badly hurt and needed help.

That's when Ivy made a decision: the next time the door opened, she would do whatever she had to do to save Courtney and free them from this place.

Chapter 54

"This seems really stupid," Fletcher whispered. They were crowded around a service entrance of the Orangelawn Shelter while Andrew worked at picking the lock.

Meg shook her head. "Dr. Foreman said they ran out of funding halfway through renovating this wing. He had us bring some boxes back here and he said no one had been here in weeks."

"We're in," Andrew said. They followed Meg up a flight of stairs and down a hall lit only by the dim trickle of twilight through the filthy skylights. The stink of fiberglass insulation hung heavily in the air.

They passed through a door, the handle of which was shimmering with some greasy unknown filth. Dante drew a handkerchief from his pocket and used it to turn the knob. He hated doing that, as it seemed like full-on mental illness, but it was better than touching that thing with his bare hand.

"This was the room," Meg whispered, pointing at a padlocked door. "There are cots in there and a long table and chairs. It's perfect."

"A padlock," Andrew said. "Your move, Fletcher."

"You have bolt cutters in the van?" Dante asked.

"Don't need 'em," Andrew said.

Fletcher was on his knees, spinning the dial. "There aren't that many possible combinations."

"You sure about that math?" Dante said. "Forty times forty times forty is like sixty-four thousand possibilities."

Andrew chuckled. "You'd think so. Except a glitch in the design means there're only a hundred. Once you find the base number, some basic third-grade math can open any padlock in under five minutes. Fletch claims he can do it in three."

"I can," Fletcher said, writing on his arm with an ink pen.

"You say that, but in Birmingham it took you seven."

"I can do it in three if nobody talks to me."

"Let's go grab our bags," Dante said to Andrew.

"No hurry. We've got at least seven minutes before the room is available."

Dante looked down at the handkerchief in his hand. There was a thick, round stain where it had touched the doorknob, but it was also filthy throughout, streaked with grime and filth, which he was sure hadn't been there that morning. He dropped it to the ground.

"There are little snakes all over this," Meg said. "Isn't that sort of satanic?" She was examining the base of the monstrance as Andrew and Fletcher deposited the rest of their belongings on a bench next to the row of metal-frame bunk beds.

"No, there are snakes everywhere on Malta," Andrew said, "especially in churches and religious buildings."

"Why?"

"Because St. Paul survived a snakebite there," Fletcher said. "It should have killed him, but he didn't even swell up. The people assumed he was a god. Acts 28." He pointed at Meg's Bible atop her suitcase. "Wait a minute! Pi alpha 19.12. That could be *Paulos Apostolos*—that's how St. Paul begins most of his books of the Bible."

"But I thought John was the patron saint of the Knights of Malta," Dante said.

"There're a lot of references to St. Paul in these

letters," Meg offered. "But what would *Paulos Apostolos* mean to the map and the monstrance?"

"Well, we've got these conflicting reports— early sources say the Knights revered the hand of St. John, while the later accounts say they left with his skull. What if the skull was just a convenient place to store the necklace while the order switched up their patron saint to Paul, the man who had seemed like a god to the Maltese?"

"But how would *Apostle Paul 19.12* tell José Fonseca where to find the diamonds?" Dante asked.

"Wait a minute." Fletcher grabbed Meg's Bible and began to flip. "*Praxeis Apostolôn.*"

"Come again?" Andrew said.

"That's the name of the book of Acts in the original Greek. Here it is, Acts 19:11–12 . . . 'God did extraordinary miracles through Paul, so that even handkerchiefs and aprons that had touched him were taken to the sick, and their illnesses were cured and the evil spirits left them.' "

"That's got to be their great relic, then," Dante said. "I mean, every document we've looked at seems to associate the necklace with a particular cloth with a distinctive round stain. What if it's all misdirection? Who would give the old cloth a second look if it's wrapped around a hundred million in diamonds?"

Fletcher nodded. "And the Alchemist was far more interested in the cloth in the altar than in what it contained. The Knights could have acquired a relic like this when they took Malta."

"A round stain," Andrew said. "That might be how you line up the cloth with the monstrance so you can shine the light through it and find the location of the ship."

Meg shook her head. "What if the Alchemist isn't after the necklace or the ship? What if he wants a cloth with the power to heal diseases?"

"I don't follow," Dante said.

"He calls himself the Alchemist. Remember what alchemy was all about: distilling things down to their essence."

Fletcher's phone rang. He glanced at the display, then looked up at Meg, eyes wide.

"What?" Meg asked. "Who is it?"

"Courtney." He answered the call on speaker. "Hello?"

"I'm looking for Fletcher Doyle." The voice was deep and resonant, the very opposite of Courtney's.

"This is he."

"Hello, Fletcher. This is Andre Foreman. I'm at the Orangelawn Shelter tonight." The tension in the room increased.

"Oh, Dr. Foreman," Fletcher said. "What can I do for you?"

"Well, a young lady named Courtney is with me. She says she was here volunteering with your group this week."

"Wait—she's here? Or there?"

"Yes." He lowered his voice a bit. "She looks like she's been through quite an ordeal. Someone has struck her, but she won't tell me who and she won't hear of calling the police or her parents. She'll only talk to you."

"We're actually not too far away," Fletcher said. "Meg and I will be there in a few minutes."

"Sounds good." *Call ended.*

"We have to wait a couple minutes at least," Fletcher said to Meg, who was hurriedly lacing up her shoes.

"And you have to look concerned but not frantic," Andrew said. "Remember what Cagliostro wrote: 'Men who live by the art of misdirection are able to overcome their emotions so as to become whatever they need to be in a given moment, not to survive, but to thrive.'"

Meg gestured at the bare, unfinished room around them. "You call this thriving?"

"I insisted she let me call someone to come get her," Dr. Foreman said, "but she made it clear that she'd run if I called anyone but you. Must be making quite an impact on these young people." He led Fletcher and Meg down a hall to a small nursery, where Courtney sat rocking slowly on a glider. The left side of her face was purple and bruised.

Meg bit her lip. Fletcher knew she was in grave danger of losing it.

Dr. Foreman said, "I'll let you talk privately."

The moment they entered the room, Courtney rushed to Fletcher and buried her face in his chest, sobbing.

Meg gave her just a moment to get it out before asking, "Where's Ivy?"

Courtney took a step back from Fletcher, rubbing at her eyes and nose with her sleeve. "She's still there. With them."

"Did you escape?"

"No, they let me out. The guy—the guy with the scar told me to find you and tell you . . ." Her chin quivered, a preamble to another crying jag.

"Tell us what?" Meg asked.

"He said you have one more day or he's going to kill Ivy."

Meg slumped to the ground, face buried in her hands.

"He said to stop screwing around looking for pirate treasure and find his prize. Whatever that means."

"Anything else?" Fletcher asked, down on one knee now, rubbing Meg's back.

"He said you're close. But close doesn't cut it."

"Listen, Courtney," Fletcher said, "do you think you could describe the trip? We could try and backtrack it in the van."

Courtney shook her head. "He blindfolded me and put these giant headphones on my ears with this awful heavy metal music."

Meg stood and wiped her face with her fingers. "The man who did that to you—did he do the same thing to Ivy?"

"I don't know," Courtney said. "After we tried to escape, he kept us in separate rooms."

Fletcher nodded. Without warning Courtney wrapped her arms around his neck and pushed her lips up to his ear.

"One more thing," she whispered. "He's listening to you. All the time. I could hear them through the wall. The man with the scar was playing all these, like, sound bites of you guys talking."

"You've delivered your message," Fletcher said. "I should take you back to your dad now."

"I'll do it," Meg said.

"No, Andrew and I will go." He opened the nursery door. "Don't worry, Gorgeous—I'll tell Brad you're thinking of him."

Chapter 55

March 21, 1791
St. Peter's Basilica, The Vatican

"Your Holiness, there are men here to discuss the matter of Count Cagliostro."

His Holiness Pope Pius VI ran his hand absently along the velvet armrest of his chair—a habit that had worn it smooth. "I am familiar with the man and his detainment by the Office of the Inquisition. Tell me the particulars."

A papal clerk referenced the document in his hand. "Cagliostro, who was baptized Giuseppe Balsamo, was detained here in Rome two years ago and charged with alchemy, heresy, and Freemasonry, as well as a variety of more, er, fantastical claims."

"Such as?"

"Such as having been a guest at the wedding in Cana where our Lord turned water to wine and having borne witness to the crucifixion."

"I assume he recanted these claims when pressure was applied?"

"No, Your Holiness. He denied that he had fabricated a single claim, nor did he admit to being Balsamo. He was sentenced to death this morning."

"And who dares to question our verdict?"

"I do not know, Your Holiness. He would not give a name."

The pope snarled, "How did he gain entrance to St. Peter's without giving a name?"

"He was escorted in by the Grand Master of the Knights of Malta. And he gave a word, rather than a name."

"What word?"

"I have been forbidden by Your Holiness from speaking this word aloud," the man said, visibly shaken. "They wait now in the antechamber."

The pope pulled at the fringe on his sleeve for a moment before saying, "Send him in."

The clerk bowed low to the ground and exited through the heavy doors, past two Swiss Guards, and approached the mysterious visitor.

He was a young man, perhaps twenty years old, dressed in a military uniform that the clerk could not identify. He was short, but his bicornered hat added to his height, as did the sense of power he exuded. He stood straight, his right hand wedged into his waistcoat.

"The Holy Father will see you," the clerk said. The visitor removed his hat and handed it to the clerk, who received it bewilderedly. He then entered the pope's chamber, closing the doors behind him.

Not more than a minute later the man came back out, snatched his hat and placed it firmly on his head, and left. When the Holy Father appeared a moment later, he looked pale.

"Put this to paper," he said, sitting on a padded bench and rubbing his temples. " 'I hereby commute, by special grace and favor, the sentence of death that is rightfully declared upon Giuseppe Balsamo, known to many as Alessandro Cagliostro. The heretic shall be perpetually imprisoned in a fortress, under constant guard and without any hope of pardon whatsoever.' " His eyes darkened. " 'But while the man may be spared the fire reserved for heretics, his books and papers shall be ceremonially and publicly burned by the executioner.' See that the Office of the Inquisition receives this message."

Chapter 56

Fletcher had texted Andrew with his own phone, summoning him and Dante to the van. When they arrived he held up a pad of paper with the words SOMEONE BUGGED written in large block letters. He took both of the cell phones from his pockets, powered them off, and set them down next to Meg's. Andrew and Dante followed suit.

Andrew pulled a crate of custom electronics from under the workbench and riffled through it until he found the Happy Scanner. He powered it up and slowly ran it over Meg's phone, then Fletcher's, then the burner from the Alchemist. The red light came on. He paused and exchanged a look with Fletcher, then resumed the scan. His own phone elicited no response, but Dante's also lit up the device, causing the red light to flash rhythmically. He pointed at Fletcher's phone and scrawled the words *listening device* on his pad, then to Dante's and wrote "GPS beacon."

Fletcher stacked the two bugged phones and

handed them to Dante. "You keep my wife safe," he said. "Andrew and I are going to take Courtney back to her dad."

Courtney, who had been slumped in the passenger seat smoking a cigarette she'd bummed from Andrew, wheeled back and shot them all an angsty look. "I don't want to go back."

"I don't care," Fletcher said.

As Andrew drove, Fletcher barraged Courtney with questions, now free of the Alchemist's listening ears.

"Did anyone use names?" he asked.

She thought for a moment. "No. They called the big guy the Alchemist, but he never called the other guys anything."

"The Alchemist—what did he look like?"

"Big. Really big. I would say almost seven feet tall. Really muscled up, long black hair down past his shoulders."

They were nearing the church. "Would it be asking too much for you to tell your dad you ran away? If you tell him you were kidnapped . . ."

She nodded. "Don't worry."

Andrew pulled up to a curb about a block away from the church and killed the engine. "You want me to come in with you?" he asked Fletcher.

"No, that's okay. Just take a second."

Andrew caught his forearm. "Listen, kid, I know you're looking for a head to bust, but don't do anything stupid. Think about Ivy."

"Don't," Fletcher said, jerking his arm away. "Don't say her name."

He and Courtney walked quickly up to the front stairs of the church, where Father Sacha sat looking out into the night, having a cigarette. He recognized them when they were ten feet away and began to rise to his feet, but Fletcher pulled her past the priest and into the church without saying a word.

The sound of revelry—shouting, screeching, and loud music—wafted up from the fellowship hall. Fletcher pulled out his phone and texted Brad. The vestibule. Right now.

A minute later Brad came rushing in, his face flushed. At the sight of Courtney, his hand went to his mouth and tears began to streak his face.

"Daddy," she said, beginning to cry as well. The two shared a long embrace.

"Are you okay?" he kept asking.

"I'm fine, I'm fine."

"Oh, thank you. Thank you, God."

Fletcher was about to leave when Brad suddenly released Courtney and went to wrap his arms around him. Fletcher caught Brad's ruddy face and shoved him, sending him stumbling backward.

"What did I do?" he asked.

"You know what you did."

Brad blinked innocently. "Whatever it was, I'm sorry. I owe you everything."

"I found a card you sent my wife," Fletcher

growled, "with a very familiar tone. She was keeping it in her Bible, Brad. Her Bible!"

Brad pulled Courtney back in and looked down at the top of her head. "I know. I was wrong to try. I was just . . . so lonely. And I'd never met you. She needed help and I was just . . ." He finally met Fletcher's gaze. "I never touched her. You have to believe me."

Fletcher glared at him silently.

"You want the house? You can have it. You brought me back my daughter. You can have whatever you want."

Fletcher took a step back. "I don't want anything from you. I was planning to come in here and put you down on the ground. But I realize now, I don't hate you. I hate what you make me see in myself." He turned and took a step, then paused and looked back at the reunited family. "I'm sorry you lost your wife, Brad. In a way, I know what that's like."

Father Sacha was gone when Fletcher came back out, and Andrew was standing were he'd been.

"You keep it together?" he asked.

"I'm fine," he said. "That guy's the least of my problems."

"That's right, kid," Andrew said, smiling. "That guy doesn't have half the class and raw talent you possess. Don't go down that road, okay? Don't throw it all away."

"What road? What are you talking about?"

"This Jesus Freak thing you're playing with. I mean, look what's come of it. Don't get me wrong; when you're Inside you do whatever it takes to get you through. Or to get you *out*. But you go telling everybody you found Jesus, you're just handing them a big fat peg. You may as well wear a T-shirt that says Easy Mark."

Fletcher walked past him, back toward the van. "That's not even how it works. You don't find Jesus. He finds you."

Andrew caught up to him and matched his stride. "Come on. It's a grift—same thing Cagliostro sold his marks. Follow my way and I'll walk you up by degrees into the presence of the Great Architect and take away your original sin."

"But what if he cut out the middle man? That's what the Bible says. Jesus *is* the middle man."

"You sound like a mark!"

Fletcher came to an abrupt stop and grabbed Andrew by the collar. "Knock it off! I need this right now, all right? Let it go!"

Andrew matched his volume. "This is important, Fletch! Your daughter needs you at the top of your game. It's time to forget this superstitious junk!"

"Oh, you got everybody pegged, huh?" Fletcher released his grip. "What about you, Andrew? What's your peg? You never told us that."

"I want you back in the game, son. I want my protégé back."

"I'm not your protégé, and I'm sure not your son. Let's just get back to the others and make a plan for tomorrow. We've got one more shot at this."

Andrew unlocked the van and the two men climbed in, Fletcher riding shotgun. The engine roared to life, and then they heard a voice behind them.

"Hand over the gun, Bishop. And both of you come back here. We're going for a ride."

The bag over Fletcher's head didn't breathe well, and it smelled strongly of sweat. He and Andrew had been instructed to lie down in the back of the van. The driver had turned the radio up full blast, and Happy's bass-heavy custom sound system was vibrating through the floor and into Fletcher's skull.

They drove for about twenty minutes. Then everything went still and silent. One of the men said to the other, "Make sure to wipe the memory on the navigation system."

"You kidding me? You think this Stone Age thing has NavStar?"

The sliding door opened, and the bags were suddenly removed.

Fletcher blinked at the light. They were inside a warehouse. The man holding the bags was older—in his seventies, maybe—wearing a button-up shirt that stretched and complained over his paunch.

"This way," the man commanded. Andrew and Fletcher followed him down a short hallway and into a large open area, at the center of which had been constructed some kind of building-within-a-building. "In here," he said, opening the door and gesturing.

They entered the conference room and took a seat. "Do you know who I am?" the man asked, sitting across the table from them.

Andrew lowered his eyes. "I think so."

"Well, I don't," Fletcher said.

"These are the people who bugged Trick's phone," Andrew said. "This guy's Marcus Brinkman, works for the Syndicate."

"Oh. You the guy who sent those thugs to the church?"

"Not directly."

"They shot Dante, you know. And my wife was there."

"That's a shame," Marcus said. "But we're wasting valuable time. You're here because of your connection to Mr. Watkins. You see—" He sat back in his chair and gave Fletcher a look. "Do you want to ask me something, Doyle?"

"Me? No, sir."

"Sure you do. You've been staring at my ears since you laid eyes on me. Yes, they're ragged. It's called cauliflower ear. Comes from my younger years as a wrestler. 'Course, nowadays wrestlers wear headgear so their ears don't wind up like mine. Should be called ear-gear, really, because it doesn't protect your skull. Then again, we've been hearing all about these football players in five-thousand-dollar helmets still getting their brains beat out."

Fletcher half shrugged. "Mr. Brinkman, sir, I'm going to go ahead and admit that you lost me a good minute ago. You said this has something to do with Dante?"

Marcus sucked his teeth for a moment. "The point, Mr. Doyle, is that if you enter the fight, you're going to wear the scars. Nobody just walks away."

"Have we entered into a fight? We sure didn't mean to."

"You threw in with Trick. That's good enough. And now he's talking about you guys and some gem heist you got on the line. Says you're after a big old diamond."

Andrew cracked his knuckles and bit his lip.

"With all due respect to you and your associates," Fletcher said, calling on his charm and his fake dimple, "we had no idea Dante was involved with the Syndicate."

"Doesn't matter," Marcus said. "I looked into you two. A couple of slick talkers. I'm sick of guys like you drifting in and out of the city. You think because you're grifters you can operate in Bella Donna's territory without permission, without paying your share? Well, you can't. It's time to pay the piper. And the clock's ticking. Trick's got just one more day, which means you've got just one more day before it's all or nothing. Under-stand?"

Fletcher opened his mouth to speak, but Andrew squeezed his shoulder and said, "We understand, sir. We'll make good."

"Glad to hear it. And you should know, this is neutral ground. Bella Donna has some respect for what you do, I guess. Wanted to make sure this was done right. My guys are gonna take you back now. You've got work to do."

Chapter 57

Andrew's eyes scanned their room at the Orangelawn Shelter, landing on the two bugged phones. He grabbed them and wordlessly walked back out to the van.

"That took awhile," Dante said. "We were starting to wonder."

"We met your friend Marcus," Fletcher said.

Dante swallowed hard, his fingers gravitating toward his Glock. Andrew came back in, shut the door quietly behind him, and glared at Dante, who glared right back.

"I don't know what's going on," Meg said, "but we don't have time for this alpha male crap. My daughter has one more day."

"We have a better chance if we cut this dead weight," Andrew said, pointing his chin at Dante.

"Don't be an idiot," Fletcher said. "We're all professionals here. We don't need to like each other, but we're already down one man and it would be stupid to lose one more."

"Fine," Andrew said, plopping down in a chair.

"Good," Fletcher said. "Now, I had some time to think in the back of that van, and I've come to a conclusion: we should focus everything on Julian Faust. He's the key. He's working against Belltower, trying to play the Knights of Malta. He seems to be collecting documents related to the necklace. And the Alchemist said we were getting close. So we need a plan. We need to work together to create a web of misdirection that gets us the diamond necklace wrapped in the magic cloth. Nothing else matters right now. Agreed?" He looked around at his three partners. Everyone nodded.

"But Faust had access to all of this," Dante said, gesturing to the letters, map, and monstrance piled on a card table, "and he hasn't found it."

"Or maybe he has," Andrew said. "Maybe the question is, where did he hide it? I say we separate Belltower from Faust. The old guy might be half checked out, but he could still know something. Fletcher, you've had the most face time with him. You and Meg work the Inside.

I'll put a wedge between them and light a fire under Faust, get him to lead me right to the package. Or at the very least, to whatever he's got on hand."

"What about me?" Dante asked.

"You can stay in the van. We're all a little sick of your tricks, Trick. I'll be pleasantly surprised if you can just stay out of our way."

Dante stormed out, tipping the monstrance as he passed it.

Fletcher righted it and followed Dante out to the sidewalk. "Hey! Can I talk to you a minute?"

Dante stopped abruptly. "I'm not sweating that clown. Don't worry. If you can use me in the van, I'll stay in the van."

"It's not about Andrew," Fletcher said. "It's about this." He held up the tube containing the map, which he had palmed against his side when he picked up the monstrance. "Something's off." He carefully pulled out the map and unrolled it, holding the back of it up against a streetlight. "What do you see?"

"Nothing. Back of the map."

"Look closer."

Dante squinted. "I can see the outline where the monstrance fits."

"Anything else?"

"Nope."

"Exactly."

"Oh," Dante said. "You think the whole

monstrance-treasure-ship deal is misdirection? Keep us off-balance?"

"I don't know if Andrew drew the outline or if the Alchemist did. I still haven't ruled out them being the same person. But I think whoever is pulling the strings here wants us to keep our eyes on the diamonds and the ship so we don't realize what's really going on with the cloth. We can rule out beams of light and all that."

Dante sat on the curb. "It does seem like he's trying to keep us off-balance, but I can't see his angle."

"Remember the letter to Grand Master Rohan? He said he was on the verge of acquiring something that would bring power to Rohan and a true elixir of life to them both."

"You're thinking alchemy? Like the Alchemist wants to distill the cloth down to its essence so he can live forever?"

Fletcher sat down next to him and began rerolling the map. "Makes the most sense to me. But really, what do we even know about the cloth? I guess it came with Paul and his companions to Malta when he was shipwrecked there."

"When the locals thought he was a god," Dante said. "You think the cloth could have helped build up his rep?"

"Couldn't hurt. I mean, how could anyone think the apostle Paul was a god? The big-shot preachers in Corinth said he was eloquent in his

426

letters, but unimpressive in person. And church tradition says he was short and ugly with a pronounced unibrow."

The two men locked eyes. "The old man in the parking lot," Dante said. "He had a cloth with a round stain on it."

"Got to be on the Alchemist's payroll," Fletcher said. "He's trying to send us some kind of message."

"No." Deep lines were drawing themselves between Dante's eyes. "I saw him in the jail. Inside. Holding that dirty cloth and wearing those robes. But nobody else noticed him." He was silent for a beat. Then he stood. "I gotta go. I'll be back in a couple hours."

Fletcher opened the door as quietly as possible. Andrew was hunched over the card table, filling in the plan. He glanced at Fletcher and returned to his work. On the top bunk, closest to the wall, he could see Meg's stocking feet. He felt a new knot form in his stomach, somehow worming its way into the midst of all the others. There was no way he could sleep here tonight—near his wife, but so far away. It would be torture. But he desperately needed sleep. He glanced at his watch: eleven thirty. He quietly closed the door and headed back to the van.

Dante rounded the corner and walked briskly past the shelter's front entrance. He had parked the

Mustang a couple blocks away, where it seemed less likely to get jacked.

"Reverend Watkins." The voice made Dante jump. He touched the handle of his gun, but then recognized the man sitting on a bench in the dark. Only every other streetlamp was on in this neighborhood—a cost-cutting measure—and Dr. Foreman had been sitting quietly under one that hadn't made the cut.

"Odd time for a walk," he said.

"Just heading to my car."

Dr. Foreman stood. "Did they get the girl back to her father?"

"I'm sorry, what?"

"Your friend Fletcher." He poked his thumb back toward the unfinished wing. "You all can stay there tonight, but I want you out tomorrow morning."

"I'm not sure what—"

"You know, you two men are trying to solve the same puzzle. You got two versions of yourself, and you don't know which is real and which is the mirage."

Dante snickered and waited for a smooth response to present itself, but it didn't.

"What do they call you? On the street?"

"Trick."

"Is that who you really are, Trick? I've heard you talk about Jesus, but you're chasing after something else, aren't you?"

"Trying to find a dirty old rag," Trick said. "Which is stupid, because I feel like a dirty old rag."

"That's good, son. We're all dirty before Jesus gets a hold of us. The Scriptures say even our most righteous deeds are like filthy rags in his sight. You could raise a billion dollars for those fatherless kids and it wouldn't do anything to clean you up. But he died for those filthy rags— all that dirt you and I did. And he'll wash you clean. Even you, Trick. If you repent and believe. Clean you up good, even give you a new name."

Chapter 58

Fletcher pulled the batteries out of the bugged phones. He was alone, so there was nothing for the Alchemist to hear, but for some reason he couldn't think straight when the place was wired.

Even with the batteries removed, his thoughts were garbled. He thought of the old man with the cloth. Even at his most fanatical in prison, Fletcher had never believed in visions and the like. Then again, what he believed was very much up for grabs at the moment, along with who he was and what he stood for.

It was all misdirection. Missed direction.

He balled up an old Michigan State hoodie of Happy's and crammed it under his head. The old man wasn't vexing him nearly so much as his Old Man, who seemed to be rallying more and more as the weeks out of prison ticked by. Inside it was somehow easier to keep him at bay, surrounded as he was by the wages of sin. Fletcher had gone to every Bible study and worship service—even led them. But even back then he knew he had been studying the behavior of the most devout inmates, filing it all away, and mirroring it back to them.

At his parole hearing he'd trotted out the big leather Bible and paired it with the dimple and the old charm. And now he didn't even pray. He wondered what a real alchemist would find if he were to boil Fletcher down to his essence, if he put all of Fletcher's words and posturing in a furnace and burned everything away but the True Him.

The side door of the van slid open, and Fletcher felt a sudden prickle of adrenaline. Then he saw Meg standing there, a pillow under one arm and a blanket under the other. She climbed into the van, laid the bedding down, and curled up next to him. Then she reached over and grabbed his hand, pulling him up to her.

They lay there, quietly snuggled together for five minutes before Meg broke the silence. "Maybe if Ivy hadn't come so early . . . if she had come after we had a chance to grow up a little more." She was quiet for another minute before adding, "I know you love us, Fletcher. I know you'd do anything for her." She squeezed his hand. "We're going to get her back."

✠

It was after midnight when Andrew stepped out of the cab and banged on the door of the Warehouse.

A sliding window opened, and the face of the man who'd van-jacked them earlier that night appeared briefly. The window closed for a moment, and he heard the door unlatch.

"How did you find the place, Bishop?" Marcus Brinkman asked.

Andrew smiled. "That van may be twenty years old, but Happy's been rigging his rides with GPS since Clinton was in office."

"I'll tell you what I told Trick. You can't talk your way out of this."

"I'm trying to talk my way in, actually. I'd like to speak with Bella Donna."

"What makes you think Bella Donna would come here?"

"There's a little room in the far corner—an office, I'm guessing. It has reinforced steel walls and a bulletproof window of one-way glass. But it's dark back there, and I could see a light on inside. And when I stumbled in the direction of that room earlier, you tensed right up." He craned his neck around Marcus. "Light's still on, by the way."

Marcus pulled his jacket back, revealing the

431

handle of a bulky pistol. "Why don't you get lost?"

"I think she'd want to hear what I have to say."

"I'm going to tell you one more time—"

An intercom on the wall crackled. "Bring him back."

Andrew was patted down and escorted to the office, where Bella Donna sat typing on a laptop.

"What is it?" she asked without looking up.

Andrew smiled slickly. "I don't know what kind of deal Trick tried to cut with you, but I can actually deliver—not just promises, but a place and a time to come and get what Fletcher and I owe you."

"Before tomorrow at sundown?"

He nodded. "Before tomorrow at sundown."

She looked up from her computer. "What exactly are we talking about here?"

"You're a beautiful lady; do you like diamonds?"

✠

The robed man stood on the poorly lit street corner, again staring at Dante as he approached.

"Paul!" Dante shouted. "*Paulos Apostolos*!" He began to run toward the apparition. As he drew near he noticed that the rag in the man's hand was no longer beige with a few dark stains. It was almost completely obscured by filth. The old man disappeared around the corner. A moment later Dante followed, but the old apostle had vanished.

Phantasmagoria—could that explain this oddly

dressed man who kept popping up everywhere? With all the technological advances since the days of the magic lantern, anything was possible —3D images, holograms. So why did that seem sillier than the simpler explanation?

The metal gate was still intact and secure in front of Broadmoor Outreach Tabernacle, although the windows behind it were broken. Dante fished out his key, and a moment later was standing amidst the wreckage. The three men had apparently continued taking out their frustrations after the grifters left, as the entire floor was now littered with debris and broken glass. He went back to the closet and grabbed an old push broom.

Walking up to the chancel, Dante picked up the bent cross and dented chalice and replaced them on the altar, then swept the floor beneath.

He dropped to his knees. "I don't talk to imaginary friends," Dante said. "And you never seemed to hear me before. But now . . . I'm in a mess. I'm going to die tomorrow if something big doesn't happen. And the one thing I keep thinking about is whether I'll be filthy or clean when I stand in your presence.

"I know you're there. I've known all along. I guess I just figured when the time came, I could talk my way in." He laughed. "You know I can talk. But I don't want that now. If you died for my dirt, then wash me. Make me clean. I don't know if we'll pull this off tomorrow. I don't even know if it's right, but I know I don't want to be filthy anymore. I want the man I pretend to be when I stand up here to be the man I really am." He wiped his face against his shirt sleeve.

"If there's any way . . . I can wait, I guess." There were no sounds of angelic choirs, no heavenly visions, no flickering candles or ghostly wind. But a moment later Dante rose, feeling lighter—so much lighter—and walked up to the big cross on the wall. He reached up and grabbed the end of the black pall he'd hung there four days earlier and felt it slide down from the cross, billowing as it fell.

Chapter 59

June 13, 1798
Valletta, Malta

"The French knights are unified in this," said the battle-scarred commander, "all two hundred of them. They will not fight against General Bonaparte."

Ferdinand von Hompesch, the Grand Master of the Knights of Malta, felt his entrails deflating. He had been elected to his position the previous summer when Emmanuel de Rohan had died after a long and illustrious term.

"But will they fight *with* Napoleon against their brother knights?" he asked.

"I think not, but I cannot say for sure. Your Eminent Highness, there are terms."

"Terms? Certainly you would not see the first German Grand Master lose all that our order has built within a year of taking office!"

"There is precedent," the commander said. "The Moslems expelled our predecessors from Jerusalem after the fall of the Christian Kingdom. Centuries later Suleiman the Turk allowed the Knights to respectfully withdraw from Rhodes. In both cases, we recovered and became even more powerful. If we know anything, we know how to adapt."

Von Hompesch shook his head. "With or without the French, our navy can cripple Napoleon's. He is headed to Egypt, I hear. If he would like any of his ships to be yet seaworthy when he arrives there, he will not spend much time feeding them to our fleet to be chewed and destroyed. Ours is the greatest navy the world has seen, and we have defeated much larger forces than this."

The commander rubbed his stubbled chin. "I am afraid it is too late for that. The French have made landfall at seven points on our shores, and the west side of the island has already surrendered to their numbers. This is a one-time offer. The general will allow us to withdraw, but we may bring only one holy relic from Jerusalem with us. The rest of our wealth will become his. If you choose not to accept, I fear it will result in the absolute destruction of our order."

The Grand Master looked out over the castle walls for a long time. "Fetch me the skull of St. John," he said.

"Sir, you mean his hand."

"No. Napoleon can keep the hand. Find me a skull in Pinto's old laboratories. It will help us spirit out our true treasure—a treasure of which only I know because Grand Master de Rohan told me of it on his deathbed. It will allow the order to start over once again, to adapt. And best of all, it is a treasure that Napoleon himself would kill ten thousand of his own men to acquire."

Chapter 60

Fletcher awoke with a start before dawn. His neck was stiffer than it had ever been, but the feeling of his wife's body, nestled into his for the first time in years, was like heaven. Then he saw Dante and Andrew sitting above him, living reminders that unless they pulled off the impossible, this would be the last day of Ivy's life.

Meg sat up and was immediately offered a paper cup of coffee.

"Okay, people, it's time," Andrew said. He handed Fletcher an electric razor.

Twenty minutes later they were all as ready as they would be, gathered in the cramped van, reviewing the plan for the day. They went through it twice, and Andrew grilled both Meg and Dante on each detail.

When he was satisfied he stood, drew in a deep breath, and let it out slowly. "This is what we do, people," he said, sounding like a football coach before the playoffs. "We play the Inside. Everything's in place. Fletcher and Meg, I rented you a Caddy. Keys are here. Anyone have any questions?"

Meg half raised her hand. "Can we pray?"

―――――

At 6:30 a.m. Fletcher was up in Happy's perch alongside William Belltower's house. The overnight security guard rounded the corner and came up the walkway. He patted two of the dogs on the head, yawned violently, and then checked his hand for the security code. Fletcher was feeling good about their chances here. This was definitely the weak link in Julian Faust's security plan.

"Okay, start walking," he said into his phone. "You need to hit the doorbell in three . . . two . . ." He ran down the embankment and jumped onto the chain-link fence, a pair of heavy-duty wire cutters in his hand. He knew he had just tripped the proximity alarm, but this part of the plan had worked before. Then again, it had been dusk then.

Meg rang the doorbell. She heard someone loudly complaining inside, then found herself face-to-face with a muscular man in his late twenties. The annoyance in his face faded instantly as his eyes flicked down to her sleeveless T-shirt and jeans and back up to her face, which was smudged with just a bit of engine grease.

"If you're here for a puppy, that was a prank," he said.

"A puppy?" She scrunched up her nose and shook her head, causing her ponytail to wobble. "Do you know how to change a tire? I got a flat just up there."

"Mr. Belltower!" he called over his shoulder. "I'll be back in fifteen minutes!" He turned back toward Meg. "Lead the way."

———

Fletcher snipped through the last link and felt his hands cramping up. He had started near the top of the fence and snipped his way to the bottom, creating something of a curtain, which he pulled back and slipped through. The dogs converged on him immediately. He popped open the peanut butter, scooping up the biggest dollops he could with rawhide and sending them off in the direction of any canine he saw. When he thought they were all occupied, he broke into a run toward the house, downgrading to a brisk walk when the faster pace seemed to recapture the dogs' attention.

Finding the phone box on the side of the house, he snipped the service line with the wire cutters, then pulled out his cell and called Andrew.

"Landline is cut."

Andrew laughed. "Probably the last time a thief will actually say those words."

Fletcher ended the call and texted Meg. **You are go.**

———

Meg felt her phone vibrate in her pocket. She held it up and walked this way and that, as if trying to get a signal.

"Excuse me? Rick?" she said to the man jacking the Cadillac up off the ground.

"Yeah?"

"Can I use your phone real quick? I don't have a signal out here."

"Sure," he said. "Calling your boyfriend?"

Meg smiled playfully and said, "I don't have a boyfriend." She accepted the phone and withdrew from the car about twenty feet, waiting until Rick was fully reengaged in his task. She quickly scrolled through the contacts and copied Faust's number onto the burner phone they'd bought that morning. Then she slid the back cover off Rick's phone, pried up the battery and removed the SIM card, and quickly reassembled it.

On her own phone she texted Andrew. **Cell is toast.** Then she switched to the burner and called Julian Faust's number.

"Hello?" came his crisp voice. Meg could hear road noise. Good.

"Hi, my name's Barb," she said in her best Baby Boomer impression. "Do you know an older man named William Bill-tower?"

"I do. Why do you ask?"

"Well, I'm by the old Hudson's building, and he's down here looking for his wife. But I think he's confused or something. The first number he gave me to call didn't even have enough digits."

Faust expelled an angry sigh. "Can you stay with him until I get there? It should only take me about twenty minutes."

"Yeah, 'cause they demolished that building years ago. It's just an empty lot."

"Will you stay with him?" Faust snapped. "I'll pay you when I arrive."

"Oh sure," Meg said. "I'll stay."

She quickly sent Andrew another text: Faust on his way, then walked back and slid Rick's phone directly into his pocket. He looked up at her and smiled, bumping his head on the wheel well.

———

Andrew read the text. He and Dante were already waiting at the corner of Gratiot and Woodward, overlooking the lot that had once housed the historic building. "And now we wait."

All was silent for thirty seconds until Dante said, "This really is a nondescript van."

Fletcher shielded his eyes against the glass and looked into the library. Belltower was sitting in an armchair, flipping through an old magazine. Fletcher knocked.

The old man unlocked and opened the door. "Who are you?" he asked.

"It's me—Jordan," Fletcher said. "You don't remember your old pal Jordan? Are you ready to go?"

Belltower smiled broadly. "Are you taking me to the lodge?"

Fletcher snapped his fingers and pointed at the old man. "I am taking you to the lodge!"

"I'll get my hat." He disappeared for a moment and returned wearing a derby and grinning ear to ear. He took a step up the walkway toward the street.

Fletcher caught his elbow. "Let's go this way," he said, pointing back toward the fence.

"Fine, fine," the old man said. As they navigated the maze of dogs, each one approached him, looking for a scratch behind the ears. They arrived at the fence, which Fletcher held open for Belltower.

"Adventurous. How fun," Belltower said.

When they were on the other side, Fletcher closed the fence back up with three plastic zip ties.

Rick had finished changing the hot lady's tire and gotten exactly the reward he'd hoped for—a number. He chuckled to himself and slid the slip of paper into his jacket pocket as he walked through the gate into the backyard.

First he noticed the dogs. Then he noticed the fence. He bolted to the side door, swiped his card, and ran inside.

"Mr. Belltower!" He felt an impending sense of danger he hadn't experienced since Afghanistan. Faust would kill him. Or fire him, at least. And then maybe kill him. He pulled out his cell phone to call his employer.

NO SIM CARD the display read. He remembered the woman fiddling with his phone and making sure he didn't look at it again. He dashed over to the landline. Dead. He closed his eyes and recalled the license plate number, writing it on his hand next to today's code. He'd memorized it, figuring he could always arrange a chance encounter somewhere if she didn't give him her digits. He reread the plate number from his hand. He was 99 percent sure that was right. Now to find a phone.

Chapter 61

Faust pulled his BMW up onto the sidewalk and hopped out, making two full laps of the lot. Finally he pulled out his phone. That's when Andrew called him from about fifty yards away.

"Hello?"

"Mr. Faust," Andrew said. "I'm afraid I have some bad news. You, sir, are being played. The old man you think is harmless and feeble is neither, and he's about to humiliate you."

"Who is this?"

"This is just a friendly warning." Andrew hung up. "GPS tracker still connected?" he asked Dante.

"Yep," he said, looking at the iPad in his lap. "Looks like he's taking the old way. If you hop on 75, we can beat him there by five minutes."

Andrew pulled the van up onto the freeway and punched the accelerator, causing a number of objects in the back to crash to the floor.

"Now who drives like an amateur?" Dante said. They drove in silence for about ten minutes.

"There're Meg and Fletch," Andrew said, pointing at the Caddy zipping along the freeway in the opposite direction.

"Why didn't they just stay there?" Dante asked.

"We want to get the old man as far away as possible, as quickly as possible. That way, even if you and I get made, we're still holding some cards."

Fifteen minutes later they pulled into the woods next to Belltower's house, covered the van with a ready-made pile of brush Happy had kept on hand for that purpose, and crawled up to his perch. Down by the house they could see the security guard pacing and hear him swearing. Dante checked his watch; the day shift was due to arrive in ten.

Just then Faust's BMW came thundering up to the house and screeched to a stop. The night security guard rushed up to meet him. Dante and Andrew watched them exchange impassioned words for a minute or two before Andrew called Faust again.

"Hello!" Faust shouted.

"You may want to look in your safe."

Faust craned his neck and looked all around. Dante and Andrew ducked down.

"The GPS tracker I placed in your rear-passenger wheel well tells me you've arrived at William Belltower's estate," Andrew said. "How are the letters you keep in his safe?"

"Good save," Dante whispered.

Reaching up under the car, Faust groped around until he found the GPS transmitter. He threw it to the ground and rushed into the house. A moment later they heard a muffled *bamph* and Faust emerged, his face completely covered in bluish-red dye.

He pushed his phone to his ear and again demanded, "Who is this?"

"I'm the man who took the letters from your safe. And they led me to something much more valuable. I've cleaned you out, Julian." He hung up.

———

Dante and Andrew followed, a few car lengths back.

"Wish we still had that GPS on him," Dante said.

"He would've made us. Anyway, *I* actually know how to tail a car."

"He's on the phone up there," Dante said. "He's not going to lead us to anything."

"No," Andrew said. "Remember his weakness. He's a control freak. If he knows where the necklace is, he'll have to see it with his own eyes. Nothing else will satisfy him."

———

"This is nice," William Belltower said. "I haven't been on a drive just for the enjoyment of it in years. No one will go with me. Julian thinks it's a waste of time."

Fletcher began another circuit around the city. "I'm glad you're enjoying yourself," he said. "Sure is a nice day." He glanced over at Meg. She checked her phone and shook her head.

"You two make a nice couple," he said. "Clara and I would always hold hands when we went for a drive. You should try it."

Fletcher reached over and squeezed Meg's trembling hand.

———

"I know where he's going," Dante announced.

"Probably Belltower's office," Andrew said.

"No, man. The lodge. He's hiding it right under their noses."

They followed him for another three blocks,

then pulled over kitty-corner from the Egyptian Mystery Rites Lodge. Sure enough, Faust was climbing out of his car, which he had parked in a fire lane. His dye-stained face drew looks from passersby. He took the stairs up to the lodge's entrance two at a time.

Dante peered through a pair of binoculars. "Does that thing really work?"

"Wait and see." Andrew cracked his window a few inches and pushed the end of the surveillance microphone into the gap. "It's directional, so there's an art to it. Happy could follow the conversation of two people walking through a crowd," he said, fiddling with a nob. "I'm not that good, but I think I can—"

"But you *do* know me!" Faust's voice suddenly filled the van. "I've been here a hundred times."

An elderly man in a brown smoking jacket held up his hands, palms out. "You are not an initiate of our lodge, and you haven't uttered the words or shown the emblems."

"*Arcana Arcanorum*," Faust said impatiently. "Those are the words. He says them with me right here next to him. Twice a week! You know me."

"You recording this?" Dante asked.

"You know it."

Another man, who could have been the first man's father, appeared in the entrance beside his fellow Mason. "But where are the emblems?" he asked. His eyes were wide, and his white hair looked like the result of a small explosion.

"I haven't got them with me," Faust said. "But I'm here on behalf of William Belltower. This is urgent."

Both lodge members shook their heads in perfect synchronization. "The Rule of Thebes and Memphis is clear," the man in the smoking jacket said. "No man may enter unaccompanied without the emblems."

"Why are you purple?" the older man asked.

"I know the emblems," Faust said, trying to keep calm.

"But you need to have them with you: the septangle and the rude ashlar. Or else you can't come in."

"I don't have time for this," Faust spat, shoving the closest man aside.

The man with the hair pulled a dainty revolver from his crested blazer, aiming it from the hip. "Just try me. I didn't back down in Korea, and I won't back down now."

Faust took an angry step back.

"Consider yourself banned from the lodge, purple man!"

Andrew exploded into laughter, pounding the steering wheel. "Call Fletcher," he said. "He's got our ticket into that place."

"On it," Dante said, pushing buttons.

"Wait," Andrew said. "Where did Faust go?"

Chapter 62

"Where are you, Fletch?" Andrew barked into the phone. "We lost Faust, but we think the necklace is in the lodge somewhere. We're up the block from the place right now." He and Dante were milling on the sidewalk, eyes peeled for Faust's white BMW or magenta face.

"Passing you now," Fletcher said. The Cadillac pulled up to a meter and Fletcher came out a moment later, jaunting up to Andrew. "This is perfect," he said. "Belltower wants nothing more than to take me into that place."

"Do it quick," Andrew said.

Fletcher opened the back door of the Cadillac and helped William Belltower out.

"We're going to the lodge?" he asked, beaming.

"Sounds great," Fletcher said.

They were at the corner waiting for the signal to change when Julian Faust came rushing up from the left, red-faced and raging. "I knew it," he said. He drew up a compact 9mm pistol and fired a shot into Belltower's chest. The old man collapsed to the ground, eyes wide, breathing labored.

Fletcher dropped to his knees and instinctively put pressure on the wound. Fletcher could see Meg rushing over from the car. He cranked his neck in every direction, but could not find Faust.

"Excuse me! I'm a doctor," someone said, and Fletcher stepped out of the way.

"I saw the shooter," someone behind him said. "He was covered in paint," came another voice. "He went that way!"

Fletcher felt Andrew's arm on his bicep, pulling him back, away from the action.

———

It was just after noon when the ambulance roared off toward Mercy Hospital, Belltower on board. Dante dodged traffic through the intersection and climbed back into the van.

"EMT says he'll probably make it," he said. "Tough old guy."

Andrew, who had been uncharacteristically quiet since returning to the van, said, "This was a tragedy, but if there's an upside, it's that Faust is out of our way. He can't show his face until that dye wears off. At least two days. Every cop in the city is looking for him."

"So what now?" Fletcher said.

"We break in there," Meg said. "We need what they've got to save Ivy, so we take it."

"Bad idea," Andrew said. "You're talking about an outpost of one of the most secret of the secret societies. Building's been there a hundred and fifty years. Who knows what the security situation is? Could be booby traps. Plus, we've got that wild man with the cowboy gun."

"So, what then?" Dante asked. "You gonna talk your way in again? That went well."

"If we can't play the Inside," Andrew said, "we turn the grift on them."

Fletcher ran his fingers through his hair. "I don't know. This is the last place I'd choose to grift. This is the Rite started by Cagliostro—a secret society with passwords, secret grips, and handshakes."

"And emblems," Dante added, "whatever those are."

"The septangle and rude ashlar," Andrew said. "And we got the password on tape. This isn't the Pentagon here. This place is the Stodge Majol. It's a bunch of gomers who get together to drink brandy and reminisce about how tough Eisenhower was."

"I've got it," Fletcher said. A smile slowly spread across his face. "Dante's going to be our ticket in there."

"Me? Are you high? That place has seen nothing but old rich white guys. You two couldn't blend in—let alone me. And now they're going to be all on edge and extra cautious."

Fletcher shrugged. "We're going to use all that to our advantage."

———

There were five cops milling about in the ER outside one particular private room while men and women in scrubs pushed past them, going in and out. Dante straightened his tie and made for that room.

"I'm sorry, sir," one of the uniformed cops said. "You can't go in there."

"Yes, I believe I can," Dante said, fishing his ordination card from his wallet. "William Belltower is in there." He held the card up for the cop to see. "Unless they overturned Freedom of Religion while I wasn't looking, Mr. Belltower has the right to a religious visit by clergy when the matter of life and death hangs in the balance."

"They're getting him ready for surgery."

"I'll only take a minute."

The policeman opened the door. "This is the minister. He wants just a moment with the patient. That possible?"

A severe-looking woman in scrubs double-checked an IV and nodded. "We'll be wheeling him into surgery in literally one minute. Be quick." She closed the door behind her.

Dante stepped up to the old man on the cart, his Oxford button-down ripped open, his undershirt cut away, and layers of gauze taped to his chest. "I'm so sorry," Dante said. "If I live through the day, I'll make it right somehow."

Fletcher had told him to look for rings first and foremost, and he immediately hit pay dirt, finding a ring on Belltower's right hand bearing a blue stone cut into a seven-sided shape. With some

451

difficulty he wriggled it off the man's finger, offering several *sorries* in the process.

With a sudden grab, Belltower was squeezing Dante's hand.

"Lord, help this man," he prayed. "Save this man."

The door opened behind him, and two men and a woman entered the room, all but shoving Dante out of the way. They unplugged and gathered a number of tubes and wires and, in a matter of seconds, Dante found himself alone in the room.

He called Fletcher, waiting back in the van. "I got the septangle, but not the other thing," he said.

"Was it in a ring?"

"Yeah, but he only had one."

"Probably a pin, then," Fletcher said. "Was he wearing his jacket?"

"No," Dante said, eyes searching the room. Under a chair in the corner, he saw a plastic bag labeled PERSONAL ITEMS. Belltower's navy jacket was on top. Pulling it from the bag, he held it up by the shoulders. "Nothing on the lapel," he said.

"Look inside. Members of secret societies often do that."

"Got it," Dante said, reaching into the interior pocket and finding the pin fastened there. It was the likeness of a block of stone, its edges rough and unfinished. He slipped it into his own pocket and left the room, again vowing that he'd return these items and praying that William Belltower would make it out of surgery alive.

✠

Ivy could hear someone moving around outside the door again. She'd been pacing, but now she stopped and put her ear to the door. She had to pee awfully bad, but she wouldn't use the bucket the man with the scar had slid to her. She wasn't an animal, after all. She needed to get him to come back in. And then she needed to get past him somehow, so she could escape and rescue her friend.

She reached into her pocket and removed one of the small glass bottles. She wrapped it many times over in toilet paper and placed it in the bottom of the bucket. Then she began to stomp on it. The third time her heel made impact, the bottom half of the bottle shattered. She carefully withdrew the top half and held it in her fist, the mouth of the bottle up near her thumb and the jagged broken end protruding out the bottom. She thought of the sudden ferocity that had marked the victor in every fight she'd seen at the Worst School in America. She needed that.

She would hold the weapon behind her back while looking small and scared. And when the man got close enough, she would give him another, much bigger scar.

Chapter 63

As Happy's van pulled up to the Church of St. John the Baptist, all the church vans were pulling out, having successfully completed a life-changing week of work camp. Fletcher ducked down at the sight of their own church's van heading home, short three chaperones and two campers.

He pulled the van up to the curb where the stone path began, leading through the garden and up to his makeshift entrance.

"Meg, take the wheel," he said. "We may need you to pick us up in front. I'll call you." He and Dante leapt from the van and ran up the path and into the church. They climbed a flight of stairs and quickly made their way through the double doors and up to the sanctuary.

The nave was empty. Before Fletcher even thought to mention it, Dante had walked right through the space where the aerosol can had revealed laser trip wires earlier in the week.

"Don't—" He reached out with both hands, but it was too late.

"What?" Dante asked, looking down at himself.

"Nothing. Let's just do this quick." Fletcher slid quickly under the altar and pulled back the levers as he had before, remembering to pull his head off to the side to avoid a collision with the drawer as it ejected. He grabbed the cloth-encased septangle and opened the flap on his bag.

"Hello again." The voice belonged to Father Sacha, who had come up from behind them through the vestry.

Fletcher momentarily deflated. "Father Sacha. I'm sorry I don't have the luxury of time right now. I'll bring this back. But right now I need it."

"I've missed you the past couple of days, Fletcher," Father Sacha said as if greeting a truant parishioner at mass. He nodded toward Dante. "And I believe I know you. A neighborhood minister, no?"

Dante nodded.

"And what have we here?" The priest gestured toward the altar relic in Fletcher's hand.

"They have my daughter. I have no choice."

"Are you ever going to ask for my help, Fletcher?"

That's when he noticed that Father Sacha's cuff links were Maltese crosses.

———

Andrew approached the abandoned office building in Dante's classic Mustang, which he was beginning to rather like. He pulled right up to the back door, threw the car into park, and jogged to the entrance, slapping it with his palm.

A man appeared from around the corner

wearing black military gear and a scar on his right cheek.

He did a double take at the sight of Andrew through the glass door. He pushed it open, demanding, "What are you doing here? You're supposed to be with the marks."

"Where's the boss, Manny?"

"Right where he said he'd be. Why?"

Andrew stepped into the building. Manny placed his hand on the holstered pistol on his hip.

"Why'd you kill Happy?" Andrew demanded.

"I didn't. Lorenza did."

"But I told you his safety was your responsibility."

Manny shrugged. "You shouldn't have let him get so close." His eyes dropped to the faux snakeskin fanny pack around Andrew's waist. "What are you doing here?" he asked again, unsnapping the retention strap on his sidearm.

"I just had to show you this." Andrew unzipped the fanny pack.

Manny laughed. "Look at that thing. Whatta you got in there? Confetti? Glitter?"

"We call it the Happy Zapper." Andrew pulled the node from the pack and shoved it into Manny's neck. The bigger man spasmed and fell to his knees, grappling for his gun, then slumped. The high whine of the battery recharging filled the room.

"It's not very stealthy," Andrew conceded,

sending another load of electrical current through him—this time in the ear. "You know, because you've got all these batteries to lug around." He patted the fanny pack.

Manny was twitching on the ground, white froth spilling from his mouth.

"You kill my friend, you kidnap my partner's daughter, and you think I'm just going to go along with it?" He pulled the pocket of the fanny pack open with one finger and checked the charge indicator. "I appreciate your patience," he said. "Takes a minute to recharge, but this last one should stop that shriveled black heart of yours."

—————

Father Sacha sat on the front pew. "You're looking for the Great and Holy Relic, I presume. Or are you just after the diamonds?"

"Both, kind of," Dante said.

Father Sacha smiled at this. "They were hidden by a predecessor of mine nearly a hundred years ago, the diamonds being an unwelcome reminder of what has gone wrong with the order and the cloth too great a temptation to alchemy." He paused and thought, pursing his lips. "I can make some calls," he said, "and have a dozen Knights of Malta—true Knights—here in a few hours."

"We'll pass," Dante said. "We've got enough creditors expecting the diamonds."

"I'm unconcerned with the necklace," the priest said, "but we must keep Fonseca's successors away from the Holy Cloth of the Apostle."

"But aren't you all on the same team?" Fletcher asked.

"Define *team*. This is a struggle that goes back hundreds of years. In the beginning the priests held precedence. We only took up arms to defend pilgrims from raiding parties. Then the fighting men took over, and we priests were only kept around to bless the conquest. My 'team' wants to undo the damage we've done. We will have men before sundown." He rose from the pew.

"That might be too late for Ivy," Fletcher said.

"I will relay the urgency. In the meantime, do what you need to do. And be careful with that."

"What about the necklace?" Fletcher asked.

"That cursed thing was forged in avarice and adultery and quickly branched out to the other deadly sins. In two hundred and fifty years it has never been the legitimate property of anyone. I'll trust you to finally do some good with it."

"I will," Fletcher said.

"I wasn't talking to you."

———

Manny was very dead—back arched, eyes bulging, mouth frozen in a final, silent scream. His gun lay six feet away, where he had thrown it while trying to draw while simultaneously grounding an enormous amount of electricity. Andrew riffled through his pockets until he found a ring of keys. Only one of them looked like it might open an office door. But which door? There were six in view and probably another twenty in the building.

He approached the first one cautiously. The most direct approach would be to knock or even to shout Ivy's name. But he was not sure where Lorenza was. Perhaps she was waiting behind one of these doors herself. She was deadly and a little touched, and she made Andrew very nervous. Best to keep this as quiet as possible.

The first door he tried was unlocked and the room empty. Same for the second. He approached the third door silently and gave the knob a twist. It didn't move. The key slid in easily and turned. He held the Happy Zapper at the ready and gave the door a push.

A few feet away stood Ivy, hands behind her back, fear and confusion all over her face. Andrew hadn't seen her since her sixth birthday, but she was unmistakably the same person. He took a step toward her.

"Ivy, it's me," he said. She was quivering. He took another step. "Remember me?"

With sudden speed, she reared back, wielding something jagged and shiny, eyes wide and crazy.

"Nonono!" Andrew said. "Don't you know me?"

She froze there for two seconds, poised to strike, the bottle in her hand shaking. Then she dropped it. She wrapped her arms around his neck and began crying into his shirt.

He picked her up and carried her out of the room, past Manny's corpse and out to the Mustang.

"How about we get you to your dad?" he said.

"Whoa," she said, loosening her grip on his neck and wiping her eyes. "Uncle Andrew, you have a cool car!"

"It's all right."

Chapter 64

"I want to help," Meg said. "What good am I in the van?"

"They don't let women in the lodge," Fletcher said. "You want to do something useful? Pray."

"I look like an idiot," Dante spat. He was wearing a tuxedo and a large white turban Meg had fashioned from a bedsheet, which had turned out more convincing than any of them had thought it would.

"Hit me with the Middle Eastern accent," Fletcher said.

"Something like thees?" Dante asked.

"Good enough."

They walked the block from the van to the lodge in silence and hoisted the large brass knocker, giving the door two solid strikes as Faust had earlier.

The man with the little revolver and big machismo answered. "Yes?"

"It is I," Dante said.

"I'm sorry?"

Dante pulled open his jacket, displaying the ring and the pin. "*Arcana Arcanorum*," he said.

The old man's face lit up. "*Secreto Secretorum*," he said, extending his hand. Dante stepped back and stared as if the outstretched hand were a dead rodent.

Fletcher sighed impatiently. "The Grand Kophta and High Priest of Egypt does not take part in the secret grips with men of a lesser degree."

"The Grand Kophta? But I've met him." He glanced at Dante's turban. "He's from North Carolina."

"The figurehead, yes," Fletcher said, annoyed. "This is our true leader, the highest master of our Rite and secret successor to Count Cagliostro, and you are offending him by leaving him standing on the stoop like a beggar."

The old man took a step back into the lodge, his face frozen in puzzlement, and waved the two men in. "Of course," he said, "the Grand Kophta. Welcome! My name is Sheridan Chambers."

"I'm afraid this is not a social visit," Fletcher said. Two men appeared in the foyer from one direction and three more from another. "We fear that your lodge has been compromised. A man was here this morning. Very pushy, trying to gain unauthorized access to the lodge."

"I think I know who you mean."

"He was . . . purple."

"Yes!"

"You have no doubt seen this man before. He told you his name was Julian Faust. However, he was born Angus McCullum. He is a thirty-third degree Mason of the Scottish Rite and is trying to steal the secrets of our ancient and primitive order to further his own vulgar lodges."

The growing number of men in the room gasped and murmured angrily to one another.

Fletcher let his eyes drift from face to face. "We believe he may have hidden a listening device somewhere in the lodge. Could you show us where he generally goes when he visits?"

"He spends most of his time with William Belltower, our Master Mason, in the parlor. Although they do like to visit the wine cellar. Belltower is something of a connoisseur."

Dante emitted a stream of gibberish.

"The Grand Kophta would like to see this cellar," Fletcher said.

"Of course." He led the two of them down a winding staircase to a room packed full of overstocked wine racks.

Fletcher took it all in.

"These over here are for everyday use," the old man said, gesturing to his right, "and these are for special occasions. They've been cataloging these."

The wine racks in question were seven feet tall and filled with dusty bottles. Then Fletcher saw a small section with little dust. He pulled the bottles down, two at a time, setting them on the floor. "Look here," he said, reaching behind the rack and pulling out a curious object. It was cast silver, Fletcher thought, and looked like a highly decorative coal shovel, consisting of a short seven-sided handle about an inch around and a scoop made to resemble a wide scallop shell, into which were etched the likenesses of a bee and a locust.

Chambers stood back, slack-jawed. "The sacred trowel! That is a sacred artifact of our lodge," he said, anger rising in his voice. "It was displayed for more than a century in an ebony case in the Great Hall until it went missing about two years ago."

Dante let loose with another barrage of gibberish. Fletcher bowed shallowly at him.

"The Grand Kophta would like to have this piece analyzed to help us find and neutralize the threat to our ancient Rite. We will return with it within the week."

Chambers nodded, his anger still smoldering.

"We thank you for your hospitality and cooperation," Fletcher said.

They mounted the stairs as quickly as possible without arousing suspicion and were out in the late-afternoon sun within a minute, artifact in hand. As they descended the concrete steps to the street, Fletcher whispered, "I know where the necklace is."

He felt his phone vibrating and pulled it out. CALL FROM THE ALCHEMIST.

"Hello."

"What happened to the phone I gave you?"

"It was sort of bugging me."

"My patience is at an end, Mr. Doyle. It is now four forty. You have until five forty to bring me what I want or I will kill your daughter." The line went dead.

"We've got one hour," Fletcher said. "We can make it."

His phone rang again—a number he didn't recognize.

"Who's this?" he said.

"Have a look to your right." It was Julian Faust. "Do you see that lovely young lady?"

Standing perfectly still on the sidewalk thirty yards away was Meg, a red dot hovering on her chest. She looked up at Fletcher, eyes red, and mouthed *I'm sorry.*

"Walk toward her," Faust said. "Both of you."

As Fletcher and Dante drew near, they could see the source of the laser dot. It came from under the half-open garage door of an abandoned transmission shop.

"Come to me, all three of you," Faust said. "Try anything funny and I'll kill her."

"I should have stayed in the van," Meg said as they approached the dark building.

"Don't worry about it," Fletcher said.

"I love you."

"I love you too." They ducked under the garage door and into the darkness.

Andrew led Ivy through the church doors and into the nave. "We'll find your dad in here." But it was empty save for two older women on kneelers, praying. They trekked from one side of the building to the other, glancing into every room and hall. "It's okay, Ivy. We just got desynchronized, that's all. I'll call him."

Chapter 65

It took Fletcher half a minute to adjust to the low light. Faust closed the garage door and turned his pistol on the three of them.

"I suppose I just conned the con men," he said, tossing a small novelty laser pointer to the ground.

"I know you," he said, locking in on Fletcher. "You're the art appraiser." He laughed cheekily. "What fun."

Fletcher's phone rang in his hand.

"Drop it," Faust said. "And kick it over to me." He stopped the skidding phone with his toe, then crushed it into oblivion with his heel. "It seems I have the upper hand. You will return my letters, the map, and the monstrance, as well as the object in your hand, and you will get me safely away from this crime scene so I can wash this ridiculous dye from my face."

Fletcher saw the shadow of a man crawling along the back wall, approaching Faust from behind. For a moment he thought it was Andrew and felt a wave of relief. Then he recognized the man.

And nothing made sense.

———

"He's still not answering," Andrew said, trying to hide his concern. He furrowed his brow, mentally running through options. "Okay, I have a few ideas where your dad might be. None of them are a good place for little girls."

"I'm not a little girl."

"You're right. Sorry. But you're safer here at the church. I'm going to go find your dad. You do me a favor and find someplace really good to hide. Somewhere no one could find you, okay?"

Ivy nodded.

"It's good to see you, Jumpin' Bean," he said, and gave her another hug. "Now go. Stay put until you hear your dad calling for you."

———

The man walked quickly, silently out of the shadows and poked the muzzle of a nickel-plated handgun to the back of Faust's head. "Actually, I have the upper hand, Julian. Drop the gun."

"What—?" Meg grappled for words. And Fletcher couldn't blame her. The man holding Faust at gunpoint was Brad Howard. Only his khakis and golf shirt had been exchanged for a tailored suit. On his finger he wore a large gold ring inlaid with a black Maltese cross.

"Brad?" Meg said, taking a step toward him, but Fletcher caught her elbow.

"I think he prefers to be called the Alchemist. Isn't that right? Or is it Cagliostro?"

The Alchemist smirked. "I'm whoever I need to be," he said, the accent from the phone calls coming and going.

"Farrington?" Faust said, turning to face him. "You're behind this?"

"You shouldn't have pushed me out, Julian."

"What choice did we have? You went mad, claimed to be a man who died two thousand years ago."

"And how do you know I didn't witness the crucifixion?" He took a deep breath, in his mouth and out his nose. "Doesn't matter now. I've moved beyond. The people of Malta thought St. Paul was a god. Just wait until they lay eyes on me."

"You're insane," Faust said.

"And you're dead." The bullet passed through the silencer, emitting a suppressed *phut,* and then through Julian Faust's head, emitting blood and skull fragments.

✠

Ivy pushed up on the trapdoor with the broom handle. From the floor she had barely been able to make contact, so she had brought over a stack of chairs and climbed up on them. Balanced precariously on her tiptoes, she gave another shove with the broom. It swung open, and a folding ladder came tipping down out of the attic, slowly at first, then picking up speed. She jumped down to the floor and pulled the chairs out of the way.

Don't think about bats, she told herself, ascending the ladder. The attic was dark and stale, the only light spilling in through a couple roof vents.

Reaching down through the opening, she gripped the ladder and pulled up. It didn't budge. She pulled harder and almost lost her footing. Her heart thudded in her chest. It was about eight feet to the floor below and a face-first free fall would be disastrous. She anchored her feet and pulled again. The ladder began to rise slowly, folding against itself. Ivy closed the trapdoor.

This was a safe place. No one knew about it but her.

And Courtney.

✠

"You kidnapped Ivy!" Meg was shouting and crying. "She loves you!"

"Blame your husband," the Alchemist said. "We had a good thing going, didn't we, Fletcher? You assume the risk—I buy what you steal. But then you had to get yourself arrested before I had everything I needed."

Fletcher ground his jaw. "I'm sorry to complicate your plans."

"A real grifter never apologizes," the Alchemist spat. "I tried to finish the project without you, but I hit the wall a couple years ago. And so I embedded myself in your life while you did time, prepared my end game. Such an easy mark."

Fletcher felt hate bubbling in his guts, dusted with awe. How flawlessly Brad had played him every day of the past six months, working his pride, drawing him back to the city and into the grift. Every comment, every smarmy smile, had been designed to turn Fletcher's peg. "Where's Ivy?" he asked.

"She's with my wife."

Meg let out a wail and clawed at her scalp.

"Oh," the Alchemist said. "I see how that could be confusing. Ivy's with my wife, Lorenza. You've met her—only you know her as Courtney. Talented actress. She can play anything from fifteen to thirty-five. Talented grifter too. She's been keeping an eye on your Ivy for the past few days . . . except when she stepped out to take care of your friend Happy."

Meg took two quick steps forward. "Take me! Take me instead of Ivy."

Fletcher grimaced. It should have been him throwing himself in harm's way, not Meg.

The Alchemist laughed. "Fletcher! Your wife just can't seem to stay away from me." He grabbed her by the arm and yanked her close, pushing the gun up to her chin. "Did you tell him about the kiss? Did you?"

Meg shook her head.

"Don't feel bad, convict. Lonely wife. Handsome, concerned friend. Who can blame her? I think I *will* take you, Meg. In addition to Ivy."

"Let her go," Fletcher said. "Take me."

"You see, I *would,* Fletcher. But you've got"—he checked his watch—"forty-six minutes to get me the package or you're all alone in this world. I'd get moving if I were you."

Chapter 66

Lorenza followed Happy's van back to the church, remaining one lane over and two cars back at all times. The marks had never seen her white Camry and they would likely not even recognize her out of character, but she did things by the book. When the van pulled up to the church, she drove right past, took a left, and parked a block up.

She had returned from a food run half an hour

earlier to find Manny dead and the girl missing. With Manny out of the equation, she would bear the Alchemist's wrath alone if she did not recover the girl. And the Alchemist's wrath was not something you walked away from. If you were lucky, you dragged yourself to the hospital. She had married him nine years earlier, when she was nineteen, and they had traveled the world together, shared adventures and experiences that most people would never dream of. But none of that would matter if she failed him now.

And so she had lain in wait at the lodge, watching from a distance, and followed them here. Maybe the girl was in the church, maybe she wasn't. But Lorenza knew just where to look first.

St. John's was deserted as Dante and Fletcher rushed in, a harvest of empty pop cans and candy wrappers the only evidence of the week's gathering. They ran up the aisle, Fletcher carrying Andrew's messenger bag.

"You sure you don't want me to call him?" Dante asked, huffing. On the way over, Fletcher had briefly returned the batteries to the two bugged phones. Dante's showed six missed calls from Andrew but no messages.

"Forget it," Fletcher said. "He's in with the Alchemist. Why else would he disappear right when we need him? Help me with this." He was at the baptismal font, trying to get a finger grip on the outside of the basin, but failing. Dante had no better luck. The symbols of locust and honey on the sacred trowel had pointed them back to St. John the Baptist, and the shell itself, being a symbol of baptism, brought them here.

"We should empty it," Dante said. "The water probably weighs thirty pounds."

"How?" Fletcher asked. "We have twenty-eight minutes before my family dies. Anyway, the men who designed this wouldn't have wanted someone sloshing holy water into a bucket, so there must be some other mechanism." He stepped back and examined the font, trying to push out the frantic thoughts crowding his mind. "Look at the pedestal. Seven-sided. I can't believe I walked right past five times."

"Give me that shovel thing," Dante said, running his finger along a slight indentation where the basin fit into the pedestal. Fletcher fished the sacred trowel out of the leather bag and handed it over. The top edge of the shell fit perfectly into the indentation, its entire six inches sliding in, shifting the basin up. He pulled down on the handle of the trowel like a lever, tipping the basin. The water poured from the font, soaking into a layer of sand in the base below.

Fletcher wrapped his arms around the basin and set it gently on the floor. "Let me see that," he said, holding a hand out toward Dante. He began digging in the wet sand with the shovel, pushing aside the mud until he had uncovered a polished stone surface with a seven-sided cavity in the center.

"Try to clear that out," he said, pawing through the bag for the altar relic.

Dante clawed the sand from the inch-deep recess. Fletcher pulled the cloth from around the septangle and used it to wipe the remaining sand from in and around the cavity. He held the relic over the recess; it was a perfect fit.

✠

Ivy had inserted herself behind an eight-foot-tall sandwich board sign advertising a week of Vacation Bible School in June of 1987. She'd been feeling increasingly claustrophobic and was considering whether she should abandon the hiding place and try to find a phone to call 911. But her dad wasn't supposed to be talking to Uncle Andrew, and she feared that such a call might lead to the police taking him away in handcuffs for another six years.

The *whump* of the trapdoor opening stole her breath. Light shone into the attic from below, and she heard someone climbing up the ladder. She heard the sound of a pull-chain, and light came from above as well. She pulled herself farther back behind the sign.

"Ivy? Are you up here?" Courtney's voice.

"I'm back here," Ivy called quietly.

"Oh, thank God." Courtney took a few steps

forward, her eyes searching. "I don't see you."

Ivy wriggled out from behind the sign and looked at her friend. Something wasn't right. She looked different. Older. "How did you get away?" she asked.

"They put me in a different room after the bathroom thing. I pried the window open and dropped to the ground. Come on, I have a car. Let's get somewhere safe."

Ivy shook her head. "No, I'm supposed to stay here."

Courtney considered this for a moment. "Okay. I'll stay with you." She found another pull-chain and gave it a tug, illuminating the attic all the more.

"Can I ask you something?" Ivy said.

"Sure."

"What happened to your black eye?"

Ivy jumped up and grabbed the top of the plywood sign, pulling it down on top of Courtney.

✠

"A 3D lock," Fletcher said, "with seven possible ways to insert the key." He studied the recess. A different word was written at each corner: *Hail, Mountain, Wormwood* . . . "I got it," he said. The seven trumpets from the book of Revelation. He turned the septangle so that the first seal lined up with the first trumpet—and all the others as well —and pushed down.

They heard a click. The two men leaned in expectantly, but nothing happened.

"It's a key," Dante said. "Maybe you have to turn it." He tried to rotate the ivory relic with his fingers. It didn't budge. "Wait, I got it!" he said, snatching up the trowel from the floor behind him. He inserted the end of the seven-sided handle into the center of the septangle and twisted. The grinding sound of stone against stone filled the church as the top of the pedestal turned forty-five degrees, then popped up six inches out of its base, revealing a hidden compartment.

Fletcher tentatively reached into the hollow and wrapped his hand around the old cloth. He gingerly withdrew it, feeling the heft of what lay within. His eyes met Dante's, and for one exhilarating moment they forgot everything else and grinned at each other like a couple of drunks.

"It's smaller than I thought," Dante said, pulling back a corner and peering in. "Hooo, that's a lot of diamonds."

Fletcher laughed and turned his attention to the cloth itself. The distinctive round stain was there, but was not a perfect circle and was far too small to line up with the monstrance. "Okay," he said, "I'm going to call the Alchemist. You may as well call Andrew back too. If he's against us, he'll know where we are soon anyway. If he's not, we're gonna need him."

"Should we find the priest first?"

"Yeah," Fletcher said. "See where we stand with that."

"You believe all that noise about knights coming to rescue us?"

"I don't know. But I'll take a long shot right now." They raced down the hall and up the stairs.

The door to the church offices was locked and all the lights off.

"You got a number for the priest?" Dante asked.

"No." Fletcher checked his watch. "We've got six minutes. I'm calling the Alchemist." He pulled out the burner phone and inserted the battery.

✠

Ivy turned and bolted for the ladder. On the third step, she felt Courtney's hand close around her ankle and she went down, slamming against the attic floor.

"Who are you, really?" Ivy asked, rising to her hands and knees.

"Name's Lorenza," she answered, grabbing a fistful of Ivy's hair, pulling her several steps away from the trapdoor and dumping her. She laughed. "I know, I know—you're tough. You told me. But get this: The guy with the scar? He was my errand boy. He answered to me."

"He didn't really hurt you?"

Lorenza scoffed. "He only stopped in a few times. It was just you and me in that building. I kept you there. And now I'm going to keep you in here. So get comfortable."

Ivy thought again about the fights she'd seen at school, about striking fast and the power of surprise. She began to sob. "I miss my mom and dad," she said through gasps and hiccups.

"Stop it," Lorenza said. "Seriously, cut it out." She took a step toward Ivy.

"But-but-but, I just—" Ivy launched herself up from the floor, trying to channel all the power of her legs into her fist. She connected with the woman's nose, feeling it crunch against her first two knuckles.

The pain in her fist caught her off guard, as did the meat of Lorenza's hand smashing into her throat. Ivy fell back to the floor, gasping for breath.

"Bad move, princess," Lorenza said. "Do you have any idea how much this nose cost?" She kicked Ivy in the ribs and walked over to an old mirror leaning against the wall to inspect her bloodied nose.

Ivy grabbed the opportunity and lurched toward the trapdoor. Lorenza sighed, annoyed. She turned and sprang on Ivy, digging a boot heel into her thigh. Ivy screamed.

"If you're going to make noise, I guess I'll have to put you to sleep," Lorenza said. She knelt down and wrapped her left arm around Ivy's throat, shutting off the air like a vise. Within a few seconds, the world began to dim.

Chapter 67

Andrew sat behind the wheel of Dante's Mustang, gazing up at the lodge of the Egyptian Mystery Rites, considering whether he should take another crack at it. He'd been everywhere else he thought Fletcher might be. He'd called him a dozen times, as well as calling Dante and Meg. It was like they'd all disappeared. Had he been made? No way to know, really, and he couldn't exactly call the Alchemist now, having killed Manny and released the girl.

His phone rang on the seat next to him. Dante.

"Where have you been?" Andrew demanded. "Listen, I—"

"No, you listen," Dante said. "We've got the necklace. Fletcher's calling the Alchemist now."

Andrew processed and reprocessed this.

"Hello?" Dante said.

"I'm here. Where are you?"

"We're at the church. Now, what'd you want to tell me?"

"Nothing. I'm headed your way now."

✠

Ivy pulled herself forward another foot, dragging Lorenza, whose grip tightened all the more. She collapsed against the floor, guessing she would lose consciousness in a matter of seconds. The floor beneath her was swimming, morphing. She could see different pictures in the wood grain. Moving pictures.

Then she saw the knothole, as big as a quarter. As big as the neck of the little bottle in her shorts pocket. Ivy pulled her arms down by her sides, wriggled her hand into her pocket, then slumped, letting her mouth hang open.

"Nighty-night," Lorenza said. She kept her grip on the girl's throat for a moment longer.

Ivy could feel the bottom of the bottle with her fingertips. She coaxed it into her hand, pulled it free, and punched it down mouth first into the knothole, snapping it off at the neck. With all her might she stabbed the jagged edge into Lorenza's arm and gave it a twist, drawing a shriek from the woman.

Shrugging off her attacker, Ivy stood, taking deep, replenishing breaths. The spinning room slowed. She gripped the bottle tightly and held it out in front of her.

Lorenza stood and examined the wound in her forearm. "I'm going to kill you for that." She drew a short but deadly looking knife from inside her boot. "We don't need you anyway. Not after today." She feigned a strike at Ivy, who flinched and took a step back onto the broken neck of the bottle growing up out of the floor like a stalagmite.

The uneven glass crunched under her foot and

sliced up through the sole of her shoe, bringing a stab of pain followed by a warm, wet feeling. She looked down for just a second and felt the heel of Lorenza's boot connecting with her sternum, launching her back through the opening in the attic floor. Her back collided with the ladder and she bounced off, landing hard on the tile.

Lorenza dropped the eight feet to the floor, landing lightly.

"I guess you forgot to pray before that little trick?" She closed one eye and held the knife casually up in front of her face, looking down the razor-sharp edge. "Time to die."

"I'm afraid I can't let you harm that innocent girl." Father Sacha stood five feet away from Lorenza and a good inch shorter, wearing his tab collar and wingtips, and she sized him up with a smirk. He swallowed hard and said, "Please just walk away and leave this holy place."

Lorenza lunged at him, driving the knife at his throat. The priest took a step toward her and snaked his arm around hers, bringing his fist up in front of her shoulder with great force and a loud *pop*. The knife clanked to the ground. Tugging her off-balance, he drove the heel of his right hand into her already broken nose, then brought her head down to meet his knee.

She fell, turning onto her stomach as Father Sacha pinned her arm behind her back.

The priest shook his head sadly. "So senseless.

What a shame." He looked from Lorenza to Ivy. "Are you okay, love?"

"I think so," Ivy said, rising tentatively and wincing at the pain in her foot. "My mom says I'm rubbery. That's why I hardly get hurt." She surveyed her former friend's broken form. "Where did you learn how to do that?"

"Some friends of mine. I'll introduce you; they should be here soon."

Lorenza grunted and tried to stand. Father Sacha twisted her arm and guided her back to the floor.

"You're Fletcher's daughter," he said. "Ivy, right?"

She nodded.

"Ivy, there's a toolbox in the closet behind you. Would you do me a favor and bring me the duct tape?"

Dante and Fletcher checked the vestry and the sacristy for Father Sacha but found no sign of him. From there they began a systematic search of the building. They were in the multipurpose room, now completely empty save for Fletcher's air mattress and duffel bag, when the Alchemist called to announce his arrival.

"Where are you?" he asked.

"Men's sleeping quarters."

"That's good," the Alchemist said. "Out of the way. Wait there."

A minute later he entered the room, holding Meg close and apparently burying the muzzle of a gun in her back.

"Where's Ivy?" Fletcher asked.

"You didn't think I'd bring them both, did you? What if you did something stupid, like call the police? Your daughter's fine, but if I don't call my man in the next half hour, he's going to kill her." He shoved Meg toward Fletcher and Dante and raised the gun.

"Your man is dead," Andrew said, approaching the Alchemist from behind, his .38 trained on him. "And Ivy's safe."

The Alchemist smiled at Fletcher. "He has a gun, doesn't he?"

Andrew pulled back the hammer.

"This is a stupid move, Andrew," the Alchemist said. "You have no play here."

"We'll see."

The Alchemist closed one eye and centered his aim on Meg. "I'll kill her."

"I'm not Fletcher," Andrew said. "You're turning the wrong peg."

"You better do something, Fletcher," the Alchemist said. "I'll kill your wife. And even if your daughter did escape, Lorenza has undoubtedly found her."

"Don't listen to him," Andrew said. "Ivy's fine. She's here in the church. Now, Meg, I need you to do something for me. I need you to get the necklace from your husband and let me see it."

Fletcher handed her the cloth and its contents. She draped the cloth over her arm and held up the necklace, letting it hang down. A few diamonds were missing here and there, but the rest was intact.

"Good," Andrew said. "You see the two outside pendants hanging from the choker? I need you to remove them both." Meg fumbled with one of them, trying to pry it out with her fingers.

"Let me help," Fletcher said, taking a step toward her.

"Stay where you are," Andrew and the Alchemist said in unison.

"You two are still playing us," Fletcher said. "Why should we believe Ivy's safe when you two have been working together since day one?"

"Mom!" They heard Ivy's voice, filled with joy, from out in the hall. Father Sacha was carrying her past the doorway, toward the stairs. Fletcher had to hold Meg back from rushing to her.

The Alchemist used the distraction to turn his gun on Andrew. The two men squared off.

"That good enough for you, Fletch?" Andrew said. "Now, the diamonds. We don't have much time."

"There's a multitool in the pocket of my jeans," Fletcher said, gesturing at his bag near the foot of the air mattress. Meg scrambled over to it and dug through the contents for a minute before locating the jeans and retrieving the tool. She tried the pliers with no luck, then flipped out the utility knife and was able to quickly detach them both.

The Alchemist chuckled. "You had that wicked blade in your luggage for one of these youth group kids to find? You really are bad at this whole domestic thing, convict."

"Shut up," Andrew said. He unbuckled the gaudy pack from around his waist and tossed it in Meg's direction. "I want you to put the rest of the necklace and the cloth in there."

"I don't know if it'll fit," she said.

"Make it fit. Stuff it in."

She struggled to close the zipper.

Father Sacha reappeared in the doorway, alone, and offered another update. Andrew and the Alchemist kept their guns trained on each other. "She'll be fine," the priest said. "And help's on the way. Ten minutes." He scurried away.

"No," Andrew said. "Help's here now." He raised his phone to his ear and said, "Come on in, guys. Left and down the hall."

Chapter 68

They heard the clomping approach of a number of men. Then they saw Marcus Brinkman, gun in hand, followed by the two mooks who had van-jacked Fletcher and Andrew the night before, and another guy—the biggest of the bunch—who forced Father Sacha into the room at gunpoint with a halfhearted, "Sorry, Father; no disrespect."

"Guns down!" Marcus said. "Both of you." The Alchemist's pistol bounced on the carpet floor while Andrew's revolver sank into Fletcher's sagging air mattress, disappearing from sight.

Marcus and his men did a quick sweep of the room, patting everyone down—including Meg, to Fletcher's great displeasure. When they had secured the room, Marcus punched a key on his phone and held it to his ear.

"It's all clear," he said.

The click of high heels on tile grew louder with each step. Bella Donna entered the room.

"Give her the diamond, Meg," Andrew said.

"Which one?"

"She'll know which one."

Meg held them both out, one in each palm. Bella Donna took the one from her right hand and held it up to the light streaming in through the window. She took a small magnifying glass from her purse and studied the gem closer. "Oh my," she finally said.

Andrew nodded. "It's what we discussed."

She strolled over to the Alchemist. "And I assume this is the man who comes with the diamond?"

The Alchemist sneered. "There are more where that came from. A lot more. And I can get them for you."

"A lot more diamonds?" she asked, dubious. "Like this? Unlikely."

"In this room. I don't think you fully appreciate what you have. They belonged to Marie Antoinette and—"

Marcus buried a fist in the Alchemist's stomach, sending him down to one knee.

"You know what I hate in a man?" Bella Donna asked. "Desperation. Besides, I honor my agreements. The four of you have settled your debt. And, Mr. Watkins, you can come back to work tomorrow."

"I appreciate that," Dante said, "but I think I'm due for a career change."

Brinkman's face soured. "No, you're not, Trick. This clears your debt, but it doesn't buy you out."

Andrew lurched forward and stomped the air mattress, vaulting the gun back into his hand. He fired two shots into Dante's chest, blasting him back onto the floor where he gasped and moaned, blood pumping from his wounds.

Four guns were instantly trained on Andrew. He dropped the .38 and threw up his hands. "He drew!" he said. "He drew on Bella Donna!"

Marcus stepped cautiously toward Dante. "Huh," he said, kicking the Glock from his hand, sending it sliding across the floor. He tilted his head and looked down into Dante's panicked eyes, flickering in and out of awareness. Dante opened his mouth to speak, but all he managed was a bubble of blood. "I didn't think you had it in you, Trick," Marcus said, his voice edged with respect. "Thought you were just talk."

"The priest called the cops," Andrew said, "right before you got here. You should go. I'll deal with all this."

Marcus looked to Bella Donna, who nodded and walked quickly out of the room. As he passed Andrew, the old enforcer said, "We're square, Bishop. But you stick to the deal. I don't want to see you anywhere near the Motor City. I don't even want to think I smell that obnoxious cologne of yours. Got it?"

He nodded, and the gunmen left, taking the Alchemist with them.

On the floor a few feet away Dante was shivering, his breaths coming short and shallow.

"I'm s-s-so cold," he managed to croak.

"Somebody get Dante a sweater," Fletcher said, offering his hand and helping him up. He grinned at Meg. "And *that,* my dear wife, is what we call pinching the gizzard." Dante held up the bulb in his left hand, attached to a small hose that disappeared under his sleeve.

Meg gawked for a moment and then laughed. "So you had blanks the whole time?"

Andrew shrugged. "A real grifter never carries live ammo." He pocketed the revolver and picked up the Alchemist's pistol from the floor.

"This one is the real deal, though," he said. The room went silent.

"Meg, why don't you come over here and buckle that pack around my waist." As she obeyed the order, Andrew announced, "Before I leave you all for good, I just want to make sure there are no hard feelings here. Everybody should be happy. All your pegs have been turned. Fletcher, you've got your kid and your wife and your life back. And you've got Jesus, whatever that's worth. Trick, you're free from the Syndicate."

"What about Happy?" Meg asked, stepping away from Andrew.

"His troubles are over. And if any of you feel like you got cheated, I leave you with the crystal, the monstrance, and the map. Feel free to go after the Maltese treasure if you like. I for one am more than content with my hundred-million-dollar necklace."

"I guess we found your real peg, didn't we?" Fletcher said. "If we boil you down to your essence, you're just another grifter willing to sell his friends for a big enough score."

"I guess so," Andrew said, "but I can live with that. Especially on a private beach with a Swiss account full to bursting."

"At least tell us the truth," Dante said. "The monstrance and the crystal have nothing to do with Cagliostro's treasure, do they? That was all misdirection. It's the cloth and the map that show the location. And I'm guessing we'll find the tube in the van empty."

Andrew didn't even blink. "Either way, this is good-bye." He backed out the door and disappeared down the hall. They heard the heavy church door close behind him.

"I was just starting to like that guy," Dante said, staring out after him.

Father Sacha reappeared in the door, helping Ivy limp along. Her parents rushed to embrace her. Then came the barrage of tears, kisses, and questions, particularly variations of "Are you okay?" and "How did you get here?"

"Uncle Andrew rescued me," she said.

Father Sacha sighed. "I wonder how much of his life that man will waste looking for a treasure that never existed."

"What are you talking about?" Fletcher asked.

"The priestly faction of the Knights of Malta laid down the clues and kept the story alive to keep the crusading set busy. We even left them a little something in the wall of the castle. The fact is, the only hidden treasures we ever had just went out that door with your friend."

"No, they didn't," Meg said, grinning. She reached into Fletcher's bag and pulled out a purple fanny pack. "Object permanence," she said. "I don't know what was in the other pack, but it was just bulky enough to pass for the necklace and the cloth."

"It was brownies," Fletcher said. "Little Debbie brownies."

Meg glanced at the door. "What if he comes back?"

Dante recovered his Glock. "We'll be ready."

"I don't think you have to worry about that." Father Sacha was leaning out into the hall, waving at someone. "Down here, fellows!"

A dozen men filed quietly into the room. Three of them wore clerical collars and the rest business casual attire. None were clad in body armor and laden with assault weapons, although four of them held handguns.

"I'm afraid you just missed the main event," Father Sacha said, "but we could use some help with the aftermath."

"I'm a doctor," a big bearded man said to Dante upon seeing his bloodied chest.

"No, no, he'll be fine," Father Sacha said. "In fact, he's the man I told you about. However, there is a young lady over here who needs some attention."

"What does that mean," Dante asked. "The guy you told them about?" Father Sacha just smiled.

The doctor determined that Ivy's foot did not need stitches—just some antibiotic ointment and a butterfly closure. And, perhaps thanks to her "rubberiness," she did not have a concussion or anything more than bumps and bruises. If she took it easy, the physician knight said, she would probably recover within a week or two. For the time being, she let her parents support her weight.

"Have I told you I love you?" Fletcher asked.

"I love you too, Dad."

Marcus Brinkman pulled his Bentley to a stop outside the Warehouse.

"This is where we part ways," Bella Donna said to the Alchemist. "I expect you of all people to understand that this is not personal."

He summoned a slick smile. "You know as well as I do that nothing's sealed up that can't be unsealed. Now let me explain why—"

She interrupted him. "Do you know what they call me?"

The Alchemist arched an eyebrow. "La Bella Donna, I believe."

"And do you know why they call me this?"

Chapter 69

June 14, 1798
Dingli Cliffs, Malta

Cagliostro sat at the highest point on the Island of Malta, enjoying what he deemed to be the most beautiful and majestic view in the world. He had thought of it often during his two years in the dungeon of the Castel Sant'Angelo, where he had remained until his death sentence was changed to a life sentence. At that time, the order was given to relocate him to the Fortress of San Leo, where he was to inhabit a cell built into the sheer cliff near the peak of a mountain.

As far as breathtaking views were concerned, one could do worse than San Leo, which was perhaps some consolation to the prisoners who were brought up to their cells in an elevator using an elaborate system of ropes and pulleys. And perhaps, as he felt the unnerving shake of the creaking apparatus carrying him up to Cagliostro's cell, the prisoner had thought something similar. No one would ever know—for Count Cagliostro had died of apoplexy on August the 26th, 1795.

Or so it was reported in *Le Moniteur Universel* and elsewhere.

In truth, the count never set foot in the fortress. Rather, with some help from a confederate, he had arranged for a condemned man to take his place, living out his days with the wind and the sun and all his needs met. Cagliostro had, in turn, taken the place of the condemned man, insofar as he was covered with a blanket and carried with a number of corpses to a mass grave.

Now he sat in the glint of the sun and thought of the untold treasures that would soon be floating in the grotto some eight hundred feet beneath him, obscured by rocks and waves. He thought about all he had done to bring his plan to fruition. He had been a charlatan and an alchemist, a count and a peasant. He had lived in the palaces of princes who showered him with anything he might desire and in prison cells that stunk of dung and death. And now he had finally arrived at the end of his Grand Design.

Fonseca was dead and so was Rohan, but he had counted on that. Time and mortality had been two of his greatest accomplices. The Knights of Malta had been stripped of nearly everything, but Cagliostro would not be ruined by revolution. Rather, he had used revolution to solidify his fortune and position in perpetuity. His eyes searched the horizon for the ship that would soon be delivering his spoils. Soon thereafter would come another ship to bring him and his treasure to America, where men were allowed to rise from nothing and chair the aristocracy—so long as they possessed enough money and worldly wisdom—and where he would be free to spread his Egyptian Freemasonry without fear of the Inquisition. He would be a world away when the evidence of his deception was erased from the memory of man, sinking to the bottom of the sea. And that was good.

The sound of people approaching brought Cagliostro to his feet. He turned and saw four men clad in military uniform and regalia. One of the men was most familiar, the shortest of the group, about the same height as Cagliostro himself.

"Your Excellency," the count said, bowing slightly. He felt his heart begin to race. This was unexpected.

"Your blade," the general said without even a greeting. "Let me see it."

Cagliostro unbuckled his sword and handed it to the general.

"This, I believe, belonged to Grand Master Pinto da Fonseca, did it not?"

"It did."

"That makes it property of the Knights of Malta," the general said, "which makes it my property." He handed the sword to the officer at his right and straightened his bicorne. "But that is not the ceremonial blade used by the Grand Masters for more than two centuries." He drew a sword from its scabbard and held it up for Cagliostro to see. It was beyond ornate, stunning as the sun glinted off the gold and gems adorning its handle. "This is the sword of La Valette. Not the sort of blade one uses in battle—only for rituals, coronations, and other special occasions."

The general took a quick step forward and slid the blade between Cagliostro's ribs and through his heart, stepping slowly forward and pushing it in until the elaborately decorated hilt pressed against the alchemist's chest.

General Bonaparte smiled. "It is so easy to manipulate a man when you know precisely what he wants." And with that, he took one more step and gave the sword a shove, causing Cagliostro to slide off its blade and plummet eight hundred feet into the Mediterranean Sea.

Chapter 70

Dante held the door for the Doyle family as they collectively limped from the multipurpose room. He had traded his blood-stained button-down for a tie-dyed T-shirt provided by Father Sacha. It read, "My life was changed at Christian Service Camp 2015."

"I was thinking of finding a pew and saying a prayer," Fletcher was saying. "I've been putting it off for a while. I'd rather not do it alone."

Leaving them behind, Dante strode down the hall, looking for Father Sacha. He found him in the vestibule talking with Dr. Andre Foreman. The two men quickly halted their conversation as he approached.

"Am I in trouble or something?" Dante asked.

"Not a bit," the priest said. "We were just discussing what might happen next, now that Dante Watkins is dead."

Dante smiled. "Born again too. None of the old baggage holding me back."

Dr. Foreman smiled. "So what's ahead?"

"Well, for starters, I'd love to see a series of very large donations made to my Father the Fatherless campaign. Like enough to buy a diamond necklace."

"I can see that happening," Father Sacha said. "Perhaps from the Hospitaler Order of St. John of Jerusalem of Rhodes and of Malta."

"But since I won't be hanging around, I should probably file some paperwork so the Clergy Forum can take over the account. There's already enough to finish off that wing at Orangelawn and a whole lot more."

"I'll happily oversee that," Dr. Foreman said.

Fletcher and his family hobbled into the vestibule, laughing and joined at the hip. Dante watched the three of them pass through the propped double doors and up the aisle of the church. They had the whole place to themselves.

"I need to ask you for one more thing," Dante said. "My little church will need someone to take over the pulpit and help them go legit. They never knew any of it. Just regular folks who love Jesus."

"I can do that do for them," the older preacher answered. "But I can do something for you too, if you're interested."

"I'm listening."

"By tomorrow night, Dante Watkins will no longer exist. You will have a new name, a Maltese passport, and will be using your gifts to plead the case of children who have been forgotten and exploited. I heard that you are good at that sort of thing."

Dante smiled. "Oh, I can talk. But I'd rather just work. I've done a lot of talking, but I haven't given much of myself to the poor and needy all around me."

"You tell me where and I'll get you hooked up," Dr. Foreman said.

"How you gonna pull that off?"

"Dr. Foreman is with the Protestant Knights of Malta," Father Sacha said, shrugging. "We let it slide."

The sight of two policemen entering the vestibule brought a heaviness to Dante's chest for just a moment. Then he saw them receive custody of a young woman from two of the Knights of Malta, one of whom displayed a badge of some sort. The woman looked like she'd been in a fight.

"Lorenza?" Dante asked.

"Her real name is Katerina Penn. She'll be extradited to England, where she's wanted for murder and fraud. After that, the French would like a crack at her."

Dante watched her disappear out the door—hands cuffed behind her back—and felt only sorrow for her. He knew how unforgiving it was Inside.

"I wouldn't mind doing some prison ministry somewhere," he said.

"I'm sure that can be arranged."

The door had almost closed when the old man in the robe slipped in. No one seemed to notice him—not even Dr. Foreman, who was less than four feet away. The man looked up at Dante, his eyes still intense, but peaceful. And while his appearance hadn't changed, Dante no longer found him ugly. In his hand was a cloth—perfectly clean and spotless. Dante thought of the words of Scripture emblazoned on his counterfeit ordination certificate: *If we confess our sins, he is faithful and just and will forgive us our sins and purify us from all unrighteousness.* He'd chosen the verse almost at random, to fill some negative space in the design. Now the words were like life.

The apostle walked through the double doors with the lightness of a messenger bearing good news and stepped quickly up the aisle toward Fletcher.

Author's Note

While promoting my book *Playing Saint* over the past year, I've often been asked how much research it entailed. My answer has been that, insofar as the plot involved an invented order of priests (the Jesuits Militant) and an imagined relic (The Crown of Marbella), there wasn't much need for research. The writing of *The Last Con*, on the other hand, was a very different story.

Much of the historical content in this book is rooted in fact. The general history of the Knights of Malta (including their evolution from monks who cared for the poor and injured to knights and warriors who battled pirates for the spoils), the Affair of the Diamond Necklace (and its role in lighting the ready fuse of revolution), and the life of Alessandro Cagliostro (born Giuseppe Balsamo) are all presented largely as they unfolded in real life—with some degree of artistic license, of course.

The Sovereign Order of the Knights of Malta does continue to exist today, their Grand Master still hold titles of prince and bishop, and the order does enjoy Sovereign Observer status at the United Nations. While it was certainly a blow, Napoleon's sound defeat of the Island of Malta did not spell the end for the order and, in fact, the Republic of Malta returned the Castel Sant'Angelo to them in 1999, bringing them back to their eponymous home. And I was fascinated to learn (after the manuscript had been completed, unfortunately) that the Sword of La Valette, with which Napoleon absconded in 1798, is currently on loan from the Louvre to the people of Malta, who would very much like to keep it permanently (there's even a petition to that effect on Face-book!).

What may be more surprising to many readers is that the Knights' accumulated wealth was indeed loaded onto great ships by Napoleon's troops and that these ships were sunk by the British fleet before the treasure could be unloaded. No more than a few coins of it has ever been recovered.

From there, however, I can cite only my imagination. To be clear, the treasures of Valletta are likely still littering the floor of the Aboukir Bay. The infamous diamond necklace is presumed to have been broken down and sold piecemeal in England. Cagliostro died in a lonely prison cell in 1795, a disgraced charlatan who seems to have begun believing his own fantastical stories. And let me state for the record that St. Paul does not physically convey forgiveness to the penitent any more than St. Peter welcomes the departed at the pearly gates. His presence in

The Last Con is meant as a symbolic device and nothing more.

More than some curious historical facts, though, what I hope you take from this book is the question that Cagliostro never really settled in his own life: which *you* is the real you? Is it the sins and habits that define you at your worst? Is it a perfect version of yourself that exists in theory only? Is it some mixture of the two, wheels continually spinning, but progress ever-elusive?

Dear reader, know this: if you have been bought by the blood of Jesus, then your identity is in his perfect righteousness. And if you have not put your faith in him, I pray that you will. That simple icon of two lines intersecting is not merely a peg to manipulate and imprison the hearts and minds of the masses; it is a reminder of the great sacrifice of Christ, which *frees* our hearts and minds from sin and death.

Live free, then, knowing that your identity—and your eternity—are secure in Him.

Soli Deo Gloria,
Rev. Zachary Bartels

Reading Group Guide

1. Fletcher finds himself hiding aspects of his life from his wife—starting with trivial things and growing more serious from there. Do you believe it is ever okay to hide aspects of your life from your spouse?

2. It may seem especially shocking to think of Dante pretending to be a pastor, even while carrying out illegal and immoral activities. At the same time, Fletcher emphasizes repeatedly that the church he was caught robbing had been "deconsecrated." But is it worse to lie about being a minister than an art appraiser? Is it better to rob a deconsecrated church than an active one? Or is lying simply lying and stealing simply stealing, regardless of the circumstances?

3. The idea of alchemy—including the use of dark arts to turn common metals into gold—seems harmless, if a little stupid, to many modern people, and yet it has been linked with sorcery throughout much of history, even punishable by death. If a friend of yours said he or she was taking an interest in alchemy, what would be your reaction? What about

Ouija boards, séances, or horoscopes? Are such interests dangerous gateways or harmless frivolities?

4. Fonseca and Cagliostro give their lives to a plan that they believe will allow them to keep the wealth they've amassed indefinitely. Do you see anyone carrying out similar plans today? What is the greatest flaw in such a plan?

5. Dante became a con man without ever deciding to do so. Likewise, Fletcher went back on the grift without directly choosing that path. Yet both had to make a conscious choice to leave that life behind. When people wind up on the wrong road, how often do you think they make a conscious choice to do so? How can you protect yourself from slowly, incrementally ending up on a destructive path?

6. Andrew taught Fletcher to ball up negative emotions inside of himself and transform them into positive ones. Is this a healthy idea when communicating with other people? When communicating with God? Have you ever had such a strategy backfire?

7. Fletcher is advised against falling back in with old friends, not only because it would

break his parole, but because it might cause him to fall back into old habits. As a rule, should believers avoid old friends who might lead them back into sin, or should they maintain contact, hoping to lead their friends to Jesus?

8. If someone were to successfully grift you, what would be your peg?

9. Fletcher wonders what would be left if someone were to burn everything away down to his very essence. According to the New Testament (I Peter 1:6–9), God is doing this now. What is he using and what will it reveal for the believer?

10. Cagliostro's séance was clearly a parlor trick. Do you think there is ever more than sleight-of-hand to such things? What would you say to someone who claimed to communicate with the dead?

11. Dr. Foreman reminds Fletcher of the distinction between godly sorrow, which "brings repentance, leads to salvation, and leaves no regret" and worldly sorrow, which "brings death" (2 Corinthians 7:10–11). In your own life, how can you distinguish between the two?

12. Throughout the book, several characters brag that they are able to become whoever they need to be in a given moment. Is that preferable to being consistent in your identity, regardless of the circumstances? Which best describes you?

Acknowledgments

The writing of a book is an unusual process, in that it's so very personal for the author, and yet such a communal effort. As my second novel goes to press, there are now even more people to be thanked for their support of my writing—too many to be listed here. However, I must name a few.

First of all, my wife Erin—an incredible writer and a source of great wisdom, encouragement, and inspiration—and my son Calvin, who thinks everything about my books is "awesome." No way I deserve either of you. My church family has been incredibly supportive as well, coming to signings by the carload, buying stacks of books to give away as gifts, and in general being the loving and engaging people they always are. (By the by, we'd love to have you worship with us any time—www.ChurchLansing.com.)

Of course, my deepest thanks also goes to my agent Ann "Annie B" Byle of Credo Communications (I'd say "Shut up!" here, but people wouldn't know it was an inside joke and might assume the worst of both of us), my awesome editor Amanda Bostic and the whole incredible team at HarperCollins Christian Fiction, and the one and only LB Norton. You all do what you do with excellence and it inspires me to do the same.

I am also indebted to the late David W. Maurer, whose book *The Big Con* has been a source of inspiration and information for every grifter story written in the past seventy years, to Adam Jones, who served as historical consultant for this book, and to Daniel Paul Kersey, for not taking it personally.

And last but never least, my boy Ted Kluck and the Gut Check Army. Don't forget to turn up the trim.

About the Author

Zachary Bartels is the author of *Playing Saint*. An award-winning preacher and Bible teacher, he serves as pastor of Judson Baptist Church in Lansing, MI, where he lives with his wife, Erin, and their son.

You can find Zachary online at
www.zacharybartels.com.
Facebook: AuthorZacharyBartels
Twitter: AuthorZBartels

Center Point Large Print
600 Brooks Road / PO Box 1
Thorndike, ME 04986-0001 USA

(207) 568-3717

US & Canada:
1 800 929-9108
www.centerpointlargeprint.com